EP WATKINS

Fields and Contrails

a novel

For my daughter

Reagan Chairs

By the late summer of 2004 the Reagan Chairs had come through their controversial infancy, cycles of fads, and legislation had firmed up. Most people ignored them unless they intended to sit in one.

Activists had pushed legislators to add warning placards, put spacing requirements in place, forbid for-profit chairs, mandate mechanical safeguards, and one by one days where the machines would not run were added: The Super Bowl, Christmas, New Years, the twenty-four hours after polls close on Federal Election days (some states added their own blackout for off-year elections). Even cities added days - usually from the local sports calendar. In a fit of nonsense, there was never the will to mandate Valentine's Day as a blackout.

Though in place for ten years before Reagan used one, they were rare and controversial. Reagan's decision in 1999 spurred Congress to take the issue up and put an end to the disconnected laws and regulations each state was developing. Cognitive tests were drafted first - though none of the congressional representatives would tie this to Reagan. A five minute waiting period - which was put in place by the developer to kill time while the booth's systems warmed up - was extended to twenty minutes.

Users who failed the cognition test could appeal from within the booth to 'judges' who were working from a call center in Utah. The judges had to pass a criminal background check during the certification phase, and maintain licensure as a notary public. Most had been at work for months before their certificate arrived. The pay and benefits package was generally well received and thought to be fair.

Automated consciousness and coercion questions were added to the inebriation scan in 2001 as additions to a trans-portation bill.

The Smithsonian and the Reagan Library struggled with one another, as only archivists can, for possession of the booth that Reagan used. It had been decommissioned within months of his use of it because the gawkers and visitors to it were interfering with the country club and the members felt that it was *déclassé* to see a shrine forming. The Smithsonian won out, the exhibit they created was heavy on oak and bunting but dodged controversy by having only a small plaque that listed bare facts to contextualize the booth. Security staff were constantly busy fending off vandalism from punkers, anar-chists, and LGBT activists. While most of the vandalism was sloganeering via paint or markers, the booth had developed a scent of urine that the cleaning crews could not overcome.

Day to day regulation of the booths was contentious. Every government layer wanted the responsibility housed with them - not least of which because of the taxation and revenue stream opportunities. Department chiefs struggled to secure the booths in their portfolio.

Legislators in Minnesota found the formula that was quickly

2

copied – they housed the oversight of the booths with the state Public Utilities Commission since the booths drew a tremendous amount of energy from the grid while operating. Aside from the Deep South states and Alaska which all went for a special appointee answering to the state's Governor.

Activists saw in the booths the ability to make shocking political statements, waves of short-lived campaigns were launched. They failed, the people who were most passionate and bought-in were the ones going into the booths, leaving people who couldn't persuade or push the movement forward as the only ones left.

Creditors sued for veto power and credit checks complaining that debtors were avoiding their obligations by using the booths. These lawsuits were what made the Catholic Church speak out for the first time on the booths. They filed a brief – echoed from pulpits across the country – that life is sacred and moneylenders should not decide who lives and dies. As of the late summer of 2004 there is no credit check to use a booth.

With the widespread adoption of email some states did trial runs using them to notify next of kin. The National Association of Letter Carriers, American Postal Workers Union, National Rural Letter Carriers' Association, the National Postal Mail Handlers Union, and the US Post Office itself jointly sued the states testing email and lobbied against this Federally and in states that hadn't done trial runs. Their argument hinged on propriety – but the rambling missives of some notes racked up considerable postage.

One novelist entered a booth in a stunt writing session. He posted up in the closest booth to his apartment with provisions and amphetamines, promoting his undertaking to friends darkly as *The Late Great American Novel.*

He had cleared one hundred and fifty three pages when the amphetamines began to wear off and boredom slouched about. Only then did he read that for his protection that everything written would be deleted from the booth's local memory and could not be copied onto external media should he not proceed.

This was put in place after a civil case brought from death row by a murderer who had been convicted because he had left an open confession typed in a booth but changed his mind. Already suspect before going into the booth, the investigators seized the confession and used it to close the case and deliver it to the prosecution.

The novelist sat stunned at his mistake. He was honest enough with himself that he knew his writing needed the marketing boost he had envisioned in order to get published.

One posthumous doctorate had been awarded when a doctoral candidate's final entry was delivered to his department chair, though the practice was quickly banned at all universities as doctoral students are inherently desperate people and it was simpler to put standards and practices in place not to award them posthumously than to do anything to reduce structural stressors on them.

A half an hour after realizing his writing would be deleted the novelist left the booth into obscurity.

Because Ronald Reagan was so intrinsically tied to the booths - both the concept and mechanics - they held a revered place among conservatives. Liberals - generally more inclined to support undertakings like this - had already been supportive. This meant that the booths fell into the rare neutral area where legislation and regulation was advanced without political maneuvering.

Two men cut past a Reagan Chair just off the property of a middling university campus. They walked across the sedate grounds, alone in the fading light. They were running late and followed desire paths pounded down to bare soil over years by thousands of students. Dirt traces through closely clipped lawns. They hustled down concrete sidewalks with competing messages chalked on them for Greek organizations, invitations spelled out in balloon fonts. Against these, in the least practiced lettering IT'S NOT TOO LATE TO REGISTER TO VOTE!!! GOTV 2004!!! Chalk dust in pink and orange, green and white, blue and red worked its way into the fading tread of their shoes.

'From a certain perspective there is a crude, unintentional, meritocracy to it,' Stephen, the elder of the two, said. White feathers poked from the seams in the black hiking vest he wore. Though fifteen minutes late, he took the opportunity to pontificate to the audience of one that he walked with. 'You can succeed coming from anywhere in it as long as you can divorce your actions from the class you come from in your head. So it is an improvement over feudalism in that respect.' He gestured as if he were miming underwater. Slow, and measured, even as he kept up the fast walking pace. Like a motion-enabled version of Exquisite Corpse. He was tall, ropey and slender from decades of outdoor work and picket lines. Stephen Robin worked as a bricklayer, employment that was flexible enough to allow him to travel while grounding him with blue-collar cachet. He was invited to speak on campus - another source of income - about the role of corporations in international relations in the latter

20th Century, and his own history of activism against them.

Paul, the younger walking with Stephen, wore a green corduroy jacket over a plaid work shirt and chinos. He led Stephen up a back access stair in the Student Union that Paul remembered from his time at the university. Some impatient student or faculty member had broken the push bar for the outside door before Paul's time and it remained open for them now. This had become a regular shortcut for those aware of it. They arrived at Student Union Room 314 to a meeting still being arranged. Paul opened the door for Stephen and walked in. The meeting organizers, the Campus Democrats, had hoped for a large turnout and delayed getting underway. As it happened each attendee could have taken five seats. Both of the Campus Libertarians were there, they normally stayed after their own meeting to heckle and argue with the Democrats during their meeting. Both groups agreed that the reason for the low turnout to their meetings was the university administration's policy that only pre-approved material could be posted on campus. For reasons that were identical, though arrived at along opposite ideological paths, both groups refused to participate in the approval process. Thus, their posters were removed almost as soon as they were put up. Since this was the issue, their reasoning provided, no one knew to attend.

The Libertarians shared the store-brand cheese puffs left over from their meeting with the Democrats. The President and Vice President of the Campus Democrats[1] pinned a *John Kerry for President* banner to the tack strip behind the front table to intermittent booing from the Libertarians.

A man close to Stephen's age, at least two decades older than any of the college students milling around, sat in the middle of the room. He wore secondhand chinos and a black hiking vest. He nodded to Stephen and smoothed down his ginger horseshoe mustache. Paul was pulled aside by the student organizer he'd been in contact with who thanked him profusely for picking him up from the bus station for them. Paul's cellphone vibrated with a text message.

6:09 p.m. Isaac Scheer
<Drinking on the way home from work is so passe. Come join me. The music is terrible. You'll love it.>

We have a moment to regard Paul alone as he is checking his phone. You'll see he's a doughy white man in his mid-twenties, glancing around shyly now that he is being described. He's tall but shrinks when put next to another man. Through some learned sleight-of-hand he accommodates his bulk so as to be the minor partner. In the walk across campus he was five foot eleven, an inch shorter than Stephen.

---

[1] Positions won with a two vote lead (6-4) in a bitterly contested election earlier in the term. The opposing ticket dropped out and joined the Campus Greens, bringing the membership of that group to four. While the fallout was brutal and brought comment from the faculty advisor, it was still one of the largest elections the group had to date. The three original members of the Campus Greens were concerned about the comparatively centrist ideologies that the former Democrats brought with them and what that would mean for their organization. One of the original Greens and the incoming Democrats began dating and the debate sputtered out.

Stand Paul alone in a cyclorama and tell him to keep his back straight and his chin up and he'd be a serviceable model for a young and poorly-remembered king. He wouldn't work as a model for one who led conquests to enlarge his inheritance, nor one who served wisely and left his subjects in awe. But if there is one who was overthrown early after earning the sobriquet *the Bloody* not for any particular acts of horror, but for mismanaging internal tensions and foreign affairs so completely as to leave the land in shambles, he'd do. Paul is very embarrassed after hearing all that, so we'll turn elsewhere.

Music filtered in from the auditorium downstairs, where the turnout for the Campus Crusade for Christ concert was beyond capacity for the room. A nervous fire inspector weighed her options as people lined up to enter the hall. Their University Approved posters depicted a stylized Knight Templar half in shadow. People swayed and waved their arms over their heads for a bowdlerized rock concert. Skim milk salvation appeared to draw a bigger crowd than watered down revolution.

She.Her

↓2 →4

We are now two hours ahead and at a bar. It was roughly a parallelogram, narrowing towards the back, built to fit on the oddly intersecting block, now standing alone with empty lots where its neighbors had been torn down years before. On one side wall was painted the bar's name, the opposite had blue paint splashed across it like a hydrant had burst on the wall, the center of the spray had the command DO WORK painted in white. Stephen has been left behind and we're following Paul's evening. He's in a crowd, listening to the bartender shout into a microphone. 'Hey! Listen up! The second car of this train goes out to Julie! That bitch cut this boy deep!' The bartender stood on an upturned five gallon bucket, addressing the dimly lit, packed, bar. 'Suck it down you bastard!' This bastard was taking a Train, a ritual started by the original customers at the bar. Rail employees who created a reverential skit dedicating whiskey shots to the pains they endured. The crowd that slowly replaced them over years kept the folkway going – Three glasses on the bar and one dumbass in front.

The man of honor raised the shot to Julie. The crowd was split between booing and cheering. Julie herself in the back of the bar with her friends booing theatrically. The bartender

9

read off the next line on the note card while handing over the third shot. Paul and Isaac sat on stools just outside of the spotlit area of the bar, cheering along.

'Oh! This last fucker has gotten more than a few of us! Shorted hours at work! Take it you working class shitstain!' The room unified in cheers. 'Who's up next? Paul? Dinares, get up here! Get up here! You've got three coming!'

'Go go go. Times wasting' Isaac pushed Paul with both hands.

'He paid for Jack, that work for you?' The bartender asked as Paul got to him. 'Clean glasses, right?' Paul nodded. 'Good, let's go. Got a stack tonight. Hey, listen up!' He yelled as he stood up. Paul's up, and he's got troubles. You want to hear about his troubles!?' The crowd cheered.

Isaac had taken Paul under his tutelage when they met in college. He was two years younger than Paul, and had met when Isaac's dealer had flunked out and he was looking for a new one. He'd been told by a mutual professor that Paul was holding, but this wasn't the case. Over the semester they realized they had common interests aside from weed and became close friends. Isaac dropped out the same semester that Paul washed out of school. Paul took the first job that would take him. Isaac went looking for candidates and by the end of that year's election cycle had filed an LLC for his one-man consulting firm. He convinced Paul to quit his job and work for him, assigning him work on campaigns Isaac had contracts with - scraping together field plans and designing literature on a clearance copy of Photoshop. Sorry, looks like we missed the first car of the train while I was talking. It was about voting. Here's the second one.

'Alright, the second one is to, what the fuck?' The bartenders were rarely amused by the lists Isaac submitted, they didn't get a good crowd reaction like breakups did. 'Nepotism? Fuck nepotism everyone.' Paul took the shot. 'This one won't be popular tonight! Paul is looking for a fight! This car is for the Karaoke Rock Stars waiting for ten o'clock to come around! Hey, Asshats, not everyone can be rock stars!' Middle fingers went up as Paul took the shot.

In the 2003 election cycle, Isaac gave Paul the title of *General Consultant* on a countywide race in a rural reelection. It came with business cards and stress hives. Isaac's status as a college dropout and aggressiveness in building his firm gave him rebel cachet with potential clients, he quickly cemented himself as a upstart heavyweight in City elections with reach into the countryside. He forced aside established media firms who took on political campaigns as side work to the multi-million dollar corporate accounts that paid their invoices on time.

'Quiet now! I've got one to add here! You aren't getting glasses, but I'm taking one for all of the staff! Cause the last car on this train that I'm adding on here is one that has flattened a whole lot of you! Paul's just the last one to do it! I mean you, the fuckers who are laughing! This final shot, the one with the little blinky red light on it that tells you you just got run the fuck over, is tabs on Dollar Night! How do you walk out on your tab on Dollar Night you blacked out bastard!?' The crowd cheered and got an admonishing index finger pointed at them, 'Everybody laughing get their credit card held behind the bar! You're not to be trusted, but thank you Paul for tipping so well when you forget to close out and I get to write it! That goes for all of you! Alright, that's it! Jon, get up here!' He matter of factly shoved Paul away from the spotlight.

'So this look.' Isaac gestured at Paul when he came back to his stool. 'Is this Golden Age pornographer or rural County Commissioner candidate and former Secretary of the regional Farm Bureau? Chinos,' Isaac pointed his whiskey sour at each item of clothing, 'Green cord sport coat, and the unfortunate plaid shirt. Going to have to say that it comes down to how many buttons you leave undone on the shirt.' Isaac took a drink, 'What's got you so your-version-of dressy dressy? But button one up, you're trending porn.'

'Had to pick up a speaker who came in for a campus Dems meeting. This activist.' Paul shrugged and trailed off. His clear tequila and Sprite sat on the bar.

'I don't get why you stay involved with them. They weren't anything when we were there, and they haven't gained any ground since. When we need volunteers we go to ONE meeting, ONE time and make them feel important then. Now you're chauffeuring people around for them. Do you buy the kids alcohol for their parties too so they think you're the cool mom?'

'With the Presidential the group is growing. This year they've got maybe twenty who have been to meetings, and double that on their mailing list. I just want to see them get support so they're not just termed out and walking into nothing.'

'Fair enough.' Isaac said, 'How's the temp job?' Paul grunted in response.

I'm going to take a moment to describe the person approaching Paul and Isaac before they see Her[2] and start talking. She is short, a punker, wearing a blue mechanics jacket, a gray v-neck dress over jeans, and running shoes. Her bangs had been lightened and dyed pink, though some time ago and now faded to a rough ombre. She squeezed in next to them at the bar. 'Paul, right? Nice first bit on Cheney, you could have reminded people to vote though.'

'I've got to take the blame for that omission actually.' Isaac interjected. 'I'm Isaac. What are you drinking?'

'Nice to meet you then. I'll have a Rum and cola, Paul.'

Isaac nudged Paul. 'Well, that's clear enough. Paul, buy the lady a drink. I'll be back shortly when the conversation needs me.'

'So,' She said as Isaac left, pushing through the crowd, 'What are you doing tonight? Watching people embarrass themselves with your buddy and going home alone?'

'Just a few and going home.'

'That's what I said. Pay attention. I'm going to find someone else to get up with tonight after this drink if you don't start picking up your end of this.' She flicked the challenge at him.

'Get up?'

'Bombing. You ever go?'

'I was into graffiti back in high school, haven't been out in years.'

'Yeah graffiti. Come on, keep up. What's with you? Your smile looks like it's going to go drink by itself leaned against

---

[2] Sarah will be referred to as She/Her throughout this piece when Paul is present. It's to bring attention to various issues in the way people see one another without caring about one another. It's very thought provoking and moving, don't you worry.

the wall.'

While Paul had filled several sketchbooks – now at the bottom of a banker's box in his apartment with other detritus of his teenage years – he had neither the ego nor talent to put the time in. He hated being the slowest runner among his friends when the police showed up – always having to rely on hiding and misdirection rather than just running away. 'I was into it back in the day. Decided if you're not on a coast you're just going to be a toy.'

'Bullshit to that. You may be a toy, but no need to slander everyone with that. Anyway, I do posters. Wheatpaste. I've got a new series that I want to get up and I'd like a lookout. Leave with me. You're dressed so square the police won't notice you.'

Isaac twisted and elbowed through the crowd back to them. 'What misanthropic architect would draw up a bathroom with no window and no fan?'

'Isaac, did I ever tell you that every time I got over in high school my friends and I got chased by the cops?'

'You have mentioned it. Didn't you hide under a squad car once?'

'Then I'm not giving you a choice. Isaac, maybe we'll see each other soon. I'm taking this one with me,' She finished Her drink and turned for the door. George Bush's face over crossed bones was stenciled on the back of Her jacket in red. Isaac elbowed Paul as he followed Her.

Paul eased into a doorway, glancing up and down the street. He put a cigarette in his mouth but left it unlit. He'd smoked a lot this evening. Headlights rounded the corner and he coughed twice, as loud as he could. The alcohol in his breath burned the air. He heard Her duck between garbage cans in the alley behind him. The police car passed as Paul flicked his lighter. Over his shoulder Jesus Saves was scratched into the steel door that Paul leaned against, in crisp typewriter script. Fresh enough that the scratches glinted unoxidized under the streetlight. The police car turned and accelerated away, Paul heard the engine race as it diminished.

'Clear?' Paul heard Her whisper.

'Oh, yeah. Clear.'

'Then say *Clear* when it's clear. Is that clear? I don't like hiding back here. There's something leaking out of this trash can.'

'Cool. Sorry.'

'Oh, *cool*. Cool now. I see.' She cuffed him on the shoulder from behind and gathered Her equipment. 'What's that? You do that?' She pointed at the scrawled graffiti.

'No. It was up there.'

'I didn't notice it before.'

She hooked his arm with Hers and kissed him. Her backpack was empty apart from masonry brushes wrapped in shopping bags. Another pedestrian heard them chuckle at a joke as they made their way into the night.

Standup Routine

↑4 ←3

5:23 a.m.

Paul lay on the bed watching Her dress. With Her back to him She slipped a dark blue shirt with a silkscreened equal sign over Her head. She spun quickly in place. Her room was cluttered with cardboard, pens, markers, canvasses, brushes, clay, lino cutting tools, razors, books on fine art, books on primitive art, books on modern art, books on ART of all kinds. Rolls of some matte plastic leaned in the corner.

A cat sat at the foot of the bed staring at Paul. Paul was hit with the thought they'd met before, and he owed the cat money. It glared and kneaded the bed at him. 'Your landlord lets you have a cat? I didn't think they did in this building.' The cat continued to knead the comforter, not breaking eye contact.

'No, no cats. But I read the lease and it doesn't bar *secret cats* and Happy Birthday is the secretest.' Paul laughed and reached to let the cat sniff at him.

'What are those rolls for?' Paul pointed to the translucent matte plastic. The cat silently leapt to the floor.

'It's mylar. I get it from the blueprinters' dumpster. Best stuff I've ever come across for stencils. Those three rolls are two years of haunting that place. This apartment catches fire those and Happy Birthday are under my arms.' She rubbed Her face quickly with her hands, up and down, 'Anyway! Get up. And get dressed. Your laying there naked is weirding me out.' She smoothed Her hair.

'What's that?'

'It's a favor. You get to sleep in a familiar warm bed tonight, with a pillow that's just right, and an indent in the mattress that fits you, and your binkie.' She picked up Paul's black leather sap from the floor and tossed it on the bed. 'Which I suppose is that thing.'

'That's my walking-home money. Seriously though, it's like five thirty in the morning and my car isn't here. It's daytime now.' He pointed at the window, gold from the sun at the horizon.

'It's not daytime because people don't stay overnight. You can go rinse off, but don't flush the condom. Tie it off and throw it in the trash like a gentleman. And I want your number, so we can see one another again.'

6:33 a.m.

Henry awoke with the sun. He sat up, blinking. He stood, stretched, and stamped his feet. He rolled his bedding, tying it with a boys' leather braided belt. He rubbed the forest detritus off his socks on the laces of his shoes before pulling them on. His camp was at the edge of a patch of woods and looked over a farm field, this year planted with soybeans. He preferred the years with corn because of the privacy offered. All of it was inedible matter to be fed to the global processors and supply chain to become food in a year or more. To the southwest traffic moved through a busy intersection with a half-empty

17

strip mall beyond. A forty minute walk would bring him to downtown. On the other side of the woods lay a members-only golf course. Henry avoided being seen on that end of the woods.

'Where to today?' Henry addressed the trees as he urinated. Catholes for waste dotted the site. One special one held a plastic coffee can with a hundred and forty three dollars in it, his entire savings.

He kneeled over a small charcoal grill, half rusted away, and lifted the cover. Blowing steadily on the coals, adding small twigs and leaves until they burst alight. Henry carefully removed the lid from a can of soup and gingerly rested it on the grating.

Pulling a cigarette from a tin, Henry lit it with a fire piston he wore on a chair around his neck. He pulled the soup from the grating and drank it in a few quick gulps. Drawing deeply on the cheap cigarette he squinted through the smoke and untied the tarp he had set up as a rain shelter and stowed his possessions underneath, checking the temperature of the grill before stowing it as well. He examined his work, satisfied that it looked like a windblown tarp caught in underbrush, then set out. Walking, miles into downtown. Locomotion older than civilization, older than the species.

8:17 a.m.

'No.'

'Please?'

'This is a small business, Sir. We operate on paper-thin margins.' A stack of pulp novels and a treatise condemning Communism credited to J. Edgar Hoover sat on the counter. 'Sir, you may not make credit card purchases for less than seven dollars.' The barista picked up a straw and smacked Paul's hand with it. 'Why do you even buy these? You don't even read them.'

'That's my business. What if I refuse to patronize this establishment, Carrie?' Paul leaned over the counter, grinning slyly.

'The quarter books and pot coffee aren't paying the bills. And you can't follow through on that promise. Here, I'll add an americano for me and that should be enough.' She rang it up and took Paul's debit card.

He looked around the room at the other customers, 'Ah coffee shop patrons, as beautiful and gloomy as ever. So many scarves.' He turned back to Carrie, 'I met someone last night.'

'Yeah? Did you act like an idiot and get nowhere?'

'No, She likes me. I even got kissed.'

'Likely story.'

'I've got to go to work. Seriously, we might go out later tonight to an art-slash-protest thing. You should come.'

'Boo to that. I've got plans. But, text me with it in case they fall through. Your vague, last-minute, half-invitations have always been terribly irresistible to me.'

11:23 a.m.

All of the temps and managers thought the project was senseless when they had time to reflect on it. And every one of them had been bored enough a hundred times over to reflect on what they were doing. The insignificance of their job was multivariate, complex, and overwhelmingly vapid. But, it was inside work, the company didn't drug test, and the checks were on time and always cleared. The forklift they had been using when Paul started had been chained to a door and the propane tank removed. It was barred now because Chuck hit and nearly toppled a support beam while racing the perimeter of the warehouse in a time trial. They'd made it to the fourth heat. The fastest perimeter lap was written in permanent marker on the roll bar.

Paul grunted as he shifted another stack of eight boxes off the red handcart. Half a days' work for the office. He hadn't bothered turning on the overhead lights in the warehouse, he'd be finished before they warmed up and the fogged skylights allowed plenty of light through besides. Coffee-table-sized flakes of mint green paint with white primer reverse showing lay where they had sloughed off the walls in drifts, those away from the walls broken from footsteps and wheeled traffic.

In haphazard rows in the center of the enormous room sat nearly nineteen thousand black plastic, weathertight, commercial filing boxes in over two thousand stacks. They were documents of all sorts from a bankrupt company being held onto for legal compliance.

Because the contract hadn't given direction otherwise at the beginning of the project three years ago the boxes and the files within were in no order, other than roughly chronological as they were marked, closed, and readied for storage. They should have been for when a creditor subpoenaed particular records, but this wasn't caught until a year in and the managers decided when they met to continue on as they were because a close review of the contract they had didn't delineate that and they were on solid footing legally.

Paul added these eight to the installation that would sit until they were hauled off for shredding. A windfall for whatever company received them then.

They were garbagemen. Inverse-archivists making a performative journal with the barest of information of the files and secured for others but pointed at a shredder and oblivion. This slow moving ritual would end years on. Unburdened, the handcart traced lazy arcs through the paint and dust as Paul made his way back to the carpeted office, popping and squeaking when it hit rusted bolts cast into the floor to hold heavy equipment that had been cut off or hammered over.

Albert finally sat down. He felt tired. No, he told himself, he wasn't tired he was nervous and his body made him sleepy when he was uncertain. The metal folding chair he sat on, the pressboard folding tables, the brown carpet tiles, some askew. He pushed one with his toe to square it up and it fell into place. The competing smells of cigarettes, air fresheners, and basement damp. He thought of the community partners he'd made contact with, the outreach he'd done. This would be the first event in this town. Wondered if anyone would turn out. If the calls and flyers were enough. Clock ticking forward. The trash was filled with the detritus of packaging from all the new art supplies, Albert made a mental note to find a recycling bin for it and that he should say that he would to the attendees. He realized people would use the bin during the training, so he stood and looked for something different to use. Looking up, Stephen was opening the door to bring poles down to the basement.

7:33 p.m.

'I'm Carrie. Paul's been my best friend for,' she paused, 'like three years now. It's nice to meet you.'

'Same yeah. You two ready to go in? I'm fucking stoked for

this.' The three walked down the stairs to the common room. Spread out on the tables that normally saw nothing more exciting than ashtrays for Alcoholics Anonymous meetings were piles of cardboard, cans of spray paint, jars of paint, brushes, stencils in all stages of completion and some used whale staplers, and scrounged fabric. Wooden poles leaned against one wall.

'These colors don't work next to one another.' the organizer, Albert, said to an attendee. He brushed his mustache absentmindedly, 'Black and red print the same in grayscale so if you get coverage no one will be able to read your sign in the paper. Just put in a white outline.'

Paul walked around the room, looking over the shoulders of the fifteen other attendees, finally choosing the circle led by Stephen who was teaching how to make the heads for giant puppets. Here out of familiarity with Stephen more than any particular choice. 'They're useful in protests, they give a vertical element and they keep things upbeat and absurd.' He bent and folded the cardboard, using his whole body to push it into shape, using a whale stapler to keep it in place.

'Good potato.' Whispered into Paul's ear. 'Are we protesting potatoes? Are they oppressing some indigenous people and I haven't heard about it? Is this because I don't listen to the BBC Overnight?' then, louder, 'Make room. I want to know about this. She sat next to Paul. As they worked alongside one another She created an accurate likeness of Rush Limbaugh as Paul stapled away at his lumpy mass of cardboard.

'Going for a potato?' Carrie said when she came over while Paul was half-heartedly stapling cardboard.

'This could be, something here. Maybe a pompadour if I make this the top?" Paul rotated the lumpy cardboard in his hand, catching his palm on a staple and began to bleed.

'I made this t-shirt. What do you think?' Carrie twirled. She had stenciled an enormous fist in red with VOTE across the knuckles in black, and spray painted it diagonally across the shirt. She gave Carrie a thumbs up from within the oversized Rush Limbaugh head she had put on. Paul was impressed.

'I'm impressed.' Paul said, impressed. 'Would you make one for me?'

The sun was low and coming through the basement windows high on the walls when Albert noticed the time. 'Alright everyone! Let's stand together and show off what we made. I need a picture to thank the people who sent me here.' People worked their way upstairs. Holding still-wet signs and banners, with lumpy puppets on wooden poles towering over them, the group stood on the church lawn, squinting into the low evening sun. Click.

1:35 a.m.

'I feel stupid.' Three men wearing browns and grays crawled the last few feet to the top of a fill dirt hill. One, Matthew, had a large gym bag on his shoulder. Nettles, burdock, bindweed, pokeweed, nightshade, and thistle - the seeds disturbed and sprouted after years laying dormant plucked and pulled at their clothes. The one in the lead, Sebastian, peered over; waiting for the bright flash of light from night watchmen. Nothing came. The wind rustled. Cars and semi trucks drove past at dizzying speeds on the Turnpike hundreds of yards across a field behind them.

Matthew could hear the roar of his heart over the sound of the vehicles.

'You guys ready?' Sebastian asked.

'Let's go.' Frank said, Matthew laughed.

'Alright, gloves? Frank, you're the pitcher. Matt, you want the honors?' Sebastian pulled an aluminum bat from the gym bag.

'No, you go. I'll keep watch.'

'A'ight.'

Franklin lined up and threw a baseball in a gentle arc towards Sebastian, who swung wildly at it. The ball thudded to the ground, rolling a short distance.

'Shit, I can't see anything' They all giggled nervously.

'You should have swiped a tee ball base, man, when you were pocketing those baseballs.' Matthew said, giggling.

'Fuck up. Hey, Frank. Man move over a couple feet to the right. I think I'll get it if the ball is silhouetted against those lights from the truck stop.'

The next pitch connected. The ball landed in the bare soil that would be a side yard. 'Throw another.' They heard the crunch of a downspout in the nearly completed development below.

'I'm going to amateur night next week.' Matthew said.

'Wet t-shirt, eh man?' Sebastian missed the pitch. 'You don't have the chest.'

'Comedy club. I've been working on my bit.'

'Maybe we should do golf instead of this?' Franklin said. Matthew stomped in the weeds behind Sebastian looking for missed balls.

'No man, THIS is American. It's right that this is how we're going about this action. Gonna get hot dogs on the way home.' The ball smacked against vinyl siding. 'Jokes! The king demands jokes! Make me laugh, jovial prole!' A french door shattered below. 'Fuck right.'

'Uh, alright. Here. So I've got a farmer's tan. But I'm not a farmer. So I prefer *body mullet.*'

'They gonna get better man?' Sebastian asked. Swing and a miss.

'Little bottles of wine make me feel like a giant wino. That was a pun. Uh, you know that over a third of pets die in shelters? And just about every old person dies in a nursing home. There's a lesson. The lesson is that *the love of a child is for shit.* I wave to people on accident. To strangers, thinking they're someone I know. But I don't stop there. I take them to lunch, we become friends. I meet their family. When eating fruit I really appreciate that I can overcome all of agricultural sciences and modern pesticide chemistry with a three second rinse under cold water.'

'I got one.' Sebastian interjected. 'Frank, you want to bat?'

'Sure man.'

'Alright. A few years back I was standing in a snow covered yard wearing brand-new, mall-bought clothes. A big overcoat and khakis. I was waiting for a goldendoodle to take a leak so I could leave for a wedding at a converted Victorian mansion. Golden doodle. Poodle and Golden Retriever. Anything crossed with a poodle becomes a doodle. Matt, your spawn if you fuck a poodle would be a mathedoodle. Don't fuck a poodle, Matt.' A bedroom window shattered. 'This dog was fucking expensive. The woman I was dating, God I was crazy about her, didn't care. Found it online, bought from a breeder. How weird is that? She gave up another dog when she moved in with her ex. That should have been a sign. Super suburban too. All sectional couches and Gray Goose. Anyway. I was standing in the snow with this dog waiting and thought to myself *Am I a yuppie?*'

25

'Yeah you fucking bougie Sebastian Waddlesworth the Fourth, yuppie fuck.' Franklin answered.

'No I mean, ALL that had come down on me after meeting her and it didn't occur to me. You know how the story ends, she dumped me a month later for her dog trainer. Dog trainer, man! How else do yuppies get dumped!? Only yuppies get dumped for dog trainers. I met the guy, he had all these big ferry dogs, or something, sled dogs, and would make them pull things in competition. Went on and on about his fucking roided out dogs. Like he buys dogs, makes them pull heavy things so he can have awards. I mean, I lost her to him but he's got to live that life which is worse than anything I could wish on him. I'm glad I sunk back into the lumpenproletariat with you assholes.'

'Did he play acoustic guitar?'

'He did, yeah.' The ball ricocheted off a roof, coming to rest in a gutter.

'That's the sign you missed man. Dude shows up in your girlfriend's life who owns an acoustic guitar and you are About To Be Single. Every time.' Matthew affected a deeper voice with a slower cadence, 'Hey babe, you want to come by and smoke up and hang out? I'll just be practicing guitar. What, your boyfriend isn't cool with it? Yeah, some guys are uptight like that. I don't get it, I'm not like that. Just whatever you want. Gonna be laying around practicing, could show you a few chords. Whatever.' Matthew paused, 'Scratch a hippie and you find a psychopath though. Fuckers are dangerous.'

'Truth.' Franklin put in. 'Alright, we got two more.'

'Alright.' Matthew started again. 'You want humbling, building on your story. Go to the bathroom midday hours away from taking a shit and wipe your ass. It's jarring. Think you're clean and all, and find out the truth.' Matthew waited,' No? Alright. You know those bus stop benches with the armrests in the center. Really skinny homeless people look at those and are like *Ooh, seatbelts! I'm sleeping safe tonight! So glad this city gives two fucks about me staying alive!*' A sliding door spiderwebbed. 'Alright, I used to be forgetful. But now I play practical jokes. Like when I played that practical joke on you and forgot to pick you up from the bus station Frank. You were leaving me voicemails like *Matt, what the fuck? Where are you? I'm cold and alone.* Gotcha, pranked, bitch.'

Sebastian took a glass bottle out of the gym bag. 'Alright guys, scout the area and pick up what you can find. Meet me at the creek where we crossed.' He unscrewed the cap and stuffed a rag into the mouth, tipping the bottle upside down to speed the wicking. 'Eeny Meeny Miney Moe. Catch a de-vel-o-per by his toe.' Sebastian looked over the houses, 'If he hollers, burn him down. Eeny Meeny Miney Moe.'

2:54 a.m.

Paul nosed through the profiles he'd found and left open as tabs. The search feature was his key. Night after long night he'd scroll through the photos of woman after woman in hopes they'd posted photos from a trip to the beach, or fooling around in their underwear, a sultry glance making eye contact with the camera, really anything that he could add to his massive, unwieldy file of marginal pornography. While he didn't seek out the profiles that were clearly faked, he was drawn to them because they held greater promise of illicit photos snuck past censors.

Returning to the search results unsated he saw one that was a blurred red swirl. He went to the profile and saw that there weren't many photos and all had been modified somehow. Inclusions, tinting, color reversal. After some time, Paul realized that the primary photo was a heavily Photoshopped eye. He went back to the profile and read:

New technology does not give you license to corrupt the language. You are an adult.
Errors of grammar are very serious offenses. You can be sent to war.
Spelling errors will also be corrected harshly. Drive.
For both you face crushing ridicule. Drink.
I loathe confrontation. Smoke.
I will not do this because I wish to discipline you. Buy porn.
I must because your grade school teacher didn't do his or her fucking job. Fuck.
It will hurt me as much as I hurt you. It's simple.
If you choose to you may send me a note. Conduct yourself as an adult.
I like interesting people.

Paul leaned back in his chair. He asked himself what he was considering. His thoughts drifted to tangential subjects. His fear of discovery, his shame. The hoard that kept growing. Carrie's reaction, or any of the other people in his life. He thought of the stranger who he had run into at a show. She had known people's names and all the information they had up online. Cornering people, she would delve into conversations with casually introduced topics that were too pointed but to have been researched. That she had disappeared a week after inviting everyone to a party that no one had gone to. Carrie mocking men who sent her photos of themselves bare-chested, or nude, hoping for her attention. The feared news reports *Local man. Over thirty-five thousand images. Pervert.*

The hoard had grown so large, and Paul had constant, ongoing access to new images and videos, that he hardly ever looked at any of what he had collected. The disorganized collection was a dragon's bedding; beautiful women of his generation available for as long as the files remained uncorrupted. Because Paul hadn't started it as an archive or an art piece - and wouldn't have maintained interest enough to continue it if he had - it was comprised solely of women he found attractive. It had outgrown Paul's rudimentary organizing effort. It was becoming a record of its own. As loosely defined, biased, and twisted as it was.

After typing several introductions and deleting them as unsatisfactory, Paul copied song lyrics and pressed *Send.*

6:37 p.m.

'That'll be four fifty four.'

Paul handed over six dollars then pushed through the crowd to Her. He found Her standing with Her eyes closed.

'Beer. Man, it's getting expensive.' He said, handing over Her draft.

'Buy it with your good looks. Anyway, shush. Don't talk. This guy is horrible and I'm letting it wash over me. I've decided to enjoy this.' A skinny teenaged boy with an inflamed pimple on his forehead was reading hesitantly off a sheet of paper at the front. Paul reassessed and decided the guy on stage could be in his mid-twenties with ongoing acne.

'I've got another new one tonight.' He coughed. 'I haven't read this for anyone before.' He waited, breathing in as he gathered his nerve. 'Silence. Is so quiet.' He looked up at

29

the crowd then quickly down to the paper, 'It's much quieter. Than a crowded room. Even when those people are sitting.' Dramatic pause, in which She snorted loudly stifling a laugh. 'Quietly. And so much quieter. Than even the vast emptiness of space. Cause space is loud. In the right frequencies. Silence.' He moved the paper to the back of the small stack he was holding.

'Three poems or five minutes!' She yelled.

'Hey, the kid isn't even' Paul paused, 'fifteen or twenty-five. He's got his whole life to improve.' Paul whispered to Her.

'Age isn't relevant. For that he's being tried as an adult. Prosecutor has a solid case. No juvie for him.' She sipped Her beer.

'This next one, my final one tonight,' He glanced at Her, 'is also about the act of writing poetry. I call it *Muse*.'

'Art should aim to, at the very very least, annoy the audience. She's cute and welcome though.' The redheaded host interrupted the boy/man citing the five minute rule that he'd hit and introduced the next person in the lineup. 'What's your take on Stephen and Albert?

'The whole *professional anarchist* thing is, something. I mean, it's interesting to meet someone who is doing that for real, and making it work.'

'A professional anarchist who is slumming and registering voters.'

'True enough. What's your take?'

'Seems genuine. Really intense though. I'm down for seeing where what they offered me goes. Registering people is cool. And when I volunteered with the Dems it was like my soul was being bludgeoned with a cosh. The script and calls and all that shit.'

The dozens of volunteer call scripts Paul had written on campaigns sprung to mind and he winced.

'You had History Methods with Zunk, right?' She asked.

'A while back.'

'Yeah. We were in class together. You slumped in every Monday and Wednesday and annoyed me. Always chatting him up like you two were friends.'

'Zunk lives,' Paul took a drink, 'that work. He and I had a good rapport outside of class.' he felt defensive.

'Uh huh. You should have seen him when you didn't come in. When he realized that everyone was there for the day he always broke out grinning.'

Loudly, spoken over the PA. 'Ronald Reagan. Should have contracted AIDS.' Pause, the room echoed. 'GRID. Pumped into. His veins. Not from cum. Soaking in his ass. Not fun. Needle in the arm. Infected transfusion. Fusion, when Hinckley put him in. The limousine.' The words staccatoed out of the small PA, without cadence. The man was weathered like a fence post, Paul thought he must have been a teen in the eighties. 'The ambush! Greatest love offering in the world! No barrier would stand. A cure! To save the President! Reagan's Disease!'

'This is fucked up.'

'Shush, this is it.'

9:30p.m.

She sat cross legged over a cutting board laid on the floor of Her bedroom holding a razor knife like a pen. She carefully sliced away at the mylar. 'Autobiographies are for suckers.' She said, apropos of nothing.

'What's that now?' Paul lay back on Her bed typing on his

31

laptop. Happy Birthday slept on the pillow next to him.

'Autobiographies. What a pompous undertaking. Biographies are where it's at. Live and be recognized.' She finished outlining Zack de la Rocha's chin on the large paper she had laid out on her cutting board. 'Why'd you quit graffiti, really?'

'I wasn't very good, you know? I didn't have an original voice. I was scared as shit of the police.' Happy Birthday stood and stretched then walked out of the room. 'It was what we were all into, but that was it.'

'You were only into it because your friends were. It could have been anything really. Just lucky it wasn't soccer or some expensive card game.'

'Yeah.' A sophomore in high school, introduced to it by two scrawny brothers - one ahead of Paul's graduating class and one behind - who brought graffiti with them upon transferring in like a gift over the Silk Road. They were silent in classes, often napping. They were indifferent to school; neither contemptuous nor, as often happens, veiling fear as contempt. They were simply set apart from it all. They alone ignored the scrum of the adolescent lek.[3] They waited for nightfall, to go out and get over. The rail town offered thousands of undeveloped opportunities, and as many approaches and escapes for people with the will. The brothers had the will.

---

[3] Lek: A breeding behavior characterized by a group of males clustering to entice one or several females. Studied in various prairie chicken populations, also seen in amphibian, fish, insect, and mammal species. The most dominant males arrange themselves closest to the females, with the other males arraying themselves around this core, while simultaneously undertaking their own courtship attempts. Teenagers are predictable.

The circle that Paul filled a gamma role in attracted the brothers as a safe place to base themselves in. It wrapped around them and to this circle their sketchbooks were opened. They explained what all these kids who had grown up in the town had missed. They sat in this tight-knit cluster of friends and became the center that all the others formed around and weighed each other by how closely they modeled their behavior, how quickly and deftly their sketchbooks filled. The Polaroids they shared. The boys at the core continued to bluster, play pranks, tell bawdy jokes, and play guitar but the presence of the brothers irreversibly kinked the path.

Blackbooks and Prismacolors showed up in backpacks. By winter break no more additions had been added to the collective. Security was discussed jokingly and reached a soft consensus. The boys acted aloof but jockeyed for position, for invitations to go out, or to trade books for edits and critique. For the boys and few girls outside of the core to sit next to one of the brothers and review his sketches for inspiration was the goal. This adulation was a trifle, the crew of two allowed guest writers in with the same calm, silent, detached, decision making that they expressed to everything else. The group felt a current stinging them that by summer the brothers would move on as smoothly as they had entered if the group didn't keep up. The first test to be taken out was to show the most promise - those with the best connections and boldest schemes, who passed around the strongest Polaroids of solo work at lunchtime. But the second was silence - any sloppiness, braggadocio, or attention seeking was anathema to them, and would earn the one exhibiting it the cold shoulder from all. The adults around hadn't seen any of this before and weren't sure if the group was doing anything worth reprimanding or illegal. To these rural high school teachers the kids didn't smell like drugs and seemed to be spending their days drawing, and while they wore dull gray hoodies and oversized jeans and none of them wore a backpack correctly they weren't nuisances in class and didn't loiter outside the school.

Paul filled blackbook after blackbook with pencilled sketches and Prismacolor pieces, taped in ACLU pamphlets on police stops, photocopied pages from textbooks on drawing, along with snappy quotes and lyrics. He modeled what he saw around him. He bought caps offline with a money order and chose the name of a session musician in a Santana CD he owned. Racked paint and panicked. Bought it when he was able to get out of town instead.

But he wasn't there in spite of all of the pretending. He was a peripheral actor. A run for him meant days of fretting and planning. Every wall in town crossed his mind as a piece, and hours were spent rolling over getting to it, driving by it and thinking how to get there at night. He flattered himself saying his approach was methodical and tactical. But in the end he had as much reason to call it on the way out, or even getting up and couldn't get the hours needed with a can in his hand. He got up. But he always bailed on the big piece, the name-maker. He never got over. Never with the brothers, never atop any structures. They all saw him for what he was. In it for the camaraderie, in it for the thrill of feeling like an outlaw artist. But he wasn't an artist, he wasn't a writer. He was a kid who was doing what his friends were doing. 'It introduced me to midcentury postmodern Brazilian authors though. And how being invisible means not wearing black.'

'For sure. Quick way to draw attention to yourself. Dress like a shadow.' A plaintive scream sounded outside the bedroom. For ten seconds it flooded Her small apartment. Wind through a long abandoned homestead on the prairie with child graves overgrown with grass outside, La Llorona's wail. Paul looked towards the door apprehensively, goose prickles on his skin and his hair standing on end. Happy Birthday stood with her back to them, staring down the dark hallway to the front of the apartment, yowling. 'Happy Birthday!' She yelled. 'Happy Birthday goddamnit you lunatic. Come here!' After a few moments Happy Birthday turned and walked into the room, she dropped a fabric toy ball from her mouth onto the ground and glanced at each human. She mewed.

'Sorry man. She's done that since I got her. I think she lost a litter or something.' The cat walked to the bed and threw one paw with claws outstretched over the other, scaling it dramatically. 'Man, I want my landlord to invest in some home defense shrubbery. I hate being on the ground floor. And how this damn mansion got cut up to make it into apartments. Being back here with that damn hallway to the rest of my place. Something outside my window with giant, poisonous spikes would be nice. Prickly pear cactus would be good, they're native. Or a pitbull bush.'

She stood, stretching, and undressed in the few steps to the bed. A neighbor pulled into their own driveway minutes later. With Her atop him, Paul saw the beam of the headlights winding across the darkened walls and ceiling of the apartment. The three lives intersected in that moment. Only one witnessed it, and it would detach for him. Falling away from the quaintly imagined linear catalogue of his life to be another aoristic memory, muscae volitante - uprooted. Impossible, once distant, to recall the overwhelming weight of the present that dimly recalled lovers once held.

'You should take off.' She said later that night. 'It's late.'

'Yeah.'

Paul used Her toothbrush, a person who had been, a few weeks before, a stranger. He looked through Her medicine cabinet as he brushed his teeth. The sample bottles of Drakkar Noir She wore sat alongside Her birth control on one shelf. He closed the mirrored door, spat in the sink, rinsed off and went back down the hallway into the bedroom.

'Alright dude, I'm out.' He said when he was finished dressing.

Her eyes opened. 'Dozed off.' She yawned. 'See you soon Call me this week sometime.'

grammateia

→4 →4

Carrie taped a countdown calendar to the living room wall. She had made it herself, and it burst with Catholic-school-graduate curlicues and other flourishes in four colors. She tore off the topmost page. In the kitchen steam curled from quinoa simmering on the stove.

'Here, why don't we get started,' Albert said. He sat cross legged on the floor in the center of the room. He adjusted an easel holding a tablet of oversized paper and brushed his ginger mustache with his left hand. Enormous jade plants badly in need of being turned huddled by the sliding glass door that opened onto the modest backyard. Carrie had organized them the first floor of a duplex to use as a meeting space. The owner came into the coffeehouse most every work day to get coffee from her and was traveling over winter. Stephen and a new crew member, Troy, sat opposite one another at a low table. Albert looked around the room, then under the table. He reached for the marker that had rolled underneath before going on. 'We should brainstorm on venues to reach young people who aren't registered to vote.'

She, Paul, and Carrie sat down at the table. Carrie took Paul's arm and wrote in small, careful script, *Anarchists have decent artistic sensibility. They tried to blow up that Gaudi thing in Spain.*

Paul twisted his arm and read it, he took Carrie's arm and wrote back in his larger, sloppier handwriting, *Too bad their aim was crap.*

She glanced over, ignoring Paul and Carrie. Saying to Albert, 'What about shows. There are a few every weekend, I might be able to get on stage ahead of the bands.'

Carrie wrote *You should reconsider your atheism. G O D*, she underlined each letter. *He tells poop jokes.*

He? Paul wrote.

Troy suggested speaking at local high schools.

Carrie responded, *Berkeley Pit. No woman would have the snow geese that died bring in the bacteria cleaning the Pit up their butts.*

Haha! Paul wrote, *So before the pit killed the geese, they shit in its eye?*

Looks like. then, *People standing on the ground complain about the social safety net.* To the group Carrie said, 'I can ask if we could do a registration drive at the coffee shop I work at.'

And people that don't believe in gravity tell others to pull themselves up by their bootstraps.

Republicans need to embrace pseudoscience. Just disbelieving science is played out.

Paul stepped away from the meeting to use the bathroom. The toilet was full of partially dissolved piss-laden paper. Stephen asked the crew not to flush unless they shat, the owner of the house had a rule against it. It was an exciting new way of revolution. Letting urine ferment was a bold, caustic, statement against authority. Ecological!

Before rejoining the crew Paul found a computer that was

sleeping. He pressed Return and logged online.

New Message from Chloe April

Subject: Cute, but unsatisfactory

Body: You've got my attention. Tell me a joke. Something original.

Chloe

Subject: Did you hear the one about the British Moose?[4]

Body: The bobby asked him "Why the soap?" And the moose looked down and asked "Why the cuffs?"

p

'If you keep looking at me like that I'm going to tell you how good you look in those jeans.' Paul said to Her walking out of the meeting.

'Don't start with me,' She snapped back, 'what was with you two writing on each other?'

'Just something we've done since we first met. It's nothing.'

'Sure it is. Makes me uncomfortable.'

'Honey, she's my best friend, it's just something we do.'

'Yeah, and best friends are people who know everything about you except what you look like naked. But you two, you two act like you want that last part to change. And don't call me *honey*, be original.'

---

[4] Moose, Graffiti Writer. A British writer who rose to notoriety by 'clean tagging' the walls of Tube stations rather than painting them. He annoyed the police because they knew to arrest him, but not necessarily what for. Chloe had to look it up. She liked that.

New Message from Chloe April

Subject: 8.25/10

Body: I'm 'grammateia' on the screen talker box. I lead a boring life and am usually around to talk. I'm also in a relationship with a boy and we are 'crazy about one another,' as they say. So if that's an issue for you, don't bother.

Chloe

ps. I hope that it's not.

Glitter

↑2 →4

The next day at work Paul bounded down the three flights of stairs out to the sidewalk on his last break of the day. He lit a cigarette and looked out at the neighborhood falling into shambles across from the gray parking lot used by the building.

For decades the building Paul stood in front of this autumn afternoon was the administrative hub of a network of factories and shipping docks stretched across the Midwest. The pangs of recession bankrupted the corporation. The business fell in stages; first to its knees spinning off the logistics and shipping division, then on its hands with the closing of the extended factory network in one day, finally collapsing completely to the ground with the shuttering of this complex. Administrators and CPAs scrambled to staunch the losses, but every sortie failed. Thousands lost their jobs in great waves that crashed upon and decimated neighborhoods - including the one Paul was idly watching. He and the rest were employed by a law firm hired by and managing the rump company formed to guide the business to an end.

Men and women who had supported their families on a single income now stitched together part-time jobs. Banks repossessed vehicles. Mortgages were called. Deputy Sheriffs came under orders.

In one attic - in a house that had been bought by a property rental enterprise at auction and rented back - a young boy and a young girl sat back to back making cards using white glue and markers, crayons and ribbon, rainbow-hued construction paper and glitter. They started the game on Valentine's Day. The girl's parents smiled when they saw them sneak art supplies up to the attic. The parents had spied on the children and deemed it harmless. The boy's father didn't know what he did after school. The boy faced his father's leather belt when he got home, a proactive punishment in case he had misbehaved.

The girl poured an expansive heart on the front of the card and, giggling, shook the can of glitter over it. She shook off the unfixed sparkles and set the canister on the windowsill beside them. The boy smiled as he felt her back move against his.

The canister shimmered and fell, emptying on the boy's head. It poured down his face, in his eyes and in his mouth. He coughed, surprised, sneezed. Glitter flew. Tears welled and he rubbed his eyes. He fell over, coughing. The girl turned, smiling, not knowing what had happened. He took her giggling for snickering. 'W-Why? Why'd you do that?' He ran, red-eyed, for the ladder down. He rubbed his raw eyes, coughing out onto the street and running home.

The girl ran after him, crying now. She missed rungs on the ladder in her haste. Calling his name down the street.

Paul was at his desk bending a large paperclip into an abstract shape. Satisfied, he set it furthest to the right in a line beginning with an unchanged paperclip. His workspace nestled neatly into an alcove. The afternoon sun and a register over his desk made it as warm as bathwater. The loud hum of rooftop machinery outside his window provided an aural cocoon; coworkers had largely given up on talking to Paul at his desk because they had to speak loudly to be heard. He risked drifting off to sleep (then off to fired) if he remained there too long. He was woken by the boss once, who luckily didn't realize he was asleep, but normally the intermittent clanging of the mechanicals outside the window brought him around. He pulled a mortgage file from the cart next to his desk. Taped alongside his monitor was a strip of paper with directions printed on it:

Enter Employee Number
   TAB
   F2
   TAB
   07
   ENTER
   12
   ENTER
   F3
   TAB
   3
   1-0 depending on file type
   ENTER
   SHIFT F2
   Enter Generated Filing Alpha Number Code
   TAB
   1

CTRL V

ENTER

Over and over. His productivity had increased since the pre-ceding month. One lunchtime he had played ignorant when a coworker suggested taking lunch together and splitting the cost of a hotel room. She and Paul had flirted since she arrived, celebrating her third wedding anniversary with a temp job while her husband looked for steadier work than he had in Nevada. Paul wasn't sure what she saw in him, but he was intrigued by the curves he saw under the prairie blouses she wore. She had been ignoring him ever since he had turned her down

He crosshatched a scrap piece of paper with correction tape until the dispenser was exhausted. Then threw the empty dispenser and the paper in the bin under his desk.

Paul stretched and went to a row of file cabinets. Counting the third one from the window, he crouched and pulled the bottom drawer out fully. He reached behind the files and stuck a small piece of folded paper to the back of the drawer with a magnet. It was the twenty-third clue in a building-wide scavenger hunt he was making unbeknownst to anyone. The fire alarm sounded. It was the third time that week that the day - some may call it a workday - had been interrupted. He walked back to his desk for cigarettes as the other employees filed out the door.

An hour later the fire department had cleared the alarm and allowed the staff back into the building. People finished their cigarettes and went inside. Paul volunteered to take the morning's files to the warehouse. Seen as a generous gesture, he enjoyed getting away from his desk and being able to get another cigarette in. The red cart followed behind as he walked down the worn out carpet to the freight elevator. The path to the warehouse was complex and he'd gotten lost often early on. Now he could do the round trip in less than a half hour including a cigarette at a loading dock that was stuck open and faced away from the office. Out onto a weedy turnaround in the open central plaza. He decided to return by a route he rarely took, pushing open the door to personnel stairs, the fallen paint thick on the stair treads. He had been through recently and scrawled a long missive on the plaster walls. He'd taken a photo when he finished, the ink still wet in places, and sent it to Her. It had been painted over but the ink from the homemade marker She had taught him to make bled through the cheap white paint a manager had found and used in an attempt to cover it.

What names do bees have for flowers? Do they revere them? Do they see themselves as fulfilling a spiritual calling when they quietly gather pollen, taking it back to pack away into holy ossuaries? Or are they production workers? Long over romance and novelty. Can both be true? Do individuals have preferences? Flowers they seek out over others? Do they argue and tease to pass the time in the evenings? Do bees have cliques? Friends? Favored co-workers? Do the oldest bees – the foragers – garner respect from the younger workers? Do they carry themselves as ragged veterans, or as seniority trades? Do the hive bees have a grudge against the older bees – their sisters – because of the risk of disease, pests, and predators they expose the hive to?

45

Paul read through it, and read it again. The paint flakes shattered under his feet and the wheels of the cart as he walked on up the stairs.

Five p.m. approaches. The employees mull around the exit, chatting. None crossed the threshold to the hall, but the workday was over. Some fingered cigarettes. Others gossip magazines. Paul's dress shirt was untucked and his tie was rolled in his satchel where he had stowed it at ten that morning. The boss stewed in his office, but he was incapable of dispersing the huddle. It formed in ones and twos at four forty and quickly swelled so that the whole office was waiting, milling, by ten till. The boss took to closing his office door at four thirty so he couldn't be seen and angrily planned the next delivery of paperwork from a distant factory.

Driving home under a still pastel sky Paul turned onto Collingwood where his small Saturn station wagon was engulfed by dozens of sport bikes. A cloud of chrome and brightly colored fiberglass wound around him. The early evening air shimmered with exhaust, the riders revved and squeaked their tires. They sped and turned the next corner. Down one block a still life; two men. One sitting on a stoop holding a baby, the second in a third floor window talking on a cordless phone, watching them. A snapshot at the red light: a man atop a Harley screaming at a young woman driving a coupe. Paul's cell phone buzzed. 'Hey you.'

'There's a show Friday. We should go.' She said.

'Yeah? Who's playing?' Paul steered with his left hand and cradled the phone against his shoulder. It was too small and slippery to do this, but he needed his right hand to shift. Paul drove past a broken-hearted alcoholic ascending the staircase to his dark apartment with his evening rations under his arm.

Unaware of Paul's dangerous juggling She went on with Her end of the conversation, 'They're called *Parasols for Ponies*, my friend Helen is the lead singer. They play showtunes, straight. Bunch of old theater kids so they know them all by heart. It's just the best show in town.

'Are they headlining? What time should we get there?'

'Helen is the headliner of my heart, but they're not Friday. It's this solo static act, *Esos*, he studies the broadcast band of the area and does live tuning between stations. I don't really want to see it. *Wolves of Paris* is good though, they're on the bill.'

'Yeah, same. Would your friend ask people to register to vote?' Paul asked, 'It would help.'

'She probably would. She's down. And it'll give me a chance to talk to her.'

'Alright, cool. So I'll see you tomorrow?'

'Yeah dude, see ya.'

Field

↑2 →1

'In the middle of the ni-i-ight.' Matthew sang quietly.

'Shut up man.' Sebastian growled.

'Sorry Mister All Revolution No Fun.' he hummed on, 'I go walkin' in my sle-e-ep.'

'Just pay attention to what you're doing.'

'You're a pay attention to what you're doing.'

Franklin pushed aside corn stalks and found the two bickering. 'I think I'm ready to go. I splashed a couple dozen square feet over here.' He was carrying an empty red five gallon jerry can of gasoline.

'Okay, I got a joke.' Matthew said as he wet down more dry stalks of corn, 'Three assholes covered in gasoline light matches in the middle of a field.'

'I know, I should have thought of that.'

'Hey man, I suggested a timed detonator.'

'You know how to build one of those?'

'I do not, no.'

'Is it ethical to use all this gas to do this? And all the smoke in the atmosphere.' Franklin mused.

'Hey man, these fields need to go. It's our duty to fuck up Roundup's shit. All these test fields are prime targets.'

Sebastian answered. 'If they didn't want them lit up they should take these fields home with them at night and lock them up.'

'Alright, I'm out.' Matthew flung his plastic jerry can in a high arc.

'Me too.' Sebastian and Franklin both tossed the cans they carried aside.

'So uh, what, light and run?'

'About all I can see working. Car is that way.' Sebastian pointed, 'Frank, you and Matt head straight back to the car. On a hundred count I'll light this patch.'

'On it.'

The fire gorged itself on the land. Tumbling black smoke climbed into the air. From miles around volunteer firefighters raced down country lanes to fire houses, sirens wailing on a mix of American-made pickup trucks and SUVs. By dawn, seven hundred acres and seven homes were scorched, with the front line still out of control. Gawkers drove to see the blaze. Power outages rolled through the area as the wooden poles were consumed, stressing the grid. A transmission substation became a battleground, with a circle of firefighters and volunteers wetting down the area, stamping out fires as airborne sparks landed in the dry grass.

Golf

→2 →3

The evening began with a nosebleed.

Paul wiped his face and a red smear stretched across his hand. Bright red opaque blood poured from his nostril and down his body, swirling down the drain with sudsy water. He closed one nostril and blew, droplets sprayed against the wall of the shower.

'Well, shit,' he muttered. He blew his nose again and again. The primitive part of Paul's brain panicked at the sight of so much blood. Of so much, specifically, of *his* blood at that. Paul fretted, the rise of emotions ramming against his reasoning. He finished his shower quickly and toweled off carefully. He twisted five squares of toilet paper in his nostril and dressed.

grammateia: She is cradling the infant, and we see the dead Jesus.

g: Can you imagine coming up with that? Simultaneously in marble.

'Who are you talking to?' She sat down on Paul's legs as he lay back on Her couch.

bkp971: like aphrodite and her dead adonis. i've got to go. talk to you later.

g: Do you realize that we're having a multimedia conversation every time we're online? We can seamlessly fact check, link to songs, videos, news articles all in real time. No one before us has had this. It's all I want. Regular conversations are so limited. So truncated.

'No one, just someone who was on my high school golf team I keep up with.' Paul's voice was tinny due to the blockage in his nose. He closed his laptop.

'It's so weird you played golf. I need your help with this sign. Can you come outside?'

g: I like your style. Goodnight.

What's your revolution?

↓4 ←4

The line had ended and newcomers had thinned. Paul thought of stashing his clipboard and going in. A homeless man walked up to Paul. 'Excuse me sir. I don't mean to bother you, but I was wondering if you had any change?'

'I don't man. Cigarette?'

'That would be a kindness.' He pulled a fire piston out, snapped it and lit the proffered cigarette. 'What's your shirt say?'

'What's your revolution?' Paul said, answering. He opened his jacket wider.

Henry stood quietly, regarding Paul and the question. 'Staying sober. What's yours?'

'Nothing that good. What's your name?'

'Henry Canfield, young man. Thank you for the cigarette.'

Paul got a drink inside. Sebastian, in his uniform of a brown hoodie, messenger jeans, and self-dyed black v-neck t-shirt and broken-down Converse, walked up to Paul. 'Dude. I'll tell you the revolution. You got a minute?' Sebastian had a two-drink look in his eyes. He steered Paul to an unoccupied corner. Paul bumped against a Reverend Powell, who muttered and glared at him through wraparound sunglasses. The TVs were turning themselves off around the bar and the staff was digging for remotes to turn them on again for the few people watching them. The opening band played so loudly that Sebastian and Paul had to yell to one another.

'The revolution has all the writers, thinkers, talkers, doers and small arms it needs!' Sebastian yelled. Waving one hand for emphasis, 'We need mortars! Like a new *Blyskawica*[5], you know!? What's up with your nose!?'

'Dude!' Paul replied, 'I don't have any idea what you're talking about!? It's Friday night, man! Let's talk about this stuff some other time!? Oh, I fell off my roof!'

'Now is the time, man! When else! I've been reading this book on Swiss guerrilla tactics, I can't shake that we need mortars![6] Off your roof!? Is this like when you said you'd gone to finishing school!?'

'Yeah! I don't think it'll ever come to that! What's that B-thing!?'

'Polish Resistance, World War Two! A submachine gun that could be made in a basic machine shop! And assembled in the field! We need to design a mortar like that! Like the Type Eighty-Nine that the Japanese had. Thousands.' he trailed off to himself, 'And who knows man! Shit is crazy and getting crazier! Paul you're a good guy but you're missing so much! Bush is just a symptom of what's going on! Yo, I hear you're working at a bank!?'

---

[5] Błyskawica (Polish: *Lightning*): WWII era submachine gun produced covertly in Poland by the resistance. Designed to be robust and simple enough to be made by machinists with regular tools. Sebastian references shit like this because he thinks it makes him sound like he's a real revolutionary. Paul doesn't know what he's talking about.

[6] See? He's ridiculous. And loud.

'Not quite! Bankruptcy, through a law firm! But, through a temp agency!'

'What do you think of it!? What are you getting paid!?'

'Eight an hour! It's dumb but inside! You looking for a job!?'

'No man! I just started at a tool and die shop in the North End!'

'Hey you!' Carrie crossed her arms as she walked up and kicked the side of Paul's foot.

'Hey! I didn't know you were going to be here! Do you mind!?' Paul indicated his lit cigarette, 'Hey man, I'm gonna go catch up with her! Talk to you later!'

'Later man! Hi Carrie!'

'Yeah! Hi Sebastian! Bye!''

Paul and Carrie found a place to stand at the back of the crowd. Just quiet enough to talk. Helen's band was on and playing *Wash That Man Right Out Of My Hair*.

'I won't light another when I'm done with this one.' Paul said.

'Eh, everyone else is. So, what are you up to? What do you think of these guys?'

'She told me about them.' Paul shrugged, 'I mean, it's good seeing a band that doesn't take itself seriously. And this is my second double. I'm feeling it.'

The Reverend Powell was in the front of the crowd, kicking wildly with his left foot and mostly hitting the beat.

'Another nosebleed?'

'Yeah, this seems to have abated for now.'

'I don't see that Lady you're kissing, She's here?'

'Up front. Big crowd too. I don't recognize a lot of these people, who are they?'

'Hipsters.' Carrie replied.

'Extras? Paul asked, mishearing.

'Yeah, extras. If they talk I've got to pay them more.' Carrie looked around, 'You want to go check out the fire? I'll drive. Let's get out of here for a bit.'

'Sure.' Paul finished his drink. 'You want to take my car.'

They walked out into the evening, Paul texting Her what he was doing. Carrie took Paul's keys and he reclined in the passenger seat. She sped up on the ramp, merging onto the highway. They crossed the river, heading south. 'Can you see anything at night?' She asked.

'I don't know.'

They drove for some time without talking. Wind buffeted the station wagon, the aged rubber door seals whistled off-key.

'This is a beautiful night.' Carrie rolled down the window and put her arm out in the windstream. 'I want to leave again.'

'Chicago?'

'No. West though. Denver, or San Francisco, or Seattle. Somewhere different than here. If only we could keep driving. Through Indiana. Cross the Mississippi by dawn. Keep going.' She twisted her palm to face the wind, her hand rose quickly, and just as quickly down. Over and over, sine waves in the night. 'But we can't. Neither of us can, singly or together. When you're young you say yes. You say yes to traveling, you say yes to new friends, you say yes to sex, you say yes to anything. I was unencumbered, I didn't know enough to care about pissing off my landlord by breaking a lease early, I cheated on boyfriends when someone charming came along. I met people because I made myself available. But I'm getting older and I'm saying no, or no is the answer so people don't even ask. No, I've got a boyfriend. No, I've got a job here that

55

may become something. No, I've got too much going on. No, no, no. The past ten years were amazing, and the next ten may be grueling.'

Paul sat quietly, just thinking about what she said but not responding. 'It's up ahead. Look.'

The smoke could be made out by the winking off and on of the stars. On the ground, flashing lights marked the emergency responders. Carrie took the exit and slowed to a stop at the top of the overpass. 'Should I try to get closer?' The smoke plumes were making the night sky flat black.

'Why not. It's burned up almost two thousand acres now, right?'

'Something like that. Couple square miles.' They approached an intersection. An orange and white sign was erected *Local Traffic Only.* As they slowed to consider this, a State Trooper sped past them, overtaking and curving wide of their car. Driving fifty, sixty miles an hour with flashing lights on. But no siren.

'I guess we should have expected this.' She said, 'We're going to be in the way out here and there's not much to see now.'

'I think so. We're pretty exposed. I don't know if there are any restrictions on being out gawking.'

'What, you think that we'll be stopped and made to present our papers?'

'That Statie didn't seem to care about us.'

'Oh yeah. I guess that's true.' She shrugged, 'Why don't we just get back to town?' Carrie turned the car around in the street towards the highway. The headlights swung over a trailer park, illuminating a sign propped against one home, *It's a boy!! Jakub*, black paint on blue.

mint green polyester

←3 ↓1

'Hey brother!' Chris, a friend of a friend who Paul had met in the spring slapped Paul on the back and rounded in for a bear hug. Forty pounds lighter than Paul, he hopped up onto his back. 'Onward Christian soldiers! Giddyap!' Chris kicked his heels into Paul to spur him forward. At first glance Chris was intimidatingly jockish; muscular, with a tall pompadour and an affinity for leaving three shirt buttons undone. But his disarming boyishness, quick wit, and aptitude for antics made him and Paul fast friends. 'Hey Carrie! Good to see you out and about!' The gentleman Chris didn't subject Carrie to any of the roughhousing, instead shaking her hand quickly and politely. 'You two feeling a shot?'

'I'm down man!'

'I got this one.' Chris said. 'Forward steed! Once more into the breach!' The three made their way to the bar.

'Mister Medvedik. Mister Dinares. Miss Newcomer. How are you all this evening?' The bartender was good. 'I see you've got your drinking suit on Chris.'

'Looks like we're having a night! I want to wrestle a cop car.' Chris replied from his thick polyester mint green suit, he pantomimed a lasso. 'How about you Mr. Patton?'

'Life is life. It keeps on coming. Shots?'

'What are you thinking?' Paul responded.

Brian Patton paused, considering the question, 'I've got something I like a lot, give me a second!' He ducked to the other side of the bar.

'Just them, I'm driving!' Carrie shouted.

'Youth'll be frittern' away,' Sang out over the speakers. 'I say your young men'll be frittern'! Frittern' away their noontime, suppertime, choretime too!'

'Words! Words are happening!' Paul yelled, 'I don't understand words right now! Three? Are we at three? Where's Trevor?' Paul tried to turn his head around to look at Chris, but failed and shuffled backwards to regain his balance. Chris waved wildly at Trevor and caught his attention.

'Not three, we're at four!'

'Well, let's make it a nice....next number up!'

'Four!' Chris, Paul and Trevor yelled in unison.

'Fore!' Chris pantomimed a golf swing, nearly tumbling them over. Trevor caught him and got them back to balance. 'Hey Paul, from this angle I can see that your Horseshoe of Doom is coming in nicely.' He traced it with his index finger.

'I swear that I will knock you into a doorframe!'

'You seeing anyone?' Chris asked.

'Yeah, She's up front somewhere. You'd like Her.' The band struck up *If I Were A Rich Man*. 'Phone, ringing phone!' Paul yelled, 'Chris, phone, left hip!'

'Roger! I'm on it!' Chris twisted around, digging in his pocket after the vibrating phone. He lost his balance and slid off of Paul's back, landing on the floor hard on his right side.

'Uff.' Chris coughed. 'This phone functions much better when I'm sober.'

'Hey you guys,' She said as She walked up, 'you see that guy dressed like sudden death stalking around? Someone told me that's Jack White.'

'Cool.' Carrie said.

'Yeah, he comes down regularly I guess. Hearing that makes this town feel like less of a shithole.' She walked off to dance.

'Man I don't like when people get down. It's hard enough.'

'Dude, if you two break up I'm going to do my damndest to give her a new last name.' Chris said from the floor.

'Oh guys!' Carrie grabbed both their shoulders, 'So the coffee house got a great review online today. They said the staff was super friendly, the space itself was the classiest in town, and singled me out! They really liked that I make leaves in the foam.'

'Oh, sure,' Paul said mockingly, 'It's cheating to review yourself. *Oh, her breath smelt of angels. And her hair was ebony silk.*'

'I didn't write the review!'

'*Her skin was the finest marble.*' Chris added, '*Like the Taj Mahal could have been if they'd really tried.*'

Carrie laughed, 'Knock it off!'

'Here you go guys, something new. I call it the *Sylvia Plath*, I'm working on a line of Suicide Shots. Dirty glasses, heads up.'

Chris clambered up and grabbed one of the glasses. The five chimed, tapped the shots on the bar, and drank.

'Damn brother! That's awe-inspiring!'

'The secret is tequila. And Rumplemintz. And Baileys. So there are a lot of secrets.' Brian said. 'Anybody get anything?' All shook their heads negative. 'Huh, I think the new guy is salting the glasses every night, I tell him not to. Paul, what's up with your face? You're dripping blood on my bar.'

'Chris cold-cocked me!' He put the empty shot glass on the bar and motioned for another drink. 'Can I get a Tony's Magic Tequila!'

'It's true. I did.' Chris kneeled on the floor, his forehead on his arms crossed on the bar top. 'We were walking in and the urge just came over me. I love you though brother!'

'I love you too man!'

You better, one of these days you're going to swing faster than me! You got a smoke?' Chris slid down to the floor. Carrie stood ignoring them, thumbing through Paul's wallet.

'Sounds delicious!' Paul pulled out his pack, gave Chris one and lit up. 'I'll be right back.'

'I feel like an asshole for bumming all the time.' He said up to Paul.

'It's easier to give you one rather than share, you damned wet smoker. How's your lady?'

'Good. She's coming out later.'

Hangover

↓3 →2

The next day, Paul's Hangover opened the curtains in Paul's apartment, sending harsh morning sunlight streaming through the windows. Paul reflected on his faith. The absolutions of acetaminophen and tall glasses of water. He reached to his nightstand for the half-empty glass of water he'd left there hours earlier. His Hangover saw this, and countered with a full blast of sunlight. Paul mewed and recoiled, pulling a pillow over his face. The Hangover stalked around the bed. Boring quickly with subtlety, it resumed beating at Paul's head with its fists. Paul's hand grabbed for the glass of water and he quietly sipped at it. Angry, his Hangover prodded him in the stomach. Paul, nauseous, sat up. The Hangover laughed and his nausea grew. Paul poured out of bed and crawled to the bathroom, finally laying on the cool tile. His Hangover followed. But it stood on the entry carpet, afraid to step on the tile. Paul shifted and his nausea abated. Paul began scrolling through text messages he'd missed, or drunkenly forgotten, to piece together the night. His Hangover saw this and grew enraged. It strode forward, forgetting its fear, and kicked him full in the torso. Paul retched, clambering to his knees and vomited in the toilet.

Paul tasted cut grass. Bile and half dissolved pills floated in the bowl. His stomach was empty.

Within the hour Paul was mobile. His Hangover returned to its home, to wait. Paul saw the clothes from the night before strewn around his apartment. By the door his rust leather jacket still held its shape, his jeans next to his bed, and the Revolution t-shirt laying on the wood floor in the kitchen area the same. Looking just as if he were invisible and laying there in them. He was relieved not to face any peculiar mysteries this morning. He'd grown sick of the series that included such titles as *The Case of The Man Who Decided He Had Too Many Doors In His Apartment*, or *So, Mustache*, and *Bathroom Sinks Full of Garden Soil: An American Tragedy.* He didn't understand why he pulled drawers out on nights like he just had. He'd given up putting them back, next time he got drunk they'd be on the floor again. He couldn't find his wallet.

12:53a.m. Carrie Catherine
   <I'm home safe and sound. You let me know you're alive?>

9:35a.m. Isaac Scheer
   <Let's get together soon. I want to talk something over with you.>

10:30a.m. Carrie Catherine
   <You coming to sign wave?>

10:47a.m. LadyLady
   <Am i picking you up or are you driving?>

11:20a.m. SENT Carrie Catherine

<Yeah. Noon?>

11:20a.m. SENT LadyLady
  <Pick me up?>
11:21a.m. Carrie Catherine
  <Oui Monsieur. How you feeling? You were pretty deep in when I left.>

11:21a.m. SENT Isaac Scheer
  <Sure man. Phone or in person?>

11:22a.m. SENT Carrie Catherine
  <I'm good. Thanks. See you soon.>

11:25a.m. Isaac Scheer
  <You just waking up now? Let's meet up, bunch of stuff.>

11:25a.m. LadyLady
  <Cool. See you in fifteen.>

11:27a.m. SENT Isaac Scheer
  <Right on, let me know.>

11:28a.m. SENT Lady Lady
  <Right on. I'll be ready.>

Forty-five minutes later, Paul stood on a busy corner. The sky was cloudless and gray from the haze of the wildfire smoke, the sun a hot yellow circle on the gray and vehicles roared by.

'And there's a voter! And there's a voter! That guy there!? He's going to register to vote right now!' She was having a ball, using long fiberglass poles to make the giant puppet point at drivers while she yelled out to traffic and made up songs. Paul hulked at one corner of the intersection. His sunglasses did little to counter the sensory overload. His Hangover - the vicious bastard - stood behind him giggling and waving diesel exhaust from a nearby idling bus towards Paul. Paul swayed slightly.

'Are you the example of what people will turn out like if they don't vote?' Carrie asked, 'Are you making this sacrifice to scare them straight? Beware Beware! For I have not voted! Do not follow my dark, haunted path!'

'Please don't talk with exclamation points, I can see them.' Paul replied. 'I am focused on sipping this water and pretending I'm lying down in a cool, dark, place.' Albert was across the intersection, taking pictures of the crew to send to his funders.

'Woo! Honk if you think voting is the superbs!' She yelled across the intersection. A car turning in front of Paul and Carrie let go with a long blast. Paul winced.

Carrie looked up at the noon sun, then at Paul. 'Quite a feat of willpower if it's working. You look like a high school production of Frankenstein, Mister Nightlife. Oh wait, here.' She pulled Paul's wallet from her pocket and handed it to him. 'I forgot to give this back to you.'

'Will you stop pickpocketing me? I thought I'd lost this.'

'Stop being annoying drunk and I'll stop getting bored and being seduced by an exciting life of crime. You weren't going to pay your tab anyway, you're welcome. I don't tip the bartenders as much as they tip themselves.'

'Thanks of sorts. Do you think I could talk Her into encouraging people to, I don't know, turn down their radios to show

64

solidarity rather than honking?'

'Doubt it.'

'Agreed. I think this is food poisoning. There was something in my drinks.'

'Yeah, it was alcohol. They were filled to the brim with the stuff.' Paul's Hangover grinned and danced a quick soft shoe tap step behind him and flicked him in the back of the head. Carrie swatted at it. 'Hm, look at all the bricks in this intersection. I bet if they were all pulled up they'd make a great homeless shelter, but instead we got them prettying up the place.' Paul grunted, acknowledging her.

'Do you remember the fight?'

'No. Well, there was, some guy?'

'Man, Paul. Your eyewitness statements are enough for an open and shut prosecution. Forget dusting for prints. Yeah, *some guy* shoved Trevor and you started screaming in his face.'

'Oh for fucks sake. Yeah, it's coming back to me.'

'Lucky Chris was there to step in and tell the guy he could fight you after him. He's a good friend. How's that scratch over your eye? Let me see.' She pulled up Paul's sunglasses and examined his face. 'It isn't too bad, but it is visible.'

They stood, Carrie waving enthusiastically at drivers. Paul holding his sign and counting slowly, over and over, to sixty in his head.

'So, tell me. In all the campaigns you've worked on, how many times did you do this human billboarding?' Carrie asked Paul.

'All of them got to this dark point. Either to cheer up the candidate or to rile up staff. Get people moving early in the morning on a big day. Not in the middle of the day on Saturday ever, for that matter.' Paul snatched a dirty look at the sun.

She hopped from one foot to another across the intersection, signing.

'So what impact did it have?'

'Oh, absolutely none. Literally no effect at all. Just done to pacify a candidate or get staff up and about. She never stops moving does She?'

'Maybe you should consider starting a faith where the main religious duty is to examine, appreciate, and find peace with one's hangover. For non-drinkers you can, what, just rough up their head and neck with a ball bat. A HOLY ball bat. For the same effect.'

'I'll take that into consideration.' His Hangover looked over at them when it heard its name mentioned. Bored, it went back to its list of times Paul had embarrassed himself to have on hand to wake Paul up with in the future.

Silence

→4 →3

'I really appreciate you sticking around. I know you've been getting hit for it.' Albert said to Stephen later on that day. He handed a joint across the low table.

'It doesn't matter. Chatter is chatter.' Seeing the joint had gone out Stephen patted his pockets for a lighter, finding matches in his black vest, 'I don't see anything happening right now, this is as good a way as any to spend the next few months. Rather here than in a squat with a bunch of trust fund crusties.'

'I know that feeling. Your first stipend will be in the next batch. What do you think of bringing Carrie and the other one on?'

'They're smart, good leaders.' Stephen passed the joint back to Albert.

'Leaders, ha!'

'Oh right, leaderless organizing. Smart,' Stephen went on, 'good lead organizers, hitting numbers. And bringing two local women on as long-term points of contact here is solid.'

'That's what I'm thinking. Think Paul and Troy will keep volunteering?'

'I expect so. What's your thinking on Paul? Troy's so new I

see that he's not a good pick.'

'He's a dilettante. Whole background in electoral politics aside from some protesting here and there. He's my third choice and I'll probably ask him if one of them turns it down - sending money back always is an issue - but I'd rather cultivate people who will be committed. Man,' Albert leaned back, 'This is a long way from the Bay.'

'Amen to that. Makes sense about Paul, nice guy but a bit. I don't know, reserved may be the right word? Did I tell you about the lecture I sat in on when I first got here?'

'No.'

'This professor, a woman,' the joint went back across the table, 'was desperate for the class to engage. Just desperate. She was verging on begging for participation. And the more she asked, the more tense and quiet the room became. It's like the whole scene was this spiral down. She pled, the class, a hundred fifty some odd people,'

'So, what, ten in non-organizer-talking-to-press numbers then?'

'Ha, yeah. None of the students broke the silence. It's like they united against her. This silent mass of kids made a fool of that professor.'

'That's wild. This is a tough town though. I believe it.'

'Yeah. It's nothing like bigger cities. But this felt generational. This one coming up now. I thought it was passivity, learned helplessness, that kept them out. But after seeing that it feels like what I'm witnessing is a new power. Like fish schooling, they acted together in their intransigence. And by default the plan is interrupted and the new power has to be acknowledged.'

'A lot better than sore feet and blisters from picket signs.'

Albert passed the joint back held in a paper clip.

'Yeah, but for fucks' sake that accomplishes something.' They looked at one another furtively,' Well... What did those students gain from refusing to engage? What are we accomplishing?' Over the nearly fifty combined years Stephen and Albert had been activists, the two had organized, supported, or participated in one hundred and thirty seven of the *198 Methods of Nonviolent Action.* 'What are your goals doing this?'

'You mean what numbers do we have to hit? I've got them somewhere, but honestly they're pretty soft. Mostly recruitment, crew building, media.'

'No I mean you, Albert, what are your goals? This summer I watched you get pepper sprayed full in the face at Brunswick and you didn't budge. You can't have bought into electoral politics now.'

'What? Holing up on a commune voting on every damn thing and living the revolution hoping regular people will grok it and join? Or protest and as soon as we're hauled off the bosses and corporatists go back into their boardrooms. They get paid to be there and do that shit, we just show up now and again and provide a sideshow. Bush or Kerry, we're going to accept it. I think you have the wrong takeaway from that lecture hall. It is passivity. People aren't going to stand up. Is that cashed, you want another?'

'No, I'm done. It's just that some of the critical comments being leveled at me are *It's here, Bush gets reelected and people will rise up and Robin is selling out to the Dems.* and on and on like that. But saying *What I was doing is going nowhere* doesn't address why you're doing, this, now.'

'We're not even connected to the Dems! For that matter, not even Soros.'

'You're the one that said to me that the truth only sometimes includes facts.'

'Only sometimes. To answer your question, Republicans and Democrats aren't different where it's important, right? But I want to see what this side of organizing looks like. And registering young people to vote, passing on organizing skills to people here, like Troy and Carrie and the rest, is going to be of benefit down the line. ACT is doing it too, to a degree. I think we're doing it better, though I wish we had their funding stream.'

'Not if you knew how that money was made.'

'Yeah, I know. But I'm learning. One of these two will win and I'm getting too old to keep on in my ways. I need to shake it up, take on some new challenges. Brunswick was pretty heart wrenching though; I mean, maybe I didn't show it, but I certainly felt it. And that bus ride back over the bridge? There were so few of us, and even fewer that were there to say anything, and not just antagonize the security forces.'

'Yeah, I don't know how to bridge the gap either. Younger anarchists are just so angry, I don't feel a connection to them. They're hard up to smash windows and get arrested. And that's bringing the hammer down. Police love that excuse to round everyone up. I feel spent.'

Migraine

←1 ←3

'What's wrong?' She blinked back to the present as Paul rolled off of her in pain.

'I don't. Hold on. Oh god, okay. I'm okay.' Paul paused, blinking, 'Sometimes when I'm close it's like a migraine hits me.'

'Is that going to happen often?'

'No, it's rare.'

'No more cigarettes for this boy,' She joked nervously, 'You're too cute to have an aneurysm.' She reached over and rubbed his shoulder.

'I should get going, my night is going to be pretty off with nausea and after effects.'

'No, it's okay, you can stay tonight.'

'Yeah?'

'Don't expect this to be a regular thing.' She hit him with a pillow, 'And no cuddling. You're a goddamn spider monkey. Hairy arms in the night.'

Paul lifted his arm to wrap around Her. The blanket exhaled and the musty smell of damp bodies and unwashed sheets wafted into the room, competing with the tang of outgassing spray cans. She pressed in against him.

71

'Mmm. You put your underwear on.' Paul mumbled into the pillow, 'We are a layer of clothing further apart than I want to be.'

'Worse people than us have made long distance relationships work. Go to sleep.'

Happy Birthday mewed and picked at the blanket. She picked up her arm to form a cavern, Happy Birthday circled and cuddled in against Her stomach and, purring, quickly fell asleep.

'So when am I going to meet your parents?' She asked.

'Ha. What's that now? You serious?'

'I don't know. I don't care. Thought it would be something you'd want.'

'It's fine. Just soon, you know?'

'Yeah, forget I mentioned it.' Before long Her breathing slowed and became deep and steady. Paul felt Her chest rising and falling under his arm. He lay looking over the top of Her head, out the bedroom window. Her newly-thrifted black hiking vest lay on the end of the bed. A sodium light cast the night in orange. He reached over to his phone.

1:35a.m. SENT Carrie Catherine
<Alcohol is a depressant>

He soon fell asleep. Soon his phone - on silent - lit and buzzed.

1:56a.m. Carrie Catherine
<Nervous system. Not mood, P. Night.>

TWO MANY YEARS IN IRAQ

←4 ↓1

'You the only one here?' Sarah asked Carrie the next evening as she walked in the door.

'Albert's at the Progressive Coordination meeting. Troy flaked.'

'That calendar thing?'

'Yeah. Hey, I've got some data entry you can share in.' Carrie picked up the stack she was working on and waved it at her.

'What about Headliners? I can get some more registrations, there's a big show tonight.'

'We're not going to be able to reach out to our people and rouse up more volunteers if this doesn't get done.'

'We're not going to have people to reach out to if we don't get registrations.' She snapped back.

'Yeah. Well, there are a couple more events, can you hit those? Paul and Stephen are out but we've got two on Adams Street that aren't covered.'

'Sure, I need the boost. It's been a shitty few days and I need to be around some energy.'

'That's fine. Go ahead.'

She loaded up her backpack with blank registrations and

pens.

'Hey, so I hear you're staff now.'

'Yeah. I like doing this, talking to people, getting them jazzed up about the election.'

'That's cool. Paul too?'

'Yeah, the temp job doesn't really do two weeks' notice so he's going to finish out the pay period and quit. Were you approached?'

'I was. I just can't leave the coffee house. But I'll still help. Got to do something, you know?'

'For sure.'

Carrie turned away from the computer and faced her. 'Do you think we're doing enough?'

'I think what we're doing is important. I guess we could be doing more.'

'Like what?'

She sat down, 'I don't know. Waving signs doesn't have an impact. Let's shut down the system.' Sarah chuckled, 'That sounds stupid to say, but I don't see any way to change anything without denying Power, power. Too bad we don't have a special law that applies to elected officials. *Anti-Constitutional Acts* – knowingly subverting the Constitution. Or make Presidents serve murder sentences after their terms are up. They're all guilty of it. Make them pay attention.'

'We need to just stop them from acting. I know how you feel. Like, that Cheney visit in July. If we could have just, I don't know.'

'Stopped the motorcade?'

'Ha, yeah. Run out in front of his car and stolen a few seconds from him.'

'That's really about all we can hope for. Spray paint NO

MORE WAR or TWO MANY YEARS IN IRAQ on the side while it's stopped. Unless you're getting arrested the actions aren't having any effect on what's going on.'

'That's what I'm seeing. New rhymes to old chants. Pun-laden signs. What's the use really, even the big puppets that everybody's excited about? It makes things more interesting visually but what does it change? I don't know.'

'Doesn't seem to have much effect. Polite protests are useless. Waving signs on weekends, it's time to just disrupt power. Honestly, I'm questioning the use of doing what we're doing, what effect it will have in November.'

'Steal their seconds.'

'Ha. Only after fighting to steal their minutes.'

'Good thought.'

'This is a groundswell. So many people are engaged. But we're not reaching the people that want it to go on.'

'It does feel like it's getting a lot less lonely here on the outside. People are waking up to what's going on. Like that memo in oh one, from Clear Channel banning songs. We've been dancing with fascism. My cousin got caught up in Stop-Loss. This stuff is oppressive, and it's happening every day. We should talk about this more, I should get going.'

'Later.'

11:10a.m. Isaac Scheer

  <Can you meet me for lunch?>

11:26a.m. SENT Isaac Scheer

  <No. I only get an hour off and i'm a ways from down-town.>

11:28a.m. Carrie Catherine

  <Salut Paul, collect voter registration avec moi, tonight au cinema?>

11:30a.m. Isaac Scheer

  <Okay. Wesley's at 5:30 or so?>

11:32a.m. SENT Carrie Catherine

  <...>

11:33a.m. SENT Carrie Catherine

  <Oui?>

11:34a.m. SENT Isaac Scheer

  <That works.>

11:36a.m. Carrie Catherine

  <Tres Bon!>

11:40a.m. Carrie Catherine

  <I forgot to ask earlier, but can you give me a ride to the train station at ... 5 tomorrow morning? I'm going to Chicago. I need to be picked up Saturday too.>

11:41a.m. Carrie Catherine

  <I know how you are about mornings, I can call you to wake you up. I'm really sorry :/ but I really need a ride.>

11:42a.m. SENT Carrie Catherine

  <Of course i will. But i will need a wake up call.>

Business Voice

↓3 ←2

Paul found Isaac sitting at the end of the wooden bar talking on his cell. Isaac waved at the stool next to him, 'Give me one minute.' Paul ordered a drink while Isaac wrapped up the conversation. 'What are you doing for work now?' He said, putting his phone into his overcoat.

'Temp still. The mortgage stuff. Though I'm getting out.'

'Into what?'

'The voter registration work. They got approval to bring me on as staff. It's short-term, but it's a bit more money, and you know, I'm actually doing something.'

'Oh, But Isaac I'm out of politics! you say. Then you're back. Then Oh, for real this time! Then you're back.'

'This is different!' Paul protested, 'It's not an electoral campaign. Registration and activism. I'm learning some stuff, I like the people I'm working with.'

'Like your girlfriend, you macktivist?' Isaac put in.

'Yeah well.' Paul swirled his whiskey and cola.

Isaac took a sip. 'You can only collect through, what, the first week of October? Then what? You've never been one to think long-term, but that's kind of ridiculous. Are you able to pay your bills as it is?

'Nothing's shut off.' Paul paused, he was floating his gas bill this month, 'There's funding through the end of November. Post filing we're going to do visibility and election protection.'

Isaac rolled his eyes. 'You've got to pick a side if you want to be taken seriously. Electeds are unnerved, and won't hire you if they think they may be protested by you later down the line. There's a career in this, obviously, and in non-profit work. Not one in grant-funded activism as far as I see. So, Labor Day is coming up.' Isaac's cell buzzed and klaxoned. He found it in the pocket of his overcoat and looked at the screen. 'I've got to take this,' He answered the call, 'This is Isaac.' His voice on the phone was a half step lower than his normal voice. Paul referred to it as Isaac's Business Voice, 'Yes, hello Commissioner.' Pause, 'I understand that, sir, but the buy is the buy. We're going up nine days starting on the twenty-fifth.' Pause, 'I know that.' Pause, 'Yes, I laid out the points at the last meeting.' Pause,' Yes. Look, we're in. This is the best price we can get. Split fifteens are simply a bad idea. Nonstarter, your ads aren't just shot and cut, they're at the stations. Like I explained. Recutting down to fifteen is just a waste of money. I know that Andrew says differently but I and the other consultants have been over this.' Pause, 'Alright, goodbye.' He hung up, and watched the screen to make sure the call ended. 'Fuck candidates and fuck their stupid fucking idiot fucking friends.' He swiveled his stool to face Paul, 'I could use your help cutting turf packets and talking to volunteers. The campaigns have like ten canvasses launching Labor Day weekend and I want you as my eyes out there as well as getting the new volunteers up to speed. Saturday and Sunday, tops. And some hours ahead with the packets. You can even sing that song you made up when you're cutting turf, I won't give you shit about it.'

'I don't know if I can. That is a big weekend for this too.' Paul paused, 'And I wouldn't be protesting people I work for. You know I see it as a continuum. I hope that I can have a line in so if issues arise I can reach out to folks that I know to do something. Have contacts inside.'

'Come on, you're my Field guy. I need your help. One weekend, get people up to speed, check over the scripts and packets, just dot the i's, you know?' Isaac took a drink, 'Plus I can give you five hundred bucks for a weekend of work. And you know as well as I do that no one sees this as a continuum. It's an antagonistic relationship, and rightly so. Community advocates and activists need to be on the side of the community and no one else. They don't HAVE anyone else. Can't be relying on people who are looking for work.'

'That much?'

'Oh Paul; I've got a statehouse race, county treasurer and that commissioner, a common pleas judge in the hinterland, and a tax levy. So you're going to be earning it.'

'I'll think about it. It'd be a tight weekend for me.'

Isaac looked over at Paul. 'Seriously? Get up at nine and work until nine, not that hard for a couple days.'

'I'll tell you tomorrow. What's happening on the campaigns?'

'Eh, plowing along. The usual candidateitis, refusing to fundraise, back and forth on approval – get this, the judge doesn't even have a website up yet. Fired three designers, won't approve anything. Not that it really matters, I've tried telling him to move on, it's too late to bother. But he keeps going back to it. I feel bad for the commissioner, his only real problem is that he talks to voters. If he'd stop doing that he'd be fine. As it is he's losing votes.'

Paul laughed. 'You certainly sweep the floor for folks no one else will touch.'

'Keep talking like that and I'll stop pulling you along.' Isaac raised an eyebrow and sipped his drink.

lightvessel

←1 ↓1

'Thanks again for this. I really appreciate it.' Carrie said as she twisted to pull her duffel bag out of the back seat of Paul's station wagon. She sat it on her lap as the car idled outside of the AMTRAK station.

'No problem. And I get to go to work on time the day I'm quitting.' Paul yawned and turned down the radio in the middle of Ivan Watson reporting on a mortar bombing in Iraq, where an interim national assembly was being chosen.

'Saturday?'

'Yeah I'll get you. There's a house party that night. We should go.'

'I think I'll be up for it. Seeing Willem and Chicago is pretty overwhelming.'

'You two are at a year now?'

'Yeah. Anniversary of sorts. Long distance is its own beast.'

'I like him though. Big turnaround from Charles. Why don't you just stay the weekend? Seems weird to spend this much money and just go through Friday.'

'I'm glad you approve of this one, you're unbearable when you don't. I couldn't get anyone to cover for me on Sunday. So I've got to be back for that. It's going to be good though. We're going to a play, *Accidental Death of an Anarchist* on Thursday. I've wanted to see it for a while now.'

'Bring me the program?'

'Will do buckaroo.' Carrie yawned, 'Funny, I need some coffee.'

'The shop is open?'

'Yeah, but if I go in there I'll get swamped with work. Oh, while you're here just do this. Oh, one more thing. Well, I should get in there, I hate to rush anything.' Carrie opened the door, 'Have a good week buddy.'

'Have fun, say hello to Willem for me.' Paul watched Carrie walk to the building. She swung the duffel onto her shoulder halfway across, causing wisps of the morning's mist to chase away over the pavement. She reached the glass door, putting her hand out and waving to trigger the sensor. Paul turned up the radio and drove off.

Paul drove casually through the city, he had over three hours to get to work and normally had to rush in minutes. He drove alongside blue delivery vans dropping off stacks of the city's daily paper. Commuters sipped coffee from spill resistant mugs. The world was crisply defined, but dimmed. The romanticised blue hour was in full effect. He saw the Googie-inspired donut diner that his grandfather frequented ahead. Its yellow deep-V roof and orange walls called to him. Realizing that he'd been heading for this diner, somehow, Paul pulled in. The burst of cinnamon-sugar heat hit him as he opened the door. The bell-like chimes of utensils on porcelain. The crowd of regulars, different men from the days his grandfather brought him, but the same.

Paul thought of those men, and his grandfather. The old regulars likely dead as well now. Most all had worked at the refinery up the road after the War. The waitress came over, order pad in hand. Paul ordered the same breakfast his grandfather had always ordered, substituting a cola for the black coffee his grandfather had taken. Did they ever know one another? Paul asked himself. Would his grandfather like the man he'd grown to be? He knew, the same way that he knew this was where he was heading, that his grandfather wouldn't respect him. Loved him, but wouldn't respect him. He didn't bother asking himself that. Would he smile, bemused, if Paul told him of his morning plans? A man who went to war out of high school, four years off of Calshot as a lamp-trimmer on the lightvessel there, married a woman whose still body he'd wake up next to almost fifty years after charming her across the Atlantic, who began working a job he'd hold until retirement before the red mark from his garrison cap faded from his forehead. Youngest son, last unmarried daughter. Took her name. His had no history that mattered to him, Paul couldn't recall at the moment what it was. All undertaken at an age younger than Paul was, sitting there on the same stool he occupied the mornings after his parents' let him stay the night.

Paul ate slowly, reading the newspaper he'd bought from the box in the breezeway. His lovely grandmother. So sweet and so sorrowful. She left everything she knew - save for her language, though American English doesn't compare to the Queen's - to marry Her GI. To a two-story house in the shadow of a refinery, a new husband, big American cars, and, eventually, several children. What would she think? Paul was descended from hard people. Good-natured, but willful and able to outwork an ox. For a great, great, grandmother that was literal according to one family legend. Any one of them

83

would scoff if they heard of Paul's life and decisions. He stood, folding the paper neatly and leaving it on the counter for the next customer. He paid, tipping heavily, and walked to his car.

Quit

↓2 ←3

'No,' Sandra said into the receiver, 'Mister Dinares, our policy is very clear on exit procedures. This was explained in the training.' Long pause, 'It is normal procedure for an officer from security to escort you off the premises under these circumstances.' Pause, 'While I understand that.' she paused, 'Mr. Dinares, you cannot return to the work site to retrieve your belongings. They will be gathered and brought here to our office where you can retrieve them during normal business hours.' Pause, she glanced at the sleeping screen of her computer. Proverb 19:21 faded to be replaced by Proverb 26:11; she made a sour face in disapproval, disliking the crudity, 'Well Mister Dinares, the appropriate procedure would have been to call us here to discuss ending your posting, not to the client directly. This could have been avoided.' Pause, 'I understand that you see him everyday, but we are your superiors here and we are who you report to in the end.' Pause, 'Looking at your file we were under the impression you were looking for a long-term posting. Perhaps in the future if you approach us for another position you'll update that.' Pause, 'Yes. Goodbye.' She hung up the phone. 'I just don't understand how some people are so thick.' Sandra said to her co-worker sitting next to her at the counter, who nodded in agreement.

'Bullshit,' Paul said to himself after hanging up. He was still in the parking lot at the office. He looked at the clock, 9:20 a.m. He'd been inside the building for fifteen minutes, and another five fuming here. He'd get a day's pay at the end of the week, aside from that he'd have to wait fifteen days for the stipend to arrive. 'How the fuck did I get fired by quitting?' He pulled out of the parking space and returned to his apartment.

9:22a.m. SENT LadyLady
  <Quit today. Want to go out for a few tonight?>

9:22a.m. SENT Trevor
  <Quit today. Want to go out for a few tonight?>

9:23a.m.SENT Isaac Scheer
  <Quit today. Want to go out for a few tonight?>

9:39a.m. LadyLady
  <Thought you were working through the end of the week? I'm busy :(Tomorrow?>

9:40a.m. Trevor
  <Sure man, when you thinking? Ot?>

9:41a.m. SENT LadyLady
  <That's fine. See you tomorrow.>

9:41a.m. Isaac Scheer
  <Transition out, eh? I'll be there. Your usual?>

9:42a.m. SENT Trevor
   <Yeah. I'm going by when they open. Meet me after work?>

Paul stripped naked after closing the door to his apartment. He looked around. His apartment was originally the kitchen for the massive mansion. A landlord had put a latch on the door going to the central hall and boxed in the door going to the dining room. Paul tended to use the door out onto the back porch that he shared with his neighbor on this side of the building. His bathroom was once a pantry. Two walls were windows - looking onto the backyard now paved for parking. It came with curtains. His bed was tucked away from the outer walls in a small alcove that he provided privacy to with a trifold bamboo screen. He made a simple lunch at the best kitchen in the building, ate, and laid in bed, hoping to nap.

9:44a.m. Trevor
   <I'm down. See you then.>

9:45a.m. LadyLady
   <I've got some posters. Could use your help late tonight...>

9:46a.m.SENT Isaac Scheer
   <Yeah. See you after work.>

9:48a.m. Isaac Scheer
   <After I work, you mean. See YOU after you're done jerking it all afternoon.>

9:50a.m. SENT LadyLady
  <Maybe, I'll let you know.>

When he woke he texted Albert.

12:10p.m. SENT Albert CREW
  <Left work, so I'm free to start early and work the rest of the week.>

12:15p.m. SENT Isaac Scheer
  <Got any quick work? I've got to make rent.>

12:30p.m. Albert CREW
  <Well, there's JFS. You can cover that weekdays.>

The blue sedan turned off the county highway, taking turns until it finally staticed over gravel on a neglected road lined with vacation homes. The driver went slowly, using the low light of dusk so they didn't have to turn on their lights. Three quarters of a mile down they turned into a small wooded lot with what was once a white house on it with an attached garage. To describe it as white now would be like a child describing tree bark as brown. Green and gray, tan and brown. Dirt and mold and moss and sun damage made the house fade away as you looked at it. In the open garage door the waiting owner stood, turning his head as the car came to a stop, brake lights flashing as he pulled the aged cord to bring the door down. Parked inside was an old VW trike conversion painted in gold flake sunburst, badly peeling.

  'Welcome everybody. There's food on in the kitchen, tacos

and hot dogs. Make a plate, use the bathroom. Just don't open the curtains.' Joshua pulled luggage from the open trunk and waved the occupants of the car towards the door to the house. 'Um. Hola. Tacos y hot dogs. Usa el baño. Mi casa et su casa!' The house itself smelled closed up, the For Sale By Owner sign was leaned against the wall in the dining room, the dirt caked to the frame falling off onto the linoleum floor. Plastic grocery bags sat around the kitchen unopened. 'Robert, can you leave these folks for a bit and help me with the boat?' The driver nodded, speaking quickly in a foreign language to the riders and picking up the tool box that Joshua gestured at. Joshua slid the metal frame glass door aside and stepped out into the back yard. He walked across the sparse, heavily shaded lawn to the dock, where an old tan Starcraft Islander sat moored. 'I wish I could upgrade the exhaust. This is still so noisy. Makes my head ache when we're out there alone on the water.' He took the tool box from Roberto and found the wire strippers.

'You put too much money into it and you won't be willing to abandon it if you need to. You'll hesitate.' Roberto said.

'I can only get so far towards a Q Ship with no budget.'

'You're the only courier that doesn't take anything, not even gas money.'

'You start taking money and you don't know what you'll do. You'll hesitate.' Joshua twisted off the splice and flicked on the dash lights. 'Can you run through the safety and landing instructions in Spanish? My, well, I'm practicing but it's not coming along very well.' He leaned back in the Captain's Chair, the boat smells of gasoline, vinyl exposed to the sun and mildewed carpet sat with him. 'Trip three. What's the story with this family? They are a family with that little kid I expect?'

'Two of the adults are related to the child.' Roberto lit a cigarette, 'The third, the woman with her hair in a bun, Elena, is traveling alone. They all know English enough, and the family doesn't know Spanish at all.' Roberto smiled, 'Seeing as they're Lebanese, but told me they appreciated you trying.' Joshua sputtered, apologizing. Roberto waved his hand at him, quieting him. 'They've had incidents that lead them to believe that they're going to be arrested soon, the Mother is suspected of money laundering for a blacklisted paramilitary group. She denies it to us, but she's been brought in for questioning twice now. Our network has confirmed their fears. It's safer for them to get up North right now, the lawyers don't think they can keep the family together if they get arrested. Our overland routes have too high a chance of interception with open files.' Robert blew smoke vertically and it wafted in the still air.

'I saw a helo when I was doing some seamanship practice.' Joshua said, 'I think the Mounties are putting eyes out on the lake.' He pet the hard plastic of the throttle. ' If they chase us, if they have a helo after us we're exposed. Those fishing poles – that was a good idea though – are concealment, not cover.'

'Tell them what you are convincingly enough and they won't see what you are. If you have fishing poles behind, bait the hooks, run spoons, go slow. Commit to it.'

'At night, running without lights?'

'It will keep you focused, and quiet.'

'Before the next run I have to figure out a top notch exhaust. I want a silencer.'

It's getting dark. I will go tell them how to be safe and what to do ashore. You should pray or prepare. They will come out to the dock when they are ready.'

'Life jackets on everybody, and check that kid twice. Make

sure every one of those people have a plan if we go down to keep that kid alive. Having a child on the boat makes me worry. Adults take risks, kids shouldn't have to.'

'In war everyone is at risk. This is a step - a dangerous step, across a chasm - but a step to safety. Their parents are choosing this and they know this is the only way to get out in time.'

Roberto stood and stepped onto the dock. He nodded at Joshua and crushed his cigarette out on the wood under his feet. He carried the butt back to the house and dropped it alongside the foundation as he stepped inside.

They came out all together, Robert closing the slider behind him. The small group of silhouettes walking down the lawn to the boat, backlit by the lights of the house. Joshua waited for them on the wooden dock, watching them in the life jackets and each carrying their luggage.

'Four hours until we land, it's thirty five miles dock to dock. We can't get up on a plane, so it's going to be choppy and slow going. And we're going to be exposed out there.' Roberto threw the lines to the dock as Joshua spoke and backed the boat out. The six cylinder engine under the deck rumbled quietly. 'Sound carries out there, so don't talk unless it's necessary.' Roberto settled in to the left hand console seat and studied the unmarked chart by a dim red light on the dash. Darkness was setting in and low on the horizon the waxing crescent moon was inching down, it would not accompany the small party as they motored towards the border halving the lake.

Elena watched across the water. Focusing on the lights she could see receding away from her to force away her nausea. She had thought enough about what put her here and couldn't

91

know, even with the preparatory conversations and briefs on what to do, what to expect. She'd taken in the guidance and memorized the statements to give when she would speak to the authorities. That was for the future, but now her life had focused into a single vinyl seat on a boat running without lights, clinging tightly to a gunwale. She sat in the rearmost portside seat. Her bag stashed in the bow cuddy ahead where the boy had gone to try to sleep. This pilot was so earnest and so stupid, she thought, both him and Roberto. Run or walk through the rain, you get just as wet. They'd be safer if they just threw on the lights and gunned it, or better, had gone during the day. Played pretend at fisherman, hidden the darker riders and had the white ones wave beer bottles at the Coast Guard. The Coast Guard would see white drunks in their binoculars and move on. Instead they sat rolling about out here, trebling or more the time on the water. She knew resenting them was unfair, turning her mind to the contents of her bag, going over everything one by one to keep herself under control. Roberto turned, telling the riders that they were crossing the border, Elena didn't feel anything at this, even being caught on the dock would be trouble enough, they would be handed off and driven along the coast to conceal their route before they could present themselves to be considered. She tried to reach down to touch the water but thought better of leaning over the side.

'I think I've got a good lead on a thirty-six footer.' Joshua said to Roberto, 'Would mean safer passage, do daylight runs, could conceal people better. It's in pieces, but maybe that's what I want, put it out at the cottage and make it my Q Ship. This thing, this is a row boat with half a roof. It's a good boat but I can feel everybody on it when it's loaded up. Radar, bolt holes, a small tender so we'd have a lot of options where to put ashore, and power – it'd be a real asset.'

'I don't know.' Roberto said, 'Nothing can outrun a heli-copter. And you're frantic about this. I've seen you, you've put everything into the gear you have. That cottage. You live like a monk. There's no woman in your life. You're going to burn out.'

Joshua pointed high to the East. 'Plane coming off Pelee. Not a Coastie. I don't think they use fixed wing planes.' He looked ahead, eyes adjusted to the dark. 'I hear what you're saying, but the revolution needs lives. Not lives spent, but lives dedicated. This is my mission.'

Elena watched the plane climb, it leveled off on the same heading as the boat. She wondered who was aboard, if they were border guards or fisherman, hunters? What else would people be doing out here, flying this late? The boat turned, the horizon ahead was dimly lit from lights ashore. Still far out of site, still two hours away. She closed her eyes, not to sleep but to close out the dullness. She heard a commotion ahead, the little boy rushed out and vomited over the transom. Roberto handed a bottle of water back to him, but the boy slouched against the engine cover. His mother smoothed his hair and said soft words to comfort him. Elena's stomach recoiled when she smelled the vomit and she was over the side of the boat herself. Angrily, she filled her mouth from her bottle of water and spat into the lake. 'It'll be smoother and faster if we just ran out the last few miles.' She said, 'There are only a few boats out here and we're suspicious floundering in the waves. Other boats are racing around, we should do that.'

'This is what we've done and what we agree is the safest.' Joshua replied.

'The Coast Guard has radar and thermal cameras. If they had one of those pointed at us we'd stand out like fireflies. They won't care if we're going fast because we'll look like everybody else.'

'We'd arrive around, what, midnight instead of two?' Roberto looked at his chart. 'You're not wrong, but it is riskier.'

'I'm for it,' the mother interjected. Her husband nodded and voiced his assent.

'There,' Elena replied, 'this isn't a democracy and this wasn't a vote, but you know what we think.' She drank from the bottle, emptying it.

Joshua nodded, and looked at Roberto. 'Pull in the lines, the fish aren't biting.' he put on the marker lights and turned the spotlight ahead to see the way. The fishing poles were taken down and stowed, the engine roared and the bow lifted as the boat lifted and planed. 'Gonna get up to thirty and run in.'

Elena smiled as the boat chopped across the lake.

'Hey! Welcome back!' Paul dropped the cigarette and ground it out with his heel. Carrie smiled at him and opened the hatch of his car, tossing her duffel in.

'So where's this party?'

'In the neighborhood, on Robinwood.' Carrie smelled faintly of diesel exhaust and commercial upholstery. Shortly, the car smelled like long distance traveling. The conversation turned to art. Wheatpasting, stencils, stickers were on Paul's mind. 'I think all art should have a political message. It's just narcissism otherwise.' Paul went on, self-righteously.

'Oh?' Carrie looked over at him as the wagon passed under a sodium streetlight. 'How is your art political?'

He stumbled through a response. 'There's that one piece, in my apartment, the black and gray one. I feel that really puts my feelings about the war out there.'

'The one in your apartment? I don't remember it.'

'It's there, on the wall across from the bathroom.' Such an unfortunate reply, here caught out posturing and she didn't even remember the piece he brought up in his defense. 'I stenciled *fey* on it, at the bottom.' If he started claiming it was hard work, that he really threw himself into it well you, reader, should know that it was an accident of overrunning paint that he expanded on. Anything more than that is just an attempt to save face.

'I really poured myself into that piece; it took me several months to complete it.'

'Mhmm.'

How was Chicago?' He asked, changing the subject.

She glanced up at the streetlights. 'The trip was the best part, in its way. I remembered the last flight I took on my way back, it was at night. Cities look just like fungus in a petri dish from the air. All mottled orange, with spots of green, red, white. Clouds softening the light. Boundaries defined when they hit water, like fungus running out of sustenance. From the train it's like you glimpse all these lives as you pass through towns. They're so different and similar.'

'Not all fungus is bad.'

'I didn't say it was, just an observation. Saturday night in the city, look at that.' She pointed to a group of young girls circling on the concrete pedestal of a lonely parking lot light. Their shadows going around and around on the asphalt.

'You describe civilization like it's a spreading fungus.' Paul said, 'You're not going to ditch off with Willem for a cabin in the high country with a composting toilet?' A quiet beat, 'I've noticed birds have lost track of time though.' He paused,' These lights everywhere are the light of dawn. Here I thought I heard them singing because I'm up too late, but what business does a bird have singing at three a.m.?'

What business you have being up at three a.m. is a good question too. And I'm not going anywhere, I can't live without my CSPAN.'

'Three a.m. I was a freshman. I'd study in the common space on my floor. I met this sophomore that lived a floor above me. She was smart, flirty, pre-vet. We hung out, nothing serious. I would get back to my room at midnight or one, she would still be studying. I remember laying awake one night. With this feeling that if I was awake at three something magical would happen.'

'And?'

Paul chuckled. 'I fell asleep. But then things tapered off. She stopped coming down as often, and finally altogether. Coincidence, I suppose. Maybe something else that I missed.'

'Do you pay attention to anything that doesn't involve good-looking women?'

'It's rare.'

'Rare enough that I don't think there's a breeding population in the wild.'

Fight

↓2 →3

They saw Her worn out red Chevy 4x4 shortbed parked on the street outside the party and angled in to parallel park ahead of it. She, or a previous owner, had screwed in plastic fender flares to hide the rusty wheelarches. Carrie looked over at the faded Victorian mansion as Paul parked. The whole neighborhood was built in a different century, when the city was on the rise. Seeing lights on on every floor and people packing every porch and balcony. 'Ugh, I don't know if I'm feeling this tonight. I'm tired and I didn't shower today.'

'Oh come one. Give me a sniff. I bet you're fine.' Before either realized how weird that was and laughed it off, Carrie picked up her arm and Paul leaned over. The smell was comforting. Her body odor was sexy. Paul's pupils dilated. 'Oh god. I'm blushing now.' he was shocked, 'You're fine though.'

'Let's go creeper.' She laughed and opened her door.

They walked in together, Paul left the beer he brought to share next to the closest cooler and went looking for Her, who was somewhere in the crowd. He found Her in the back garden, surrounded by spectators. That's all anyone was when She was telling a story, an audience. She didn't allow for dialogue.

They were all laughing and She was close to yelling to be heard over the music. She saw 'Paul! Hey! Over here!' Waving. She punched his arm and leaned in for a kiss when he got to her. 'Where have you been?'

'Picking up Carrie.'

'No prob,' She spun him around to make introductions.' Pauls, guys. Guys, Pauls. Pauls is going to be a congressman one day, say hi Pauls.'

A beat too late Paul responded with 'Only after you're a senator, sweetheart. Hi everybody.'

'Right right. You want to smoke? Trevor is over by the diving board.' She pinched his butt as he walked away, picking up the story where she left off.

He found Trevor, Sebastian and his friends, and some guy he didn't recognize standing on the bare soil of the recently filled pool. Sebastian nodded at him and offered Paul the bong he held.

'Don't let me interrupt the rotation. How you folks doing?'

'Life's good man,' Matthew said. 'What have you been up to?'

'Registering voters down at JFS and Swayne Field. Since Wednesday I think I got over a hundred and fifty new ones.'

Franklin, Matthew and the new guy chuckled.

'That's cool man,' Trevor took a hit burble burble burble. Paul noticed the stranger wore a small flash drive like a medallion on a beaded chain around his neck. 'I'm going to be out of town for a few weeks, got a drive coming to a close. I think we're going to get a new unit.' burble burble burble. Trevor handed the bong to Paul.

'That's great news man,' Paul said. ' How big is the plant?' Paul burbled.

'Close to three hundred, this is our third go.'

'Try and try again.' Paul put in, 'You take this union and like it!' they laughed, 'Take it! Take it!'

Trevor swatted him. 'This is our first time getting to a vote jackass.''

Franklin burbled. 'Man, I don't know how you do it Paul. Buying into this system. It's not sustainable. Growth forever and ever.' burble burble burble 'And the politicians prop it up.'

Troy joined the group. 'How'd you do today?' He wore a black hiking vest as well.

'Thirty new registrations. You?'

'Forty, I spoke to a couple classes of seniors.'

'Right on.' Paul began feeling the effects, the film was playing slower. They heard a girl in a dark red beret screaming the lyrics to *Solidarity Forever*, her friends grabbed her and wrestled her towards the driveway. Sebastian, Troy and Trevor, along with some others in the crowd, joined in singing until they couldn't hear her calling back.

'For the union makes us strong! Woo.' Troy said. 'We're doing our part guys. Up to Kerry and Edwards to win it.'

'You guys are too much man!' Franklin yelled. 'Class collaborator here,' Pointing at Trevor. 'This guy props up the establishment,' Pointing at Paul, 'look at that fucking button. Rainbow Kerry/Edwards? Are you serious? They're nowhere on gay rights. And this guy.' He pointed at Troy. Holding eye contact for long seconds. 'I don't get it. I'm going to find a beer.' He walked off. Matthew and the stranger moved off as well.

Rifts were opening up. Continuity flickered for Paul. Every few seconds there was a black frame, a glitch. 'I think every person has the right to rob their own bank, even out the fees we're charged.' He said. Paul loathed getting this stoned in public. The rest of the party he'd have to constantly check himself and wouldn't enjoy his night. He felt claustrophobic standing in the open backyard. 'I think I'm going to go find a beer too guys.' He ran into Her almost as soon as he turned around. He kissed Her full on the mouth wrapping his arms around Her waist. Paul picked Her up off the ground, still kissing. She smacked at his shoulders until he put Her down.

'I hate being picked up.'

– flicker flicker –

Paul nuzzled Her hair and muttered how beautiful She was. She laughed and he ran his fingers through Her hair, smelling baby powder and the men's cologne She wore. He remembered what he was looking for and walked towards the house.

'Oh the adorable activist couple. Changing the world to-gether. Gah, now I taste vomit.' Carrie gagged theatrically – flicker flicker – standing on the back porch in front of a beer cooler.

'What? Because we're stupid over one another?' Paul reached around her and pulled out a bottle from the cooler. It wasn't a twist off cap, he looked around methodically for a bottle opener.

'No Paul, you're just stupid. Maybe over Her, it's hard to tell with you two, you seesaw. One moment She's all moon eyes at you and you're pushing Her away, the next She's ignoring you and all you do is follow Her around like a puppy.'

The party went on around them, people brushed by as they slid deeper into an argument neither one was looking for.

'That isn't fair.' Paul was patting with both hands on the

railing, searching, but forgetting what for. 'It's complicated.'

'Oh come on. This is you ever since I've known you.' - flicker - 'You seek out the ones that'll dump you.' Carrie stood a step above Paul putting them at eye level. 'You treat yourself like a placeholder' - flicker flicker - 'A bookmark.' Paul saw a bottle opener on the railing, just out of reach. 'You deserve better than that. The women you date do too.'

'Deserve. Deserve is such, such a funny little word.'

'You know what I mean.'

'What do I deserve though?' - flicker - 'What does anyone? Whenever I hear someone say that word my head cocks to the side. I've had so many opportunities that I've squandered, that any new ones are suffocating. So many open ended possibilities that I've screwed up by being too immature, or just an idiot. I don't know.' He paused, the bottle opener was gone. Annoyed, he caught the cap on the railing and pushed down, it flew into the bushes and he took a drink. 'It's strange realizing people you've forgotten about have been the main factors in your life. Nudges here and there.' - flicker - 'Spending time at this place with these people rather than some other place with different people. Who knows, if I'd gone to lunch at noon instead of one some Tuesday four years ago I might be somewhere completely different now. If I'd been single at that point.'

'At what point?'

'At any point!' he waved his hands, 'Longest it's been was about four months since I graduated high school, and that was by choice.'

'I remember. You think people made you who you are, and you're not one of them?' She said softly.

- flicker - 'Something like that. All the people I've dated, their friends and families. People who aren't in my life any more. Holidays with people whose names I don't remember, rather than my family. To have the direction of one's life defined so heavily and consistently by outside forces. It's, I don't know.'

'Hey Paul?' He looked up at a beautiful oval face, oversized mushroom red knit hat and black coat. Blonde hair flying everywhere on the breeze. She held the screen door open. 'Hi Carrie. Hey, we clogged up the sink making candles and I can't find James.' – flicker – 'Can you help?'

Paul spent the next hour under the kitchen sink up to his elbows in black sludge, breaking apart hunks of wax until the line was clear and it finally drained.

Paul ended the night curled behind a green corduroy sofa. Carrie drove his wagon home just after midnight. Before she left she wrote on his arm that she'd pick him up in the morning. Paul's girlfriend left at two, enlisting Trevor to help find him. They weren't successful, someone had knocked a comforter over him and he was hidden.

3:35 a.m. SENT Carrie Catherine
  <You mabebne se lf xonssnious about mt face whme you look atbwme>

3:38 a.m. SENT Carrie Catherine
  <You knw if you wolud date me h woludmt have to find craayies>

3:41a.m. Carrie Catherine
  <Knock that shit off. Seriously.>

3:44a.m. Carrie Catherine

<Go to sleep, P. You've got a proof, not a BAC. I'll pick you up tomorrow.>

linggdraft.exe

↑1 ↑4

'So, you think it's ready?' Matthew asked the stranger, W., as they made their way to the front yard, past Carrie and Paul fighting.

'I think so. Having some trouble with getting it to propagate. I think we should round up the guys and give it a run. It might fun up the night.' Matthew rounded back. W. stood looking at the residential street, sipping his beer. They soon appeared, Matthew, Sebastian and Franklin. Troy followed but was told quietly and firmly that he wasn't welcome.

'I think we should put this off.' Franklin said as they walked down the block.

'Why's that?' W. asked.

'That Troy guy's a cop. He was plainclothes pointing people out when I was arrested last year.'

'Dude! You let us smoke with him right there and you knew that shit?' Sebastian yelled at Franklin.

'What the fuck's he going to do at a party?' Franklin shrugged his shoulders. 'I don't think he gives a shit about us, he's obviously looking at that thing Paul's doing. Not gonna blow it on a couple of dingy pot heads.'

'I guess.' Sebastian looked back over his shoulder, 'You'd

think with all the funds pouring in for Homeland Security they could finally afford some uniforms for those guys. This is almost abusive, sending those poor detectives out in their street clothes to look for criminals.' They laughed. 'With not even a badge on their chest to put electrical tape over. Oh! Jokes! Hey, Matt! How was amateur night?'

'Amateur night? He doesn't have the chest for it.' W. noted. 'I choked.'

'What do you guys think?' Sebastian asked. 'Skip it for tonight?'

'I'm ready now. No one knows where we're going. Tomorrow, or the next night, they might.' W. answered. Grunts of agreement. 'So that's it.'

They came to an overgrown lot, Sebastian moved to the front and pulled aside a particle board panel and the others ducked into the darkened basement. Their paranoia was palpable. They took out small, single LED flashlights used for finding keyholes in the dark and shone them at their feet. Sebastian replaced the panel, pulling it in position from the inside and followed the rest slowly up the stairs. Every scuffle and intaken breath was cacophony, the scrape of their shoes over the dusty wood floor a table being dragged across a room.

They went upstairs to an abandoned office. It was stripped, aside from a halogen lamp and a silver tarp covering lumpy shapes. An extension cord running in from the back window ran under the tarp. 'Check for light leaks before we go on.' W. said in the dark.

'For real? We were just here the,' Matthew began to say. 'Do it.'

The four circled the room, checking the caulking and rags they had put in around the boarded up windows. 'No change.

Blackout.' Sebastian said after checking the seal around the power cord. Outside it was disguised amongst ivy, laying in tall grass once it reached the ground. W. turned on the halogen lamp enough to flood the room with dim yellow light, then pulled aside the silver tarp covering the improvised work station.

'Alright.' They all looked at a computer tower sitting on a metal folding chair. A tube display warmed to life atop a second folding chair that it shared with a keyboard and mouse. W. sat cross-legged on the bare floor and pulled a small netbook from his satchel. He opened it and powered it on. He intently read the screen, the flash drive plugged into one port. They'd assembled this station over the course of two months. Leaving it for a month after it was ready. Only watching for activity from a distance. 'Seb,' W. looked up from the screen, 'You're SCRAM. Matt, you're count.'

'Oh right,' Sebastian left the room and returned with a large fire extinguisher. He checked the pin and the pressure. 'Good here.'

'Alright, here's what you'll see. This isn't final. I've got to make sure the screen goes dark and I've got some issues with propagation. But I'm leaving it as is so we can observe.' He plugged the flash drive into the tower. He ran linggdraft.exe. 'Alright, logging out, that should launch it.'

Matthew leaned back against a wall. Franklin began rolling a cigarette. Sebastian and W. stared intently at the screen. They waited.

All the programs on the tower quickly opened. They'd liberated it, along with the monitor and keyboard, from a dumpster behind a dorm on campus. Word processing, porn, music, downloaded games, homework and letters filled the screen. 'So, my guess is this is about average load for files and programs.' The fan kicked on, whirring contentedly. 'The final will have a forty minute delay before running after logging out, but the screen is locked same as final. Files start being deleted as soon as the programs are opened.' W. swept the mouse, the cursor was locked. Soon, the whir faded. 'Fans off. Matt, start counting.'

Five minutes went by, Sebastian put the back of his hand against the metal case. 'Warm, nothing bad.' He leaned on the fire extinguisher.

Twelve minutes passed, and the tower was too hot to touch. 'We got smoke.' W. said.

'No, that's.' Sebastian looked back at Franklin smoking. 'Damnit Frank! We're doing something here.'

Ten minutes later a thin line of smoke seeped from the upper vents in the case. 'Smoke.' W. said, leaning back.

'Twenty five minutes, thereabouts, from the fans going down.' Matthew said.

'So about an hour after people leave for the day we're looking at fires starting.' Franklin noted.

'Yup. Perfect. How are we on the email side?' W. asked.

'I still don't get, like, what's stopping the janitor from just shutting everything off before it gets hot enough? People may still be in the office an hour after normal work.' Sebastian asked. 'Plus, every one of these will have fire suppression above them.'

'Like a janitor would dare fuck with a Colonel's desk, or a Congressman's.' W. replied. 'A lot of them will be under desks, may have paper files set on them. Unless the room they're in was upgraded to CO_2, there should be enough to keep going. Hell, since it's email accounts, this will get running at homes without any automatic extinguishers. And remember, this is worldwide. We've got random chance on our side. Once there's enough smoke to trigger suppression systems the computers are toasted and there should be a lot of secondary issues underway.'

'So when are we going to have the final worm?' Franklin asked.

'It'll be ready soon. Keep bulking those gov and mil emails for the launch list.' W. replied. He clipped the chain back around his neck. 'And knock the amateur-hour ELF shit off. I know what you guys are getting up to and it's endangering everything. That cop might be looking at us, might be looking at your friend. But they're pissed off, and they're looking. Just because the news hasn't picked up that it was an action doesn't mean the cops aren't investigating. Tighten the fuck up.'

OAC 4301:1-1-49

↓4 ←3

The next day. 'Excuse me, sir.' Henry was dismissed with a wave. 'You have a blessed day.' He walked on 'Hello, ma'am. Don't mean to bother you.' She ignored him. 'Have a good day.' He stood at a crosswalk, wondering whether to continue East or turn South to walk through the office district. Even on Sundays it sometimes paid off. 'Excuse me, sir.' This conversation netted seventy-five cents. 'Got to ask everybody you see.' He said to himself. ' Hello, sir! If you have a minute. I don't mean to bother you, but you see I need a dollar.' fifteen cents. 'God bless you.'

He rattled the change in his pocket, up to one dollar and ninety three cents. 'What's the price? Thirty twice. Plus a bundle for inflation.' Henry ducked into an alley, pulling a rumpled cigarette from behind his ear he snapped the fire piston. He leaned against painted brick and exhaled. Looking down he saw a quarter. 'Thank you. ' He scooped it up and took another drag on his cigarette. 'Almost there baby bear.'

Within the hour Henry was at his favorite bodega with enough change to make his morning drunk. It sold on Sundays to regulars, in violation of OAC 4301:1-1-49. He frequented it because they carried his preferred wine, which was becoming rarer and rarer among carryouts in his pedestrian world. Once, a few years back, they stopped stocking it. Henry kicked over a display of snack cakes and twisted his ankle when he slipped storming out. The cashier shouted at him not to come back, threatening to bring down the police. Henry returned two days later, limping, carrying a handwritten petition signed by himself and four other homeless men who promised to purchase enough of the stuff to justify them stocking it. This day he left with a bottle, loose cigarettes, a hot dog slathered in ketchup, and was still thirteen cents up.

Roll

←3 ↓2

bkp971: you you. what are you up to this monday?

grammateia: Looking at what classes I need to register for to wrap my degree up.

b: now?

g: Yeah. I'm bad at life and didn't do it in the Spring.

g: Still, May 2005 I'll be out.

g: What are you doing right now?

b: putting together some lit. actually, which of these do you like better?

Paul sent her photos of three cards that Isaac had given him to model the literature off of.

g: The second one. Are these what you're making? I'm confused.

b: no, just copying off them. whats your degree in?

g: Art History/Psychology

g: Copying? Sounds like trouble.

b: there ain't no plagarizin in politics sweet pea.

b: ive seen ads that are shot for shot, line for line remakes. i was straight impressed when i saw them

b: and what i'm doing. really, only so many ways you can arrange red, white, and blue on a piece of card stock.

g: That's true. So you do graphic design?

b: only at the local campaign level...it's not a high bar to reach. between a decent array of examples and having a wisp of talent i can put out better work than anyone else in the area.

g: Ooh, cocky. I like that.

b: haha. it's true! when there's a vacuum pretty much anything can fill it. i'm not saying i'm good. just that no one else is either.

g: Weird industry.

b: politics is the stronghold of the amateur. there are pros, but because of how the system is set up (like, fifty valid signatures and a pocket change filing fee to be a congressional candidate) there will be candidates and staff with every level of skill running for everything.

b: they usually don't find support but sometimes they get lucky. and at the local level there are no pros, there's not enough money in it.

b: or a staffer wins one race and gets hired into a government job with the candidate they worked for. so that takes them out.

b: unless there's already a cabal running the place. that'll keep staff on the outside.

g: What's that now?

b: just sometimes you run into bougie insiders who really run things. suits and smiles. they get the electeds to hire on their friends rather than the people who just ran the campaign. hit my head against that wall once.

Sometimes the revolution just needs someone to do the damned dishes. Paul looked at the linoleum counter overflowing with dirty cookware. He took off his jacket and began tackling the mess. Albert arrived a short time later with several boxes of new literature for them to distribute. He split the tape and started portioning out roughly fifty pieces at a time, turning each set ninety degrees as he built it up. 'Did we get new registration forms?' Paul asked.

'The Secretary of State should have mailed those by now. Keep using photocopies until those come in. Do you still have the connection to make more?'

'I think we're good. Probably shouldn't push it though.'

'Noted. Where are you going tonight?'

'Not sure, I'm going to follow Her lead. She knows where people are.'

Albert looked over at Paul, who was turned away from him at the sink. 'Okay then. Can you bring the new guy with you and show him the ropes?'

Later that night She and Paul met at Carrie's apartment. 'Communists are always going on about permanent revolution, but the capitalists made it stick.' Carrie said. 'It's like everyone in this country is obsessed with pioneers and outsiders and that we gunned down Brits to become a country.'

'Hey now.' Paul said.

'For real! We're stuck on revolutionaries and rabble rousers. The conservatives - who don't want anything to change - most of all. Strutting around like we're tolerating the government and any one tax increase or levy is King George trying to sneak back into power.'

'I hear you.' She took a hit from the bowl and passed it to Carrie. The ember faded. 'The anti-war movement is DOA unless the draft comes back. We need everybody afraid for their lives to get them off their asses. There are plenty moving but we need them all.'

'Wait.' Paul said slowly, 'I think that's the opposite of what she said.'

'Yeah maybe. But it's true too.' She replied.

'Where's your head at about graffiti and the election?' Carrie asked Her. 'You papering anything special for it?'

'Kinda.' She said. 'I'm careful about my profile, you know? Like, I don't want to change it up too much, might bring down attention. I don't know. You know, all this graffiti that goes up. Not my stuff, but what gets thrown up on rail cars. The audience for it is rural conservatives. How weird is that? Suburban and city kids run out in the night to throw up wonderfully exuberant pieces on rail stock that ends up being towed behind flashing gates all over flyover country. What do those people think waiting for trains to pass? More,' She lowered her voice in imitation of Rush Limbaugh, 'Downfall of America! Do their kids get excited, glimpsing the world beyond their experience?'

Paul lurched to his feet. 'We're flyover country. Fields and contrails overhead. You think anybody gives a shit about us because we're living in a city?' The floor retracted. She glanced up at him. He rotated in place and identified the bathroom door. His nervous system was under-dampened, his movements were difficult and irregular. Without option he acclimated to the loose response, like steering a bicycle made from rebar. He made his way towards the targeted door in diminishing overcorrections. His eyes focused on the door, but his carriage swerved side to side, like the trail of a beagle after the scent of a pheasant.

He hit the doorframe and rolled inside. He closed the door and pressed at the doorknob until he heard it lock. He felt through the darkness, tapping his fingertips against the wall.

He felt the buttons of the light switch, but lost them. Again, tap, tap, tap. He left fingerprints in lazy circles. Tap tap, and he found it. He got a firm grip on the antique brass faceplate with his fingertips. His bare toes clutched at the basketweave tile floor searching for purchase as if the gravity had gone out finally pressing the light on and in an instant disappearing the darkness.

The mirror. Paul's reflections stood before him. It held perfectly still. Slowly it raised its left hand and waved at Paul. He waved back. The reflection put their arm down.

'Shit.' Carrie said, seeing Paul had left.

'What's wrong?' She asked.

'Just. I'll give it a minute. Sometimes it's nothing. Since you two are dating you should know. Don't let him be alone around mirrors when he's high.'

'He was hitting it pretty hard.'

'Yeah, well. You're dating, good you noticed that too.'

'Who are you?' Two hazel flies darted, synchronized, over the mirror while waiting for a reply. 'Who is this person I'm riding in?'

'Paul Urban Dinares. He'll always answer to that name.' He was rolled back on his heels at the sound of his name. Paul came back to rest flat-footed.

'Always?'

'Far as I know.' His reflection shrugged. Paul saw it had one hand down the front of his pants.

'Then who are you? What's your business here?'

'The Devil.' Paul's eyes widened. Both he and his reflection gasped. His reflection, though, then laughed. 'I'm just fucking with you. You're so easy. You take everything too seriously. risum teneatis, amici? Right?' Making a face, pausing for a reaction. 'Seriously?' He dropped his hands to his side in the mirror, frowning. 'That's pretty basic Latin. Oh, I forgot. Nevermind. It was a clever reference wasted on you.'

'Hey Dracula. I can hear you talking in there.' Carrie knocked on the door. 'Open up.'

'Someone's at the door.' The reflection looked over.

   'It's Carrie.'

   'Oh! I like Carrie! And how's the girlfriend? What's Her name again?'

   'Not sure where it's going, but She's good.' Carrie was still knocking outside the door.

   'Funny, it sounded like those pronouns were capitalized.'

'Stop ignoring me and open this door!' Carrie pounded her fist at the door.

   'Is he crazy?' She asked Carrie, quietly, thinking She wouldn't be overheard.

'She thinks you're crazy. Bit of advice, you should knock off the weird shit.'

   'Good thought.' Paul regarded his reflection in the few moments while it wasn't paying attention to him. 'Who are you though, really?'

'He's not crazy. He just gets in these reveries. Paul! Hey! Open up! Get out of my bathroom!'

Squaring up and making eye contact. 'All these distractions. I can't tell you now. You are, however, exactly who you pretend to be and no more. All of you are.'

'Won't tell me, you mean.'

'You're right, I won't tell you who I am if you're too stupid to come talk without making a spectacle.'

'Fuck you.'

'Whatever. You're fundamentally unlovable. Your natural condition is alone. You're really not worth my time. See you soon.'

'I'm okay.' Paul said loud enough to be heard. 'I'll be out in a moment.' Paul flushed the toilet and ran water over his hands. His genitals were sore. He'd been rolling his penis and scrotum in his hand like an exercise device. He soaped his hands and rinsed them.

He opened the door. Carrie leaned against the wall with her arms crossed. 'She's putting away the weed.'

'Do you have a pen?' Paul asked her. He saw one on a shelf in the short hallway and took her forearm. *I take so much from you*, he wrote.

Carrie took the pen and wrote *You give too*.

'What's that about? If there's something going on between you two I want to know about it.' She said, seeing them.

'It's really nothing. Paul and I met at a loud,'

'Very loud.'

'Yeah, very loud party and couldn't talk. He found a pen and said hello. We kept it up for a while and it tapered off.' She paused. 'But it felt weird talking, so we got back to it.'

'I guess. It's just weird you two are, are, handling one another all the time.'

'Yeah. I get that. And both of us will pay more attention. At this point it's just habit, you know?'

'Habit.' Paul echoed. 'I have something.' He mumbled. 'He began again, louder. 'I have something I wrote. You should read it.' He enunciated carefully and motioned towards his satchel.

The Chorus sings of the nationalist shooting a paper aristocrat in the throat, his commoner wife in the stomach. On the paving stones where their blood fell snakes grew and fled to dark recesses to brood and sulk. They emerged to blood and a transformed world. The Gorgon was dead, and with it the gilt and pageantry of the passed age. The dark-suited asps were free to consume and grow fat. Stripped of their filial heraldry, the conglomerates ravage without border. their affected humility needs none of the pomp or ceremony, content to simply gather their treasure. The struggle we face is with the spawn of the long-dead Medusa. Claiming Gavrilo as our Perseus striking at the serpents, wearing masks in lieu of silvered shield.

'Do you actually believe any of this?' She asked. 'You're all about elections.'

'I mean, I don't know. Felt good to write.'

'I'm think I'm going to get home.' She said. 'Paul, I'll give you a ride.'

Game

↓2 →1

grammateia: So, I've come up with a game.

bkp971: game? do tell.

g: I watched this video that Arthur C. Clarke filmed, like in the mid-nineties, on fractals last night and haven't stopped thinking about it.

g: I had a dream last night.

Albert had everyone sit together in the living room. 'I was on a conference call with the funders today. They're directing staff in all cities to focus less on voter registration and more on media. Which, I have to admit, we've completely dropped the ball on here.'

b: i think that i've seen that

'So what about the work we've done?' She asked. 'Are we just turning those in and dropping that? No follow through?'

g: I saw two lines running out from a single point, they dodged back and forth, up and down.

g: Going two up, then three right, one down. Like that. That make sense?

b: yeah i follow you.

'I get you feel that way, but we're looking at ensuring our part of this is known. There's a lot of money being spent and

119

credit needs to be given.' Albert replied.

    g: It was beautiful. Like, I felt for the lines, they tried to grow and expand. It was like they were chasing around. There's a simple formula for the Drunkard's Walk. Average distance traveled in a step multiplied by the square root of the number of steps.

    g: My mother and I played a game when I was little. We just called it the dot game, you took turns connecting dots in a grid with lines.

    g: This reminded me of it.

'What Albert and I have discussed is focusing on street theatre. Costumes, signs, more times with banners.' Stephen put in. 'We'll notify the press and work to get coverage.'

    b: then what? how is it a game?

    g: It faded. I didn't wake up from it, but it changed.

    g: It needs a win condition, obviously. I think trapping the other side is the only thing that makes sense.

'Is that really the best use of our time? Aren't there. I don't know, more aggressive actions we can take?' Troy asked. The others were quiet, unsure of how to respond.

    g: But here's the thing I want to try. Tomorrow, take notes of every number you see that isn't in some sort of obvious list – No elevator buttons for instance – and we'll give it a shot.

    b: sure i can do that.

'Paul, can you get us a media list?' Albert asked.

'Sure. How far afield?'

    g: I'm really excited about this. Are you busy? I want to get the ideas out while I've got someone to talk to about it.

'Toledo media market at least. If you can get statewide, or at least Columbus papers, that would be ideal.'

    b: i'll listen. in a meeting, but i can respond.

'No problem.'

g: Okay. So we end up with a bunch of numbers. 5 through 0 will be converted to 1,2,3,4 by 0=1, 9=2, 8=3, 7=4. 5 and 6 will cycle opposite one another. That should keep the distances manageable. It won't be as beautiful as Levy flight - sigh - but it's a necessary compromise and should mimic brownian motion.

Paul searched online for what she was talking about.

g: The ones I've been doing today don't cut down the distances.

g: So, that's distance traveled. Now for direction.

g: ...

g: Honestly, direction is a stumper. I'll figure it out.

g: I found this eight-sided die on the ground outside my building. Maybe roll for direction?

g: But to set up, the numbers are out in a communal pot, and pulled out.

b: i don't really see the "game" here.

b: it has been a lon gtine since i flunked calculus though.

g: Yeah. Well. I'm mulling over What is desire? What are we after? How much of our lives, our paths, are directed by random chance? You play this game and every move you and your opponent will make is laid out at the beginning. It appears you're moving under your own volition, but it's

g: It's decided for you. You don't have control.

g: Other assorted rules. You can cross over your own line, but if you approach your opponents you reverse course and travel the remainder of your move after getting to one space from your opponent's line.

b: is that really how you see things? as random chance, or predetermined paths we follow unknowingly? that's pretty dour...

g: Neither person can cross the other's line. So the goal is to deny your opponent any room - pin them in. They'll only have the space they already have.

g: I guess I do feel this way. I mean, I make a lot of choices, but what are they predicated on? My experiences, advice I've been given. Also based on experiences. Observations. Everything has one chance to be true. Where we are determines what it is.

g: And all of those things come from random chance and encounters. So they're negated, really.

g: What are we but the products of unforeseen encounters and events?

g: Though the paths do have some beauty along the way. As well as looked back on.

Gerry

←3 ↓2

Henry quickly looked away when he realized the danger he was in. To the side, out the large windows looking out over the street; not down. Never down. He'd mouthed his way into a fight with Gerry – 'Ger the Bear' – when the guy had first came around, and learned his lesson. Fucker was crazy. Over nothing, for nothing. And he didn't stop. Gerry was a loner and mostly sold stolen phones to the bodegas, and anything that he could pry loose to anyone he could. Though he avoided the scrap yards for some reason. He supplemented his income by ripping off other homeless, which aside from his temper, meant he was a terror to most of the men. Gerry was bad enough, but the Bear was who Henry just made eye contact with. Gerry moved on. He was walking down the line from the front to the back. Henry touched the rib, healed now, but it was a long time coming around. He saw Todd ahead of him in line, nodded. Todd was good people, got in from Nebraska for some work with his brother that dried up before he was in the state. Stranded, he hated the life. And wasn't much cut out for it. Gerry's presence in the grub line put people on edge. The staff and volunteers were picking up on it. 'Everyone. If we could just tighten up this line we're getting clumps of people up here getting served and it's slowing everything down.' The lead volunteer said to the room.

Henry hated days when he ended up here for a meal and couldn't pay for one himself. Funny how Todd always bitched about being stranded, how his brother had fucked him over and got him stuck so far from home. Like it was his brother's fault the IRS had decided to look into the landscaping business while Todd was taking the Greyhound in. Henry asked him once what the difference was. Sure he had rented a trailer, a home, back there. But wasn't he stranded there just the same? Work was shit, not like that changed. Women wouldn't look at him, not like that changed. And liquor is sold here same as anywhere. The weather here is milder too. Todd had cuffed him and hadn't talk for few hours that afternoon. Henry had tried to bring him around, he'd get out soon, find a steady job, get housed. Todd sulked and refused to engage him. That was last year this time, Henry remembered.

'Season's changing.' They reclined in the grassy lot across from the building after they ate. Passing back and forth a bottle from the bodega a block over.

'You need not wonder why. You've only got one winter in, haven't you?' Henry asked.

'Yeah. What do you have planned?'

'Got a Deputy in Wood County that I'm on good terms with. I just have to track him down if it gets bad. He'll charge me with enough to be inside through the worst. It helps clear up some of the minor shit that never gets gone. Don't pull that shit here though.' Henry cautioned. 'I've been in this jail and it is nothing, nothing, I want to do again. The rural one is better in every way.' Henry took a pull from the bottle. 'You got to get to de Paul – just not when the Bear is in there ripping them off – and get some good boots and socks first thing. You can get by with everything else halfway, it'll be miserable, but bad feet will kill you.' Henry glanced over at the parking lot of the bar behind them. It looked like it was going to be busy for a Tuesday. 'That go in the Navy and those big beds didn't prepare you for this, now did it?'

'Beds?' Todd chuckled. 'Air Force got beds. And prepare me for what? When I wasn't puking I was palleting missiles. Not a lot of call for that out here.'

'What happened to that lawnmower you had? Still running?'

'Still running somewhere.' Todd leaned back on his elbows. 'Pawned it.'

'Ah fuck.'

Gerry had grabbed another man on the sidewalk outside the front door of the center. 'Hey! Is that Willy?' Henry heard behind him. Gerry had ahold of Willy's canvas coat with both hands and slammed him into the window. The entire pane, more than seven feet tall, rattled. Henry saw the reflected world shimmer.

'Yeah.' Henry, Todd and others on the lawn watched the fight – well – beating. Willy was on the ground curling in a ball, arms up over his face. Gerry kicked him in the stomach over and over. A boot connected to Willy's arm, smashing him in the face. Henry took a sip. A staffer ran out to the sidewalk, cellphone to her face, yelling to 911.

911 ALERT . PHYSICAL FIGHT(IN PROGRESS) . 19 ST/MADI-SON AV, TO <19,1900> . CHERRY ST FOOD SVRCS 08/31/2004 17:25

'That guy is bad news.' Volunteers and staff rushed out, some pushing people away from forming a circle, the more experienced ones looking for men they knew to intervene. Henry shrugged, motioning that he was on the wrong side of the street when he was waved over.

A cruiser arrived. Sirens screaming up the street. The police driving it hopped the curb, his partner jumping out before he stopped. She took out her Taser and held it at her waist, shouting to everyone to step back. The officer driving got out and did the same. Gerry still kicked at Willy, his back to the police.

'You ever see someone hit by one of those things?' Henry asked.

'No, what happens?'

'Well, for this particular piece of shit, not nearly enough.' Gerry's head snapped up. He collapsed, spasming, the barbs buried deep in the muscles of his back. 'I wish they'd, this once, go back to night sticks and go to town. It's a good show anyway.'

'Happy Stryker, Motherfucker!' Henry said as the car pulled away. Todd and others within earshot laughed.

Ganzfeld

↓4 ←4

'I appreciate you letting me getting to know this program.' Carrie said. 'I think it's a skill I should have. You know?'

'Yeah. No problem,' Paul laid back on his couch reading *Callahan's Crosstime Saloon.* Police sirens in the distance. He'd agreed to teach Carrie to use Photoshop on his antique copy. Half an hour before she arrived he'd brought up the program and went looking for a sample image for her to use. He realized, to his horror with the short time he had, that there wasn't a single non-pornographic image on his computer. Panicked, he rushed to transfer everything off the computer and scrub the disc clean. Just as she knocked at his door he was done. 'I'm sorry the copy I've got is so old. It's good enough for what I do, but the newer versions are a lot more powerful and user friendly. Nice vest, by the way, you damned anarchist.'

'Ha! You like it? Figured since everyone else has one I might as well get one.'

'I guess I should get one too then, since it's a uniform.'

'Check that shopping bag by the door.'

'Seriously?'

'Hey,' she looked over at him, 'I found them both at

Goodwill. You're welcome. I wanted to thank you for taking the time today.' Carrie looked at the computer when it sounded. 'Oh, looks like you got a new message from Chloe April. Who's that? The name doesn't sound familiar.'

'A friend. Just ignore it. I forgot to log out of my stuff. Can you do that now?'

'Yeah. Did I tell you Willem is getting into Static?'

'Oh no, really? Did he just tune between stations and make you sit in a dark apartment? How far into it is he?'

'He just got a recording from a Scapa Flow steel studio before I got there. It was expensive, they got the steel and set it up to avoid radiation from nuclear tests and are charging for it. Ten hours. He played a bunch for me when I was there.'

'What did you think?'

'I hallucinated voices. Willem said that's the Ganzfeld Effect and I needed to fight that and focus on the static. I made him shut it off.'

'So he's not going to get into pure notes then? He's into the static?'

The devotees split early - those that listened to static and those that listened to pure tones. Each quickly fractured further. The statics splitting first to live and recorded static. The drawback from live static is the risk of intrusion from terrestrial broadcasts interrupting the noise. Scapa Steel studios were the standard for recorded static, though were challenged by surplus weather balloon launches to get static from the edge of space. Digital static was looked down on but the small subset who followed it claimed it was the most honest static. Recordings of industrial noise and electronic interference, were lumped in when conversation turned to it but seen as very different to those inside.

'Yeah. He's got some headphones coming that are just breathtakingly expensive.'

Pure tones followers split into analog and digital. About forty percent curated their favorites to listen to but the rest resisted this and pressed others not to be sentimental. Runners were those that listened to 20 Hz to 20k Hz runs exclusively, most pure tone aficionados *Run the 20s* at least once - a ten hour recording of a rise in pitch from low to high. It was a mark of unserious people to hold onto recordings of tones your hearing has degraded below. Pinks were interested in the variety of colors of noise, and were referred to as such regardless of where their particular interest fell. Most bonded over an early interest in the mains hum - the AC electrical harmonic. Interestingly, there was no strong correlation between interest in pure tones and those with perfect pitch.

'So She and I are going out to a movie this weekend.'

'Oh yeah?'

'Yeah. Well, She's obviously unsettled. So, you know like I've done before, just reaching out to show Her I'm no threat. Plus, you know, we agree on a lot of stuff and I want to talk to Her more about it.'

'Right on. That's cool.'

'You be good to this one. I could throw a stone out this window and hit one of your exes, you need to slow down.'

'That's why I don't throw stones out my windows. How do you explain that to a judge?'

Registrations

↓1 →2

'Tori, listen.' Stephen sat in the small living room leaning over the table. 'I don't care what mom and dad think, for the last time. You're important to me, don't screw things up by relaying messages for them. It just gives them the chance not to make a decision and makes you their runner.' He paused. Albert walked out of the bathroom and listened to the conversation. He walked over to Stephen sitting cross-legged on the floor and leaned down, kissing him on the bare spot on top of his head. 'How's Hong Kong treating you? And Roger and the boys?' Pause, he smiled. 'Well let me know what they want for the holidays. I'll get it out in time.' Stephen reached up and squeezed Albert's forearm. 'I'm good. In Ohio actually. Registering people to vote.' He laughed. 'No, I'm not going to get maced. I'm playing it safe this fall. The police are okay with things that don't matter.' Pause, 'I love you too. Thanks for calling and have a good morning over there. Rake in that proletariat capital.' He laughed. 'I will. Bye sis.'

'How'd that go?'

'Good. She's still wrapped up in family drama. Though she's getting better.'

Albert started setting up clipboards 'So, Troy.' Albert trailed

130

off his question. Each got at least a dozen sheets of paper printed with the Crew logo at the top and space for contact info for twenty, the names would be added to the voter file they were creating. So as to show any elected officials who landed in the crosshairs just how many people the bloc represented. As well as around fifty cardstock voter registrations. Albert was measuring them by judging the thickness of the stack.

'Yeah. You were right.' Stephen shrugged his shoulders. 'He isn't coming back. Nice that he flaked rather than trying to arrest me.'

'You just can't spot them, can you? You should get better at it. It's always the eager, reliable ones that you have to suspect. With your reputation, infiltrators are the people who follow you in the door in a new city.'

'I just bore them away rather than try to spot them. You should put in a request with the county mounties for the half of the list that he walked off with. That's what bothers me when this happens. Are you going to catch heat from the funders?'

'No. I already explained it to them. They're happy that the main station and the paper came out to the press conference. Maintaining the list just isn't a priority right now.'

library

←3 →4

Matthew stretched and yawned. He sat at a pressboard desk in the downtown library camouflaged as homeless with a sailor's watchcap pulled low and a tattered Marine poncho on. The thrifted glasses were giving him a headache though. Students and homeless sat at terminals around him. He checked the time remaining on his session - logged in with a card under a fake ID that Franklin had secured - thirty-five minutes. He wished he could log in for another session, but this was peak time, as W. insisted, and people milled around waiting for terminals to open up. Enough time to take down the emails from staffers from one more office. Franklin and Sebastian were doing the same at other libraries. Matthew thought it was stupid that W. insisted they take down the names longhand rather than copying them into a text document. Could introduce unforced errors. 'Whatever.' Matthew mumbled and got back to it.

Senator

→3 ↓4

Arlington, Virginia. Morning of Thursday, September Second. He woke early again, earlier than his habit of four thirty. The sneezing fit came on immediately. Three days now of this, he thought. And working all day with that little prick Santorum to look forward to. Should have begged off and gone to the convention. He sighed. Got to leave a note for Patricia asking if she got a dog or something. He didn't get along with the new housekeeper, what's her name was better. His eyes welled up with tears, over and over massive sneezes shook his body. Milk, milk has helped before for whatever reason. He swung his feet out from under the quilt and found his slippers. Standing, he pulled on a dressing gown. Sneezing, he made his way out of the bedroom towards the stairs.

At the top of the townhouse stair he sneezed the hardest of the morning. The sudden spike in blood pressure blew out a berry aneurysm deep in his brain. His empty body tilted forward, tumbling down the stairs. The head smacked against the wooden stair railing, the wall, and the stairs as the body pinwheeled. A framed and signed photo of Gerald Ford fell, shattering the glass. The body came to rest at the bottom of the stairs with its head slumped forward. It lay in the informal foyer sitting back against the front door with limbs askew. Simply one death from natural causes.

street theatre

←1 ↓1

'So we've got a new focus for Labor Day. We've been asked to canvass the largest parade in our area and get as many people signed on to the petition against Issue One as we can.' Albert said at the nightly meeting. 'Before you say anything, all states we're active in with the DOMA stuff on the ballot are doing this.' Two new volunteers crowded around the small living room, bringing the crew up to eight. 'We've got to push back on it. We're thinking maybe street theatre to get their attention? Press notice?'

'What is that going to entail?' Carrie asked.

Albert nodded his head as he replied. 'Ideas would be appreciated. I think it should be something focused on the war to draw people in, then we can have people circulate through the crowd.

'On Labor Day?' One of the new volunteers asked.

'That sounds fucking awesome. Oh hey, did you hear that Senator Ciolek was found dead today? She added. 'He was a Republican, pretty moderate. Not sure if that might do anything?'

'Who is that?' Albert asked.

'Oh I heard that too,' Carrie interjected, 'He's our senior

135

Senator, they found him in his apartment in Washington. It was a home invasion or something? The story I read was that he was pretty beat up and police are investigating.'

'Probably should steer clear of it.' Stephen said. 'Maybe Abu Ghraib or something that's clear-cut.'

Special

→1 ↓4

Paradiddle-diddle and a triple stroke roll. Paul listened
for a syncopated follow-up. No more claps were forthcoming.
Nine quick snaps in the middle of the night without a rejoinder.
Gunfire, same as country nights.

The next day, he found himself walking downtown near Isaac
Scheer's office. 'You hear the news about Ciolek?' Isaac asked
when Paul sat down.

'Yeah, home invasion? Something like that?'

'No, that was nothing, it was natural causes. The guy was
pretty good at what he did, all things considered. When he was
mayor he worked some magic in Cleveland. Times change,
one less moderate R in DC. All of them that are going to go
for his seat are going to present themselves to the right of
Goebbels. You should get onto one of the primary campaigns
for our guys. They'll be staffing up now. Chatter is that Sexton
is serious. McAllen too.'

'Why bother? Working in the field for state senate candidates and county commissioner candidates is a lot different
than a senate race. I wouldn't know where to start. Plus I've
got the crew I'm working with and that's something.'

'What are you afraid of? Everyone quits campaigns. Regis-tering people to vote is what,'

'We kind of stopped that part of it.' Paul interrupted.

'Registering? What are you doing then?'

'Well.' Paul broke eye contact. 'Street theatre, and list building.'

'Ha, fucking grants. Fucking great great grandkids of robber barons thinking they're doing something for the world. The Medicis at least had flair. You're doing bullshit. You're doing grant funded nothing. You don't really have a job right now. Do yourself a favor and make some calls. No one is going to entrust you with the success or failure of any part of the campaign. Just do what they ask and put it on your resume. It'll be great, and you'll be a lot more valuable to me after.'

'Isaac, I'm not,' Paul paused, 'well you remember the stupid stuff.'

'Falling asleep in your car on the day of the election? Yeah. But incompetence is a venial sin, just give yourself space to get better and attach yourself to a few winning campaigns all will be forgiven. Now tell me which of these fonts I should use. I hate doing layout.' Isaac turned down the static he was listening to.

'You do a full run yet?' Paul asked.

'No. Not yet. What I'm reading is you've really got to prepare, obviously. I mean, ten hours is a fucking long time. I think by the new year I will be ready. Going to do it here not at home.' The conversation turned to work, but they chatted about banalities, about beautiful women neither of them would ever bed, about projects they had both started and they had yet to finish. Paul sat with his jaw cradled in his cupped hand. Isaac nodded to emphasize a point and it caused

Paul to bob his head sympathetically. Over his desk Isaac had framed a sheet of blue **By air mail Par avion** etiquette that the post office used. He claimed to any that asked that it was the closest to perfect graphic design that he had seen. It was concise, handsome and confident in its role.

'So why doesn't the Governor just appoint one of them? I mean, it'd make our lives a whole lot harder, but it makes sense.'

'Ha, cause he likes to wave his dick around and that would stop quick if he crossed either side of that party. He's weeeaak.' Isaac drew out the word. ' Appoint anyone and he's dead. This has nothing to do with Democrats, they're sure to keep the seat. And by staying out - not appointing someone who would be the Senator for a few weeks and run as the incumbent - he lets nature take its course and things will stay named after him when he's dead.'

'Is it that certain they'll get it?' To Paul, it felt like when he and Isaac spoke his friend was testing out bon mots and witticisms to be used later on more established company. This was mere defensiveness on Paul's part. Isaac peppered his statements with references to obscure candidates, literary figures and allusions to lyrics; but often when they spoke, Paul was ignorant of the majority of what he was referring to. He didn't mind, and had been practicing acting as if he caught the meaning for years.

'Well, anyone can lose. But this is a tough year and their bench is deeper than ours. That may benefit if blood is drawn in the primary, but it's unlikely. Who knows, roll the dice.'

Paul's phone buzzed. It was Albert. 'What I want is a button on my phone that introduces static and interference so I can get out of conversations that are dragging on too long.' Paul said.

'Are you still doing that thing where you keep the back-lighting off on your phone? What was that 'To save power?' When will you join modern society? How old is that thing? I bet you're still worried about minutes, aren't you? You don't even have a keyboard on it.'

'A couple of years. But look! It has a flashlight!'

'Hey 1998, the future is now. What good is a flashlight?'

'Says the man in the brightly lit room.'

Le

→3 ↓4

That evening, at the crew HQ, Paul's cell phone rang. An unknown number with a 202 area code. He stepped through the sliding door to the back yard before answering.

'Is this Paul Dinares?' A woman's voice asked.

'Yes, who is this?'

'Hi Paul, my name is Chelsea. People call me Le. I'm a Deputy Field Director for Thomas Sexton's campaign for Senate. I'm sorry to call so late, but I just came on and we're staffing up as fast as we can. I assume you have heard about Senator Ciolek's untimely death recently?'

'Yes.'

'Well, Congressman Sexton is going to announce his candidacy Tuesday and I am working on forming a field team for this part of Ohio. Your name was recommended to me, can you make yourself available to work on this campaign through December?'

'What would that entail?'

'I've got the Congressional districts for the western half of Ohio. I need someone to be my deputy in Northwest Ohio to ensure we win these districts in the primary and in the general.'

'I need a day or two to think about it. If I can I can be available by the end of the week. Does that work for you?'

'No. We need folks now. I need you to get back to me by tomorrow, Sunday, end of business.' Le said. 'Also, when you call have a list of three potential office spaces I can look at in Toledo.'

Paul looked at the phone after the call ended. He leaned against the porch railing and lit a cigarette.

smoke detectors

←3 ↓4

Henry hefted a battery operated Sawzall from the back of Dave's rusty white panel van. Todd and two other men - Mitch and Dusty - did the same. They formed a half circle around the back of the van, regarding one another. Todd stubbed out his cigarette. Dave nodded and the five kuroko turned as one to the shuttered elementary school. Mitch, the youngest, jogged ahead with bolt cutters to the entry they'd chosen.

Dave, the last to enter, closed the door softly. They listened down the hallways cast in twilight by the sodium lights outside. Henry looked into a classroom, still decorated for kindergarten with brightly colored toys and posters every-where. A carpet lay on the floor decorated like a town with a road running through it. Plastic trucks sat on it. He thought of the last time he saw one like it, dropping off Timothy. Building, he mused, action. Really a verb. They're never finished and start dying when they're locked up and unoccupied. He backed out of the room and followed the others to the basement, hitting the trigger on the saw once. Just five months since it was reported that it was closed and already water sat on the floor, plaster crunching underfoot. By the time he caught up Dave was already rounding back up the stairs shaking his head. Someone else had already gotten to the copper in the basement. Henry shook his head. It would be a long night to make this run worthwhile. He headed out looking for the cafeteria, motioning Dusty to follow. Henry listened to the melancholic chirping of the smoke detectors. All over the school, someone with more time than Henry would probably easily discern a pattern in it. They start doing that at eight volts, he recalled from a past life. Talking to one another, asking 'Why?' 'Didn't we do a good job?' 'Did they forget that?' 'Will they ever come back for us?' He shook his head. No, he thought. The teachers are gone, the students too. They're never coming back. You've got us from here on. Until some junkie comes through and rips you all down and pieces you out for a couple bucks.

Henry smiled. He pointed to Dusty, then towards where they had split off from the rest. Dusty turned and jogged to find them. Henry pried a sink loose from the wall then cut in, exposing the copper lines. Water poured over the floor as he began cutting the pipe into manageable sections, tossing the lengths into a pile. The others filtered in as Dusty found them, soon several hundred pounds of copper was ready to go with more added as walls were opened up. Going for shy of three large a ton, the night was made.

Go for it

↓1 ↓4

He went back inside and woke his laptop. He leaned back against the arm of the couch, his feet out before him, staring at the home screen on his browser. His phone buzzed.

10:11p.m. Carrie Catherine
<If you feel you should. Go for it. I'm not upset.>

Springer

←2 ↓2

Paul parked and examined the campaign office. Enormous, and long vacant, so very cheap. The upper floor was a false story, low-ceilinged and only good for storage, though windows rimmed it. The windows along the sides had been replaced with glass block, some busted out on the outside by bored drunks but still secure. The floor to ceiling storefront windows had a hand lettered sign telling passersby the number of days left to register. He was glad his contact had this open and he was able to pass it up, good to start off a job with a solid win. Through the window Paul saw a stocky woman pacing on the phone, arguing with someone. A VW trike with a springer fork sat on the sidewalk outside the front door. Garish and aged gold sunburst paint covered the fiberglass body. A ball hitch hung off the back.

Inside, Paul saw all of the chairs scattered around the room had been stenciled with the numbers of union locals: 50, 75, 14, Council 8. The folding tables were certain to have similar on their undersides. These donated supplies were comfortable, familiar. Paul expected that everything visible had been cajoled out of someone who paid dues. She was yelling now, the person on the other end of the phone had failed to deliver on a promise made and was catching hell for it. An enduring, muscular stockiness described her frame. Paul imagined her playing rugby or roller derby with aplomb. A few small objects had been unpacked from the bankers box sitting on the battered steel desk by the front window. A fist-sized glass teardrop - Paul didn't know what it was called - with black and white diamonds on a spindle spun quietly in a ray of light sat next to an open laptop.

'Clear!' yelled a man standing on the top of a ladder with his upper torso lost in the drop ceiling. A sharp *Thwap!* followed. Paul flinched. The man hooted and looked down, noticing him. He smiled. 'Hey how ya doin? This your workstation we're putting in here?' Paul saw him remove a crossbow from the ceiling. Mid-century style with a wooden stock. 'Fastest way to wire across a building this size. Can you give me a hand? I need to feed the wire through.'

The woman hung up and looked at Paul. 'Paul? You're Paul.' She walked over and shook his hand. 'I'm Le, you aren't what I pictured on the phone. This is a good space, the others were crap. It's bigger than HQ actually. You might want to just bar off areas so it doesn't feel empty. I like that it's across from the local Dem office. That'll be handy for vols. You have a station wagon, right?' Paul nodded, surprised at how fast she spoke. The man leapt down from the ladder and went to the back of the office. 'Good to know. I need you to get walk lists. Super D's. We're going to be the first to file. Call Columbus.'

'What's that on the desk?'

'A radiometer. I spent a year and a half in a basement and I'm never going back to it. I felt like a mule in a salt mine. I won't take a desk that doesn't make that thing spin any slower than it is now.' She looked out the window. 'I'll be splitting time here. Here's the number to Columbus. Once you get the lists I'll log you in to the reporting side. I need you to split your day scheduling shifts and going out yourself.'

'Did you hear that another candidate just announced from Akron?' The man shouted from the back. 'A woman, she's a higher up at Goodyear. Y'all can't leave Labor Day alone.' Said the man as he quickly tied the wire and launched cord together with a double sheet bend.

Paul decided to make a joke. 'Akron? She could get Mark Mothersbaugh's endorsement. Imagine the campaign ads.' Neither laughed.

'So that's three now for Democrats? Right? Her, that McAllen guy is getting in, and your guy. Hey, Paul, will you pull on that line hanging there? Go slow.' The man directed.

Targeting

→4 ←2

'So who are you targeting?' Ken asked. He spoke into a microphone setting on his contemporary-style steel desk, with two monitors glowing on it. A database with dozens of searchable categories sat open on one. He'd selected everything Paul needed before he finished listing them. Oh, just Dem supervoters in those four wards? That's it?' Pause. 'What about middle income white males who drive American cars and are between the ages of forty-seven and fifty-six who have at least an associates degree? Those that have Sunday delivery of the Blade? And have not lived outside of that county?' Pause. 'Just the basics. Yeah. Alright, I'll get that over to you now. Get it done.' He hung up the phone. 'Most expensive and comprehensive voter database and targeting software in history and fucking field people come in here *Ooh nah, I want just lists of people that have voted cause technology is scurrrry.*' Ken mocked to the empty office. 'At least direct mail is putting this to some use.'

nunatak

←2 →3

Paul walked up the driveway of the modest, white, two-story home. He saw that the door of the garage behind the house was open. Paul tapped the clipboard he carried against his leg and announced his presence with a loud, but not shouted, 'Hello.'

A man's voice chastised Paul almost immediately. 'Shush out there, you'll rile her up again.' An elderly man stood up from the worn steel patio chair he was sitting in, he had been invisible sitting in the garage. The man flicked the cigarette he held in his hand into a nearby coffee can and walked out of the shadows. The advanced age stated by the wispy white hairs circling his head was belied by the jaunty, effortless way he approached the young man standing in his driveway. 'Cooled off today, don't expect you enjoyed being out in the heat yesterday. How can I help you?'

'Hi sir. Are you Allyn Stuart? I'm here with the McAllen campai...sorry. Hi, I'm here with the Thomas Sexton campaign. He's running in the Democratic primary for Senate. Did you see his announcement in the news today? Do you know who you will be voting for this November?'

'I don't suppose I do. I would happily vote for whoever you

decide that you're helping.' The old mans' eye glinted as he teased Paul. 'Didn't two Democrats announce today?'

'Yeah, but I'm here with Thomas Sexton. He's running to be our next senator and he needs your vote. What issues are important to you in the upcoming election?'

'Well, I suppose what is on my mind right now is the environment.'

'What would you like your senator to do about that?'

'Clean up the sludge pond I found Snowflake in. Do you think my senator will do that if I ask him?'

'I'm sorry?'

'Sorry, I'm feeling ornery. Here, you can meet the reason why. I'll toss her a rat and she won't be too upset you're eyeing her.' Paul followed as Allyn led him back to the garage, stepping around the car backed out in the drive. A mottled shape clattered at Paul from a table in the center of the garage. Allyn reached into a cooler and tossed a white rat on the table. Paul heard a soft tap of the carcass landing. His eyes adjusted and he was startled to see an enormous owl standing atop a circular, blood smeared, dining room table. The bird eyed him over its shoulder, one clawed foot gripping the rat. Paul thought of Happy Birthday. Well, Happy Birthday crossed with a snake. Angry. Far from the wind-battered nunataks and long twilight of the shelterless North.

'A fellow found her in a sludge pond by the refinery.' Allyn said softly, 'She was covered in oil and had given up by the time I got there. She wasn't doing too good but he knew that I'd look after her so he called me to get her out. I put on my waders and went after her, she was too far gone to bother fighting me. Ruined the waders mucking through there.' Allyn paused, watching the bird as it plucked at the rat. Even more softly he said. 'Worth it though.'

Paul was shocked speechless. The bird was the largest he had ever seen alive in person. It stood on the table with a soft leather thong binding its legs and brought its attention back to the rat. Its black-tipped feathers were oil stained, he wouldn't have recognized it without the explanation. Using its spats-covered talons, the owl got the head of the rat into its mouth. Then, in a few quick motions, it flipped its head back and swallowed the rat whole.

'I expect you're wondering if this is legal. I'm not sure really. I will be calling the zoo, I want her to be healthy first. She nearly took my finger off yesterday, she's getting quick. I suspect she's about ready. If I had called them when I first saw her they might have just put her down. I've been feeding her plenty and I sit out here and let her chat me up. All she says is 'Clak-clak-clak' mostly, sometimes she rattles at me, but she's not preening herself when I'm here so she's not getting any of that in her belly. She's almost all molted out now; between that and my wife's dish soap, she'll be okay.' Allyn trailed off as his attention focused on the bird, he forgot Paul was there. Snowflake had finished eating and hopped across the table closer to the two men. She squared up on them and flexed her wings, nearly spanning the six foot diameter table that she stood on. She clicked her beak twice and turned her head as she tucked her wings away. In case either were unsure of just whom they were addressing she wanted them to know that she was royalty, in spite of her current circumstances. 'So, what should I know about Thomas?' The owl regarded Paul through narrowed eyes.

Paul blinked, lost, he had delivered similar raps hundreds of times, but never with a yellow-eyed predator staring him down and heckling. 'We're voting on both senators this year, but one is a primary on November second. The general election is in December for that one, Sexton's election. I'm circulating a petition to get him on the ballot.' Snowflake clattered at him, then turned away.

'Mhm.' Allyn signed the petition. 'Well, thank you, young man. I will be watching the news. I hope that your boy wins.'

Master's

↑4 ←4

'Hey! Yeah, hey! You registered to vote?' She yelled to
to group of men walking down the sidewalk. Two shook
their heads no. 'Then get over here!' Carrie followed with
her clipboard to keep it quick. 'Alright, just fill out what's
highlighted, we'll get it in to the Board of Elections. You going
to vote November Second?'

'You ever think of being a community organizer? You're
good at this.' Carrie asked after they'd gotten all the guys to
register. She had badgered the three who hadn't responded
and thought they were by noting that if they were unsure, they
weren't.

'Eh. I was never good at team sports.' She shrugged.

'I mean, we've got one that's doing good work here in town.'
Carrie put the completed forms at the bottom of the stack.
'And this is what they do, rile people up, get them motivated.
And it's year-round.'

'Maybe. I try to focus on what's here, rather than what's
next. I'm thinking of traveling next year anyway.'

'Fair enough. Where to?'

'Parasols for Ponies is setting up a tour up through Buffalo,
then Nashville, Saint Louis, uh, I forget, but it's shaping up

to be three to four months. And while we're out there I'd be working to make connections and add dates. Helen asked me to make sure they get paid at each stop. Promoters have this nasty habit of disappearing before the headliner is on.'

'That's cool. It feels good to be back to registering people to vote.'

'Truth. I was getting sort of down about it. Like we were spinning our wheels. What are you doing when this is over?'

'I'm thinking of applying to get my Masters. Public Policy. Pittsburgh, Detroit, Chicago, even looking down in Tennessee. Not certain if I can get funding, that's the big one.'

'Always seems to be.'

W154.y0uw343.43r3

↓4 →4

'Hey Paul, I need a password for you so you can have a login.' Le said over the phone.

'Sure. Are you ready? Capital W, one, five, four, period, lowercase y, zero, u, w, three, four three, period, four, three, r, three.' He waited, 'Uh, want me to repeat it?'

'What the fuck is that?'

'It's secure, I took a song title and leeted it. It's a pretty good system.'

'What? You just veered off into nonsense and I'm not engaging with that. How am I going to get on your account if I need to? How are you going to?'

'Well it's what I use.'

'Here's your password. Democrat Zero Zero Four. Capital D.'

Max

→2 ↓3

Max carefully placed strips of toilet paper to cover the entire seat. He loosened his tie and removed it, unbuttoned his dress shirt and hung it on the hook along with his coat. If he had been wearing a t-shirt he would not have had to do that, but casual dress wasn't an option for him. He lowered his pants and sat on the pressed wood pulp seat. He let out a tremendous fart before his bowel moved its contents into the toilet bowl, uncaring about the noise and smell he was creating. He sat in the sickly sweet sulfur stench of his lactose intolerance. Planning that if anyone were to enter the bathroom he would dally where he was until they left. The anonymity provided by his black dress pant cuffs gave him that luxury. He began reading over the graffiti written by idle hands; Jesus Saves in neat typewriter script, homoeroticism couched in aggressive homophobia, phone numbers, and crude drawings of women. He relaxed and thought about what his day entailed.

shares

↓1 →3

Henry woke long after sunrise. He groaned and rolled onto his back. He shaded his eyes and saw a half empty bottle within reach. He finished what was left and sat up. Todd lay sleeping a few yards away. Bottles were strewn around the camp, he hadn't even made it to his mattress. Henry sat up and stretched, his shoulder, back, and hips were raging from the awkward way he had slept. The day was cool and threatened rain. He stood and made his way to the grill, stoking the fire and rolling several hot dogs on the grate, along with setting a pot of water to warm. He patted himself down, crumpled in his coat pocket was what was left of his share. He counted it. Ninety five. He snorted. Five men, five shares is how it should be. But Dave took one for the equipment, and one for leading it and taking the risk with the scrap yard. Seven ways, all that copper and aluminum. Henry walked over to the cat hole and looked at Todd who had stopped snoring but was still asleep. Stupid to bring anyone here, Henry admonished himself. But Todd was good people, and they had been celebrating. He quietly dug the can up and put in seventy five dollars. He buried it again and smoothed leaves over the spot. Satisfied with the work, he walked over to Todd. 'Hey! Todd! Wake up!

Coffee and hot dogs! Extra ketchup! Better than the shit on shingles you got in the Navy.' Todd grunted and rolled over away from him.

BOE

↑2 →2

Albert looked from the folder filled with registrations to the clerk, dumbfounded. 'What do you mean you can't accept these?'

'Oh, no sir, we can take them. They won't be entered though. The Secretary of State issued a directive. We can no longer process any registrations that aren't on eighty weight paper.'

'I've been here a dozen times with no problems. What's eighty weight paper?'

'I'm not certain, I think it's like cardstock.' The phone at the counter rang. 'One moment.' She picked up the receiver. 'Board of Elections.' Pause. Albert fidgeted, angry. 'Yes, let me transfer you.'

'Can I get the correct ones from you? We were supposed to get them from the state weeks ago and they never came.'

'Well, ours are incorrect. So we're not distributing them right now.'

'You recognize that that is ludicrous. Right? What about the ones we've turned in already?'Albert thought of the hundreds at the house, printed on whatever paper was in the copy machine.

'Those are under review by our attorney, we may send them

new forms to fill out.'

'Send them new forms!? We have less than four weeks to register people!'

'Sir, please lower your voice.'

'Who's in charge here?'

'The Director and Deputy Director are meeting with our attorney right now. On this matter.'

'So no one? Is there anyone here that can answer some questions? This is ridiculous and throws a lot into chaos.'

I'm sorry sir. I will give them a message when they return if you wish.' Albert turned and stormed out, dialing the funders on the way to the elevators.

slang

→3 ↓4

grammateia: Tell me something

bkp971: hm, well, i'm working as field staff for a senate race, that's exciting. making phone calls right now from the office.

b: it's a big challenge

g: I would imagine so. Are you concerned about calling random people from your own phone?

b: Nah. Our burners came in, so I'm calling on one of those.

g: Burners? Really?

b: what's funny about that?

g: What else have you misappropriated from street culture?

g: You found a use for 'chickenhead,' yet?

b: HA. well i'll be cutting turf for the canvass this weekend and then training peopleon an effective rap.

g: Are there any books on your desk?

b: unfortunately, no

b: well, there is one in the drawer. i brought it to read when I had time, "dante's inferno."

g: How far are you?

b: i read up to canto five a few weeks ago, but haven't had time to read it since then g: That reminds me. I'm working on a painting. The title is 'The City of Dis on Satan's back. Floating in the Lake of Fire.'

b: that is more descriptive that even prog rock is allowed to be

6:30p.m. Carrie Catherine
<OMG FUCK KEN BLACKWELL>

g: I have a vision of the tortures in Hell taking place in Dis, and that the city is founded on Satan. He's drowning facedown. The cellars and basements and dungeons are bored into his flesh. He forms an island and the demons, his servants, torment him as they do their work.

6:32p.m. SENT Carrie Catherine
<I heard. What a crazy thinh. Got some respect for how little a shit he gives for society or law though>

b: that's something i haven't heard before. is religion important to you?

g: Only the symbols, really. Only the symbols.

conference call

→4 ↓1

'This is Jamie. Who all do we have with us?' The campaign manager leaned back in her chair. Across the conference table Max sat doodling on a pad of legal paper. She took a sip of coffee. They were in a first floor conference room in the state headquarters for the Sexton campaign. A two story red-brick box in Columbus, appended to the front facing the road were four white columns and a peak forming a cheap portico in an attempt to read as class. It was surrounded on three sides by blacktop that merged with concrete and asphalt from the neighboring properties. A grass strip soaked in hazardous lawn chemicals bordered one side. The parking lot was filled with cars, the majority Ohio and Virginia plates.

'Vincent, Mail.' from the triangular conference call speaker in the center of the table.

'Polling.'

'Data and Targeting.' Pause. 'Ken.'

'Fred Ryan, General Consultant.'

'Allison Williams, Field.'

'Walter. With Gina, and Irene, Finance.'

'Okay, we're waiting for Congressman Sexton to join us.

Max who was cut loose on request of the DSCC[7] to run Earned Media is here with me.' The door opened. Sexton walked in and sat at the head of the table.

Another caller dinged in. 'This is Steve Foliot. Congressman Sexton's Chief of Staff.'

Max looked up. 'That's nice, you're on personal time, right?'

'Not only that, but I'm even on my personal Blackberry instead of my work one. I'll be your Political department. How you been Max? Really appreciate the D S coming on this early. I can't thank you enough.'

'Good Steve, glad to be helping out. The Congressman has joined us.'

'Hello everyone. I need to get back to call time, so can we make this as quick as possible?'

'I love when candidates say things like that. I'm tearing up.' Gina said to laughter.

'Alright, we are going to keep this on point.' Jamie led the meeting, 'Field report, then finance, and media. I'll talk to everyone else offline.'

'Field here.' Allison started, 'We need one k signatures to file, we have been collecting for two full days now. We've made sixteen hundred eleven knocks and collected one hundred and three verified signatures. So just over ten percent to minimum. Our regionals are doing double duty,'

'Are we going to run into any issue with the directive?' Sexton interrupted to ask.

'No, that only affects new registrants. We're targeting D supervoters. Um, okay, we're just over fifty percent staffed

---

[7]   DSCC Democratic Senatorial Campaign Committee

on Field side. Three regions; I'm running Columbus, I've got two Deputies. Le's turf is western Ohio and has filled five of seven regional slots. Charles is in the east and has filled three of his eight. I've got two of my three. We'll adapt regions if we expand our staff.'

'So we're weakest in the East? Where two of my opponents are from?'

'There are the Republicans too. Maxie, Congressman from 2, the other one was originally from Mansfield, Maguire. Though he's a C-bus hack now.' Steve put in. 'We're doubling down on that. We've got the resumes and will be staffed up by weeks-end. That's my report.'

Two dragons flew in and settled at the end of the conference table. One set down a cribbage board and started shuffling a deck of cards. The second lit two cigarettes and handed one over. It offered one to Max, who waved it off.

'Thanks Allison. I just want to be clear on a couple points. This directive from, what's the Secretary of State's name here?'

'Blackwell. J Kenneth' Steve said. The second dragon scored a ten on its first card. The partner was annoyed and ashed on the carpet.

'Thanks. It has no effect on us at this juncture. We'll be running into it soon enough when we're putting together the persuasion and turnout universes, but with the Special it's still going to barely affect us. Ken and our attorney are working on that. And it appears there are going to be some lawsuits from other parties - League of Women Voters, maybe others. I'm on top of this. And as for Field, we knew going in that McAllen would have an edge on us; he's a populist, he's in-state, and he's a bomb thrower. We're going to have a solid Field team, we *have* a solid Field team, and we're going to dominate on fundraising and getting our message out. Okay, Walter?'

'One more thing.' Steve jumped in, 'We've got a proven candidate. McAllen hasn't run or won anything higher than State Senate. And dropping State from that title is something he isn't ready for.'

'Fundraising is ramping up. Our candidate has good name rec and an established fundraising operation. We're here to supplement that and make sure we're hitting our goals. We've got a lot coming up, but we're in a good place. With our attorney we are almost ready to switch the campaign account and committee over. As it stands, the Congressman is coming in with a million and a half in the warchest. Since Friday he's raised just under fifty-five thousand. Like I said, this team knows their stuff and the candidate is making hard asks. We're getting some hesitance from donors in-state, so we're focusing elsewhere until we can break through.'

'Let me know what I can do to assist that switchover. That is top priority.' Steve said.

'Will do.'

'What's the name of the committee?' Max asked.

'Sexton for Ohio.' Jamie replied. 'You're up Max.'

'Alright, so the announcement got stepped on. Unforced error on the part of both campaigns. Terrie won the day when she announced. Maybe we should set up a shared calendar or something. But we're moving on.'

'You should have been here on Labor Day.' Sexton pulled a slender blue and white pen from his coat pocket and clicked it several times while rolling his chair back.

Max turned to look at him. 'Well, I wish I could have been, but that decision was made over my pay grade. Near future, we'll be rolling out a five point plan over the next week with surrogates. Fred I'd like to go over the fine issues with you offline. Also whether we're budgeted for staff in my department. I'm not going to be able to go everywhere.'

'We'll discuss that offline. Could you send the plan to the team when it's ready, along with the trip schedule?' Jamie replied.

'Yep.

'I'd like to see it too.' Sexton added.

'Sure.'

'Fred, any closing thoughts?' Jamie asked.

'We should have Paid Media, television and radio, on by tomorrow. Still photos, old material, and stock footage but it'll carry until we can get a shoot. I've got two proposals for oppo, waiting for a third one that I expect by EOD tomorrow. We're working on freeing up political staff from DC. That's it.'

'Who are we getting books on?' Steve asked.

'Unfortunately, it's going to be everyone.' Fred replied. 'I can't justify cutting any out to save costs when the race is so wide open.'

'Can we buy recent op books off anyone friendly?' Gina asked.

'I'll ask around, but I'd only be comfortable doing that if I trust who did the work. And for Terrie we need our stuff. She's your biggest problem getting through if she's serious about this. Your contrast isn't big enough. The Republicans, maybe if we can put feelers out. Update them ourselves for the General.'

'Alright everyone.' Jamie said. 'I think we just set a record for a con call. Talk to you all tomorrow.'

The participants hung up. Ken, the last one on, heard the dragon with the deck of cards warm up a saxaphone and start in on hold music.

SCRAM

→1 →1

'We're ready to go?' Sebastian and the others sat in the foreman's office of an abandoned factory. The door was propped open. The shop floor, a level below them, was visible through the broken out and dirty window behind Franklin's head. Each had a cigarette and reclined in chairs they'd brought in. On the desk four computer towers sat, still too hot to touch, covered in white monoammonium phosphate powder. One empty extinguisher was laying on the catwalk outside of the office. Another sat next to Franklin. A crisis had just occurred, their nonchalance belied how aggravated they were.

W. shook his head. 'We're not ready.'

'But this one was successful.' Sebastian protested.

'Ha.' Franklin laughed. 'Having to smash windows so we can breathe is successful?'

Matthew laughed. 'Yeah. I fucking cut my hand. Can we do the next one in a room bigger than this hovel?'

'Give it up Matt! SCRAM Team Fuck The World.' Franklin put his fist out and they fist-bumped.

'The test was successful. It jumped.' Sebastian turned in his chair. 'We know it can replicate. I'm comfortable with the

170

program. It's all the rest that we've let falter.'

'What do we need to be ready then?' Matthew asked.

'One.' W. ticked off on his fingers. 'The launch list isn't big enough. Two. We don't have locations prepped Three. Enough supplies Four. Or enough firepower. We can't have our asses hanging out to the wind when we're the ones that know it's coming.'

'Fuck man. We'll raid the stuff with everyone else. You want to be a damn king after?' Matthew said. 'We'll prove we've got the stuff to be part of the new society by proving we got the stuff. Already got inside information.'

'That's just foolish.' W. said. 'Seb, where are you on making the mortar?'

'Can't seem to get time alone in the shop.' Sebastian shrugged. 'But I've got the pieces cut and prepped as much as I could do at home.'

'Ammunition?'

'Got to scope out the reserve post.'

canvass

↓4 →1

Paul leaned against his station wagon waiting for the volunteers to arrive. It was a perfect day for a canvass, and he had confirmed four. He checked the time and decided he had enough to smoke a cigarette. As he was lighting one, a cruiser pulled into the lot and parked. Paul glanced over, impassive. Annoyed, he took a drag and stubbed the cigarette out, setting the nearly untouched butt on the front tire so the cop didn't see him littering. The officer stepped out and walked up to him.

'Can I get your license, sir?'

Paul pulled out his wallet and handed the card over. 'Here you are, sir. Do you need my registration?'

'Not right now. Please remain here. Do not enter your car. I'll be right back with this.' The officer returned to his cruiser. Minutes went by, Paul folded his arms and looked around. He was embarrassed. Cars drove by, he saw kids in the back of an SUV point at him. Finally the officer got out and walked back over. 'The library is closed. We've gotten a couple of calls. What are you doing loitering here?'

'I'm campaign staff for one of the Senate candidates.' Paul was careful to remain vague. 'I'm meeting volunteers here to go and talk to voters here in Sylvania and circulate petitions.'

'Can I see your license?'

Paul reached for his wallet, a confused look on his face.

'No, the one you got from the station to solicit here. Did you pay the fee and get the license to peddle?'

'We're not going to be selling anything, this is political speech.'

'I'm not trying to get into a Constitutional argument with you. I want to know if you are complying with the laws here.'

'I'm not aware of them, sir. I can call the campaign manager in Columbus to find out right now.' Paul knew this game. 'They'll call the Congressman and make sure that is, or was, filed appropriately. It'll just take a few minutes, sir.'

The officer paused, considering what he just heard. A car pulled into the lot and parked. Paul, for once, wished volunteers were late. Another vehicle, a van, pulled in behind it. The officer walked back to his cruiser and sat with the door open, talking on the CB. The volunteers stayed in their cars, one made eye contact with Paul. He put his palms up, made an exasperated face, and shook his head. Universally known as 'Nothing to worry about. Simple misunderstanding. It'll be wrapped up soon.'

The officer closed the door and drove over to Paul. 'You're fine. Call the station when you're in Sylvania so that we know how to respond to calls and don't have to come out unnecessarily.'

'Thank you sir.'

And today, Democratic candidate for the Senate Patrick McAllen issued a challenge to his rival in the Special Primary Congressman Thomas Sexton to, as he put it, beat him at a 'shoot off' at a Dayton area gun club. This is in response to calls made by the Sexton campaign to likely voters in this contentious Democratic primary raising doubts about McAllen's voting record on gun issues. There has been no response from the Sexton campaign team so far this afternoon.

Sexton stormed into the office with his driver trailing behind him, they had been crisscrossing the Southwest part of the state going to events since the early morning: a hastily called meeting with leadership from a rural county, to a press conference, along with interspersed private meetings with big donors and union officials. Max followed them in and slowed down as he was passing Le. When the candidate was out of hearing he leaned over her shoulder and whispered, 'I can sum him up in two words. *Tom wants.* Equestrians have solutions for horses that are pasture sour.' They heard Sexton berating Jamie in her office. 'But I'd make him into glue.'

Directive

→2 ↓2

'We've got a problem. I don't know what's going to come of this.' Albert sat at the low table. Carrie, Stephen and two volunteers sat with him. Others who couldn't fit on the couches. She was out, skipping the meeting disgusted with the news. 'This directive means we're effectively shut down. It's not ethical, or useful, to collect registrations and tell people they can vote if we don't know they will be able to.'

'So what do we do in the mean time?' Carrie asked.

'We could organize a rally?' A volunteer said.

'That's something. Right at the Board of Elections.' Stephen said. 'We could mobilize the list we collected, get people marching. In line with the directives?'

'No, anything too aggressive might hurt us. It sounds like this Blackwell guy is looking for someone to push back.'

'Can we do voter protection?' Carrie asked. 'Maybe organize attorneys to watch the polls and be ready to challenge? A lot of law students have gotten through by studying at the coffee shop. I can get in touch with them.'

'I don't know what the laws say about that. We can look into it. But that's also at the end. We can't spin our wheels organizing towards Election Day, we've got to be a presence now.'

Starships like jellyfish

↓3 ↑2

'Hey dude. You busy?' She walked in the open front door of the office, looking around. Paul was by himself, making calls to potential volunteers. He hung up and closed his laptop.

<u>grammateia</u>: It was a weird dream. Starships like jellyfish hanging in the sky.

'I can take a few minutes, Sunday night is a good time to call though.'

'What's that smell? It reeks in here.'

'Someone jammed stinkbombs in the door and they got crushed when I opened up this morning. I think they got some into the vent on the side of the building.' Paul paused, 'The grate may have been busted already. I don't remember. Tried airing it out but it's designed to stick.'

'That's some really childish bullshit.'

'Yeah. It's the game. What's up?'

'I'm just frustrated.' She pulled a chair over to Paul's desk. 'Round and around we go, I am not feeling this. It doesn't feel like we're accomplishing anything. You know? How do you stick to it, this looks awful.' She waved around the empty office.

'I guess I look at the long term impact. Get people mobilized, maybe get an elected official in who I agree with. It's worth the tedium.'

'And the aggravation. I got your text about being stopped.'

'Yeah, not the first time it's happened.'

She laughed. 'It's what you get for going to the suburbs, man. You got to stay away from places that know what corn looks like on the stalk.' She walked around the room, opening a box of green and gold Sexton for Ohio yard signs. She grimaced. 'These are ugly.'

Paul looked over at her. 'Oh, yeah, not the best. Slacktivists love them though. My boss told me to only give them out to volunteers after they complete a shift. Pretty good advice I thought.' He cocked his head. 'You remember I grew up in the country right? Fields surrounded my house.'

'Guess it slipped my mind. You want to go out tonight? Maybe get up on an overpass. I want to say something about this.'

'I can't. Would be a news story if I got arrested now.'

'I guess.' She walked to the front of the office, watched homeless people walk to a food kitchen a block up. 'That party headquarters across the street?'

'Yeah.'

'Fuck all good what we're doing does for those guys.'

Paul walked up to the window, putting his arms around Her. He rested his chin on the top of Her head. 'Better than doing nothing. We're on the right side. Not like conservatives even see homeless people.'

'I'm going to go on tour with Helen after the new year.'

'Paul furrowed his brow. 'Yeah?'

'Yeah. I need to get out, get some miles under me. I'm suffocating in this town.'

'How long will you be gone?'

'At least three months. Maybe longer. Why don't you travel more? I need to.' She pulled away from him. and turned. 'I mean, I get antsy if I haven't lived in two different time zones in a year, you know?'

'I planned to get out after graduation, to go to one of the coasts.'

'Why didn't you?'

'I couldn't afford it mostly, couldn't save up enough. Just worked and waited for college to start.'

'You were doing it wrong. I've never saved up. Just made it happen. Like this. Hooked up with people traveling through, found people somewhere I wanted to see. Found work and a house that'd take me in. I've stuck around here a good year longer than I intended to.'

'I can't imagine being far away from my parents. I'm too poor to travel on a moment's notice and if something happened to one of them I would need to be here.'

'You're not poor, you're just broke. But I guess I get that. Just, this town is a weird place to land forever. '

'Well, growing up base to base means you sort of see the country as your hometown. Right, you Army brat.'

'Air Force. Yeah. I guess so. But still, here?'

The street was darkening, dusk was settling and the lit up office was becoming a quiet refuge of light. 'When I was growing up, I'd look at the Toledo skyline on the horizon.' She chuckled. 'Seriously, how was I to know any better? It was big, I didn't have anything to compare it to, you know? Downtown was visible from the side yard. And that was miles and miles away. It was so far outside of my experience.' They walked back to his desk, She sat down and put Her feet up.

'There was this big tree, I don't know what kind, it's dead now. I'd climb up in the branches and try to imagine what their lives were like. All the stories on TV and movies about city life I thought were happening there. It was filled with thousands of stories, opportunities, danger. I asked what I'd have to do to break into that, to work in those buildings. Become part of that and be one of the people looking out over the countryside.'

'I guess I get that.' She said. 'I mean. I didn't really connect with anyone cause everybody was transient. It wasn't even like we could get used to one another for a whole school year sometimes.'

'Yeah, I was a lonely kid too. My parents moved to the country because they didn't like the suburbs. So the closest neighbors my age were a country mile away. It was isolating. I ended up reading past my age, learning all sorts of words I guessed at the pronunciation of. And hanging on to solo play much longer than I should have. Lost a lot of friends over the years. Sort of the opposite of your experience. Instead of people mixing up and moving around, it's like everyone moves on from here. Everyone leaves. Except me. I'm still here.'

Paul's Stand Up: I've been a child myself. Most adults share that experience. I grew up in the country, which means that I grew up by myself. My parents - wishing for well-socialized, friendly offspring - decided the best thing to do would be to move fifteen minutes away from the nearest town (population 1,100 and change) and both have full-time jobs. Thing is about having access to an enormous library as a kid is that you learn all sorts of words, and what they don't tell you on Reading Rainbow is that pronunciation is a mug's game. Like Echelon.

That's a meaty word. If Echelon comes up in conversation, it is a pretty substantive one. Not just in the checkout line making small-talk with the clerk. The thing is, I pronounced it ek-eh-lon until I got corrected four years ago. So that made me break out in a cold sweat realizing that people for years, in every Echelon conversation, left confused and wondering if they'd been taken advantage by some sort of idiot savant.

'That why you're so gregarious now? Make sure people remember you?'

'Is that why you are?'

'When do you get off work?'

'Stopping calls at eight thirty, conference call at nine. So nine forty five or so.'

'What are you talking about on the calls?'

'Kerry is coming to town, and so is my candidate. Trying to get vols out to petition and attend a presser. Turnout is looking great.'

'Right on. Well, I'm going to go. Give me a call sometime this week. Cool?'

'Yeah.' They kissed, eyes closed. Holding it for a dozen heartbeats under the fluorescent lights. She picked up Her backpack and walked out to Her truck.

Clutch

↓2 →2

'Ohio.' Max said. 'The northernmost Southern state.'

'Hey, it wasn't until two Ohioans were put in charge that the Civil War was brought to an end.' Chelsea snapped back.

'True, I forgot that Sherman was from here. He was a genuine gentleman bastard. I love him. When we studied the Civil War in high school I wrote about his March to the Sea. We need more folks like that. You guys had that Senator that NASA sent up for a victory lap, too? Right?'

'Yeah, but don't talk bad about John if you want to make friends around here. Not only is he a patented National Hero, he's a Democrat.' Chelsea scanned the crowd, Sexton should be arriving. The sun was setting and the line outside the hanger stretched for a quarter mile. 'Why didn't you bring the candidate? What's his ETA?'

Max looked at his watch. 'Ten minutes.' Chelsea harumphed.

'McAllen's working the line.'

'Which one is he? Point him out.'

'The tall one shaking hands. In the suit. Two o'clock. By the AfAm guy with the clipboard.'

'Oh shit.'

'What?'

'That's my regional right next to him. Paul, get the fuck away from there.' She willed him to turn away and move on down the line.

'Le! Puppets, dead ahead. Other side of the fence.'

'Yeah, what's that all about?'

'Seen it out in Cali. Something new with protests. Surprised they made their way here so quickly though. Your state is more advanced than I suspected. Do you have my-crow-wave-zuh too?'

'Why'd we get you? Does the Dee Ess really hate Sexton?'

'I'm the best, just watch. Word is you are too. Nice of Kaptur to cut you loose for this. She trying to make friends?'

'Eh, I took a leave myself.' Though she was chatting, Chelsea scanned the line intently, watching the volunteers she'd been introduced to. 'I don't fit in on the Hill. I'm thinking of moving on.'

'Toledo Toledo. You've got Gloria Steinem, and Ben Willard too, right?'

'I've always asked why more wasn't made of President Bartlett's war record.' Chelsea saw a volunteer sit down chatting, making a mental note of it.

'Would have if he'd run against my candidate in the primary. What's with that TOLEDO PRID sign on the way in here over the highway? Did wonders for my morale.'

'I asked my regional the same thing. I guess the mayor got fixated on letting everyone know that Toledoans love their town so he had that cast up. Those letters weigh about five hundred pounds apiece. And once it was delivered he sent some city workers out to install it. They wrestled with it all day and got that far. Then it was five and they clocked out.'

183

'Then what?'

Chelsea shrugged. 'The next day they went to their next assignment, and the next after that. It's been TOLEDO PRID for three or four months now. How far out is the candidate? Shouldn't we be at the lot?'

'No, Jamie's with him. Told me to meet her here.' He pointed straight down.

'The CM is driving the candidate around? That's weird.'

'Stop-gap. We'll get a driver.' His cell buzzed.

12:10p.m. Jamie Caulfield CM SEXTON
<Just parked. How's the crowd?>

'Ah, he's here.'

'We got to get him to clutch?'

'No, and neither are on stage. Kerry's folks are hands-off. Where are we on signatures to file?'

'This is such a waste. Why are you all even here? Too many bosses not doing enough work. As of last night we've exceeded our goal. So they're being checked now.'

'Lot of Democratic primary voters out there, Le. Sexton was calling on the drive over, so it's not like he's really wasting his time. And I've got him a one on one with the political guy for the daily here.'

Chelsea rolled her eyes and went back to scanning the crowd.

'What was DC like when the news hit? I was here but heard there was a lockdown?' Le asked.

'Yeah, when they thought a Senator was beaten to death in his Hill apartment the Capitol Police got really fucking serious and brought the gates down. I ended up smoking out my office window cause I couldn't get outside. But inside an hour - too late to stop the first editions of the stories about it - they'd realized what happened and dropped the response.' Max shrugged, 'But a District-spanning lockdown is better memorial than flags at half staff or twenty-one gun salutes. I hope for it when I go.' Soon, the candidate's airplane taxied up. Stairs were rolled up and the hatch opened. The Senator stepped out and waved to the reception. He walked down to a group of no-name dignitaries waiting expectantly at the base. Local affiliates filmed. The blue-white lights suspended from the steel framework of the hanger chased away all shadows. The crowd was cast in stark relief, waving and holding up signs.

Lightweight

↑4 →3

Max threw his arm around Paul when the team returned to the office. 'All I know about Toledo is the bar in Adams Morgan. If that is an accurate reproduction of this place, I'm going to enjoy the times I'm here.'

'I would be surprised if it is, I'm sorry to say.' Paul replied.

'Well that changes things. Do you have any good bars close by? I come up with my best ideas when surrounded by drunks, they're some of the smartest people I get to deal with. Who's from here? What should I know about this town? Got any peculiar colloquialisms?'

'There are some good ones a street up.'

'Good man.' Max looked in the back. Sexton was wrapping up a chat with volunteers and taking pictures with them. Jamie was on her phone talking near the photocopier.

'You got a report to make, right? Hurry that up and show me around.'

After locking up for the evening, Paul, Le and Max made their way to Adams Street. Jamie and Sexton had left an hour earlier to their respective hotels. 'You live here, maybe you haven't noticed this.' Max said. 'Half the places here are racial slurs:

Gino's, Cooley, Beaners. It must be a trip being a minority here. For years I've wanted to open a place called *NINA's Pub*, maybe this in the town to do it in. Hey Le, what hotel we staying in again?'

'Something, I forget. They're union.'

'Is downtown within stumbling distance, Paul? Can I leave my car at the office?'

'Stumbling distance?'

'As opposed to walking. It's about half as far.'

'Ha. Yeah. We should head to Wesley's then. Couple block straight shot to the hotels down there. And no, you shouldn't leave your car at the office overnight.'

'I'm telling you guys, it's eerie here though.' Paul pointed with his drink. 'Past cycles I've felt this shift. Several times. Like the wind blew everyone else away with the leaves. It comes to me in late afternoon. when I'm out in the countryside going house to house. And everything is still. I always knock on the doors, afraid that no one will ever be home. Just me and the crunching leaves.'

'Well you're a fun one.' Max sipped his neat whiskey. 'Hey, you got a temple in this town?'

'A synagogue? Yeah.'

'Okay, good. I wasn't sure. I need to go tomorrow. Some-times in these towns that turn off the traffic lights on the weekends you can't find one.'

Chelsea was slumped over, staring at the light reflecting on the rim of her glass. 'So distinct. So beautiful. Sharply define black lines crisscrossing yellow.' She focused and unfocused. Then, carefully, focused and made the orbs grow and shrink. 'Look through the ice in your glass. It's its own

187

sort of kaleidoscope. Don't you fucking forget it. More real than reality. Sharp.' She thought to herself. Without moving her head she glanced around, saw scratches and wear marks of glasses and coasters over the wooden counter. 'I'll tell you this,' Chelsea said, straightening up. 'Once every four years the only place to be in the autumn is Ohio. We're lucky to be here right now. The leaves are falling all over the country, but no one is paying any attention to Indiana or Oregon, everyone know how they'll vote.'

'Whoa! She's back with us folks.'

'But we're not on the Presidential?' Paul asked.

Chelsea thought about that. 'Point still applies.' She slumped back down. 'Nother. Clean glass too, none of the creepy shit.' She waved the empty glass at the bartender.

'Hey lightweight, may want to hold off on the third. You've still got to find your hotel room when we get back. How's crowd for the presser looking like tomorrow?'

'Good, good.' Chelsea replied, head on her arm. 'Twenty-three confirmed. I did some of the confirmation calls myself. This regional here isn't a bullshitter.' Straightening one arm to point at Paul. 'Hey, what's your department shaping up like, Max? Am I going to have to deal with more of you catty bitches? Could we bell you or something so we get a warning you're around?'

'Right now just me. Which is not what I was led to believe coming on. A whole fucking state of eleven million and me.' He sipped his drink. 'I mean, I still outnumber it. But this is ridiculous.'

'That's rough.' Paul said.

'Make it happen. Organize yourself some, whatever.' mumbled Chelsea, her attention on the television. 'Is that a suicide booth across the street?'

'Yeah it is.' Paul answered.

'Yeah.' Max said, 'They're going to let me staff up by October, but for now it's me.'

'This close to bars? Most places got spacing requirements, keep those out of entertainment districts.' Le said from the crook of her arm.

'I think that one has a breathalyzer in it. I don't know for sure though. Never took a close look inside. I think the drunks use it as a urinal for the most part. Someone broke the door on it a while back.'

'Oh my god you two are the fucking worst.' Max interrupted. 'We should do shots! Shots instead of the two of you talking anymore! Come on, where's the bartender? Clean glasses!'

Call me

→3 ↓4

8:35 a.m. Le Boss

<Hey. I had to head out. Something came up. Call me.>

8:37 a.m. Le Boss

<Scratch that. Go get any oppo on the cand from Mansfield the local guy, Isaac, has. Go before going to the office.>

8:38 a.m. Le Boss

<TOP PRIORITY. Call me on the way over.>

8:51 a.m.

<Will do.>

8:53 a.m. Le Boss

<Check in with Max. Presser at 11.>

Paul toweled off and dressed. Living five minutes from work has its advantages, even when the boss doesn't change the day before it started.

anti-lef

↓4 →3

Isaac opened the door of his office and looked Paul up and down. 'When I see you I wonder what your clothes shopping experience is. Do you, as I suspect, pick something off the rack at your little thrift store and hold it out at arms length and ask yourself *Would the caretakers of a mentally ill person dress them in this?* And then if the answer is no, I suspect, you put it back.'

'This is my good shirt!'

'That may be a true statement, but it is not the defense you think it is. Not a lot of people could pull that off, but you didn't. This is what you wear to work?' Isaac asked.

'It is, and for good reason. I look presentable and trustworthy. An up and comer.' Paul saw Isaac was pointing at his shoes. 'Wait, are you making fun of my EZ Striders again?'

'Oh, I haven't seen past this, this whatever, that drapes your torso. Come inside, I don't want the other people on this floor seeing this outside my door, I've got a reputation to keep up. What is that color, *Spanish Shame*?[8] My opinion on your footwear choices is a matter of public record. You look like a

---

[8] *vergüenza ajena*: Shame felt on behalf of another.

191

wastrel that needs five bucks for *the bus*. What are you doing here? Don't you have work? The real political operatives expect you to show up on time, they aren't pushovers like me. Or did you expect your outfit to get you out of that? Oh, I'm sorry, the plane I inhabit now doesn't have time as you know it.'

'I was going to work, they sent me here.' Paul explained. 'They want an op research book on Maguire.'

'I don't have anything like that.'

'I know, and I said that. But he ran against Ross for Auditor and, and since you're a big wig in these parts and you worked on his campaign, well. They expect you to have one.'

'Big wigs are just useless merkins. I don't have one, I did mail for the guy for fucks' sake. Tell them to make a new one. They have to get Sexton through the primary before that's an issue anyway.'

'Apparently he wants to see a report on his *real opposition* this evening.'

'Pfft. I'm glad we don't settle this by asking who thinks they're invulnerable and will win and we go ahead and ask voters their opinion. Why did they send you, and not call? I'm not some hick scratching about politics in a one-room schoolhouse. Got to give me some respect.'

'Because I am supposed to use my friendship to secure the file, I gather.'

'What a bunch of shitbags. Well I don't have it. You can tell them that. Oh wait, Maguire has half a dozen churches around the city where all the grandma's think he's a member of the congregation because they saw him twice a year before his move to Columbus. You know, the holiday church circuit. He's pretty clean. Why don't we smoke and you can tell me how things are going?'

Paul and Isaac sat on the fire escape, leaning back against the half empty office building. looking out over the brick city.

'I hear from my network of spies that the party is just not going to commit resources, as long as there are two viable candidates in the race.' Isaac passed the joint to Paul. 'So rather than cajole someone out they're going to let a primary air all our dirty laundry for a general a few weeks later and let the Republicans rehash fresh copy against whoever squeaks out. The people that run this organization are dipshits sometimes.' Isaac paused, regarding a car being parked below. '*Hail to the Chief* just doesn't get me like the theme song to *The West Wing*.'

'Yeah, it really makes the chest swell. I got a box of t-shirts yesterday, every fucking one was extra large. When did that ever become standard practice?'

'A little person can fit into a big shirt, but not the opposite. You know that.'

'Yeah, but they look like clowns. I've seen volunteers that look like sail boats. Or the smart ones who tuck it in to hide its size and the bottom of the sleeves are at their waist and their torso is all lumpy. I'm just saying, if campaigns want people to wear the clothes, they should buy more sizes.'

'Whine whine whine, you wear it for a few hours, rep a candidate, and get to spend the rest of the day screwing off at festivals. Tough life. We should commission Sorkin's guy rewrite all our national music.'

'Here's what I want to make. An inflatable podium. Just like, in a briefcase with a little pump. *fft fft fft fft* and stick on some velcro veneer panels and boom.'

'Better than the monsters we deal with now, and that idea you had back when we first met. Vinyl stickers to go over undercar lights?' They both laughed at the memory, 'Oh Isaac,' he lowered his voice and drawled, 'Like, we just need to figure the math out once, then make waves and dragons and flames and shit on it. Like, sell it to boy racers. Make the decals so when they're on the ground they're proportional. C'mon man.' laughing. Both Isaac and Paul lowered their voices when doing an impression of the other, Isaac drawled, Paul enunciated.

'In retrospect, I think I'd rather be broke than suffer the embarrassment of making millions that way.'

'The idea *may* have made millions, but it would be spread out across all the bastards that'd rip you off a week after it hit market. You know, have you ever tried drinking while remaining completely stationary? It's totally sublime. You feel clever, witty, and most importantly: only charmingly intoxicated.'

'Until you stand up for a piss and smash your face into your knee. Done that. This is great weed, where did this come from?' Down below a sugarloaf shaped woman huddled with a lamppost near a Reagan Chair. She quietly shuffled off as Paul fixed on her.

'The usual routes, we got lucky. Did you hear that Homeland Security is going to be screening space tourists for possible terrorists? I read that and thought of you.'

'Isaac. I want you to know something. If I were approached by a representative from NASA and told I could be an astronaut if I gave up everything; you'd never see me again. They're not taking the proper tack on this privatization of space. None of the nascent spaceports are allowing people that show up with a duffle bag and a dream to start poking around. *Danger ahead: Please fill out release form completely.* Right now we're at the U-Boat phase of space travel. Smelly, sweaty bodies with corroded steel separating us from destruction. We need to work with that.'

'What do you think private space travelers should be called? Feels like they should have their own term doesn't it? Corpronauts? Copronauts? Maybe you should have given in to the pressure to be an engineer rather than bumble towards a liberal arts degree. You could have made that speaker system for Boomers that broadcasts an inverse of the sound they're producing to cancel it out.

'I still think that would work.'

Should NASA or NSA show up, flick the joint before continuing any conversation with them about job prospects.'

'I really should have. Like my idea for a funnel wind turbine? Had that sitting right here, with the wind speed getting all, higher. I've never learned how to roll these? The best I can do is less effective than just crumpling the paper around the weed.' Paul closed his eyes. 'How can this feeling be illegal?'

Isaac emptied his lungs slowly. 'Venturi Principle. Great unanswered questions. Legaler and legaler though. You know there's a lunar eclipse coming up, end of October? Not one of the good ones, but, you know, something.'

'Yeah, I read that. I told you about when all the kids at my elementary had to stay inside. We missed a solar eclipse.

'The good ones.' Isaac interrupted.

Paul went on, 'The administrators were freaked out that someone would get hurt.'

'Yeah, you told me that. I remember that. We made these viewers out of sheets of cardboard at my school.'

'I wonder how anyone got out of that place.' Paul sipped his coffee. Unconsciously pulling his lips and cheeks taut as he swallowed. A soft animal form ebbed in the competing waves in the mug. It rocked, expanded, and was gone.

'At least they didn't have you all bang pots and pans to scare off the dragon.' Isaac said. 'I think that an RFID tag embedded in ticket stubs would be great to market. Imagine going to the urinal and have the audio from the movie you're watching play to you over tightly focused, directional speakers. People wouldn't miss anything and they'd want to know how it works.'

'You have any new fun sockpuppet accounts?'

Isaac used a law directory from 1977 he'd found to create names and create the kernels of personas. 'No, playing them all straight right now. I think I crossed over to useless crank with too many when I was enjoying myself in retrospect. They are enthusiastic about all the candidates that have paid my invoices though.'

'What is your fixation on social media? People using that aren't voting in local elections.'

'Listen Paul, we're all going to be uploaded to the machine consciousness at some point. Social network are just the first iteration of that and I am ready for it.'

'I keep thinking, our generation's grandchildren will be mining our landfills and mocking us for what we throw away.'

'Capitalism is reborn in every generation.'

'You still measuring your life in girlfriend units instead of years? *That was during the Alice Era, Isaac.*'

'Ugh, on that. She and I have stopped having sex.'

'Oh I'm sorry man. How long has this been going on?'

'I don't know, a while now. I barely see Her. She came by the other day. but, I don't know. She doesn't like the campaign, doesn't see the importance; why I'm spending so much time and energy on it.'

'Are you going to break up?'

'I don't know, no reason to. Might as well keep going.'

'What we're doing is difficult to convey to someone that hasn't lived it. If it makes you feel better, I realized that I have old man shins. I got out of the shower and toweled off and there they were - bald and shiny, like my swim coach's at JCC when I was a kid.'

'You were never promised youth, Isaac. How were you just able to notice this change? I saw your scaly shins when we went biking last summer.'

'Yeah, but I thought the shred I had would hold out longer than it has. And this doesn't sneak up on you, I've just accepted the reality. Unlike you and your hairline.'

'I've been wondering why old ass white conservatives aren't raring to go and call AfAm parents Mom and Dad. Like, they get that words are okay in certain contexts or among certain people.'

'It's that they really, really, really are desperate to go back to using the n-word openly.'

'Well duh.'

'You know. I don't trust people that own boats. Boat people. With anchors in their front yards, Corona Christmas lights, Cabo Wabo margaritas. I don't trust them, their worst days are like our Thursdays. They act like every day is just one from the weekend. Unsettles me. They have no context, you know?' Isaac looked out over the old brick part of the city. 'I won't rest until I get you to check out static. I've got a CD with some great stuff on it, and it's easy to get into. Not intimidating.

Do you have a good set of headphones?'

'No. Had some, lost them in a breakup.'

'Jessica?'

'No, before her.'

'I'll lend you a set.'

Max's alarm sounded, he quickly set it for another fifteen minute cycle and went back to sleep reclined in his rental car. He was parked in the outlot of a regional grocery store. The sun warmed the car to the temperature of bathwater, Max sweated slightly. He looked at the sky. Gray, smoke or regular clouds, Max couldn't tell, drifted against it. He loved being one of the people out driving in the middle of the day. Eating in their cars, driving on business from one location to another. He had been doing this for years to nap safely by not allowing himself to fall too deeply asleep. His phone buzzed with a text, he responded. He considered calling it and driving on to Cleveland, but didn't want to. He went back to sleep.

'Hey, before you go.' Carrie stopped Sarah as they were walking out the driveway of the Crew's house. 'I've got something I want to submit. A letter to the editor. About Issue One. Can you give me feedback on it? It's one long sarcastic metaphor and you're better than anyone I know at crafting that sort of message.'

'Sure yeah.' Sarah leaned against the fender of her truck. 'Got a hard copy of it?'

'Yeah.' Carrie pulled it out of her satchel, folded it once, and handed it over. 'Just let me know? I want to get it in soon.'

She read:

I met a friend for coffee today, and while we were waiting for our caffeine he started ranting about something I didn't even notice happen.

"Did you see that?" He asked sharply.

"What?" I looked around, confused.

"That guy, I think he's a lef." Raising his voice on the last word in an attempt to make the other guy hear. In a lower voice he continued. "He was stirring his coffee, with his LEFT hand. Plus, he has his wallet in his back pocket on the left side, it's a sign among those sort of people."

I smiled uncomfortably, not understanding where he was going. "What guy? What?" It had been years since I had heard anybody say something like that – and, well, honestly – it was a bit jarring, especially since I thought I knew my friend. All the time we'd known one another he'd never made a sinistrophobic comment.

He didn't notice how uncomfortable he was making this quick coffee. "I hate when left-handed people act like we're supposed to think they're normal. God, it's so disgusting. I mean, I don't care if they are or not, but they shouldn't flaunt it. It's gross. They hold scissors all crooked."

I saw a gleam in his eye. I didn't try to interrupt him at that. I knew where this was coming from. I went to a rural school as well, and the guys would accuse one another of being left-handed all the time. I lost interest in sports because any time I threw the ball and it went crooked or my form wasn't right I'd get taunted with, "You throw like a girl! You leffer!" They'd yell stuff like that back and forth all day. The adults in charge rarely stopped them, even though there were left-handers teaching. Though, in retrospect, they had to be careful to conceal it from the students if they were going to stay employed. The administrators were cool with left-handers teaching as long as they were discreet. Even Boy Scouts, we played Smear the Laggot and the Scoutmasters didn't care, until Mike's arm was broken in a nasty tackle. Those teenage boys were depressingly imaginative in their taunts though: lef, leffy, cacky-hander, molly-dooker; it went on and on, and on, and got more offensive than I'd like to go into here. I nearly hit a guy when he rolled in on me to say this girl we knew was a Leffer Effer. I'm not even left, I mean, I know people that are, but I don't need that sort of hate in my life. Guys would play grabass in the locker room; running around naked, snapping towels at one another and trying to establish who was really "left" and just pretending they were "right." Some guys went on and on accusing others, to a point where the other rights got bored and sick of being whipped with wet towels and started to question if the rights who were still at it were REALLY right handed.

I found a table by the window and the diatribe continued. "It's okay if they are left. As long as they don't flaunt it. That's what I hate. I don't need to be walking in the park with my nephew and have to explain to him why someone is throwing a football with the wrong hand."

"Down in Cincinnati there is that group, Citizens for Community Values, that is trying to get that thing on the ballot." I mentioned vaguely. I didn't really care, I was bored and I was looking out the window at the backside of a guy strutting down the sidewalk.

"Oh yeah, the "Defense of Right-Handedness Act." I hope that passes. These leffys are always trying to get special rights. Like we need to respect their, their lifestyle choice." My friend said that with more disgust that he had initially said lef. "It's in the Bible you know. It's right there in "sin." Sinister means "Left." Right has five letters in it, like a hand has fingers." My friend went on, he looked around furtively while he stirred his coffee. "Sinister means "Left." Right has five letters in it, like a hand has fingers." My friend went on. "Lefs have always been trouble, going back

200

to ancient times." The biological arguments all seemed to ignore how many right-handed couples go for left-handed behaviors sometimes, I thought silently.

"Jesus is not quoted saying anything against it." I had read that somewhere, some leftist group had been pamphleting on campus about the ballot initiative this year. Since I was forced to think about it I wondered why people would get so bent out of shape about which hand someone brushes their teeth with. Or even why people focus on a couple of disjointed lines in their holy book rather than the overarching themes of compassion and service. Whatever, I sipped my coffee.

My friend retorted. "Yeah, well He never said anything about incest, so is that okay?" If I had been paying attention over the years I would have seen that coming, that rejoinder is pretty common. The Bible mentions left-handedness twenty-five times, all in the negative; that floated up from a muddy memory out of Sunday School. "They didn't used to allow this in schools. But these lefty liberals got in there and into government and told teachers they couldn't stop it. My grandpa acted left when he was a kid, but his teacher smacked him around until he wrote right."

"So you're a conservative then?" People only get this weird about handedness growing up in really strict households. Somehow conservatism got wrapped up with being sinistrophobic; this hard-right wing was in charge, and had tipped the balance in the two-thousand Presidential election, and with this anti-lef ballot initiative in eleven states hoped to do it again in two-thousand and four. What I thought was funny was these same guys lust after lefty and ambi ladies. My friend - for instance - when he was in the mood, because he'd talk about it All. The. Time. Personally, gross. I don't care, but I guess it's hot for a woman to be lef. Not my thing though.

"Yeah, I'm old-fashioned. It's our culture now that is turning out all these left-handers."

All this talk was distracting from the topic I invited my friend to coffee to talk about. Which would be: Me. I was even starting to become annoyed with the lefs myself because they had hijacked the conversation. From somewhere I remembered that I had heard that seven, or maybe even ten percent of the population was left-handed; and that didn't take into account people that are ambi, and those that experimented with left-handedness in college after high school - where they'd be snapped with rulers - before going on to be right-handed. Though those folks are usually pretty good people.

"They die sooner, you know. There are fewer elderly people that are left-handed than younger people. Percentage-wise. It's dangerous. Being left-handed." I chose not to note his earlier point that schools used to abuse left-handed people might maybe skew the number of elderly people who are left-handed. "Geneticists haven't found a "left-gene," it's a choice." He mumbled, stirring his coffee.

Since the conversation was utterly, and forever, irrevocably, not going the direction I wanted it to (ME) I decided to participate. "Left-handedness has been observed in nature, you know. Scientists have observed monkeys, penguins, dogs, ducks, zebras all using their left...appendage. And pretty much every dolphin is ambi."

"We're better than animals, aren't we? It's unnatural. I'm glad the military bans lefs. They're perverts. We don't need those creeps. I mean, all firearms are DESIGNED for right-handed shooters. It's dangerous and bad for morale to have a lefty on the front lines."

I noticed that my friend was stirring his coffee with his left hand while he was talking. I chuckled and didn't mention it. He'd just get all defensive. How weird was that? Am I alone, has anyone else heard sinistrophobic comments recently? I hope that Ohioans see through the ignorance and vote against the anti-lef legislation that CCV is pushing.

'It's fine. I see what you're going for.[9] Bit long, maybe cut it down. I don't know what the rules are about these things. It's kind of heavy-handed.'

'Yeah, thanks. Well. I'll revise it. What are you up to this evening?'

'Going out. I scouted an underpass that's open. I'll catch you later.' She got in her truck and drove off.

---

[9] Interesting note for you. *I see what you're going for* is the most dismissive feedback one can give in the English language.

Alone

←3 ↓2

Henry awoke. The night was clear, and cool. A breeze rippled the tarp protecting him from the weather. He broke out in a sweat, straining to listen. Something had woken him. He was drunk, and now pissed at himself for it. Slowly, slowly, slowly he reached for the iron pipe at the head of his mattress. His fingers brushed it. He heard snuffling coming from the other side of the site. He turned his head and saw a dog, no, a coyote near the cooler he kept food in. Henry gripped the pipe tightly and pulled it back under the blankets. He lay still and watched. The coyote worried the cooler; tipping it over, biting it and pawing at it, whining. Frustrated, it began circling, sniffing the ground. It found an empty hot dog wrapper and pinned it to the ground with a paw, licking the plastic. Henry saw movement out of the corner of his eye, another coyote padded up softly. Larger, it moved with certainty. It sniffed the breeze, Henry was upwind. It looked straight at him, its ears went back and it snarled. The first coyote looked up at it, then at Henry. It crouched and barked at him. Henry flung the blankets off and rolled out from under the tarp. He jumped to his feet and screamed at the coyotes. The first bolted into the field immediately. The second stared him down, snarling.

Henry screamed and strode forward, the coyote broke and ran.

BTT

→2 ↑2

Sarah turned off the truck, putting it into first gear. Parked off a gravel access drive she let her eyes adjust to the night. She rolled down the window and took a few deep breaths. The night breeze toyed with her hair. She tied it back with a bandanna. She reached across the bench seat and pulled the backpack to her and cracked the door – having pulled the bulb of the dome lights shortly after buying the truck –and stepped out. She locked the cab and tied the key inside the tongue of her shoe. One mile to the site by the route she had memorized. She jogged quietly, stopping often to listen. Bats chirped overhead.

The underpass was quiet. A few pieces were up, half-talented three color burners surrounded by tags. Empties were strewn around. Sarah sat down her backpack and got to work, layering wheat paste on a bare section of wall. The night drifted by, she was coating a piece with an extra layer when she heard men talking close by. 'Fuck.' She jogged over to her backpack and rolled up the papers.

'Hey you.' She heard from behind.

'Yeah man, you're not where you belong dude.' from ahead. She looked up and over, two ahead, one behind. She heard rattle cans tap in the satchel the loner had. She stood with her back to the wall and threw the backpack over her shoulder. She held the bucket of paste loose in her hand. The one that spoke ahead of her pulled a youth size ball bat out of his backpack, his partner's satchel bulged from spray cans, they sounded as he stepped.

'So fuckwit, you got something to say for yourself? You're here fucking up our walls. You covered anything I'm going to beat your ass.' From the loner. They closed in.

'What are you guys? I saw the pieces down here, figured there's enough space for everybody. Check it out. Nothing I put up covers anything here.'

'Ha, a girl. You're trespassing here, little bitch. Blood Thirsty Tags.' the first to speak, the leader, said. He pointed to a stylized Krylon can, the three dots eyes, the can split open with shredded steel forming the gaping mouth. 'You got no right to get up here.'

'Yeah.' The one with the bat tapped her with it; not enough to bruise, but she knew why. They were ramping themselves up for violence. She closed her eyes for a moment and took in a breath.

'Bloodthirsty is one word, guys.' Ball bat was first. She swung the bucket of paste in a great arc and down on his head. Quickly shoving him into his neighbor, towards the tracks. She rotated, the leader was on her, grabbing her shoulder. She brought her knee up. He went on tiptoes, further, one foot left the ground. His yell died in his throat, a near empty squeak of air got out. He tumbled to the brown grass. She jumped over the tangle of men she created and ran for the woods. She heard them yelling and ran hard, putting as much distance she could between them. She felt the ground drop

207

away and followed it. She lay on the forest floor, looking back. She saw the beam of flashlights, two, coming up out of the underpass. They scanned the woods and came in, back and forth. 'Fucking amateurs.' She stood and jogged deeper into the woods, looking back often. She checked her bearing and turned towards where the truck was. She worried, a mile wasn't far and they knew the direction she'd taken off. Plus the pieces she had up. She chastised herself, worried about future retribution. She worried the sap she carried in her left hand.

'No one fucking does that!' He came barreling out of a thicket to her right. The leader, his arms out. 'I'm gonna fucking kill you!'

Her arm came around. Her body following the nine and a half ounces of leather, steel and lead. His head snapped around, his body followed. Landing on his shoulder. He groaned, tried to sit up, collapsed back down.

'That's my walking home money, motherfucker. You touch me or I ever fucking see your face I'll have all your balls. Don't fucking get up till those idiots find you.' She jogged off.

At his apartment Paul put the high-end over-ear headphones on and laid on his floor like Isaac instructed, the CD player on his stomach. He craned his head forward to find play and put his thumb on the button. He laid his head back and pressed it. Immediately loud static roared. He turned the volume down and got comfortable. Legs together, eyes closed, like a body being prepared for mummification. The static crackled in his head, filling the aqueous humor in his eyes, foaming in his mouth. The static went on. Minutes in, he heard voices drifting in. He'd been warned about the Ganzfeld issue and tried to blank his mind – to force his brain to stop looking for pattern in the noise. He drifted off to sleep before the second track played, the static following him into his dreams.

Paul wakes to a small get-together in his apartment. His ex there with him, she hadn't given back her key and let herself in through the back door. She walks over to Paul and starts regaling him with stories of the new guy, what he buys for her, where they go, what a 'perfect boyfriend' he is. She's aggressive with Paul and forthright in a way she'd never been before. She always spoke in coded language before. Paul stands, asking her to leave. She pulls him into the library, with green glass shades disappearing into the distance. She gestures at the top she wore. Ruby, knit with an open weave. Exposing her breasts. She said she wears it for him. Not Paul, but him. Paul tells her she has to leave, that she has to get out. She does, smirking. Paul follows her down the back stair. It's raining, the backyard smooth brown glass, roaring like the sea. Paul walks across it, calling her name. Not l'esprit de l'escalier, but its sister, l'esprit du rêve. The truth in dreams.

He stands over Paul shaking the collar of brass bells that he holds in his left hand. Tall in his gray suit with a wide brimmed hat shadowing his face he thrust the collar back and forth out from his body jing jing jing jing twice a second.

Paul turned on the bathroom light and stared in the mirror, transfixed. Red weals covered his entire torso. He had been woken up by his hands mindlessly scratching and scratching. It felt wonderful, but in the dark he could feel his skin reacting. Now he saw deep crimson tracks had followed the paths of his fingernails. He touched the welts now with the pads of his fingertips and could feel his skin swelling, a clear line of demarcation separated infected skin from non. He couldn't understand why this kept happening. He brushed away the tears and blew his nose, looking into the mirror again. In less than a minute, as Paul watched, his lower lip swelled to the size of a cherry on the right side. Transfixed and curious he found a straight needle and set it in a dish of rubbing alcohol. He stared at his reflection, his hands mirrored and absentmindedly scratching his stomach and chest forming richly colored patterns, engorged with blood everywhere he touched. He picked up the needle and drove it straight into the most swollen part of his lip, hoping to at least understand what was happening, and at best drain it. A yellow tinged, clear fluid bubbled and leaked onto his chin. Even though he winced in preparation no pain registered besides the slight tingling of the overtaxed flesh.

Together

→1 ↓4

'How's life?' Todd asked, leaning against the bodega.

'Same is.' Henry took a pull of Thunderbird. 'You?'

'Got ripped off at the shelter. Had my roll in a dirty ass pair of socks and some motherfucker stole it while I was sleeping.' Todd sipped his forty.

'Fuck man, how much?'

'Thirty-six bucks.'

'What happened to the rest?'

'The rest?'

'From the job?'

'Oh, yeah. Lot of it was gone.'

'I hear ya.' Henry took another drink. 'You know. I had a run in with some coyotes last night. I've been thinking. You want to set up at my camp? It'd be safer for both of us.'

'Are we going to get run off? You go through a lot of trouble to keep that place secret.'

'No, the farmer is cool with me. His shed caught fire last year and he found me hollering and spraying it down with his garden hose. Could have taken out his house.' Henry took another drink. 'Well, he was cool with me once the fire investigator came back and told him it was electrical up in the wall and not arson. So yeah, no problems there. It'd be good to have another pair of eyes, and fists, around.'

'Coyotes, eh?'

'Yeah, they were just scrounging. I got sloppy and left trash around. We keep some discipline and it's a good spot. And no fights or getting ripped off.'

'Right on.' He sipped. 'I think that'd be alright. At least until the winter hits.'

'It's a deal then.' Henry finished his bottle. 'Meet me up at the kitchen about an hour before sunset. We'll get fed and head out. And try to find a tarp today. I'm going to get to work.'

'Ask everybody you see. Later.' Todd nodded and looked up at the sky.

Staff

↓4 ↓1

'I'm serious, McAllen is having a press conference in an hour. I need a tracker.' Max lowered his voice as an elderly volunteer walked in from the reception area looking to find an unused phone to call voters from.

'You can't do that in a primary Max.' Chelsea whispered.

'You know what says I can't do this in a primary? Fuck says I can't. They were tracking our press conference on monster truck rally subsidies yesterday.' Max stared at Chelsea, daring her silently to question the necessity of that initiative, and told her again, 'Give me Paul. He's up there. I only need him for two, three hours at the outside.'

'You can't know it was one of McAllen's people. In any case, that's irrelevant. No, No, No. Find someone else.' Chelsea broke eye contact. 'Field has work to do. Go away.'

'I know it was one of McAllen's. I know the smell of exhaustion and desperation that staffers exude. Bathing and sport coats can't hide it, staffers aren't domesticated. Just think about it, there isn't any staff that I can use Chelsea,' He waved his arms, gesturing at his nonexistent staff, 'I need Paul to get to the site. I need him because he won't be recognized. Seriously, it's less than an hour until it starts, he has to leave.'

'No, Paul has work to do. I have work that I need Paul to do. You can't just swing through here and take staff whenever you stop jerking it back there and decide to annoy the electorate.'

'Jamie gave me the okay. Look if I could do this some other way I would, but I can't. You know that. Don't be obstinate, I'm not the one shitting on you all the time. You know I would help if I could.'

'Fine, fucking fine. Just to be clear, we're not your gophers Max. Field isn't just staff for everyone else. You have to say it.'

'I'm not going to say it. What is Paul's number? I need to prep him.'

'Say it, you know the deal. He's mine and you know he won't put shoes on if I tell him he can't.' Chelsea, agitated, picked a folder up off her desk, thumbed through it, and looked around for a different spot to put it down.

'We don't have time for this.' Max looked furtively around the room.

Chelsea taunted, 'The only way you're going to get him is if you tell me.'

'Fuck you. Talking to you is like pissing in a urinal while wearing shorts.'

'What?'

'Splashback. You're splashback. On the front of my thighs.'

'Oh. Who run Bartertown, Max?'

'I don't have time for this.'

'Oh, Jamie. I'm a little bitch and didn't get that video I promised you.' Chelsea taunted in a falsetto. 'I was busy bashing the candle.'

'What?'

'It's slang for jerking it.'

Max mumbled.

'What's that? All I heard was Whap Whap Whap.'

'Master Blaster run Bartertown.'

'Thank you. Embargo lifted. Just remember who runs this place.' Chelsea smiled and seethed.

'Now, please, give me Blaster.'

Phone

↓2 →3

Paul was soon speeding south down the expressway with his right hand through the strap on a camcorder. The sky was gray from wildfire smoke. The diffuse sunlight cast a twilight pall over the fields. The million year random walk intercepted here at the end. While largely contained, the fire was still burning in sections covering hundreds of acres each. Fire investigators had released a statement that there was evidence of arson. Max had run through what to do and told Paul to hustle. He eyed the speedometer, wondering what he could say if he were pulled over, 'I'm late for a press conference, Officer,' and how horribly that would play if it were reported. He slowed down, enough that the needle was hanging just under 75 mph. He pressed buttons on the camera, wishing it to turn on. Max had stashed it in the office, one in every office in fact, but had failed to include the instructions. His cell phone rang.

'Where are you?' Max asked.

'On my way. I'm about, about seven, ten, minutes away.'

'It starts in five, can you speed?'

'I am speeding, I am going as fast as I can.'

'No you're not. Go faster.'

'I will, I'll get your video. You won't miss anything.'

'That's what I need to hear my man. Good job out there.' Max hung up. Paul scanned the road and pressed the large red button on the camcorder. Nothing happened. After rotating a dial Paul had a blue test screen, then video of the passenger compartment of his station wagon. Satisfied he set the camcorder down and paid attention to the road ahead.

10:47 a.m. Le Boss

<Remember. You've got a canvass launch and phone bank. Don't put on airs because you're helping media>

'What's the number on that phone?' Franklin asked Matthew as they smoked in the foreman's office.

Matthew sat down his beer and picked up the phone setting on top of the computer tower and gave him the number, and then asked why.

'Just want to try something. W. gave me this.' Franklin held a small black plastic box, a switch and a button – all sourced from Radio Shack – were screwed into holes that had been drilled in. The plastic thread from the drill stuck out from under the switch. It had a rough circular pattern of holes drilled in one end that hadn't been cleaned after drilling.

'What is that thing?'

'It should be fun if it works. Go out on the catwalk. I'm going to call you.'

Matthew went outside and around the corner on the metal catwalk holding the phone in front of him. It started ringing and he answered the call, bringing the phone up to his ear. Franklin yelled out to just hold it in front of him. He looked back at Franklin through the glass and saw he was holding the box to the pickup and pressed the button. The phone in his hand screeched. Startled, he dropped it, the phone bounced

217

once and fell to the floor below. The speaker twittered and cut out before it hit the ground. Franklin threw his head back laughing.

'What the fuck is that thing?' Matthew said coming back into the office.

'It sends a tone that I can't hear on this end but it distorts just inside the range of hearing on the other end. And it runs so loud it overcharges the speaker in a few seconds and fucks it up. We should go find it to see if you can hear anything or if it's busted.'

'What's this for?'

'Proof of concept? I don't know. Like that key fob that he gave Seb that cycles through TVs turning them off. It's just good to make something work.'

That afternoon, after the press conference was done, Paul walked down a country road, realizing what a bad plan it was to park his car and walk the targets. Structures towered in the East with the bottoms obscured by the woodlots that blurred together. Grain silos, central complexes for farmers for miles around. Gray concrete with bright metal fittings. Overhead perfectly straight contrails crossed. The sooty wind blew corn husks across the road. He walked on, three houses on this stretch and he'd double back for the car. Miles ahead, straight ahead, obscured by the distance and the haze, he saw an accident at a juncture. A truck had hit another and both were off into the field. The drivers were standing talking. Paul decided not to act. Birds sang high low from the wires overhead. Ahead on the left some children were playing on the gravel drive of the house he had to go to next. His phone rang – Le Boss

'Where are you? I'm at the office. I need you here.'

'I'm out on turf, Le.'

'Why are you on turf? You should be here.'

'I couldn't get anyone to walk today so I decided to take some packets out.'

'Well that's just being bad at your job. How far away are you? I need you to come back.'

'I'm west, Fulton County. County Road D.'

'D? No name?'

'Just D. Disco D.'

'Get back here. I'll wait. Hurry.'

Chelsea had her head down on her desk with her fingers interlaced over it when Paul walked in the door. She sat up and a red pressure mark was visible on her forehead.

'You okay Le?' Paul asked.

'I just interviewed forty people for the paid canvass.'

'We're doing a paid canvass now?'

'Starting tomorrow. And maybe paid calls. We're not getting the volunteers we need here. Well, here and everywhere. Don't take it personal. So at least they're pivoting and not just yelling. They haven't stopped yelling, but action is action.'

'What's that mean for me?'

'Keep the paid canvassers and volunteers away from one another and don't talk to volunteers about the paid side.' Le said. 'You're going to have to report on any that aren't doing the job and we'll bring others in. It's not going to be a big crew, five, six people. College kids.'

'What about the calls?'

'Still have shift goals. You won't see the paid dialers. They're a call center out of Nebraska or Idaho or something.

Don't worry about that. You don't know anything if people ask. Do that part and box it up. We'll eat shit when the finance reports come out but want to keep it tight until we have to deal with it.'

'I have a phonebank tomorrow night.'

'How many confirmed.'

'Four, one firm. So one actually.'

Defiance

←3 ↑1

'Thank you, it's great being here in Defiance again.' Sexton spoke without referring to his notes, he had his speech for the day's events memorized. A fact that he was quite proud of.

'Did you tell him we're in Paulding County?' Brian, the bodyman and driver, asked Max. They both leaned against a cinderblock wall painted white. In front of them was a pressboard folding table with campaign literature arranged on it.

'No, seeing that he just spoke to the Defiance County Democratic Party, I thought I could trust him not to fuck this up.' Max whispered. The crowd buzzed quietly, Sexton thought that it was for his stance on Ohio Issue One, a divisive constitutional amendment that had popular support in the rural counties.

'And I feel that marriage is between a man and a woman, and should remain so. I would support a DOMA law if proposed during my term as your Senator.' Sexton continued. 'Though mine is an unpopular stance, I believe that good people must take a stand for what is right. That's defiance, Defiance County, defiant stance. I don't answer to DC.' Sexton thrust his jaw out. Max stared at Thomas' throat, wondering how much space there was in his esophagus and if it would accommodate a waterproof tape player if he shoved one down there to play speeches instead of letting the candidate talk. One attendee raised her hand, she wanted to ask about this whole Defiance County business.

'This was going well until the beginning when it started.' Max mumbled to himself while rubbing his left hand across the bridge of his nose. Brian heard him, but didn't respond.

A piece of tape holding blue crepe paper ribbon to the wall let go behind candidate Sexton causing a loop to slump down.

Wild Hunt

↓4 ←3

grammateia: I win!

Bkp971: that's all you, zero me now

g: I think I prefer love

b: i need to practice? how do i win?

g: Look for better numbers

g: Have you heard about 'Wild Hunt' mythology?

b: some. it's a european myth, connntected with thunder-storms and pulling witnesses along?

g: Yes. Disconnected fables of fairies tossing curses down upon mortals. Streaming across the sky, forcing people to follow and driving them insane.

g: I love names like 'Wild Hunt.' They are so earthy and brutish.

b: fairies were seen as sinister through much of history. fey is a partner to berserk.

g: Yes, and we have Disney to thank for diluting that and providing boring teenage girls with something to sketch in their notebooks.

b: haha

g: I was a boring teenage girl sketching in my notebook
So I'm speaking from broad experience.

b: are you listening to any music?

g: Mars Volta, Jack just bought me a new copy.

g: I accidentally ran over my first one.

b: why don't you use normal quote marks?

g: 'This?'

b: yeah

g: It's just more elegant.

'You good for the night? It's going to get cold.' Henry asked Todd as they sat beside one another in front of a dying fire.

'Yeah.' He kicked dirt at the fire, making it sputter. 'I think I'm going to go to sleep. Heard about some work clearing brush. Should last a week or so. Could be enough for a ticket back.'

'Good, man. Good for you.'

Todd stood and walked over to his bedding. He finished the bottle he carried and spun it into the woods. Soon he was snoring.

Henry looked into the fire, feeding branches until it licked at the night air. He took a sip from the bottle he had and stretched his leg out, massaging the worn muscles. He stood, stretching, and turned for the field. He walked out into the soybeans. He was careful to avoid crushing any, though he left a trail of disturbed plants behind him. A dark line in the night, no longer uniform.

He stopped. Cars murmured softly, brakes talking as the stoplight turned. He stretched his left arm out, fingers loose, and brought his right around the waist of no partner. Hairy leaves brushed against his pant legs. He swayed and sang, 'Casey would waltz with a strawberry blonde. And the band played on.'   Henry waltzed in small circles, his scratchy baritone carrying over the field, 'He'd glide 'cross the floor with the girl he adored. And the band played on. But his brain was so loaded it nearly exploded. The poor girl would shake with alarm. He'd ne'er leave the girl with the strawberry curls.' His arms fell to his sides, 'And the band played on.'

Henry laid on the loose soil between two rows, watching the sky. A dead satellite tumbled, flashing, crossing near his zenith. He cupped his hands behind his head, elbows pointed out to each side. Henry reached up and across hundreds of years. He took flyspeck Sadalmelik between his thumb and forefinger, burning himself badly. He pulled himself closer, examining it, shaking it out. His eyes watered and he let Ganymede go back to his cups. Henry stood and walked back to the camp, where the fire was all but extinguished.

Old Hollywood

→4 →4

Four paid canvassers piled into Paul's station wagon. 'Okay, so I'll drop you guys off and meet you at that same spot at sundown. If anyone wants a yard sign make a clear note. You all have my phone number?' The college students mumbled assent and nodded. 'Who wants to go through the rap with me? Why don't we run through it a few times before we hit the doors?' They acquiesced, partnered, and got out.

Paul left them and drove to the union hall. As he parked he looked across the street at a vacant building that had once housed a dental clinic, the decorative grasses that had been planted among oval river pebbles now shaded the eaves. He set up in a conference room that still smelled of the adhesive under the carpet squares, call sheets and scripts like place settings at each phone. A jumble of phone lines crowded in under the door to the main hall. It was filled to capacity with the elected officials, party chairs, bureaucrats, opinion leaders, bullies, fools, geniuses, long time operatives - though no one liked them; they often looked harried and always spoke as if Doom were ready to descend - that had been carried through nestled in non-bargaining positions offices from City to Federal level, drunks, adulterers, and straight up lucky bastards, who comprised the party people worth inviting from the fourteen counties around when the state chairman was in town.

On this side of the door, no volunteers were making calls. Paul watched the wall clock, he went through his confirmations; getting answering machines, 'Oh! Was that tonight?' one chewed him out because he hadn't gotten his yard sign yet, and the last call he made rang and rang, the elderly woman didn't have an answering machine and was right then sitting in the main room listening to the speech, she had been waved in with a gaggle of people from Mansfield. She was somewhat confused, but elated to be part of it all the same, having never seen so many people she recognized from TV in one place before.

The chairman took to the podium. 'As we begin tonight, I want to take a few minutes to address the upcoming special election.' Reverb whistled, a sound technician ran for the board and quickly adjusted levels. 'Now,' he glared at the tech, squaring up to deliver the next section like the Old Hollywood star he imagined himself to be like, 'A lot of us here are on the ballot and working hard on our own campaigns. Columbus is supporting you in every way we can.' Paul leaned against the door, listening. The speech was hard to understand because of the conversation two men were having that were leaned against the wall just by the door. 'Senator Ciolek's passing is a sad day for our state,' 'Like I said to my boy, he's twenty-two and needs to straighten out his life.' 'for all our differences, he always took my call. And I feel he' 'Getting drunk is alright, we've all gotten sloppy; but you can't make a life out of it.' 'working class. Or as I call it, The Workers' Class. A lot different than this new crop we've got. I see this as an opportunity to make our case to Ohio, why a Democrat should take' 'You did right, did he listen?' 'the Democratic Party is the right one for them!' He waited, a brief pause and then clapping erupted. 'The fight in the general will be, as they say, nasty, brutish,' 'This guy man, what a prick.' The elderly volunteer turned and shushed them. Paul tapped two caffeine pills into his palm and took them. 'and BACK to the polls in December! Before making this decision I've talked this over with a lot of people in this room' - a lie - 'and around the state' - an exaggeration at the very least - 'and my responsibility as party chair has led me to make the call to endorse Congressman Tom Sexton. He's the right one for us! He's the right one for Ohio! and we need to unite to send him to Washington!' Another delay, then clapping. 'We'll be making a formal announcement later this week, but I wanted you here to know first.'

Fight the Future PAC

↓2 →1

'So they just wandered around for three hours because you forgot your phone in the car?' Chelsea asked, 'Okay, this is how we're going to do this. If I can't bury this in my report I'll tell Jamie that the directions were wrong and that's why you dropped them off in the wrong neighborhood. We need to be a team here and we can't start throwing one another under the bus.' Long pause. 'Don't apologize, this is something we have to fix. I can't have Jamie doing it. She'll tell me to fire you and I need you here. Big changes afoot. I'll have more information on the conference call tonight, but short version is that the FD, Allison, got herself fired. You don't need to know why. I'm taking over as FD and I need a regional to step up to my position as Deputy Field Director. It's double duty. You're the most competent of the lot. Also, get back to the office as soon as you can, Max and Sexton just got to town up there.'

'Hey, so I heard something. It's important, I think.'

'I don't have time, got to get on a call. Patented Twenty First Century Campaign In A Box, means we're filling our time on overlapping fucking conference calls. Text me or mention it on our call tonight if it's relevant.'

Fight the Future PAC, a pro-global warming advocacy group, announced their support for Congressman Maxie's bid for Senate in the Ohio Special Election. From their statement 'Global warming is inevitable and we believe something to be embraced. The people and governments of the Great Lakes Watershed should stage themselves for the vast economic opportunities for their region that will come with a warming Earth. Congressman Maxie has shown the leadership we need in Congress, and we are committing ten million dollars to an independent expenditure to educate Ohioans about this important issue.'

Report

←2 ↓4

Paul parked on the street outside the office. All the lights were on and the door was open, but the front was empty. He walked through and found Max and the candidate standing behind the building by the dumpster, smoking. They were discussing the press event the next morning, Paul waited for them to notice he had something to say.

Paul blurted out, 'They're supporting us!'

'What's that?' Sexton asked. He and Paul had never spoken.

'The party, I just overheard the state chairman at an insider meeting, he asked everyone to throw their support behind us in the primary.'

'Really?' Max looked at Paul, narrowing his eyes. 'Have you told anyone else?'

'No, I just got back from there.'

'Well, that certainly makes things different, doesn't it?' Thomas mused. He tapped the side of his nose four times with the index finger of his unoccupied hand.

'I hope so. What else did he say?' Max asked.

'He asked all the candidates to support us, and I think that the state party is going to put

money and people at our disposal.'

'That is good news.' Thomas thought for a moment, 'McAllen is going to throw a fit when he hears about this. And Terrie is going to denounce us as back scratching cavemen in a press conference.'

'Well, you know as well as I do boss, McAllen has too many issues he has to keep out of

the news to be viable: his company isn't out of bankruptcy yet, and no one wants that fundraising clusterfuck in '89 to define our party's candidate.' Max added. 'And, well, we're working on Terrie.'

Thomas looked at Paul, 'What's your name again? Sorry, it's been a long day.'

'Paul, sir. I'm working on the field team.'

'Alright Paul, thanks for bringing this to me.' With that Thomas glanced down the alley

and back, a quiet signal that Paul's time in his presence was over. Paul walked inside the office and started typing up his daily report for Chelsea. Twenty minutes go by, Paul hears the back door slam and Max walks out from the back office.

'Listen, you're stopping your work and coming to get a drink with me.' Max said to Paul.

'I've got a call.'

'Chelsea isn't here, Deputy Droopy; so I got rank around here and I'm forcing you to

enjoy yourself. I sent the Congressman off to the hotel in my car.'

'Thanks.' Paul quickly finished his report and sent it out.

District

↓4 ←3

'I have been tracking your movements young man. You like whiskey neat? Any time I'm out of the District I drink it, it's too simple for anyone to fuck up.' The bartender looks over his shoulder sharply. 'Not you my good man, elsewhere. Other places have had this issue. And a broken heart takes time to heal. Two please. We'll take dirty glasses, let's see if there is anything out there.'

The late show pantomimed, muted, on the televisions above the bar. Music played, tuned to the local Rock format station. Regulars huddled in clusters or alone, ignoring them.

'You know, I came to realize pretty early on that the candidate has no responsibility to

address any issue that won't win them votes.' Max said. 'News coverage over the course of the campaign is limited, right, so we're going to be lucky to have anchors talking over video of Sexton twice a week at the best of times. So he's not going to use that time talking about anything that doesn't move him towards getting elected, if he does as I say. And the man couldn't fuck a dead deer without assistance.' he stopped, 'I shouldn't have said that to you. Beyond that, the candidates' time is limited, and they need to spend nine tenths of their day fundraising, one twentieth talking to the press, and one twentieth prepping to talk to the press.' Max paused, 'Though the bastards usually cut into all of it to spend time with their families.' he sat quietly a few moments and without looking away from the closed captioning Max went on, 'This is how I know when I have to work: if a sex scandal breaks and it has a woman involved besides the wife it isn't a Republican's problem, it's mine.' The bartender came over with the whiskeys, setting them on coasters and moving away. 'And on the trail if someone leaves the day of the election off a piece of lit that other people are going to be handing out on election day, that is not my problem.' Max took a sip. 'However, if somebody from the campaign talks to the press, besides me or the candidate whose cock I'm holding, it is a huge problem for me; because I have to spend valuable time deciding how I'm going to make that person's life miserable.' he paused, 'I guess what I see makes a campaign work effectively is when people keep focused, swim in their own lane. You know? It helps me keep my positive attitude.'

'My experience has been different. The campaigns I've been on have been local and everyone wore different hats. Over the course of one day I could be designing lit, doorknocking, prepping volunteers, talking to press and chatting up possible donors at an evening event. A staff at all is very new in my experience.' Paul sipped his whiskey. 'Oh, got one.'

'What'cha feel?'

'Sad. Heartbroken.' Paul coughed, 'I think this might be Steph after Trevor dumped her. God damn, I hate getting these.' He began tearing up, the raw emotion washing over him. Somewhere between the glass and alcohol strong emotions bonded. It was believed that the alcohol worked as the mechanism. There wasn't any use for it because it couldn't happen intentionally and faded in a few uses after being deposited. Most wanted their glasses cleaned but there were enough that were curious or interested that most bartenders asked or respected preferences. 'Lucky bastard, it's the only way I know how to feel. Too bad that no one hits it when they're feeling great about something, but such is life. Actually,' he sipped the whiskey, 'I've got something, it's pretty cleared out though, getting old. A bit of regret. You know what your problem is Paul, you don't make impressions on people. Does your dog forget who you are when you go to work? Ah, that was cruel, forget I said it.' He leaned back, listening intently, 'Bartender! How many quarters did my grandma put in the jukebox? Cause she's been dead for 15 years. Whoa, wow this guy was a dick.' Some believed that personalities transferred, but this was just superstition drunks passed around.

'Really? I couldn't tell it wasn't you.'

'Hey, I'm looking out for you. Like, the last time I was up I used your computer to print off a press release. I saw what you have written at the bottom of the screen.' Max took a sip.

'You saw that?'

'*Keep your head down. Do your job. Don't talk. Don't fuck up.* That's decent advice,

friend.' Another sip.

'Stuff just gets out of hand, you know? Overwhelming, I'm trying to stay on top of it all.' Paul said.

'I know. Hey man, I need some time to myself so I can decide how we're going to win this thing tomorrow. I'll pay for your drink, but I need some alone time.' With that Paul was dismissed.

Talk

↓2 →1

Paul sat sidesaddle on the bicycle that his neighbor had secured to the painted handrail outside of their apartment. She sat leaning against the railing, both smoking. A brown tomato plant sat withered in a pot between them, the dehydrated soil pulled away from the sides. The soil from the pot Paul's neighbor bought the plant in stood proud of the rest by at least an inch. His neighbor had given up on gardening, and now it was covered in cigarette butts.

'So what's Happy Birthday up to?'

'Oh you know, I got a new chair from Goodwill and she is ecstatic to have something new to put her butt on. She is doing it right now I expect, contentedly. She's so domesticated.'

'The Crew?'

'This and that, we're not building the base that our goal was; but we have close to three thousand contacts, I don't know how many registrations. They're all held up though, we're not sure what to do with them. Albert is flipping his shit, he was threatened with getting his grant pulled. We had to put an event together and fire off a bunch of photos to pacify them. We endorsed McAllen too. Came from national.' She said, glancing at Paul.

'I'm not surprised. He's a populist Dem.'

'Why aren't you working for him then? He's the only one who's said anything worthwhile.'

'Yeah.' Paul chuckled. 'Well my guy did a presser suggesting there be tax credits for monster truck rallies to encourage economic development to get more tourist dollars.'

'Yeah, that's what I mean.' She interrupted, 'He's a suit. A corporate, milquetoast, suit.'

'He isn't that bad. He's just a centrist Dem.' Paul got defensive.

'Sure, and he hasn't said shit about the war, hasn't said shit about gay rights, hasn't said shit about anything. Fuck on gay rights, that bastard is FOR Issue 1. My sister forwarded me a news article where he's talking about it. This is two thousand and four, why is he talking about anything BUT those things? What? *End America's Dependence On Foreign Tires* and tariffs? Fucks' sake. Why are you helping him?'

'Listen, I...'

'What?'

'This work isn't that simple. It's not like being on the outside. You've got to decide who to work for not because you agree with everything they say, but because they can get elected and the things you agree on are important. And we have to get in now and move things to where we want them, this is the only party that can do right.'

'There are plenty of parties. Anybody can win.'

'No, anybody can lose.' Paul retorted, 'A win takes a lot more. And I mean party that can win.'

'Yeah, then why are there so many lazy bullshitters elected to office?'

'Well that's because of a fundamental flaw in our electoral

system. It's been there since the beginning. They can't both lose. Someone has to win every election. No matter what.'

She laughed, 'I wish they could sometimes.'

'Me too. Even some that I've worked for.'

'So you're going to be out of town more?'

'Yeah, twice a week to Columbus.' Paul took a drag on his cigarette.

'What's the pay raise? Who's taking over your job?'

'No. I'm uh, I'm going to be doing it. There isn't time to hire anybody new.'

'Are you serious? You're not even getting paid more, are you?'

'What's your issue with this? Is your spirit animal *two alley cats fighting*? This is just how it is, things need to be done.'

'That's just a line you've been sold.' She shivered and pulled the vest closed around her chest, 'It's getting so chilly.'

'Fall is here.'

'Hear the yell.' She paused, 'You know Albert is pissed at you. Said that you're doing what all the rest have. Giving up movement organizing to work in electoral politics because you want the easy way out.'

'That's not fair. I've been doing this work for years.'

'It's just his take. He's just known you for the past few months.'

'Still. So have you. He's writing me off over something that's totally unfounded.'

'What did you expect? That you'd just get a pass because you're special?'

'I don't know. It's just unfair is all.'

'Christ, you're such a wimp.'

'Whatever.' He flicked the cigarette end into the bushes.

'I'm going to bed, I've got to get to Columbus by nine. I'll see you later.' He walked towards the door to his apartment.

'Yeah, later.' She stretched and walked to Her truck, driving off.

Interference

→3 ↑2

Paul closed the door. An apartment filled with things forgotten or left behind by former lovers. And suddenly they were all there. With him. Passing through rooms they'd walked through one after the other, laughing, cursing, sleeping. Paul went through his night silently. Masturbating, showering, smoking, buzzing the internet. Chloe wasn't online, he sent her a hello in case she did become available. The women that had been there and the memories carrying them were thick as he walked from room to room.

The radio did nothing to mask it. 91.7 was static, he never remembered to find one that would get the station. He went to the porch and the chill was too much. Distraction may have held the day, but the lonely night was another matter. Instead, past lovers elbowed him for space. Told him what they had become for leaving him, how happy they were for moving on. *Because you weren't enough, and he's what I want*, drifted the answer without a question. Another cigarette. The last empty bottle was set on the nightstand. 'I did love you, I wish I was more mature. I wish I could have held it together.' Trying the radio again, still too much static for distraction, the BBC overnight was at the threshold of understanding, anything else is shouting into a blanket. News would have at least grounded Paul in the present, though the musical interludes dredge up their own memories. Sleep came finally, where others who wouldn't speak to him in life explained their decisions in his dreams.

Update

↑3 ↑3

'You know what realpolitik is?' Chelsea fumed, 'It's not any bullshit of backstabbing and making yourself look good in front of the candidate. It's not getting the title of *Fundraising Director* and getting a percentage if the campaign wins. It's going to these boring, backwoods county meetings that field staff always has to do. It's door knocking. It's phone banking into counties that haven't elected a Democrat in a generation.'

'What happened?' Paul asked. They were sitting at a pressboard conference table in a nearly bare side office. Phone cords tracked across the floor and over the table. Chelsea and Paul both had their laptops open in front of them. Beside Chelsea her John Henry's Hammer paper calendar lay open, she was against the shift to electronic calendars, and used her paper calendar aggressively. Boxes of unassigned laptops were stored against one wall. In the main room a dozen staffers were clustered around more borrowed conference tables, typing away, drinking coffee, planning, plotting. The daily grindhouse of a campaign rushing to the finish.

'Nothing.' She banged away at the keyboard as if it would yield what she was after. After a few moments Chelsea spoke again, 'They won't give me any money and expect me to

243

perform fucking miracles. I just want vans on Election Day, to expand the paid canvass. Or at least I want to be told what I can't have. Right now I beg and scrounge and no one is telling me what is out of bounds. The field plan is a fantasy and no one is acknowledging it, our targets are just the Taco Bell menu put in a different order and renamed, I know you've noticed that. We need to put resources into our ground game. So I keep asking and nothing comes, but no one says *No*. It's always like this. I don't know why I'm so angry about it. I'm not surprised. Maybe if I stopped getting angry then I'd bail on Field.'

'Can we get vans from unions?'

'No.' she snapped,'They're off limits.' Chelsea glared at the spreadsheet, pissed off at it. 'The Building Trades are behind us, we think, but are waiting until the general to put anything in. And the rest are following their lead.' She resumed clattering away, the 3 key, sick of the way it was being treated, jolted loose and hit Paul in the eye.

'Ow! Fuck.' He covered his watering eye with his hands. The 3 key lay satisfied on the carpet against the wall.

'Sorry.' she gave up on the spreadsheet for the time being and closed her laptop. 'You okay?'

'Yeah.' he blinked theatrically, then wiped away the tears on his sleeve.

'We need to talk, you got us into some shit. You can't tell the candidate something like we got endorsed. You know the shitstorm that came down on me last night after he called Jamie and chewed her out?' She stood and looked around the room for the key.

'I had no idea. I was just, excited. I thought I should report it as soon as I could.'

'Well, Tom was pissed and questioning Jamie as to why *she* didn't know. *Jamie* was pissed that Field was gabbing. *I'm* pissed that you didn't tell me. And Max was pissed that he had to talk the candidate down from letting top staff go instead of filing his petitions at the Secretary of State and smiling for the cameras this morning. Your job was saved in there. You're welcome.'

The drinks with Max the night before recontextualized themselves quickly in Paul's mind. 'So, what's happening now?'

'And she had the gall to chew me out for being on time to the morning conference, everyone else was early so it looked like I was late. I wanted to point out that I could have lit a fucking match when I left last night and blown it out this morning.' she snorted, 'Nothing, as usual. Max went to the mat for you. I did too, not that that mattered. Just stay in your lane alright? We've only got a little ways to go.' her phone rang, 'This is Le. Yes, I'll be there in twenty minutes.' Pause, 'I'm wearing a light blue vest.' Chelsea nodded a few times. 'Okay, color blind. Well, uh, it'll be a gray vest.' She winced. 'Okay, see you then.'

'That is, without a doubt the stupidest thing I've ever heard you say.' Paul said.

'Thank you, Mister Sassy Sassafras. I've got to go, what are you doing right now?'

Paul glanced at his laptop and minimized the chat window. 'Updating the volunteer recruitment spreadsheet.'

'Okay, keep at that. Something else. Sexton wants all staff on the doors this week. Top to bottom, everyone paid by the campaign directly. A shift a day. It's a massive waste of time and everyone pushed back on him. He's adamant. He'd make the contractors do it if he could. He is going to be looking at the reports himself, we can't fake them and he won't budge. So do it, we've got no choice. And no missing conference calls, I don't care if John Kerry himself wants his feet rubbed. I need the soft report on time, not just an emailed hard report. Max said it was important, as he is wont to do, but I really want to yell at you. Don't let it happen again. I've got to go, get back to Toledo, get on doors, we'll talk this evening. Do me a favor before you go and find that 3 key and put it somewhere I can find it. I use it too much to do without.' She walked out of the room, Paul followed hearing Ken, irate, in his office. Chelsea leaned against the door to listen.

'Question for you. Did it prompt you to download a new version?' Pause, 'I didn't ask if it prompted you today. Has it?' Pause, 'Okay then. So yesterday you should have.' Pause, 'I don't know what to tell you, the prompts are there for a reason.' Pause, 'Just because you only saw it once doesn't mean it's not prompting. Did you see my email Saturday saying this was coming up?' Pause, 'I understand weekends are busy and you can't get to everything, but, you did see it and ignore it?' Pause, 'Okay, well, all you can do is download the new version and install it.' Long pause, 'Well, yes. This session can't be saved.' Longer pause, 'Well you can take down your notes by hand, but it can't go into the server.' They could hear the fed up organizer shouting. 'Listen dickhead! You're the only one in the state who has had this problem! That means I'm not the issue here. You are. Write it down, memorize it, have a volunteer do it, I don't care. Make it happen. Goodbye.'

'Fuck it Ken, if that's how draconian you're going to be.' Chelsea said, 'You know when I get on there I just put my laptop on a shelf at eye level and stand there shouting talking points at it.' Ken laughed, 'Hell, I don't even turn it on sometimes.'

'You should do that to yard signs. They matter.'

'Nah, I'd have to put on pants to do that. Only one organizer in the state screwed up? I've never heard of that.'

'Well, no. But if I told any of them that there are others they start whining above their station. Got to keep them feeling alone and scared.'

lawn mower

→1 ↓2

Henry shut off the lawnmower. It coughed and spun down. The owner of the property, Harold, walked out of his house when he heard the mower stop. 'That's going to be the last time this season. Come back when the leaves are down okay?' He reached out his hand. Henry went to shake it, then realized he was only being paid. They'd never shaken hands. He took the money.

'I appreciate the work.'

'I appreciate not having to do it myself. You taking care of yourself?'

'Yeah, got a place that works for me. Making money.'

'Well, there's another twenty in there. You've done a good job this summer. Put the mower away, I've got to take off. See you in a few weeks.' Harold walked to his late-model Saab and started the engine. He powered down the window, 'Do you want a ride back to town?'

'No sir, I'll just put this away and I'll make it back on my own. Thank you.' Harold waited until the garage door was down to drive off.

Reports from all over Ohio's rural counties that robo-calls have been launched against Congressman Maxie. Two different calls appear to have been launched: in the first a woman says that he has ignored important family values, and goes on to say that he has not pushed a Pro-Life agenda. In the second a man says that Maxie will take guns from hunters, that he voted for a gun ban. Congressman Maxie did vote for a limitation on firearms sales that was an addition to a larger bill, one which Republicans in Congress at the time were split on as a poison pill, or alternately, unenforceable. More as this develops.

house cleaner

↓4 ↓1

Matthew looked over the bannister to the downstairs living room. His coworkers were busy, one pushing dirty water around the wood floor with a mop that had lost half its rope, the other dusting the mantle. He turned back to the vacuum and heard glass break. A family photo had been knocked to the floor through carelessness. He turned on the vacuum, its high whine drowned out all further noises from downstairs.

He'd caught a tremendous amount of shit from Sebastian and Franklin when he took this job but had, happily, ignored them. Matthew found he enjoyed it. Cleaning houses, putting things in order; it was such a jarring break from his life that he reveled in it. W. had pushed him to steal information or valuables but he'd refused, claiming the job acted as cover. Seeing the way the wealthy lived was a good way to keep up his class-consciousness, he would admit when being especially honest with himself. He swept the vacuum over the berber carpet, running it close by the edge. On his knees, he used the extension hose to clear corners and around the trim. The family's chocolate lab, Hunter, barked and spun in his crate. Matthew turned off the vacuum and Hunter calmed down, barking several more times before understanding the noise had ceased. Matthew walked in the room, Hunter wagging his tail and pushing up against the wire bars. Matthew pet him and looked around the room. Some son, it smelled like a teenage boy. The musty smell of body odor and mid-shelf cologne. And socks, all the goddamn socks. At least he didn't have to pull together the laundry today, Matthew thought. Glossy prints of pop stars hung on the walls, printed en masse and distributed as fast as possible before their first single had ceased regular play and their relevance began sinking. Plaid boxers were strewn around, a dozen that Matthew could see. A *Maxim* lay open on the undone bed, teenage boundary challenging at its most archetypal. Hunter barked, wanting more attention. Matthew petted him again while telling him to relax and went back to the vacuum.

carbon

←3 →4

Paul walked under the curbside shade trees in the lunchbox section of a suburb that plateaued economically and began to slowly decline. Carbon on the air, of a recent fire, muted by rain. *tap tap tap*, the clipboard said against his thigh as he walked.

He stood on the cast concrete porch in front of a brick and cedar siding home. He looked through the glass casual door out the back of the house. *tap tap tap*, the corner of his clipboard on the aluminum frame, sounding loudly. Through the two sets of glass doors like lenses in a telescope sat a sun-faded swing set on recently cut grass at the edge of an overturned field. A dimly lit kitchen table silhouetted in the frame. In the distance beyond, tall concrete grain silos tall beside railroad tracks. Woodlots. No one home, and barely secured. *What a depressing place to play*, Paul thought, not registering that he grew up with a similar view. The stiff, carbon-scented, breeze rocking the plastic seats. Piles of clouds moved quickly overhead. Paul's phone buzzed in his pocket, reminding him he had voicemails constantly, like it always did in spotty service areas.

tap tap tap. Tuesday afternoon, empty houses.

Cars and SUVs wheezed by. Paul rounded the block and saw the source of the scent in the air, a house had burned. Sun-grayed particleboard covered the windows, blue tarp over the roof. Carbonized lives knocked loose by the breeze. Paul smelled a smile from a vacation to the Florida Keys. Posed, captured, developed, seen once, boxed, burned, inhaled. *tap tap tap*, down the block under the bright orange sky.

The circular drive looped at a cemetery, headstones laid out in short grass. No fence, just asphalt drawing the boundary. Beyond, a culvert wide enough for it to be mowed and a worn out office park. Paul read names as he walked past, and back down the other end of the street where the houses were.

puzzle pieces

↑2 ↓2

'Are you sure you mailed my box of campaign nerves? It still hasn't arrived. You didn't send it COD, did you?' Max listened. 'Shh, missing is for puzzle pieces and socks. Not people.' Max sat alone in the office, reclining, his feet up on the folding table he used as a desk. Yellow light cast long shadows through the blinds. His laptop was a flashlight in the dark. 'Whatever. I feel whatever I'm allowed to feel during your prolonged absence.' He idly picked at a fingernail, 'It is *your* prolonged absence. I'm here, you're gone.' he listened, 'Well how am I supposed to know you didn't leave DC, I'm in Ohio.' pause, 'Again you're missing me. So I'm a puzzle piece now, a missing puzzle piece? You know what I charge to consult? I'm going to send you invoices for all the time taken up with thinking about you. Get me a nice convertible.' pause, 'I may be able to get back for a couple days. The best part of living with someone is watching them get ready for their day and I miss that like a puzzle piece.' pause, 'Got one candidate to drop out, well, not going to file,' pause, 'Yeah, Wood's out, Terrie. She'll announce it tomorrow or the next day.' quick pause, 'No, you can't print that.' pause, 'No, especially not as *a source close to the campaign.* It'd be better to quote me, doing that means they'd have to come find me. I'd probably be put in charge of finding me too. I'll be hinterland Hanssen out here. Go do reporting if you want to run it, I'm not your source.' pause, 'Oh we've had this conversation, I don't care if the race is a sausage fest now. You don't know her; she's Thatcher – Rice even, just proving that women are just as awful as men.' long pause, 'I will not take it back, it's true. That's equality, you're jerks too. Nothing magical about sitting to piss.' long pause, Max laughed, 'I concede that point. But as a dyed in the wool partisan, we're better off with her out of contention.' pause, 'NO! Stop asking to quote me.' long pause, 'You should write about this. Next cycle I'm staffing an entire campaign with single moms. I don't know any other demographic who, across the board, has their shit together more. Responsible, they get deadlines and repercussions, campaign stress is nothing. We'll just get daycare, already do it for the candidate.' pause, 'No, not the candidate's kids. I mean candidates are children and get babysat.' pause, 'Stress is unlived energy rotting. Run and create while you got it.' pause, 'I love you too. Talk soon.' pause, 'Thanks.' A simple phatic response on Max's part. 'Goodnight Bee.' Max ended the call. The banner he set on his Campaign phone appeared on the screen before he slipped it into his pocket: *Politely Say Nothing.* He sat quietly for a moment, regarding the ceiling tiles. Max pulled his phone out again and dialed Paul. 'Hey.' pause, 'We're running a campaign here, you shouldn't be sleeping at this time of night anyway.' pause, 'I'm calling because you're going to drive Sexton down here on Thursday morning. He's got a fundraiser up your way tomorrow. We've got a driver up there but we need one to get him back in the morning, so clean your car out. I'll email you the details. Later.' He hung up and crossed his hands over his stomach, leaning far back in the chair.

New Message from Max Cowell
   Subject: ACTION: Thursday Itinerary
   Body: Thursday you're going to drive Congressman Sexton to the Columbus Dispatch from Toledo. You'll meet the Congressman at his hotel. Print out the attached daily schedule and read it NOW and put it in a folder in your vehicle, NOW. Print out the attached FR calls NOW and put them in the folder you're putting in your vehicle. Wear a tie. I can see you right now and you're not. Here is a link to tying ties.

When: *__4:15 a.m.__* at Grand Plaza
   Where: 444 N. Summit

To: 34 S. 3rd St. enter through front door
   Arrive by: *__6:45 a.m.__* (2 hr. 30 min. drive)
   Meeting: Gina from Finance. She will escort Sexton in and
   accompany him. Do not leave until you see Gina speak with Sexton. You alone then drive to Columbus campaign office, no further responsibilities with the candidate.

I'll be in T-ledo for a few days, coming in when I can. I want to see the sights.

Don't speed. Don't touch the radio. Sexton will be making fundraising calls from 7 on. Don't make small talk. And clean your car. And wear a tie. And, most importantly, <u>and</u>.

hugs and kisses, Max

9:12 a.m. Isaac Scheer
  <I should have hid behind your bed
  and said "Should you need us." last
  time I saw you.>

9:13 a.m. Isaac Scheer
  <...dance party with Hoggle.>

9:15 a.m. Isaac Scheer
  <Come by today. Got some info you'll want.>

'For the first time in my life, last night a pretty lady slid her number across the bar at me. I didn't know what to do, so I cracked a joke about how awkward it was.' Isaac stabbed at a cardboard box with a reproduction Zulu Iklwa he kept in the office. When he bought it he had an entire theory on the massive technological breakthrough it represented through the change by Shaka and how he wanted it to symbolize his approach to the work. Since then he has left it leaned in corners and plays with it as he is now, 'Was not the reaction she wanted. Not sure what I should do next with it. She was really pretty.'

'Ah well.' Paul laid across the couch in Isaac's office. 'What do you have for me? I've got to get in, staff is coming in at noon and I've got to give them their daily.'

'Look at you, little boy all grown up. Why, I remember when you sat on that very couch and didn't know what you were going to do with your life last week. Now you're a DFD without the pay and have staffers of your own.' His desk chair creaked as he sat up, he turned down the static he had playing, 'Since you insist on responsibility, I just heard from one of my spies

257

that McAllen has gotten the endorsement from the county party. They're going to have a special vote at the meeting tomorrow. And Lucas isn't the only one, he's liable to get Wood and Allen before the end of the week. He's working Mansfield.'

'Against the state party? They can't do that.'

'Bylaws are, fungible. And enough go out together they have strength. He's been working them all hard. And he's got fertile turf here, Lou has some grudge against Sexton from way back.'

'Lou's got a problem with Sexton?' Lou Martel was a long-time – decades on – fixer for the local powers. Largely aligned with the Building Trades, he'd parlayed a law degree – never bothering with the Bar – and credit for the first Democratic Mayoral win in two decades in the late forties into running sinecures in government, paid board appointments, and union consultancies. Whatever the delay or breakdown they broke loose and projects closed when he came in. Isaac and Paul had stumbled into being crosswise with Lou when they broke onto the scene, and suffered for it. He was a bad enemy to have in the region.

'Yeah. Lou. And all that entails. Watch yourself. Seems McAllen is going after the second tier counties himself and with intermediaries, trying to use a thorough Field push to get through.' he moved around files on his desk and produced a four inch by nine inch push card and spun it over to Paul. 'There, the slate piece. It's a proof, so you can't have it. I shouldn't have it and I don't want it getting out of my sight.'

Paul looked at what he held in his hands. Green and black, printed on glossy white cardstock. The bold green *Patrick McAllen for U.S. Senate (special primary)* was second, below *John*

Kerry and John Edwards for President/Vice President. He turned it over in his hands, the stodgy layout surprised him. 'This is local then? They're going against the state endorsement?'

'Sometimes the amateurish design is cover. It's rare, mostly because that is offensively provincial. I'd have to burn any computer I designed that dreck on. Check out the turtle though,' Isaac pantomimed a turtle with his overlapping hands, 'that's a Columbus printer. I would surmise that his campaign firmed up endorsements and staged those, you're going to want to see where else those drop. McAllen has seven county endorsements since the state went for Sexton, breakaways could cause some trouble. Fuck, five of them are up here, you catching flak for that?'

'No. Can I call this in right now?'

'One more thing, have you heard the nickname the McAllen campaign has gotten?'

'We're the only campaign in Toledo. We set up across the street from their fucking HQ, added their dipshit candidates to our doorknocking rap and they're going to put out a slate card with McAllen's fucking name on it!?' Max was livid, he was shouting into Chelsea's phone while stomping around the Columbus headquarters. 'The Fuck is McAllen's Army!?' Jamie waved her arm until she got Max's attention, then gestured for him to quiet down, she was on the phone herself with the state party chair and the Congressman, the latter could be heard yelling expletives directed at both of them. Max looked around, 'Who else here has heard his campaign being called McAllen's Army?' One of the Regional Field Directors, Jen, for Southeast raised her hand, worried she was going to be yelled at. Max grunted.

Ken wheeled out into the common area from his office, his legs outstretched from kicking off, 'Yeah here. I have.'

'Anyone think to share it?'

'Nah,' Ken kicked off a folding table and rolled back into his office.

'You're all high-level staff. Except for you Jen, I'm not yelling at you. I need to know this to be able to do my job, people. I've got to go up there and yell at people, not Media's job but no one else thinks it's theirs. Fucking Toledo is taking up way too much of my time, why does every election have a Pareto region?'

5 p.m. LadyLady
<Come here.>

Paul set the phone back down on the desk and read one of the latest blog posts on the race. Sexton had a slight lead over McAllen, with Wood trailing.

Paul opened the door to Her apartment and found Her lying face down on the shag throw carpet, completely naked. She didn't acknowledge him but continued as She was doing, running both hands over the synthetic fibers, slowly. He smelled marijuana.

'What are you doing?' Paul asked.

She, facedown, continued running Her hands over the carpet. She responded lazily, 'Déjà vu is caused by misfiring synapses.' muffled by the carpet, 'The neural network gets discombobulated and your brain processes current input as memory.' Happy Birthday stared at them, seemingly disinterestedly, from her position on the couch.

'Right as far as I know.' Paul saw Her pipe and the ornate wooden box on the table as he sat down next to the cat, who noted his intrusion on her space.

'I've never experienced it before.'

'I haven't either.' Paul was fine with that. He found the doe-eyed statements made by people coming out of a déjà vu experience to be extraordinarily tedious to listen to.

'I read that you can induce the experience. My friend got me some high-grade stuff, cost me plenty. It did it. I did it, I've felt it for an hour now. Everything I've done I've already done.'

'That's very special, perhaps you should write these things down.' Paul mocked. 'Why are you doing that with your hands?'

'It feels intense, it's better than sex. I was walking across the carpet and I couldn't stop.

You should try this with me, there's some left. It's scary at first, but you just have to ride it out.'

'Right now? I can't. I've got stuff to do, early tomorrow. I've got to be out of here by four.'

'Bike For The Future is coming through town this week. They're making good time but may head south before coming in. The Crew is setting up an event for them.'

'They're the ones registering people on the ride across the country?'

'The same. Carrie is trying to pull together a show this weekend and get them to come in then.' More slow brushing on the carpet. Paul was aroused and annoyed.

'That sounds cool. Anything I can do?'

'No. Albert doesn't want you around. I'm just telling you what we're up to. I don't think you should come out.'

'Well fine. Anyone speak up for me?'

'Don't get upset. I'm sorry I brought it up. Try to get in a good place. I want you to try this with me.'

'I don't know. I've got work and should head back to my place. I'm not going to be any fun.'

'Come on, you're all straight laced since you started working on this campaign. Have fun

with me.' She brushed the shag carpeting again. She sighed and rolled over slowly onto Her back and raised Herself up onto Her elbows. Her skin was reddened with a negative imprint of the carpet, from Her face, over Her small breasts, down to the tops of Her feet.

→4 ↑3

Paul slid his hand under a blanket that had been thrown over the couch. He scratched at the fabric with his fingernails. Happy Birthday's irises expanded, she pushed her face close to the cushion and her body tensed. Happy Birthday jerked her head side to side like a pan fish realizing it's been hooked. 'Blanket monster.' Happy Birthday pounced on Paul's hand and bit at the blanket. Paul tickled her stomach, 'Oh no, blankat monstar!' Happy Birthday began kicking furiously with both her back legs as she held on with her front paws.

She awakens to a cherenkov blue[10] orb drifting in the cold. Paul stretches and feels her roots snaking deeply into the

---

[10] Cherenkov radiation is a rather pretty blue color. It's caused by charged particles given off by underwater nuclear reactions moving faster than the speed of light in water and agitating the particles they hit. You can see it yourself by visiting the Reed Research Reactor in Portland, OR. Most other nuclear reactor operators will take a dim view of your request.

rib of the whale. She is dumb but not alone. Around her sisters sit housing their primitive mates. They sway by inches each way in the current. The abyssal plain stretches in impossible loneliness for hundreds of miles in every direction around the hoary carcass. Corrupted rumors of the sun don't reach the plain, and the worm couldn't have believed them even if they had. Paul knows herself by feel and by scent, color and shape were inexplicable to her and three hundred thousand generations of ancestors. The mute detritus of the upper world slowly drifts onto the seats in the empty theatre, staining the worn velvet. The orb bobbing and searching over her. She feels a tug, terrifyingly, trying to retract, muscles pulling plumes into her body cavity. Her sisters retract in an instant.

Paul snorted as he awoke, terrified he was still there. He exhaled as he laid his head back

down. She mumbled unintelligibly beside him. He pulled a pillow close to his body under the blanket. The alarm clock hovered in the dark bedroom next to his face. Paul fell back to sleep.

The clock read four ten. Paul was fully awake on the first ring of his phone. Adrenaline coursed through his system, contesting the THC already in his bloodstream. The caller ID was from a Columbus area code. 'Hello sir.' Paul said. She rolled over next to him, but stayed asleep. Paul stood up in his underwear, his eyes adjusting in the darkness. Abject terror is a fantastic alarm clock. 'Yes I am, I'm just,' Paul pushed his leg though his Chinos in the dark, 'I'm just about fifteen minutes away, I had to stop to get gas. Are you ready to go?' pause, 'Oh, yes I do, I just thought I would stop to put a few dollars in while I had the chance. I've been on *E* for a while,' he winced, and buttoned his shirt one-handed. He was thankful he'd thought to top off the tank before coming over the night before. Her alarm tripped on. He had hit the snooze button three times since it had first gone off. 'No sir, I just started the car, that was my radio. Yes sir, I'll be there momentarily.' Paul thanked the candidate and clicked off. He kissed Her, who waved him off and mumbled 'Spider monkey,' without waking.

He shook his head and opened Her fridge. The only caffeinated items inside were two cans of cola. Paul grabbed both and headed out the door.

Paul turned into the parking lot at four twenty three and saw Thomas Sexton standing in the vestibule of the hotel talking on the phone. He felt slightly fuzzy, but wasn't sure if that was due to just waking or what he had smoked with Her hours earlier. Paul wasn't used to any after effects from pot and was unsettled. He pulled up to the front entrance, waiting. The daily schedule sat on the passenger seat. Sexton continued to talk, looking out at the street. Paul wasn't sure what to do, finally, he opened the car door leaving the engine idling. He approached the entry and waved at the candidate. Sexton nodded his head and pointed at his small luggage. He regarded Paul's Saturn like a housecat would look at unfamiliar food in its dish. He continued to talk on the phone about the day's plans as he lowered himself into the passenger's seat. Paul put the luggage in the back of the station wagon and got in the driver's seat.

'So why do I have to meet with him? The screening committee made it pretty clear that I wasn't getting their endorsement.' pause, 'Uh huh, uh huh. Well, I understand that. I just don't want to waste my first couple hours back in Columbus after this meeting with a union president whose union isn't going to endorse me. Can't I meet...' he trailed off as Jamie talked over him. Paul adjusted the mirrors and pulled out of the parking lot, heading towards the interstate that would take them to Columbus, 'No, the driver was here. Late, but we're on the road now. What's his name?' He lowered the phone, 'What's your name?'

'Paul, sir. We met once. I'm the DFD up here.' he had set them behind twenty minutes and still felt like he wasn't fully awake.

'Oh right.' His attention went back to the phone. Thomas carefully pulled at the fabric on the left knee of his pant leg. 'I don't want Paul driving me again. What about the Dispatch, who should I look out for?'

They passed the mosque, floodlights on its minarets in the early morning. 'Okay, so she's announcing this morning then? I thought it was going to be this afternoon. You know how I like things. You keep changing my schedule it throws my whole day off.' Paul stayed with traffic, wondering what reaction he'd provoke by opening a can of soda. He decided not to.

The Congressman chewed at the fingernails of his free hand and rubbed the raggedness on the passenger seat. Paul realized he hadn't felt fully awake for days, maybe longer. He was functioning at a lower level than usual, his body adjusted to the stress by slowing down. The exhaustion and long hours meant sleep came to him immediately whenever he wasn't working. The week before he found himself asleep sitting in his station wagon, the seat belt retracted against his armpit. He had dozed off while connecting it. He passed several vehicles before settling in the right lane for the long drive.

Henry pounded on the glass door of the bodega. They were late opening. He pulled a cigarette out from his coat pocket and lit it, feeling aggrieved. He peered in, his bandaged hand shading his eyes to see further into the room. The counterman, Johnny/Jaareh, flicked him off; not looking up from counting the drawer. 'Come on, man! This ain't right!' he yelled, hitting the door again. 'Sign says you open at eight!' A patrol car turned the corner and Henry walked off.

Steam

↓2 →2

Albert woke with Stephen's arm laying across his chest. He carefully picked it up so as not to wake him up and slid off the bed to shower. He turned the water as hot as possible; a luxury during Maine winters he couldn't shake off, in spite of years of working to conserve energy and resources. One that he'd responded sheepishly about when confronted in the past. The small bathroom filled with steam quickly and he stepped into the shower stall. He thought of his day, the deadline to register was less than two weeks off with no resolution yet on what a registration legally was. Rumor had different boards were ignoring or interpreting the directive differently. But that unsettled him. This is what they wanted, he thought, chaos, fear, uncertainty. Freeze the opposition in questions about what to do.

ibi evacua

↑3 ↓2

Max ran into the common office from the back and yelled at Irene to turn the volume up on the TV that was always running on the table next to her, they heard the story that had Max so excited.

'...nounced from Akron that she will not seek to be the Democratic nominee in the race for the recently opened Senate seat, attributing her decision to a bitter campaign. This ends the chance that the first female Ohio Senator would be elected this election season. No endorsement was made of either Democratic candidate in the race. The press conference was held on the steps of the building where the 1851 Women's Convention was convened, where, one month ago, she announced her candidacy and just days until ballots are to be printed. Representatives from both of the remaining Democratic campaigns have expressed to this station their respect for Mrs. Wood.'

'Oh what a bunch of horse shit, she got a six year board appointment where she has to do
     nothing and here she is saying there is a hostile fucking atmosphere.' Jamie said just loud enough to be heard by

Sexton's Chief of Staff, Steve. They sat together watching the announcement themselves in the back office, 'She just got in to be bought off. She gets a pension and a salary just for being a pain in the ass for a month.'

'Ubi pus, ibi evacua.' Steve thought for a moment, 'Easiest way to the nomination is to give everyone else a route out. But she went and poisoned the well for us in Summit County, maybe with women across the state.'

'I'll talk with Fred and Polling to find out what we should do from here out. Max has reported that media from Akron are not taking this well, supporters have called in saying she was forced out.'

'Why the theater?'

'She's going to play it to the end, can't start acting like it's fine. Too bad McAllen won't take the same offer. Max will handle the press on this, I've got confidence in him. Please do add this to the poll, I want to see where things stand. I'm going to need the Congressman for an hour when he gets back here, then I'm going to DC. Are there any calls you need me to make while I'm on the ground?'

'Want to scream at some county chairs for me?'

'Gladly.'

'Well, I've got to go fondle reporters and put our frame on this. Hey Chels, you and Blaster get online and go to the blogs as I call them out. Say nice things about us.' Max paused, 'And my hair, nice things about us and my hair. And hide your damn IP's.' He walked down the hallway, without turning he added, 'Like *God decided to give angora another go, that it wasn't shiny enough.* What's that smell?'

'You want us to write that?' Paul asked.

'No, come here.' He sniffed his way around the hallway, stopping in front of the door to the basement. Max hesitated, waving Paul over.

'This is going to be bad, isn't it?' Paul asked. Chelsea and the DFD for Eastern Ohio, Charles, followed.

'I expect so. How's your gag reflex?' The four of them stood, waiting for someone else to make the first move. Chelsea covered her nose and mouth with her hands and opened the door.

144 units mayonnaise
  96 units buttermilk
  24 units powdered cultured buttermilk blend
  24 units finely chopped fresh parsley
  24 units finely chopped celery leaves
  6 units lemon juice
  6 units Dijon mustard
  3 units onion powder
  1 unit dried dillweed

Normally, the preceding is a recipe for Ranch dressing, such a Midwestern dietary staple that future anthropologists will dub ours the *Ranch Culture*, as they do the *Mound Builders* who lived in the Midwest eons earlier. Here, it is a list of half of the contents of the basement miasma, raw sewage comprising the other half. The dressing and condiment bottling plant half a mile away – through a series of unfortunate accidents – overloaded the sewer three days before and now with the encouragement of a light rain the contents are bursting out of the sewer pipes and tens of thousands of people, including our intrepid campaign staff, are vomiting at the sight and most importantly, the stench. You're welcome, by the way, that I do not deign to go into any more detail of this horrific affair. I have some pretty good descriptions that I will forgo.

Albert answered his phone from the living room table that had become his work station. Sarah and Carrie sat in the dining room sorting literature. The couch by the front door was piled with black hiking vests. Stephen was in the bedroom, on the phone. 'Yeah, it's good to hear you're doing a story on it. I think it's outrageous.' Albert said, pausing, 'Yeah, thanks.' He hung up. 'The local media is covering Blackwell's directive about registrations, the station I talked to wants someone to speak, they'll come here. This is a big opportunity.'

Sarah looked at Albert and Carrie. 'No, not me. I don't go in front of news cameras.'

'Stephen and I aren't local, we can't do it. It'd ring false. We need someone local, we can give you the talking points.'

'I don't see why I need to do it.' Carrie set down the literature in her hand, not so angry as to lose her place counting, 'I'm always the one that has to field this stuff.'

'You're great on TV Carrie, and it's important that messaging comes from locals. It's more genuine. I'm going to call the national team and see what we should say.'

'I don't feel comfortable just parroting someone else's words. And why do we need them anyway? They're not here. If I'm going to have to speak, I know this issue.'

'So we can stay consistent nationally.' Albert said, while dialing.

'This isn't a national issue, it's the Ohio Secretary of State.' Carrie, her defenses falling before Albert ignoring

271

her protests.

'We just need you to do this, you're a great spokesperso - yes? Hi, David. Got a media opportunity.' Albert stood and walked out of the room, the conversation fading after him.

'Sorry dude.' She said as he left.

'Just not fair, I'm thrust out all the time.' Carrie finished counting the literature and laid back on the floor.

'I mean, you know I would. I just...'

'Yeah, I know how you feel about being recorded.' She sat up and smoothed down her cardigan. 'Sounds like they're on the way. I'm going to read up on where everything stands so I'm ready.'

'It's local press, they don't know enough to set up any gotcha questions. It'll probably just be a cameraman on his fifth of fifteen assignments.'

'Yeah. Still. Going to prepare. Thanks.' Carrie turned on her laptop and took it into the hallway to sit.

Factory

→3 ↓4

A realtor escorted two men through a vacant factory. Harper, was in her early thirties, and wore a silk blouse with a blazer over a matching knee length skirt. Her shoes were the sort you seek out after hard lessons about construction sites. The men were dressed in heavy-weight chinos. Both wore flannel shirts, with heavy, expensive looking, overcoats. They carried flashlights to see into the gloom. 'As you can see, there is a lot of room to expand here on the shop floor, and you've got two wings off of this, the east wall is all loading docks, west is warehouse space.' the real estate agent said.

'How motivated would you say the owner is?' The middle-aged, younger, man asked.

'I'd say very. Bought this as an investment property six years ago. We've worked with him on keeping it secure and of course, available.' She lit up the foreman's office with her flashlight.

'Looks like a fire.' The elderly man said. He pointed his light at the office. His son was a softy, he'd always thought. Didn't know how to pick out things the agent didn't have any control over to bring out when the negotiations were going. 'I'm going to go take a look at it, you never know what sort of slipshod electrical work can come up in factories. Would be a fortune to fix.'

'Dad, we'll have the inspector look at all that. We're here to see if this is even the right fit for the expansion.'

'I'm here to see what our money might look like if we turn it into this place. Come on, it's just a flight up and these stairs don't look too,' he glanced slyly at the real estate agent, 'likely to collapse.' The father and son went up the expanded steel stairs, seeing discarded extinguishers laying on the catwalk. The real estate agent, Harper, stayed on the shop floor, shouting out amenities the location had. The father led, he nudged the open door further open with his boot.

'Looks like some sort of prank?' the son said. The towers stood, gutted and twisted. Blackened by fire, in the center of the room.

'Looks like something. Doesn't look like a vagrant fire, though somebody that shouldn't be in here got in here. That's something to remember for later, who knows where people have been.' He looked around the room and nearly whispered. 'Don't touch anything.'

'You like this building?'

'Yeah I like this one. I think it'd be perfect for us. Why else do you think I'm looking for anything wrong with it to ponder loudly?' The father paused, looking at the computer towers. 'This concerns me. Really. I'm going to call Phil. You remember Phil, worked a couple summers then went to the Academy?'

'Yeah, Phil's a good guy. That was nearly twenty years ago when he worked for us. I don't think it's necessary to bother the police though, Dad. Some kids were just playing with lighter fluid and some old computers. Nothing more to it. We should look at the rest of the building.'

'Phil's kept in touch, he's a captain now. Good one too. I don't like the looks of this. Let's go tell the agent. She'll probably try to talk us out of it. I wouldn't put it past one of them to bury dead schoolkids themselves if they came on a pile of them in a property they were trying to move. Ruthless people. So no contradicting me when we get down. I want to do this.'

'I understand, Dad. I'll keep quiet.'

'Thanks, son.'

OUT OF MINUTES

↓2 →1

The next day, Paul saw a homeless man sat leaned back against the door of the campaign office as he pulled in to park. Paul parked and locked his car, mulling over how to deal with the situation. He walked towards the man in a curve, afraid of confrontation. In the distance he heard the vacuum rattle of an air-cooled VW engine approaching. Henry looked up and took a brown cigarette out of his mouth. 'Hello young man. I remember you. What's your revolution?'

'Hi. Yeah, sober, right?'

'Well, the revolution is suffering setbacks. Worried the soldiers are cuing up *Those Were The Days* on the PA.'

Joshua pulled onto the sidewalk at a curb cut and parked his trike near the two of them. He turned it off and leaned over the handlebars. 'Hello gentlemen. What's happening today?'

'Thanks for coming in Joshua.' Paul said, Henry still hadn't moved.

'Hey guy. No disrespect, but this guy here is expecting people and you're in the way of the door. Can you swing round back and I'll bring you a beer?' Joshua said as he swung his leg over the saddle. Paul smiled, the question had been asked and he didn't have to do it.

'Yeah I can do that. I'm okay to sit in back?' Henry grunted as he got up, first on one knee, then both hands on that knee to push himself up standing. 'You won't have a problem with that?'

'Yeah that's fine.' Paul answered.

Paul and Joshua went inside. Paul set up his computer and then to the file of current call sheets. Joshua went to the burner phones.

'How many you expecting today?'

'Eight to twelve.' Paul said. 'Hoping we're going to catch up to goal tonight. Le is coming in too.' Paul looked at the clock. 'Actually, she should be here anytime.'

Le walked in the door, talking with two volunteers. Follow-ing behind them and stopping cautiously inside the doorway was a skinny young man wearing bike messenger jeans and a brown t-shirt that had *Defend Fallujah* over an RPG embla-zoned on the chest. He made eye contact with Paul before looking back down at his shoes. He nervously scratched at his wide Mohawk that flopped over his scalp.

'Hey dude, what can I do for you?' Paul picked up and held a stack of walk lists against his stomach. He glanced at it and held an arbitrarily spot carefully with his index finger. This was in case Paul wanted to cut the conversation short, his strategy involved looking harried and rushed.

'Can I volunteer here?'

'Yeah,' Paul said, 'what sort of things would you like to do? We have a phone bank starting in a little bit.'

'Whatever, I'd like to help.' The young man replied.

'Paul, hey, I need you for a second.' Chelsea yelled out. When Paul was at her desk she pinched his fat roll between her thumb and index finger and said in a low voice, 'Put him on a phone, alone, in the back making calls. Do not send him canvassing, do not let him be seen by anyone else. Got it?'

'Yes, ow. Fine. That's what I was going to do.'

'You have any other phones?' Joshua asked loudly, These aren't working.' Paul panicked. Chelsea cut off the volunteer and walked over. Joshua held multiple phones in each hand, all with OUT OF MINUTES on the screen. 'Sorry brother, all of the phones in the box are like this.'

'Fuck.' Paul said.

Le grabbed both of them and pulled them aside.

'Shut up. Tell me what's going on.'

'You're all out of minutes on these phones.'

'Minutes? What the fuck 1998, the future is now. Why aren't these on for a month?'

'I don't know.' Paul took one, no I think they are, they just expired.'

Shut up. Fix it, call in and reup. I'll ask people to get started with their own phones. You go. Now.'

Later, after Paul returned and the volunteers were settled he and Chelsea sat at their desks. Paul patted himself down, looked in his desk and found a cardboard box that was light when it shouldn't have been. 'I'm out of cigarettes.'

'Nice to know, does that mean you're going to work a full hour? Jibed Chelsea. She was studying a large map of her region, wards were color coded, 'Blue is base, Pink is Per-sua-sion. I'm a fan of a-llit-er-ation.' she said in a sing-song.

'Sir, can you help me here.' One of the older volunteers, a regular now, waved Paul over.'

'I'm writing down things that they say are important to them. I think the campaign should keep track of what they think. Will you make sure that the campaign takes this information up?'

'Great, thank you for doing that.' Paul looked at the paper call sheets spread on the table around her. Scrawled on all the pages she'd gotten through were notes on the conversation she had with each person. Paul went back to his desk.

'It's important for you to know that that guy likes to fish. And he's a three. Do you want anything from the store? I'm going to run up to the bodega.'

'Threes are Midwestern Nos. I only care about Ones that audibly orgasm when they hear Sexton's name. Get me something syrupy and caffeinated. And, Paul, hurry, my phone hasn't gone off in ten minutes and I feel that there is a crisis brewing somewhere.'

Paul walked onto the sidewalk and saw a volunteer walk into the Democratic Party

headquarters across the street. He cut across a mowed lot abutting the property, the grass

remaining flattened where he stepped, already prepared for winter none of it had the energy to

spring back. Two Astro vans sped past Paul as he was stepping into the street. He noticed that

the sliding doors on both were open slightly, held closed from the inside. He regained the curb

and stepped into a vacant parking lot. The vans bounced over the sidewalk in front of the

convenience store that Paul was heading for. Men wearing black riot uniforms dumped out of

the two vans and began running for the two doorways of the building. From both ends of

Jefferson came police cars, streaming from the river were

marked cars with their sirens alight,

from the museum came unmarked cars – some black, some bronze – and just as silent as the vans.

Paul still walked towards the tableau. He notices a sugarloaf shaped woman on the

sidewalk ahead of him, reaching up to write on the reverse of a No Parking sign. A man in a brown coat ran out the front door of the store, elbowing one of the police officers in the neck.

There are shouts, and punctuating these a single gunshot. The man crumples before three officers, one of whom is yelling 'A D! A D! A D!' again and again. They drop to their knees and attend to him together. Paul sees another man step out the side door, he turns his head towards the front of the building to see if he can walk away. The officers are prepared and immediately bludgeon and arrest him.

The woman turns towards Paul and smiles. Her smile trips something in Paul who yells to her to get down and then proceeds to throw himself on the broken concrete underneath his feet.

When Paul got back he found Joshua standing behind the office listening to Henry. 'So yeah, the moon landing photos were faked. But not how people think they were. See, the cameras brought with the astronauts had crosshairs etched into the lens. But in some photos they're missing. You're too young to remember,' Henry looked at Paul, 'this guys does,' gesturing at Joshua, 'but we had shitty cameras back then. They got damaged passing through the radiation belt on Apollo Eleven and NASA doctored the photos they released when the astronauts[11] came back down so they weren't embarrassed. Can't go to the moon and come back with nothing, right? We had to show the world we were better than the Russians, they were kicking our ass up to then. We couldn't just ask people to take our word for it because they went to pick up the photos at the one-hour and everything was blurry, overexposed and discolored. So NASA touched up the photos and made due. Well, then they compared the costs of sending more up - and fixing the cameras and shielding - versus not doing that. So all the missions after Eleven did a big loop and came down and they just filmed it in the desert. They faked it.' Henry paused, 'So just those first two actually were there. All of the astronauts that went past orbit are going blind from the same radiation.'

---

[11] Astronaut. From Greek. 'Astron,' star and 'nautes' which means sailor. Sailors of the stars. How romantic. The Soviets weren't held back by any feelings of humility, they dubbed their rocket riders 'Cosmonauts.' One translation of 'Cosmos' is Orderly Universe, so 'Sailors of an Orderly Universe.' They were bringing order to society so it was natural for them to export the same off of Earth.

ASAP

→3 ↓1

Max stood with Jamie in their campaign's amen corner at the debate – the only one that had been agreed to before the special election for all four candidates. Headquarters staff that had been tasked with the event worked around them. The other campaigns had spaces across the back wall with them. Locals filed in and took seats in the auditorium. Centered in the room was the press. Max was fixated on one who was stood in the side nearest them. The reporter was so flawless that she was deindividualized. She regarded the room through long eyelashes, her bright blue irises flashed when something new came to her attention. She lacked the minor flaws and asymmetricalities that really are what allow people to recognize one another. Max held his breath as he examined her profile. She had tied her hair back into a ponytail, allowing her profile to be seen without obstruction. The strap of her camera forced her fleece jacket into the cleavage of her breasts. Her press pass laid off center over one breast. Everything was proportional, her lips were plump. Her tongue pushed out a small pocket at the center of her mouth, she exhaled air and created a pink bubble.

'What's wrong with you?' Jamie asked, her phone buzzing

in her pocket. 'You need to look, I don't know, less like this. We're getting B-Rolled right now.' She gestured to a cameraman who was getting footage of the crowd.

'Hm, nothing, Nothing. What's up?' Max looked away from the reporter. The bubble had popped, she was chewing as she was writing.

'What's the plan with the gaggle afterwards? We letting him wade in or tighten up and feed the press in as we can peel them apart?'

'Throw him to the wolves. He'll be fine. With all four filed here I don't think they'll deal with too much handling anyway. Do we have anyone in the green room with him? Ten minutes until they walk out.'

grammateia: How would you do it? Excluding the booths from consideration.

  bkp971: well, there is rope

  g: Isn't that ghastly?

  g: clawing at the noose struggling for breath? yeah...

  g: Drowning would be out then

  b: sure. when my wisdom teeth were taken out i started fighting as the gas took hold. I could only feel my eyes and began to panic. that's how i picture going by pills. i read about a man, a woodsman, whose child died. in the winter he left his house and laid down in the snow on a mountain.

  g: That's beautiful

  b: that's why i still remember it

  g: Ethan Frome and Maggie tried to kill themselves on a sled. Intentionally driving it into a tree.

  g: Didn't go well for them, as I recall.

  g: I can't imagine doing it with a gun, it's so traumatic.

b: i just saw someone get shot. well, i think so, it happened fast.

b: i don't think it was a taser or anthing. The police raided a convenience store when i was walking up to it. guy ran out and hit a police officer. i heard a crack.

g: Are you okay?

b: yeah, i don't feel anything about it really. was scary in the moment

b: but it's over and i don't feel anything now. it didn't touch me at all.

g: van Gogh shot himself in the chest

g: such an interesting choice.

b: there was some guy that helped with the oklahoma city bombings or something that cut his hand off with a chainsaw

g: Stepping into traffic. My uncle had someone do that to him. He swerved and sideswiped a car with a family in it. This was before I was born and he's still rattled by it. Says he thinks about the guy making eye contact with him, he can't shake it.

g: Have you ever tried?

b: no. not seriously. there were performative acts in the throes of acute depression.

b: but not seriously. you?

g: Yes.

g: Easter Sunday last year. I had slashed at my one wrist. I hadn't opened the vein yet. My

roommate came back and stopped me. She asked what was wrong.

g: I told her that my fiancé had dumped me, we had dated since high school, picked the same college. And he just said 'This isn't right.' and was done with me. I had been sobbing incoherently with the suicide help line for a half hour when she showed up.

g: Isn't Easter a wonderful day to have an anniversary like that on? It's always moving around and changing. It doesn't make any sense at all.

g: So, she stopped me. And I slowly got better. During summer semester I woke up early for class by chance and walked across campus, there was still dew on the grass it was so early, I decided to swing by a professor's office to see if he was in - we spoke once after I got dumped and he mentioned that he wanted to know how I was doing.

g: I went to his office and he wasn't in. However, there was a book sale and I picked up some great books and chatted with another professor in the department and a grad student. I went back to my room and dropped off the books, smoked a delicious cigarette as I walked to class. I was sitting there during lecture and realized that if I had done it, if my roommate hadn't come back early or if I had hung up on the help line I wouldn't have been there at that moment, my body would have been in a drawer, or on a trolley being readied to be put in a furnace. That was such a perfect morning and I would have missed it.

g: My body would have been rotting, that is hard to accept. Oblivion is one thing, to know that your carriage would moulder and become a monstrosity is unsettling.

b: i'm sorry.

g: It's past. I'm okay. Well, I'm better now.

b: i wish i could hold you

g: Me too. I would like that.

g: xoxo

g: You read the story of the Minotaur? Theseus? Black sails? Aegean Sea? etc.

g: I have a theory he did that to off his king-dad so he could take the throne. It's like half a day or longer across the sea in modern times. No one could not notice black sails for that long.'

b: you should ge tthat to interpol ASAP. you've cracked the case.

g: Oh! So I've decided on what my tattoo is going to be!

b: what's that?

g: Kepler's Three Laws. They can be described visually quite easily and the mathematics involved in them is sublime. I want to get them between my shoulder blades.

b: it's been a while...

g: 1 Describes the orbital path of every celestial body. (It's an ellipse!)

g: 2 As an object orbits the distance traveled varies, but the area of the triangle formed by

measuring two points the same length of time apart is equal. So another ellipse with two shaded triangles within.

g: And finally 3 the orbital period of an object changes in predictable way based on its distance from the sun.

g: So diagrams and shading and basic labels. I'm really excited for it.

Side of the Road

↑1 ↓4

Max watched the speedometer. It fell, line by line, towards zero. From ahead, under the hood, the engine clunked every time he let off the gas. Coasting was doom. Max chuckled, thinking what a miserable metaphor he was given. He touched the gas, the engine revved, uncertainly. Beside him, Congressman Sexton was on a call, trying to part some donor from their money. The highway was busy, large trucks pressed ahead along with smaller passenger cars. People cruised comfortably in SUVs ignoring everyone around. He heard the call wrapping up. Just then, the dash lights dimmed. 'Fuck.' Max muttered. Sexton hung up. 'Congressman, hold off on the next call. We may have an issue here. I'm going to call ahead and see if we can get another car to meet us.'

Sexton stopped writing his notes from the call. 'I'm doing well, Max. I need to keep this going.' He said coolly, without looking up.

'I understand, sir.' The car shuddered. 'But something is wrong with the car.' An SUV cut them off, jerking into the right lane to get around a slower vehicle in the left. Max slammed on the brake and the engine died without his foot on the accelerator. The power steering went out, he muscled

287

the wheel over and came to a stop on the shoulder. The semi truck behind them blew its air horn as it flew past.

'What the fuck are you doing!' Sexton yelled. He swatted Max, open handed, on the back of the head.

'Don't touch me!' Max snapped. 'Listen, I'm going to call and get a car here, we'll take care of this. Just relax.'

'You almost got us killed! You need to get it together!' 'Please. I'm taking care of this.' Max dialed Jamie, the back of his head stinging from being struck.

'Is that Jamie? Put me on the phone with her!'

'One moment. I need to tell her what's going on.'

'Fine! I'll call her!' Sexton dialed Jamie himself. She answered Max's call.

'Jamie, we need a car ASAP at,' Max looked up. 'We're a mile north of Carey on 23 South.' he paused, 'Yeah, the Congressman is calling you too.' Pause, 'Yes, he's here with me. He's quite upset. Our car broke down.'

'Tell her to answer my call! Jamie, pick up the phone!'

'I'll put you on the line Congressman. Jamie, I need you to dispatch someone now. We're stranded here.' pause, 'Okay, thank you. Bye.' He hung up.

'Did you just fucking hang up!' Sexton yelled.

'I did. You need to calm down.' Max turned, unhooking his seat belt. He reached into the wheel well and pulled the lever to open the hood. 'This situation is handled. You want to keep making calls, go ahead. I'm going to go look at the engine.' He opened the car door. The blast of a passing car swept inside the vehicle, tossing the papers on Sexton's lap into the air.

'You get back in here!' Sexton yelled as Max slammed the door shut. Sexton threw open his door and got out. 'Don't you fucking close the door on me! I'm your boss and I'm a member of Congress. How dare you.' He growled.

Max opened the hood, ignoring the congressman. He hooked the brace and glared at the engine. 'I really don't know what the fuck I'm doing here. I have no idea what any of this is.' Max said to himself.

'This is unacceptable.' Sexton dialed Jamie again. She answered and he launched into berating her. Max looked over at him, Sexton kicked an unidentifiable piece of another car laying on the berm. He stormed back to Max, hanging up on Jamie. 'How the fuck did you do this!?' he screamed.

'We've got this under control. Please go sit in the car, there is a staffer on the way already.' Max closed the hood, his obligatory action as a man to at least look at the engine satisfied.

Sexton patted his jacket, then his pants' pockets. 'Where's my pen?' He ran to the passenger door, 'Where's my pen!?'

'Pen?' Max followed, curious.

'My pen! Are you ■■■■■■■■ or something? The blue one I've always got on me. It's lucky.' Max guffawed at that. 'Lucky. Yeah it must be with us then.' 'Don't mock me or it'll go poorly for you. It's got to be in here, I had it while I was making calls until your ■■■■■■■■[12] maneuver that stranded us here.' Sexton knelt next to the car, throwing call sheets onto the back seat as he searched the wheel well.

'Don't use language like that.'

---

[12] I originally had this said in these places. I grappled with it and included it as the character is abusive and this is how certain people spoke at the time. But it nagged at me. I've decided to pull it as it is harmful and the action can be stated rather than laid out in the text. I think it's better to end these things and not memorialize them in any way.

'Shut up.' Sexton stood, brushing himself off, then jabbed a finger into Max's chest. 'We are late! And you did this! And I am your boss, and you are an incompetent employee. Got that?'

Max saw the pen, wedged in the crevice of the seat where the seatback met the bottom. In one smooth motion, he reached around Sexton, grabbed the pen, and flourished it in the Congressman's face. 'Found your pen! And fuck you Tom!' He threw it overhand, it spun end over end, a blur. The semi truck that disintegrated it blasted its horn as it roared past.

'What the fuck!' Sexton screamed. You fucking piece of shit.' He swung wildly at Max, hitting him in the chest. Max's fat absorbed it, and the following blows. 'Fucking shit! I'll fucking end you!'

'No!' Max shouted, his booming bass matching the traffic. 'No you won't you fucking asshole!' Sexton was caught off guard, he was quiet for a moment. 'That's right you shut your fucking mouth you no-name two-termer. I am here doing a favor, and it's not to you. You fucking TOUCH me again, or cross me in any fucking way between now and the election I will, I promise you, end you in disgrace.' Sexton moved to speak, anger welling up. 'Keep your fuckwit mouth shut. I am your only hope to win. You understand that? And I will take it all away like,' he snapped his fingers, 'that. You've gotten away with this bullshit for too long because you are like this to terrified staffers who are afraid for their jobs and the reputation they'll have if they fuck up. You wield your bullshit power and we've tried to reel you in, soften you, insulate staff from you. Well that ends, you fucking shape up, now. I'm not afraid of you, and you know my resume and all the people I can call. I'll ruin you. In the past ten minutes you have crossed every goddamn line I can even think of and if you do one more fucking thing not only will you lose, I will fucking have you primaried and you'll see every dollar coming from anyone with any name other than Sexton dry up. You got that?'

'You can't talk to me like that, you-' Max slapped Sexton, open handed, a red mark appearing immediately. 'You fucking call me Sir. You got that? Your threats are nothing. Look at me.' Sexton glared at him, 'Yeah. Look at me when I say this. Ask yourself if you want me to start calling in favors against you. Think hard on that before opening your goddamn shit-filled mouth, you fuck. I have had to work for some real shitheels, and you are one of the worst. You are abusive to staff, you are disrespectful to people supporting your ambition. And you don't deserve to win for that. You say the wrong thing and your ambition ends, right here.'

Sexton stared at Max. Max squared up on Sexton, waiting. Traffic sped past, oblivious. 'I'm going to sit in the car.' Sexton said finally, turned, and shut himself in. He stared at Max and locked the doors. Max pulled out a cigarette and chain smoked in the polluted air until relief arrived.

cathole

↑3 ↓2

Henry reached the woods his camp was in, turning off the road and stepping through the bushes. He and Todd were beginning to form a desire path here, he could see where they were creating a trail. He made a note to bring it up with him. They had to stop using the same spot to cut through and vary it more. He walked through the woods, pushing through the underbrush and reached his site. He saw a plastic coffee can sitting next to the excavated cathole it came from. He knew. He saw in that moment. Todd suspected or saw, robbed him and is at the Greyhound downtown with a ticket in his hand back to Nebraska. Henry was torn, he ran to the coffee can so its emptiness would rack across his vision. He kicked it, screaming. It sailed into the woods. He had the cash in his pocket and no more. All he had saved was lost. He ran around the camp, tearing at tarps and clothes, throwing anything he couldn't break with his hands. Screaming.

The sun dimmed to orange, Henry looked towards it and had to make a decision. His rage had faded. He walked back through the underbrush towards the road and turned towards the gas station when he reached the edge of the woods.

Henry didn't like buying this close to his camp. He didn't want people to see him here, didn't want them to recognize him. *Don't owe people money where you live. Don't beg for money where you live. Don't buy drugs where you live. Be invisible where you live.* But he needed to drink. Needed to forget so later he could recoup and rebuild. He walked into the gas station. A maroon sedan was parked at the nearest pump, teenage boys stood around it laughing with one filling it up. One of the boys elbowed another and pointed at Henry. Henry didn't make eye contact, but walked towards the small store.

'Grandpa, we need a hand.' He heard them yell out as he passed. One, the one that had been elbowed, jogged over. 'Hey grandpa, buy us some beer.'

Henry stopped. 'I don't do that. You're gonna have to find someone else.'

'No grandpa, it's okay. Buy us some beer and we'll pay you for it.' He laughed.

Henry looked at the glass door, the clerk wasn't in sight. He looked at the boy holding out the proffered cash.

'Just buy us two cases of Bud, SoCo if they got it, and a pack of Reds.' He laughed, 'Keep the rest.'

Henry looked at the cash and he'd have nearly twenty left over. He reached out and pocketed the money, turning away from the boy.

When he came out, the boys had parked beside the block wall of the gas station. He handed over the alcohol and cigarettes. His own was in his coat pocket.

TPD 38.3 Rev. 4/95(e)

NARRATIVE: Oh the listed date and time this Detective was assigned to the above felonious assault. Victim was already transported to Regional Medical College. Victim was and remains unconscious. This Detective oversaw securing crime scene, collection of evidence and photography. All evidence is in Main Evidence following chain of custody filed under this report number.

After witness and evidence collection the following timeline has been developed by this Detective. Suspect interviews have not proceeded as all suspects have retained counsel. Victim, Henry Canfield, homeless, 50s (HC) was approached or did approach the four suspects: Kevin [redacted], 15 Clay [redacted], 16 Jon [redacted] (owner and driver of dark red Oldsmobile Aurora), 16 Jake [redacted], 17 all High School students at [redacted] a nearby suburban high school. They agreed to pay HC for alcohol and cigarettes. After this transaction, they asked HC for a place to party and drink, offering more money. This was overheard by Witness 2, DF, who was pumping gas. HC brought them to his camp within walking distance. Jon parked his vehicle on the roadside leaving the hazard lights on. Witness 3, MB and Witness 4, WS, saw the vehicle at this time. At the campsite, Jake produced a small amount of marijuana and cocaine. Suspect had an empty vial when arrested. The toxicology report from the victim shows the presence of nicotine, alcohol, marijuana, and cocaine. None of the suspects have submitted to testing. It is unclear what led to the escalation to violence, but the suspects attacked the victim with bare hands and items around his campsite. Blood and DNA from the victim has been collected from the Oldsmobile Aurora that is in impound. The victim was robbed for the money he had on his person. Trophies were taken from the campsite and the victim's body including a fire piston and personal photos. These were found in the car, on the suspects, and school lockers.

No suspects are cooperating with the investigation. The parents and counsel for the suspects have blocked searches of the suspects' homes.

Paul woke up to the ringing of his phone and answered his alarm clock. 'I have seven minutes until my alarm goes off. I'm not early yet.' He said into the receiver once he found his phone.

'Get down here right now.' It was earlier than Paul was supposed to be there, so he didn't get the terse call from Chelsea because he had overslept. 'Party Headquarters was burglarized last night. The police need a statement from you. We were the last people here last night.'

A sharp catch in his side forced him to gasp and lean over as he made his way to the bathroom sink. 'Did they come into the campaign office?' He stretched his back carefully and looked into the mirror, trying to decide if he needed to shave or if he could skip that again this morning. He has a headache along with a sore throat. He couldn't tell if it was a hangover or a cold coming on.

'No, but they think we were being watched.' Paul looked at his mail. One thick envelope was his absentee ballot. Another envelope marked Return Service Requested was from the county Republican Party. He let the others drop and brought those into the office with him.

A uniformed police officer stared at Paul as he slowed to park, he approached Paul and Chelsea. 'Ma'am, is this Paul Dinares?'

'Yes officer, that's me.' Paul said. He looked at Chelsea and she shrugged the span of an eyebrow.

'I'm Officer Huntley. Can you come over here please, I have a few questions that would be best discussed privately.' The patrol officer asked Paul to sit in the open bay of an idling van. Another officer was already waiting for them there.

'Can you tell me where you were last night?' The second officer asked.

'Well, after we wrapped up for the night I went to my apartment. What is your name?'

'Do you live with anyone?'

'No, it's just a small studio.'

'What time was this?'

'Late. After midnight. Le and I left together. Am I a suspect?'

'No, we're just trying to understand what happened. I'm Officer Osorio. We'll find who did this, the forensics team is dusting for prints right now. Tell me about your arrest in two thousand and three.' On the eve of invasion in March of 2003 Paul had driven to Chicago with friends and sat in jail for a weekend with a baton induced concussion until the gaolers decided that the uprising was quelled, and the judges decided that the charges were bogus.

'It's funny you both ended up as police. Seems obvious, with a first name like Officer.' Osorio actually would have laughed at that if they hadn't trained themselves a stone-face. 'In two thousand and three I was at a protest, no charges came of the arrest.'

The first officer who was standing outside the open door of the van asked. 'Do you feel resentment towards the government? Did you know that the alarm wasn't set last night?'

'I don't work in the building that was broken into, I work across the street.'

'Your boss found this morning that the alarm wasn't set on your office either.' the second officer continued.

Paul realized he'd drank too much at the office and forgot to set the alarm. Le had been too.

'Until recently you were associating with some pretty radical people. Did you know that Stephen Robin has been convicted of felony Breaking and Entering?'

'I'm not surprised, though I would bet the motive wasn't criminal.'

'It is still a crime. Maybe you don't respect that. I should tell you that all of the petty cash, and there is quite a bit, is still inside. But three computers are gone, the only three computers with all of the unrecoverable donor and voter data.'

'You're accusing me of something. I was working across the street and then I went home last night, I haven't been inside that office in over a week.'

'You shouldn't be nervous. Why are you nervous? We're just trying to understand what happened. We think they knew beforehand what to take. Do you have any ideas who might have wanted to help them?'

The police relented and wound down their questioning of Paul. Paul noticed there was no forensics team in the building as he watched the police wrap up their questions and photography from the office. They drove away and volunteers started coming in later in the morning.

Paul noticed that the *Defend Fallujah* volunteer, Brandon, had a small yellow pad that he'd brought in and was taking down notes in it. Paul walked over and read over his shoulder. Today, Brandon was wearing a homemade shirt, a game of hangman with the letters spelling CHENEY IS A TRAITOR. Paul saw they were phone numbers. 'What are you doing with these?' Paul picked up the pad. The top had *CCCP* written on it fewer than a dozen numbers in different color ink were written down.

'It's a particular disconnect message. It's different than all the rest. It sounds like it was recorded by a random secretary in 1970's Soviet Russia and hasn't been updated since. Like this one,' he pulled the pad around and dialed the number in and called it. He turned on the speaker. The recording was fuzzy, like it was recorded off of a recording. The message faded out and came back about halfway through. It played twice and cut out *and try* both times. *You've reached a number that is no longer in service. Please check the number ... again* Each word was enmeshed in heavy fuzz. The disconnect tone at the end was variable. Paul wasn't sure what to make of it, or the volunteer. He needed the numbers Brandon put up.

'How are your calls going otherwise?' he asked.

'Yeah fine. Weird though, right? I'm trying to find more of those.'

Paul walked away. He went to Le's desk, 'Can you watch this phone bank? I need to get out. I'm going to go walk a packet.'

'I'm wrapping up the statewide Tick-Tock for Election Day. Just because I work from your office sometimes doesn't mean I'm here. Hey, that letter you got. Good catch. Those are landing all over. We're trying to figure out what it means. HQ is thinking general intimidation with that text about warrants and felonies. They tend to be landing with minority voters - AfAm and Hispanic/Latino though. Funny you got one.'

'My last name being Dinares people think that a lot. No connection though. Plus I live in a high density AfAm and Dem voting area. Must have overlapped enough on their targeting.

She noticed the look on Paul's face. 'Go ahead. Go walk. Just try to be back quickly. Don't be out all afternoon.'

The street Paul found was full of postwar houses. Vinyl and aluminum siding in whites, blues, and yellows, aluminum awnings, aluminum scrollwork faux columns, aluminum screen doors, American flags on aluminum poles. Blue sky above. The street looked the same fifty years prior. The first leaves were down, scattered across the grass, street, and sidewalks. Pumpkins sat on cast concrete porches. In the gutters lay plastic wrappers and other detritus that might excite an archaeologist in the far future. No one came to the door when he tapped with the clipboard. He left Sexton lit behind, tucked in wherever he could find secure purchase for it from the wind. He looked in the sky as he walked and watched a wispy cloud visibly grow into a pillowy cumulus over just a minute, isolated against the crisp blue sky.

'Hey! You do this!?' Paul heard someone shout from behind him. He turned and a man was walking towards him in loose cotton boxer shorts with a plaid pattern and a grayed V-neck t-shirt. On his feet he had old tennis shoes without socks. He waved Sexton lit in front of him towards Paul. 'Yeah asshole. This yours?'

'I'm sorry. If you don't want that I can take it back or you can throw it away.'

'Go fuck yourself. You put this on my door and it held down my doorbell and woke me up, Asshole.' He crumpled it up and threw it at Paul, his penis flopping out of his boxers with the

299

motion.

'I'm sorry,' Paul laughed, 'I'm sorry. I've got to go.' Paul turned and jogged off as the guy went on yelling at him.

'Kerry's out.' Isaac said bluntly when Paul picked up his call.

'What? You've got to be kidding me.' Paul started his car and pulled out of where he was parked and headed towards the office.

'Public polls are out. He's up by three and he's been up by three. That's not enough. It's not going to happen. Four more years.'

'I can't believe that.'

'Being realistic is better in this game. Statewide polls are fuzzy but I would call it for McAllen too unless you guys do something big these last few weeks.'

Pokeweed

↑4 ←1

Paul and Brandon were alone in the office. Le had to leave for an emergency in Cleveland. She'd left a note for Paul: *I sprayed bleach on the mess growing on the toilet and it coughed and slapped me. CLEAN YOUR OFFICE* Other volunteers had drifted off. Brandon was clearly working to add to his list and suffering voters picking up in order to add to it.

grammateia: Talk to me talk to me talk to me, darling.

bkp971: good evening. how are you?

g: A night on my balcony watching what stars aren't drowned out by the lights in the lot here and drinking tea that is perfectly brewed. I also have a blanket.

b: that sounds lovely

g: It is lovely.

b: tell me something

g: Figure out who you are and be as much of that person as you can stand.

g: I have been thinking about sonnets.

g: The dream I woke up from was me trapped underwater. In my dream I knew I could breathe underwater and could get my leg unpinned if I just worked at it. But I still woke up in a panic.

g: Very annoying. I was annoyed all morning. But sonnets!

b: in high shcoolw e had to write a short response to sonnet 18 in english class.

g: I don't think anyone loves like that anymore. Or maybe they didn't then. It was a job, after all. There's that unrequited love poet who refused to meet his muse when she reached out.

g: I think most people are acting like kittens, looking for body heat to share.

g: And maybe calling that love.

b: that's beautiful. you're a doorbell.

g: I'm a figment of your imagination love. xoxo

b: What are you afraid of?

g: Spiders. I'm afraid of them wrapping their spindly legs around me under this blanket.

g: Spooning.

b: weird...

g: Actually. I'm afraid I won't accomplish as much as a snail.

g: I have a lovely snail shell here. I don't know what kind it is. It's glassy, dots of browns and tans over white, a thousand different shades. Inside the base white darkens to a lovely lilac.

g: This snail lived its entire life making this. Years building it. It made one perfect thing and left it for us. It has billions of family wide across the globe and deep stretching back eons all, each, labored or laboring to make one perfect thing.

g: I, and you, and everyone. None of us will leave anything as perfect as this snail. None of us are this dedicated. And that scares me.

Brandon hung up the phone, 'It's not suppertime, I'm interrupting bedtime, ma'am!' He said after making sure it was disconnected.

'You want a drink?' Paul asked. He was tallying up call attempts and contacts simultaneously, responding in the chat when he reached three digits and paused to write his counts down and reset to zero. He'd do a second pass counting 1's for Sexton and 5's against.

b: i'm going to have to get going. will you be around later?

'Sure yeah. Beer in the fridge, right?'

'I got a bottle here. You can have beer if you want. But whiskey is an option.'

g: Maybe? The computer is ruining my night vision so I'm really just sodium-lamp-watching. But we can talk from bed if I do go in.

'I'm twenty, you cool?'

Paul hadn't considered this. 'Reward for a supervol man. I'm not a bouncer.' He went to the kitchenette and found two clean coffee mugs. He took these to his desk and poured a fair amount of whiskey in each. He brought a mug and a beer to Brandon, setting them down on the desk. 'What's your bike?'

'Old Cannondale my roommate left when he moved out. He owed me money and offered that.

The bicycle veered between the desks. 'Underdamped control response," Paul said, blinking. He overcorrected, bumping over telephone cables duct-taped to the floor. On the down-stroke his pedal caught the lip of a steel wastebasket. Pressing down he upset the weight distribution and tumbled everything to the floor.

He lay still. Brandon's helmet that had been sitting in his head unfastened rotated slowly to a stop after hitting a desk. Paul propped himself up on his elbows and looked at his twisted body, his right shin ached from where it was pinned to the floor by the frame of the bicycle. He sighed and extracted himself.

Paul looked at the glass on the bar, half full of tequila and Sprite - *Tony's Magic Tequila* that was concocted from a misheard order and given to Paul being a regular who would drink anything. He liked it and had been ordering it. He'd infrequently ordered by its alternate, casually racist, name *Dos Tequila Especiala De Tony.* He was alone at the bar, not bothering to call anyone to meet up.

He remembered the night they met here. They both found their way to putting their foot on the other's stool. They pushed off, rocking together as they talked. Their legs rubbing on one another. He remembered her weighing her kick off his boot, then spinning and laughing.

In his hands he held the Pain. The color of Pokeweed root - sallow gray, damp, and bruised. Not hot burning pain, but slow and persistent. This had been given to him by Jessica, maybe it was Mark that gave it to her. Probably, thinking back to how she talked about that ex. Paul would carry it until he left it with someone, maybe She would get it, or mix Hers with his and they would each walk away with a conglomeration of each. This game of hot potato, how ancient could some parts of it be? Paul licked it and the hot rubbing alcohol knives burned and constricted his oral mucosa as it spread. He reached for his drink to wash away the feeling. He thought back to Pain he'd carried and given to others. What Andrea had left him he'd given to Finch. Here's Jessica's, but before that he had given Nicole's to Abby. He loathed tallying up the number, Isaac teased him with guesses. Less than his age, he paused and against his will counted, no, Sh probably brought the total one past his age. Probably more. Lindsay Two - Lindsay Windows versus Lindsay Dos per Isaac - Paul hoped she had shaken off the Pain he'd left with her. Genderless, sometimes combined, sometimes one walked away with the Pain of both and the other left free of it. Rare enough, they dissolved. Sometimes people stayed together after, sometimes they split up - that was what they needed from the relationship.

God knows what I'm leaving here, Paul thought. 'You're going to want to clean this glass right away Tony!' Paul yelled to the bartender who'd gone to the back, 'Don't play with it.' Paul went to his car, forgetting his tab. He started the Saturn and did a slow U-turn in the street. He drove slowly the few blocks to his apartment. The BBC overnight on the radio. Something caught his eye in the road ahead, a flash of white. He slowed and stopped. His headlights brightened what the streetlights had highlighted, some flat object in the road. Paul got out of his car, leaving the engine running and the door open. He walked ahead and saw on the ground a flattened wire basket, maybe for a bicycle or carry basket. It had been plastic or vinyl dipped, wear points showed with metal coming through. A small green binder clip was nestled near one corner. Paul picked it up, staring at it in the headlights. The wires retained some part of their form but were crushed and overlapping. Sone washers had been brazed on before the white coating, Paul wasn't sure what their function was. A handle wire maybe had come loose on one end and added an important element to the overall form. Paul walked back to his car carrying it, he'd decided it was art and would display it in his apartment.

Morning

→2 ←3

Paul woke the next morning with the garbage art on the bed next to him. His body ached, much more than normal. He'd left his phone off charge and plugged it in as he sat up. He went to his bathroom and felt like his entire body was a charley horse. He pressed two fingers into his trapezius to massage it and felt the muscle simply part under pressure and his fingers slide deep behind his collarbone. He screamed in pain. That's when he remembered what happened. He went to his front door, he'd not only left it unlocked, it had swung open. He stepped out onto the porch and down the street saw his car. He'd driven up onto the curb and the passenger side wheel and tire assembly was turned perpendicular to the car. The entire spindle and, Paul didn't know what all it was, had broken off and the car was immobilized. He'd walked the few yards to his apartment after the crash. A patrol car was next to it with its lights on and the officers were out looking at the car taking notes.

'You're all very important, so I don't want to make a mistake by thanking anyone here and leaving people out. But thank you all for being here.' Thomas Sexton turned to greet the elected officials, union leaders, and other dignitaries who had come out for his press conference. This greeting he'd settled on because he rarely knew more than half the people he appeared with, and the flattery kept anyone from being suspicious. There is something about a good pander. People get annoyed watching other people being pandered to. And being pandered to poorly. It's like PDA, great to be inside of. Max stood behind the arc of reporters, well away from the focus of the cameras. He watched the reporters and listened to the candidate. The nods, the glances, what was being scribbled down and what wasn't. He saw the cameraman for one station, one that could afford equipment by the call sign on the camera, with a microphone taped to a golf iron. A low number, 3 or 4, Max reckoned. Long shaft. The lower edge of his trench coat stirred in the breeze, but he was still. He affected a stern, blank gaze as he heard the statement he wrote read off. The two trackers from the two Republican campaigns held up identical handheld cameras and stood by one another, bored. Max wondered if they were from the same shop and just hired out on opposing campaigns.

11:03 a.m. Jamie Caulfield CM SEXTON
   <Your presser isn't by train tracks, is it?>

11:04 a.m. SENT
   <I'm sorry. What?>

11:04 a.m. Jamie Caulfield CM SEXTON
   <It'd be easier to talk. But there's a runaway train up by you. Lorain. Right now. I'm watching it on the news.>

Max looked around and saw the railroad overpass that sat next to the union hall.

'I'm not like my opponent, well any of my opponents.' Sexton laughed as he went on. 'I'm not going to talk about the war here, that's too important to sully in a campaign. I want to talk to you about,' Max walked towards the train tracks, looking in each direction. Nothing. Sirens in the distance. Instinct raised his head to examine the direction of the noise and its threat level. Placing him at the same operating level as a gazelle. Far, far away down the track to the, he thought, east, he saw flashing lights. He looked over his shoulder at the ongoing press conference. Rarely would the person who gets blamed for things going badly get credit when they go well, Max thought. He turned and walked back down the slope towards the press conference, thinking. Charles, the DFD he'd deputized to help today was wearing a Sexton t-shirt over his plaid dress shirt. 'And I believe that we *should* consider a ban on fried foods, specifically named foods like Snickers and Twinkies, at County Fairs. I don't know where my vote would fall on it, but it does deserve serious consideration in the Senate.' Well, he's wrapping up, Max thought. The sirens were getting louder, but still far away. Sexton, up there trying to be anything to everyone. Should he cut him off? Max asked himself. The shiny end of the camera is the dangerous end. Sometimes action can only lead to making the situation worse, and you just have to accept as bad as it is, that's the best you get.

'Could you speak on your proposal on banning first trimester abortions?' Four Iron asked.

'Yes, I think women should have more time to contemplate the decision, so that's why I've released a proposal on second and third trimester abortions.'

'And the Republican, Maguire, saying that that isn't far enough, that only third trimester abortions should be legal? How do you respond to that?'

'Well we disagree on that and I look forward to debating this before voters in the General in a few weeks.'

A pickup truck locked its tires as it slammed to a stop in the parking lot. A uniformed sheriff deputy jumped out of their personal truck. They reached back in, knocking their campaign hat off, taking a pump action shotgun from a gun rack in the cab and ran between Sexton and the cameras towards the railroad tracks. Max's decision was made.

'Alright everyone!' Max cleared the distance on the lawn and cut in front of the cameras, 'We're wrapped here! The Congressman has to get to his next event!' he moved between Sexton and the cameras and tried pushing him towards their car. Sexton was considerably smaller than Max but was planted solidly in the ground. 'No more questions! Thank you everyone! Goodbye!' Max waved one hand to scratch the event. The trackers didn't even have their cameras up, they'd turned to watch the Deputy and the train. The train was visible now, empty and pulling a short mixed line of boxcars, flatbeds, and one tanker. It was moving fast under power towards them. The very special people whose names weren't read off began moving, some panicking. The Building Trades leaders were the only ones calm. They looked around nonchalantly, laughing, they dealt with worse daily. The deputy jogged towards the train, shotgun coming up to their shoulder. The cameras were being repositioned, taken off the tripods to be put on shoulders. All the cameramen saw this as their brass ring.

Sexton was still speaking, his mouth running over his speech even as he swung his head around at the chaotic scene and he moved for cover. The deputy began firing at the brake line. 'And I want to announce as well my opposition to Ohio Issue One!' He shouted as he moved behind the crowd of endorsers. 'This issue is an obvious coordinated power grab by the Bush campaign to shore up support in battleground states! Ohio and Ohioans deserve better. GLBT Ohioans should know I support them!'

Detective

→3 ↓1

The Detective walked quietly down the center of the factory floor in early afternoon. The realtor was furious, but bowed to the pressure of the badge and a developing sale. The Detective paused. A call to her colleague had led to him calling her. He was SWAT and his policing went towards flashbangs and breaching tools. Sniffing wasn't in his portfolio. It was all that was in hers.

She turned slowly around, thinking of what was described to her. There, that was the foreman's office. She wasn't ready to go there. Glass panes the size of a sheet of paper to watch work going on down here, dirty, broken. She walked underneath, then to the back of the factory, touching nothing. She walked slowly, head turning side to side, stopping, varying her direction left and right to subtle cues that pulled at her. Finally she came to the broken out window in a side door down the row of locked docks. It had been replaced with plexiglass and taped at the top. The Detective knew that they were banking on a bored contract security guard doing a round of the building overlooking this. She took a photo on her phone, for notes, not evidence. She walked back to the foreman's office, turning on a small flashlight. Beer bottles were laying, most smashed, around the wall. A different glint caught her eye and she walked over. A cheap flip phone was laying open in a drainage trench. She looked up at the underside of the floor of the office and the catwalk above.

Two hours later, a police cameraman and crime scene crew were quietly working, photographing *in situ*, bagging, and labeling what they found. Blue shirts were around too, but it was a small detachment. Not a full lockdown. The Detective was back in the center of the factory floor watching the slow, patient, inexorable, work unfold when she heard a latch click come from the back of the building. She turned her head just as Matthew turned the corner. A donut in his mouth, eleven more in the box in one hand, and a twelve pack of beer in the other.

Matthew sat in an interrogation room. Painted, and painted, and painted concrete walls, a steel door (painted) with a small window embedded with mesh, a sturdy table, and mismatched chairs. On the police side they had casters. Matthew's was wooden. He was cuffed, but they had turned them around so he could put his hands in his lap. Recording devices, one overt, others hidden, some broken, were built into the room. The fluorescent light above buzzed steadily.

'We have quite a lot to talk about Matthew.' The Detective said. She sat back in her chair, the squeak as the spring compressed and chirps as metal rubbed on metal loudly taking up space in the room.

'Lawyer, dawg.[13]' Matthew said sarcastically.

'Woof woof. One's on the way then. Since I can't question you, I'll just talk about what I know.'

Matthew stared at her impassively.

'What I know is that you walked into a building that was being used to test a weapon through a door that had been prepared in advance and used regularly. So you did not come in by accident, you were bringing snacks for the work today.' She paused, her notes were on her lap but they were a prop, 'Your fingerprints are on some breathtakingly damning pieces of evidence from crime scenes all over the region. And you've been named by our informant as a principal in the enterprise.'

'You don't have an informant.'

'Thirty five thousand acres burned, millions in property damage. Injuries. Injuries to firefighters. No lives lost, well no people. Lot of livestock. And those hard drives we pulled out of those towers are on their way to Quantico where they've got some really amazing tech and patient investigators. You know they have an award there for whoever gets into the harddrive that's in the worst shape? It's like the America's Cup, it only changes hands when a new challenge comes along. I know one more thing, Matthew. I took one of those bottles you spread around there, one with your fingerprints on it. We're stocked with some special moonshine here, Jimmy Red Corn. This beautiful pomegranate corn. It can pull an emotional imprint out that'll leave you.' She paused, 'Well, we use it and it works and we tend not to talk about it with people who

---

[13] A request that once tested in Louisiana would be found to mean that Matthew requested a dog who is a lawyer. And thus not a valid request so any statements are admissible. If you need a lawyer, miscreants, request one properly! Don't play fuck around with your rights in a police state.

aren't police except when it's important.' She looked him in the eyes and set her notes on the table between them. 'I took a sip, Matthew, from that bottle. One of yours. They've gone too far. You're caught up in this and you don't think it's right. You're not ready for what they're doing.'

'Doesn't sound like me.'

'It is you. I'm not going to qualify this. We have them in other rooms and we're going to start deciding who to take the hammer to.' She sat back again, 'I don't want it to be you, Matt.'

Matthew stared at her. His face furrowing.

'That's right. They didn't bring donuts, but yes. We got them. Ours is now in the break room eating and writing up his report for today's activities.'

'I don't want to cooperate with you.' Matthew snapped. 'You can't offer me shit. You're not a DA, you go around with your nightstick and knock loose people to feed to the maw. If this goes to court you can ONLY testify against me. I'm in this with my eyes open.'

'I understand you don't trust police, Matt. Honestly, enough of that's true for me to be surprised you know that. But think on this before I come back. Have you ever, literally ever, heard of the cooperating member of a conspiracy being dealt with more harshly? You don't have to trust me. Just ask yourself that.'

'You're not the only force around. Word spreads on turn-coats. I'll be vilified by my comrades. And rightly so. I'd do it to a turncoat.'

'Decades stretch on. Lonely years add onto lonely years, Matt. And that's for us out here. They come slowly. Inside, the years are longer, and they come slower. But when you hear the judge say the number they're taking from you, you see them in that moment – stretching forward into your life. All at once. They aren't paced out. I've been told by plenty that I still keep up with. I know that's true.' She stood to leave, picking up her notes. She rapped on the door with her knuckle. As the door opened, she was knocked aside. Matthew had leapt across the table. He caught the officer outside the door in the jaw with a sloppy double fisted punch, he reeled and fell against the wall. The Detective regained her balance and jumped into the hallway, watching Matthew flick his head around, here on the upper floor of the main station. Officers of all ranks were running towards them, the Detective realized because she was yelling for backup. She saw Matthew and screamed for someone to stop him, tackle him, trip him. She started running. He had made a decision. He was running towards the end of the room. A clear line was before him, the stretch shortening in long strides. Decades compressed to years, years to months, months to days, days to hours, hours to minutes and finally to just a few remaining seconds. She'd often seen the streetlight silhouetted out that window and idly thought about it during the long overnights. How it was like her condo, to be up here at treetop level and the different perspective it offered. Matthew's back was to the Detective, running for the plate glass window, a halo from the streetlight surrounding him. He pushed off and twisted in midair to put one shoulder forward and tuck his head. Something remembered from high school football, the Detective thought, as she watched him crash through.

9:09 a.m. Carrie Catherine
<I miss your face. Come to the shop.

Let's catch up.>

10:27 p.m.

'Where's your car?' Carrie asked Paul when he walked in. He'd parked the small SUV in the spot outside the coffee shop. They were alone, he'd come between rushes. Carrie had a GRE guide open and was marking up the pages. She was backlit by the fluorescent light of the kitchen behind her, in her white t-shirt - fancy one somehow, thick fabric and fitted, green apron, and her short dark bob pulled back in a stub ponytail. Paul was hit, once again, with how beautiful she was.

'Engine seized. Oil leak I didn't know about. Had to borrow that from my parents.' He walked stiffly to the counter. The brass bell over the door rang as it closed behind Paul.

'Oh, okay. That's rough to hear. You have money for that?'

'I'll make it work.'

'Well this one's on me. You're going to have to start saving your dimes and dollars.' Carrie sensed the shape of the lie but didn't know what to press on. 'Have a seat, I'll bring this around when I'm done.'

'The Masters is really happening, isn't it? Have you applied yet?' Paul asked when Carrie put the two coffees down, prepared identically, and sat across from Paul.

'Need to take the GRE. But yeah, I'm doing it.'

'That's good. You deserve it.'

Carrie smiled, 'Someone I care about once told me that deserve is a funny little word. I keep thinking about that.'

'Sometimes we do, and you should be working in policy. You're someone who should be on official side. How's Willem?'

'Good. Hoping I get accepted somewhere in Chicago obvi-

316

ously.' She paused, 'Halloween is coming!' Paul and Carrie had cemented their bond over their shared love of Halloween and going in costumes that were only funny to them. In 2002 they had arrived with Paul as a zombie, as he explained over and over through the night, the time when he felt like a zombie - just after waking and before his shower. He wore sandals, underwear, and a towel around his waist. People complained to him all night that he was making *them* cold, he smoked and went on about Herd Warmth. Carrie was *A DJ aspiring to reach Ibiza* and had wired a coin battery and a white LED to hang over one eye, wore a flight suit she found, and carried LPs she had thrifted. People complained the light was blinding them all night. It faced away from her eye so she wasn't bothered by it. 'Do you have any idea of what you want to go as?' The next year, he was a *Horse from Equus* wearing a brown turtleneck and messenger jeans with a handmade copper wire horsehead with plastic autumn leaves for a mane. Carrie was *The Main Character From Your Film School Roommate's Junior Year Submission.* She wore a black turtleneck and black jeans with a half-face mask she had painted to look wooden. She carried Isaac's Iklwa Paul had borrowed for her and a yellow boa around her shoulders. She didn't speak all night. Their imaginations were charged by turtlenecks in particular. That year, Paul had found a floppy-necked mottled tan turtleneck at the thrift store and considered *Psychiatrist that got too into LSD in the 70s.* 'I'm thinking of going as *All Of My Burnout Uncles*, they all dress alike so it'd be easy to put together.'

'I haven't thought about it actually. Been busy.' Halloween sat days ahead of the General election every year, a heart-breaking torment for Paul. Though invariably he forsook his duties and got blackout drunk.

'Did you hear about what happened at the downtown station last night?'

'Someone fell from the roof?'

'Or was thrown from a window.' Carrie looked to the street, 'Now that you aren't around I'm really starting to like Her.'

'Cute. Thanks.' Paul winced, his back was taut with a spasm. He receded into the hardy potted plants by the front window: prosaic plants for the most part but some Avocados grown from seed, even several coffee trees and *Camellia sinensis* sought out in an attempt to market the coffee shop. Each had a color-coded tag with its desired water condition by the owner who was good at plants, but didn't trust themselves.

'Did you get hurt? You look like you're in pain.'

'Just messed up my back.'

'But really, I'm not teasing you. I see what you see in Her. She acts differently when you aren't around. I think that She's afraid of how She's perceived as part of a couple and you make Her self conscious of that – which exacerbates it. When you aren't there, when She only has to present Herself, She is funny and whipsmart. I hope that is the side that you see. We're talking about starting a pirate radio station this winter. Broadcast local shows out live to get attention. Run old punk and protest songs from here and other countries. Full read-throughs of banned books. We're thinking the call sign XPRT. Expert but also X-Pirate and Pirate Radio Toledo. Works on several levels.'

'You should broadcast static. Mess with the fanboys' heads. Make them question what's real.'

'We've got things we want to say.'

I'm sorry. I know. I wasn't saying you don't. You're right though. I need to call Her. We haven't seen one another in a while.'

'Yeah, She's said that. Quite a while. You two are still together? You're not both sparing my feelings are you?'

'I haven't broken up with Her.' Paul shrugged.

'The Crew is going to the Cheney protest Thursday. He's speaking at a hockey rink out in the suburbs.'

'Oh yeah? You be safe, okay? They don't mess around.'

'I will be. I know you worry. I'll text when we wrap.' Carrie looked at her coffee cup, empty on the table. 'I should get back to cleaning in the back while I've got the shop to myself. Are you okay Paul? You're really acting like you did when things got bad.'

'I am. I'll be fine.' Paul said.

'Give me your arm.' Carrie pulled a permanent marker from her apron. She wrote a message on Paul's outstretched forearm. She looked up at him when she was finished and said as she stood up. 'Call your girlfriend, okay? Don't just forget you have one again. She's a catch.'

Air Raid

2:34 p.m.

'Blood. I'm picturing you covered in blood.' Chelsea said, rubbing her eyes.

'Look, this wasn't my decision. I am powerless here.' Max stood at Chelsea's desk in the Columbus headquarters. He put his hand on the red megaphone she kept there. 'Is it my blood?'

Her hands dropped, clasping on the desk. 'Your blood. It's comforting.' She rocked her head to emphasize as she spoke. 'Look at you, standing there powerless to do anything about this and covered in blood.'

'I am powerless. Covered in blood and powerless. But you are the only department with staff, Le. Well, internally, excluding the consultants and their shops. Well, and finance but they will actually physically assault me. I truly don't understand why cycle after cycle you hear about statewide races and decide to take on the task of talking to a state full of, what this go ten, eleven million, people one by one? But I am up against reporters goddamnit, and they get curious and start digging if we don't bore them away from the good stuff with press conferences. I need district staff to talk through the

press and do my job. The call was made for me to transition.'
Le cut Max off.

'Poach. Rob. Theft.' Chelsea reached up and grabbed Max's
lapel with one hand, reaching with her other, 'I'm going to
put my hand inside your mouth until you stop talking. Or
breathing.'

Max swatted her away. '*Transition*, two of your competent
people post primary to my department.' Max paused, 'I'm
fucking by myself here Le! Me against a state of eleven million!
It's always easier for Field to hire. You know this. You can
train up good people to replace them. And in a couple weeks
every campaign is going to dump their staff out on the streets.
You can have your pick then. Please don't give me shit over
this. This isn't what I wanted, but it's all I am getting.'

'Who are you taking, or do I get a say?'

'I mean, honestly, I want the two that I've been impressed
with so far. Your guy in Cleveland, Charles, who helped when
the train fucked everything, and Nikki in Cinci. I'll get them
some travel podiums that can break down and a press list. I
want to start cross training them soon. I mean, ask them too,
they might not want it.'

'So a key DFD and a top RFD. Thank you. Good choices.
And they're lecterns, not podiums. Blood, you're covered in
blood.'

'Can we talk about something else or do you need me to give
you space for a while.'

Chelsea had a small beige calculator on her desk. She'd
picked it up years before and it traveled with her. It was made
for small retail shops, had tax keys that could be preset. She
had been adding and subtracting numbers randomly to try to
reach zero. The only clear rule limiting what she was doing

was she tried to use the same number of digits as the sum got smaller. 'I am honestly not doing anything at the moment. I can talk.'

'What, did I interrupt you looking at smut?'

'No, that's different and better.'

'The production company that Maguire was using just dropped them and switched to Maxie. I've never heard of this happening, and get this, they're using footage from a shoot with Maguire in an ad for Maxie. This all fucking hit just now.'

'Before or after you took a carving knife to slice up my team.'

'Well, before.' Max shrugged. 'I've got to decide if we put out a statement. I don't think so, but it's just completely fucked. I'm trying to figure out what motivated that. Why would anyone work with them again?'

'Maybe Maguire is in freefall? Rats jumping. Reporters mention they're desperate?'

'More time and more resources. The battle cry of every losing campaign. But no, radio silence. Everything indicates they're ticking along over there. What's today for you?'

'Got to go up 23 to Toledo Pareto, overnight there, then Cleveland. I prefer to go clockwise around the state.'

'If the big guy comes in today, steer clear. You hear him on the line with Jamie, don't get caught out. Be like one of those pigeons quick on the wing when a hawk shows up. Okay?'

3:34 a.m.

Paul got to the office, the alarm company had called him. He said he'd respond and not to call the police. It wasn't that late, three thirty. He still felt drunk, but not seriously so. The front window to the right of the door was smashed, the radiometer that Chelsea had left on her desk was broken, papers – call sheets, notes, flyers – were blowing in the street. Paul put his key in the door and felt his key jam, the vandals had broken a key off in the cylinder. He walked around back of the building and in the halogen floodlight saw that the back door was seized as well. He noticed Jesus Saves written in permanent marker on the steel door amongst other tags. He realized that whoever did this may still be around, and his mom's SUV was unlocked and running on the street. He walked back towards the street, away from the dark of the back of the building. Feeling eyes on him, feeling static brushing the skin of his back pushing him forward. He saw that there were tire tracks on the sidewalk at the front door, wide, maybe a pickup truck. Maybe the vandals had done a burnout? Maybe it was unrelated. He got in the SUV and locked the doors. He turned the heat up. He texted Chelsea, he texted Isaac.

'Hey, what are you doing right now? I need your local expertise.' Chelsea said as she unpacked her satchel, she looked at the plywood over the window opening and thought better of it, repacking her computer.

'What's up?' Paul asked from his desk.

'We're staffing up the paid canvass for GOTV weekend. You and I need to get flyers out. We're going canvasser hunting.'

'Oh this is definitely where we need to be. This is student housing.' Paul said as they pulled into a complex. His legs were up at an awkward angle because the passenger footwell of Le's car had hundreds of pieces of lit from a variety of campaigns and other garbage piled in it.

'What makes you say that?'

'Look at the cars. They're all coupes and small four doors. A few small pickups. That's too homogenous to be anything but just college students in these apartments.'

'I hadn't noticed that, good call.'

They drove past a Mustang. 'His parents let him pick out his own car.'

grammateia: I want to see you.

g: Come up the night of the eclipse. Let's watch it together. It'll be a nice thing to share.

'Hey, so why don't we get out of here. No one else feels the need to stick around apparently.' Chelsea said, seeing that it was after eleven, 'Want to go get some breakfast before splitting for the night?'

'I know exactly where we need to go.' Paul said.

They walked into the turquoise diner and sat at a linoleum table. Above their heads greasy photos of classic cars filled the space, the frames screwed into the wall. A waitress with a blurry rose tattooed on her forearm asked them for their orders. Chelsea leaned over the table when the waitress walked away. 'I hate that when you go to a diner, for the rest of the day everyone you meet knows where you've been. How the grease clings and overpowers every other scent on you and your clothes the moment you step into one.'

'I'm going to run to the bathroom. Paul stood and went to the back of the diner. A sugarloaf shaped woman opened the unisex bathroom door as Paul approached. She and Paul made eye contact. He recognized her, but didn't say anything. He saw her walk unnoticed past the cash register, a rare enough thing, and out the glass door.[14]

He saw Jesus Saves scratched into the glass of the mirror in neat typewriter script. Finishing, he went back to the booth. Le was on her phone in a heated argument.

'Both you bitches need *after* couples counseling. Go to a therapist and learn how to stay broken up. Alright, my buddy is back, I got to go. Stop, and I mean stop, answering her texts.' Chelsea ended the call and tucked her phone away in her satchel. 'Sorry about that. My ex can't stop sleeping with her ex and calls me when she dumps her, again and again. Good friend but fucking unbearable to listen to over and over.'

'Joshua is a trip. Can you believe how he rolled up?' Chelsea said.

'He told me that trike is his year-round vehicle. He taught himself knitting to make mittens that go over the handlebars. I noticed the ball hitch. Did not expect to see it pulling a trailer with sheets of plywood and two by fours.'

'You're lucky you got a vol like that. Guys like that keep campaigns going all over the country.'

'Listen. So, ever since I received my first book report in elementary school I have always attempted to challenge the assignment.' Absentmindedly Paul wrapped his straw wrapper into a loose overhand knot and pulled it until it tore. He hoped that it would tear without knotting, the superstition said she'd be thinking about him. 'It started with a flourished

---

[14] The sugarloaf shaped woman and her graffiti come from a tossed off joke in what I think was, *The Art of Getting Over: Graffiti at the Millennium* though I can't find it now. It stuck with me and I wanted to expand on it here.

The End taking up two thirds of the third page of a three page book report and by high school adapted to where I rewrote arguments and statements so as to never cross over the second half of the last page.'

'That's very carefully orchestrated. You remember I'm your boss." Chelsea replied.

'Oh yeah, I didn't think it was a big deal telling you. It became obsessive. Just sharing. Also, I never bought a pen or pencil in college. Just by looking ahead of me while I walked I was able to pick up everything I needed off the ground.' Paul sectioned off a portion of his scrambled eggs, pushing it through the sickly sweet ketchup on the edge of his plate. Chemically, it was nearly identical to his soda. A lone cigarette sat in the red tin ashtray, thin curls of smoke rose from it, adding to the dusty atmosphere.

'That's because you're cheaper than a sparrow. I've seen that phone of yours.' Chelsea teased. 'Ketchup is like a racist joke as a condiment." Chelsea motioned towards the edge of Paul's plate. 'It's tasteless, offensive, and always comes out when white people are around. So, okay, I got something like your story. When I was in college,' Chelsea paused, 'on the first paper in every class my freshman year I added *I am in need of inserting fourteen words at this point in the narrative.* Everyone caught it and circled it or made a joke but it slipped by one professor, on the first paper. The next paper I turned in the last half was Lorem Ipsum, I did that thinking I could claim I submitted the wrong copy of my paper, that I do that to know how much I have left while working. Escaped his notice. Every paper I turned in to him after that was two introductory pages and one conclusion page wrapped around ten pages of Lorem Ipsum. He was a lecherous creep who made us buy his self-published textbook though, so I have no regrets. Freed up a lot of time for other classes too.'

'Le. How is it out there? What's going to happen?'

'Field doesn't get to know. But it's tight. McAllen's field campaign is brutal and almost all vols. We're outraising them four, five to one, up with the Republicans. We're dominating on-air. But I give more credence to field work.' She paused, 'Well obviously.'

'What about the General?'

'That's what I'm worried about. McAllen doesn't poll well against either Maxie or Maguire. I think he'd walk us into a loss.'

'Do you know what happens after the Primary? Staff?'

'My plan is to condense the regions. What you'll see is a smaller region and more staff. Not just the paid canvass but RFDs etc. Some other assignment shake ups will hit our department.' She sighed, 'But that's this work.'

'What about the RFDs you kept having report to you when you moved up? That's been somewhat odd honestly.'

'Yeah, no, you're right. It was a bad call and I should have turned them all over to you. But that'll be formalized and cleaned up after November 2.'

'Do you know the word aleatory, Le?'

'No, what's that?'

'It's used in law. Gambling, chance outcomes, are all aleatory contracts. It's tying your future to a chance outcome. That's our life.'

'Every election, it's a win loss binary that we pass through, and our options, our lives, on the other side are different because of that moment.'

'Yeah, exactly.'

'I like that.'

'What's the most powerful dream you've ever had?' Paul asked. 'One that stuck with you?'

'Oh, I don't remember. Usually by the time I'm done brushing my teeth it's forgotten. What about you?'

'I don't remember very many dreams, but there is one I've never been able to forget. In it I was a child in London and the city was under bombardment by a German air raid. My family and our neighbors ran from our house with its blackout curtains and descended into a dark Tube station bomb shelter. I sat with my family on a crude bench affixed to the wall. The lights were turned on, but flickered and I saw the tunnel walls were olive drab. A figure came down the stairs, leaning on an air raid warden. He had a gas rattle in his hand. The warden sat the old man next to me, he leaned back against the tunnel wall.' Paul paused to take a deep drag of his cigarette, knocking off the long cylinder of ash that had formed while it sat resting on the ashtray.

'The old man radiated sincerity and calm, the next thing I remembered was he wasn't leaning but sat upright with his nicked cane out ahead of him and a war-worn frayed suit on. A dust colored fedora sat on his head, he was a gentleman and no Jerry Heinkel could have rushed him. A bomb exploded on the surface as I was watching him and I recoiled in fright, the booming shock subsided and the lights returned. I looked around and saw the old man. He had been watching me and smiled, carefully he removed one gnarled hand from his cane and pointed to my clenched fists with a finger nearly doubled back on itself from arthritis. I opened them and on my palm there was a tiny doll. I looked closer and it was me the moment before, curled up with a horrified

328

expression on my face. He rolled the hand he pointed at me and opened it. On his palm lay a doll just like mine, with the old man's face contorted in screaming agony. I looked at him, incredulous, as calm as he seemed when I saw him up until it began and moments afterwards. He leaned over and I could hear his whisper over the fresh explosions. His breath smelt of stale air. He grinned so slightly I could hardly notice it and said, 'See how silly all of us look in the moment we are about to die?' Paul paused, dragging on his cigarette. 'I've thought about that dream often and I want to believe that that old man was God.'

Chelsea looked at Paul and said, 'Christ, and you wonder why the union guys don't like you. Do you talk like that all the time? Have you been to England?'

'Used to spend summers there, my grandmother is British and my dad is as well. Both immigrants. My mom and dad met when she was back visiting family.'

'Well not real immigrants. Right? Like, they're not Hispanic.'

'We've had to do the same paperwork, the wrong administration and we're fucked too. But yeah, people say that a lot.'

'I want you to come down midstate this week for a fundraiser. You deserve a night at the top, and we need people wearing suits looking tough and capable. Get a suit and practice your face.'

At 11:58 p.m. Henry Canfield, (54 years old. No Permanent Residence, No Known Occupation. Born in Perry County, Kentucky April 9, 1950. One son, Timothy Bauer, estranged.) succumbed to his injuries in the ICU of the regional Medical

College. His remains were transferred to the County Coroner (elected position) and the office of the County Prosecutor (elected position) was notified, where the junior prosecutor assigned to the case updated the charging documents on his assailants. His body would be held at the morgue for a set time in order to allow family to claim it. This won't happen, and they will be cremated and placed in an urn at a municipally funded wall in the city cemetery.

Prank

→1 ↓3

'Hey guys, I was talking with Stephen this afternoon and he had a great idea. We're going to do some street theater at the protest.' Albert said at the nightly meeting.

'What is that going to look like?' Carrie asked.

Albert nodded his head as he replied. 'Rush Limbaugh said something recently, that Abu Ghraib was no worse than hazing. Like, it's a fraternity prank. Stephen's thinking basing a skit around that. Like *TORTURE U* cheerleading uniforms and foam core masks of the administration neocons, It's pretty great stuff.'

'That sounds fucking awesome.' She said.[15]

---

[15] This is real and too good as-is to fictionalize. All credit to Jeff Grubler and his group *The Ronald Reagan Home for the Criminally Insane*. It's his skit, he ran it at J20 protest and elsewhere.

name recognition

→3 ↓4

Paul stood in an oak paneled room. The walls were fes-
tooned with framed photos of the home's family members
shaking hands with dozens of notable people; a tenth, maybe,
were recognizable to Paul. Decades were documented there.
Among them were awards, plaques, letters of recognition
and all sorts of ways organizations say *Thanks!* The I Love
Me room, and a good example of one – a picture of it maybe
hanging on some meta brag wall on a higher plane. He picked
up a glass egg, metallic Pyrex glinted, swirled inside. A
sandblasted dedication on the base named it as an award for
Woman of the Year 1993 from a civic organization with a name
so general as to be unidentifiable.

'You, put down what you're stealing. I'm reporting you, you
bastard.'

'Hey Max.' Paul turned and saw Max at the door with an
overweight beagle sniffing the air next to him. Paul set the
award down carefully on the shelf.

'Have you seen our candidate? He's got a speech and no one
can find him.'

'No, I haven't been in the main areas.'

'Okay, keep an eye out for him, it's important. You know, you're a lucky chump. I'm sorry you had to be here, but the host wouldn't do this without senior staff present. Just sweat if you want me to tell you how to look like one. You get to see the good parts though! What do you think of this place? See that shotgun? Thing is like six grand. I bet it has never been shot.' He sat down his tumbler and took the shotgun down from the wall and broke open the action. 'Yeah, I think that's the case, don't really know what I'm looking for here. This thing has more leaves and shrubbery carved on it than are in the front yard. She bought this estate to blast away at rabbits and upland game birds like true landed gentry but didn't have the heart to do it. Anyone tell you about this place?'

'No, Le told me some of it. Mostly said I was here to help fill out our presence.'

'Well I'll give you the dish.' Max noticed a hidden door and teased it open with his fingernails. He peeked inside, it was a tiny closet and the audiovisual nexus for the entire house sat within. 'The host, Edward, lived here with his mother until last year when she passed. She was a real sweetheart. All she wanted was to be thought well of.' He shut the door carefully. 'And she raised gobs of money for the party. Raising money, that's a quick way to go about being remembered fondly. Didn't really care much about her husbands though, they came and went. She left one around here, according to legend. The box of ashes came back from the funeral home, she set it aside and forgot about it. Was going to scatter the ashes somewhere. She had a standing reward payable to any guest who could find it. It led to a lot of otherwise decent people rummaging in closets, but that may have been her having fun. How many people would you say are here?'

'I don't know. Go out and count the legs, divide by two. That'll get you close.'

At Max's feet the beagle farted noisily. Max looked down. 'It's the old lady's dog. He keeps doing that. I don't know what they feed him here. He might be filching cat food. He won't leave me alone. And I can't just blame the dog when it happens. It's too obvious.' Max sighed and gently nudged the dog away from him with the side of his shoe as he hung the shotgun up. It farted as it was being pushed and sidled back to him, leaning against his leg. 'Oh for fucks sake. I have donors to talk to.'

'I'll sit with him.'

'Try. I tried to lock him in another room, but he found his way out and tracked me down.' Max made for the door. Quicker than either expected the beagle bolted and got there with him, nearly tripping Max. 'Goddamnit,' he muttered as the door closed. Paul followed out of the trophy room, wandering down the passage. He'd been told to be around, but stay out of the way and not engage with anyone beyond formalities. Music came from ahead, a waltz or something. Violins going slow. Buzzy, an old tape. He turned into the room, nearly empty. Three clusters of people stood around the ballroom, talking. Max in one, the beagle leaning against his leg. The murmur of dozens of conversations filtered from upstairs, where the main crowd was, people drifted out of the reception area into the rest of the house, but it was largely empty aside from catering staff and guests who were tired of small talk. Campaign staff stood out in this crowd. Even the higher-ups. Like bleached, ironed, and carefully folded dish rags; dishevelledness hung on them beyond the reach of any effort. Paul had dressed up - as best he could, on clear orders

- but felt ratty around the edges when he saw the caterers, a feeling that only grew when he saw the guests and host. He made his way towards the hors-d'oeuvres table, attempting to remain unremarked. A young dark-haired woman stood there, regarding the bruschetta suspiciously. She looked familiar to Paul but he didn't follow the thought.

'It's October, tomatoes.' she said. She wore crème yellow, a ball gown of some sort that fell to the floor. Threads hung loose from the seams.

'I'm sorry?' Paul picked up a small plate and tiny fork, looking at his options. Meatballs in brown gravy - a staple at fundraisers that Paul had grown to covet - were absent. They were far too pedestrian for this ensemble.

'It's October and there are tomatoes all over this table. How far do you think they traveled to get here? I bet they taste like diesel exhaust. Which could be fine, but that should be listed on the card. Tomate d'échappement.'

Paul stood, lost for words, as he tried to come up with anything to say.

'Don't bother.'

'Don't bother?'

'Don't bother trying to be clever. Not what I was looking for. Just talking to myself and you walked up.' She placed several roasted mushrooms on her plate, and questioned the smoked eggs. 'You should try the pâté, it's grovelingly decadent. Not totally unlike mid-range oysters.' She took a slice of smoked egg, but didn't seem happy about it. 'I have quite a lot of hope for the anchovy butter on these mushrooms, and someone will hear about it if I'm disappointed.' Paul filled his plate and moved towards the trophy room, to hide. He ran directly into her, knocking the plate from her hand. He heard a ripping sound, the tulle of her dress was under his foot. 'Oh non, mon amuse-bouche!' The plate scattered the food on the floor, and spun down in smaller circles. A waiter came over to clean it up. 'I just met you and you're making me frown.' She snatched the plate from Paul's hand and set it on the table, then gestured for him to follow as she walked towards the hallway. 'I don't get to eat, you don't get to eat.'

'I'm so sorry!'

'Don't worry about it. I'll staple the fabric back up. No drama. What's your name and occupation?'

'I'm Paul, I'm staff, for the campaign. You remind me of someone I know. What about you?'

'Terrible, terrible. I don't suggest opening with that. An ex, perhaps, close friend you are afraid to pursue? I hear it all the time. Got *cousin* once and I'm terrified to unpack that.' They walked down the hall. 'I'm Lily. Occupation: on leave from university to volunteer on this glorious Senate campaign.'

'Where are we going?'

'To smoke. You've got cigarettes on you.'

'Do I smell like them?'

'No, it's a nine out of ten chance with campaign staff.'

'Are you staff?'

'No, I'm here with my dad, Tom.'

'Tom who?'

'Sexton, your candidate.'

'Oh, oh that Tom.' Paul's heart sunk. Her face crystallized in his memory from thousands of lit pieces he'd distributed of Sexton standing with his family. 'Yeah, I work on the campaign.' He paused, groping for something to say. 'He's doing well.'

'Yeah, his name recognition is tops.' She opened the glass

door onto the patio. 'Don't worry, I'm just going to tease you about it, won't repeat it to anyone. Had my fill of gossip on this campaign. I swear on a hastily produced filter cigarette.'

Paul handed over a cigarette and she flicked her thumb in the standard *Light too?* gesture. The door opened behind them, Chelsea peeked out. 'Paul.' she whispered. 'Oh, hey, Lily.'

'Hey Chels.' Lily said, Chelsea grimaced.

'Paul, I need you in here.'

Paul stubbed out his just-lit cigarette in a potted plant and went inside, leaving Lily on the patio. Chelsea stood with Congressman Sexton, holding his elbow. Paul was shocked, Sexton had been concealed from view on the patio behind the wall.

'Paul!' Sexton's voice was smooth, gracious, and inviting. Nothing like the high strung twit he'd met. 'Good to see you again. We need you in Northwest, it's the most important part of the state.'

'Hello, sir. Thank you.'

'Paul, I need your help.' Chelsea pleaded. Sexton, ignored, said *Yes son, good job* and looked around, his eyes sparkling in the light. 'Something's wrong, he's *on* and I don't know what to do. I just took him by the arm and this happened. He'll go anywhere I lead.'

'Le, he's... He's right here.'

'No he's not. Look.' She turned him around her in a circle. He beamed at Paul when he was pointed back at him. 'He's gone Beltway on us. Can't you see it? He remembered your name, man! Has that ever happened before? It's this fucking elbow.' She pointed where she was holding his arm.

'Can you let him go?' Paul asked.

Lily opened the door behind them. 'Hey Tommy.'

337

'lil' Lil, you should call your daddy, Dad. Give him a kiss though.' She pecked him on the cheek. Photographers could check their white balance on his smile.

'Hi Lily,' Chelsea was sweating, trying to back away. Sexton backed away beside her, smiling.

'Lily, can we have a minute?'

She winked and walked to the trophy room. 'Let me know when you want my help.'

'I can't just let him go. He'll go back to who he is and fire me.' Her palm sweat made a spreading dark spot on the elbow of Sexton's jacket.

'Chelsea, ONE, we can't be having this conversation here. Senior staff is everywhere.'

'I know that Paul, because *I'm* senior staff. I have an idea. I'll shove him through a door and close it behind him. He'll come to and won't see me.'

Paul considered this. It actually sounded like it'd work. 'That actually sounds like it'd work.'

'It better, I've had an hour to come up with it.'

'An hour?'

'An hour. Maybe an hour. It's felt like an hour.'

'No one's confronted you?'

'We were hiding. I stood out on the lawn with him, there's a garden out there with shrubbery that conceals it from the house.'

Paul blinked, his brain catching up.

'Look, I panicked! I also got overwhelmed by the power and...'

'And?'

'Walked him around a bit. Out to the road and back. He shook hands with a raccoon.'

Both their cell phones buzzed, Paul pulled his phone out. It was a text from Max. 'It says SEXTON EMERGENCY WE NEED TO FIND HIM All caps no punctuation. Trophy room, now.'

Chelsea and Paul hustled the few steps to the door. Sexton, beside them, strode pridefully in league eating steps. Paul closed the door behind them. Lily pointed the shotgun at them.

'Lil, now,' Sexton's sonorous voice, tinged with good-natured humor, 'That's a beautiful firearm, mid Twentieth Century English field gun.' he was slowing and building to a crescendo, '28 gauge. *Craftsmanship. Real craftsmanship. The kind that we can-*'

'Pew pew. Quiet Daddy.' His voice tapered off and he glanced around the room, taking in all of the artifacts, linking each one to an effective and charming anecdote. She slung the shotgun up over her shoulder.

'Can you help us?' Paul asked.

'Yeah, this is nothing to worry about. His roommate discovered this in college. Passed the secret to my Mom, made him into the man he is today.' She tilted her head over to one side. 'We like to think this is the real him, and the hot mess he is otherwise is something else. None of the DC staff told you about this?'

'College is something every American parent should be able to hope for for their chi-'

'Shut up, Daddy.'

'That's my girl.' Sexton winked at her. There was an audible ping.

'No, I don't know what we're dealing with here.' Chelsea's face was red, sweat beading. She was panicking.

'Oh yeah, I remember. There are national security implications or something. The reason the NSA keeps him off the juicy committees. Or is it *on* the juicy committees?' Lily shrugged. Heavy footsteps sounded outside the door.

'AV closet, behind you.' Paul tapped the hidden door, and grabbed Sexton by the shoulder. 'Hold on to him!' Chelsea followed him into the closet, shutting it behind them.

Lily tossed the shotgun to Paul who caught it, leveled at Lily's waist, as Max opened the door.

'Lily, hello.'

'Hey, a million.' She leaned over to Paul, 'Everyone else shortens his name to Max, I prefer the other part – A Million. It's far more specific.'

'What are you doing screwing around in here?' Max took in the scene. 'ARE you screwing around in here? Are you being menaced? Paul, keep the gun on her. Most people don't think to just after meeting her to their detriment. You're a fast learner. I'm asking you what you're doing here. Did you get my text?'

'I was showing him my sweet new kicks.' Lily lifted up her dress slightly, sticking out a robin's egg blue and white hightop trainer. 'Well? What do you think?'

'You look like a cake in that dress.' Paul said.

'Fair enough.'

'Paul,' Max gave Lily a whole kraken of side eye. 'We can't find Sexton and it's getting weird out there. The donors are getting restless. We've got everyone looking for the Congressman. Have you seen Chelsea? Jamie is apoplectic. Walter and Gina from Finance are running around. Anyway, as charming as Lily can be, I need you looking for Thomas. Start in the bathrooms on this floor. Hell, he might be in a closet somewhere.'

'Crudités?' Lily said. An aside to Paul, 'I went back to the table.'

Max sighed, 'That wasn't anything veiled, just hyperbole. I'm freaking out a bit.'

'No no. Crudités, raw veggies. Want some? I made a plate.' She proffered a plate of sliced cucumber, carrot, and celery. She took one and munched on it, looking at Paul.

'Anyway. You've got orders. Keep me up to date.' Max slammed the door behind him. Paul opened the closet door.

'There's no handle in there.' Chelsea said, dazed. 'Bit, pho-bic, of hot, tiny rooms with no handles and bosses spouting aphorisms. Never knew that.'

'I don't know Latin, otherwise I'd tell you what that phobia is.' Lily waved the plate in small circles at Chelsea.

'You said you can help us get out of this?' Chelsea asked.

'Yes. Oh, that smell.' The beagle was scratching plaintively, whimpering, at the door to be let out. Paul opened the door a crack so it could go find Max. It ran, cropdusting, after him.

'We need to get coffee in him. Hot, fresh, coffee. Otherwise he won't wake up right.'

'Wait, we had an idea.' Paul explained.

'That actually sounds like it'd work too.' Lily said, after considering it.

'No issues with not waking up right?'

'Eh, screw it. Let's find a door and shove him through!'

'*We'll stand on a threshold. Together, looking forward. Our choices open bef -*'

'Shut up, Daddy. I'm fine with it being a second floor balcony if you keep it up.'

'Oh, Lily.' Grin, flash off the tooth like a camera bulb.

Paul opened the door. Max was walking back towards him,

he stepped out into the hall and closed the door quickly behind him.

'Lets smoke. C'mon.' Max opened the door to the patio and walked out onto the lawn. He stood smoking when Paul caught up to him. Paul walked over the closely trimmed grass and stood next to him silently. Max took a drag as the mingled sounds of jazz music and conversations seeped out of the house. The beagle, now laying at Max's feet, farted in its sleep. The exertion made it shift. It groaned softly and farted.

'So Paul, this is a good evening to talk about motivations. Is it not?' Max asked.

'Aren't we looking for the Congressman?' Paul shrugged, looking at the periodic lights marking transmission towers and other structures around the horizon.

'Fuck him. He'll turn up, we got money out as chum.' Max looked at his glass. 'Rosé wine. Boat people drink this stuff, nobody likes boat people.'

'How'd you get it?'

'Standard route. Bottle via bartender. They're out of everything better. I'm told that in spite of all evidence, it is filled with alcohol.' He took a drink 'So, anyway, I went to high school in Arizona. One thing about Arizona, one of many, is their disregard for Daylight Savings Time. I don't think that they have ever participated in it. That taught me that even time is a political decision. Now here I am.' He gestured expansively. The beagle farted itself awake. It shook its head, stood on its short legs and began sniffing around. Maxed looked at it and regarded his entire career and where a flatulent, elderly, supposed hunting dog would enter into it.

'Dmitry Belyaev could give you a more effective dog in twenty generations.' Paul gestured at the animal. It languidly wagged its tail and rubbed its face on the grass. Max grunted in assent. 'Going to go back in, see what I can find.'

'Yeah, solid. I'll be right in, going to circle the house.'

They walked down the long downstairs rear hallway to the back stairs. Paul in front, followed by Chelsea/Tom, then Lily with her crudités. Empty, this hallway led to the garage, a back bathroom, and some rooms used for storage of seasonal decorations. Each season had its own room. Just before the stair was another hallway. 'I can go ahead and scout it out?' Lily offered.

'Let's stick together Daphne.'

'Okay Velma.'

'Are you sure we're okay from Max?' Chelsea asked.

'Yeah, he seemed zoned out. I think he'll be a while.'

Paul turned the corner, Jamie walking towards him. She waved and called out to him. Chelsea shoved Sexton into SUMMER and attempted to look nonchalant with her hand inside the room. Lily stood in front of her, blocking as best she could. She didn't attempt to look nonchalant, she was the personification of it, she was ur-nchalant. Cool was a hyper little brother listening to all the music she listened to while going through school living under the reputation she'd left with the teachers. She nibbled on a carrot stick.

'Lily.' Jamie nodded, conveying that it was an effort.

'Veggies? They're nearly room temperature.'

'No.' She was finished talking at the candidate's daughter. She looked at her staff, 'You two know what's going on?' Lily began humming *Allison* by Elvis Costello in the only way it could be hummed at a person, aggressively. Jamie shot her a

343

dirty look.

'Yeah, we're looking for the Congressman. Enlisted Lily to help. Where do you need him?' Chelsea was brief. Paul noted her *business voice*, the one she adopted on phone calls, was now in play. She was a pro.

'Upstairs, in the main reception room. The host is stalling. Find him and get him up there. He was supposed to be on ten minutes ago.' She looked at Lily, then at Chelsea, 'I'll check in with you later. Just, good luck.' She left down the hallway, knocking on the door to the bathroom, saying *Thomas?* and going in. As soon as she was out of sight, Chelsea yanked Sexton out of the storage room. He wore a straw sun hat with an oversized brim and cheap beach-stand sunglasses. Under his free arm was a grayed cardboard box with cancelled postage on it. Unopened. Paul remembered what Max had said about husbands left around.

'Summer. *IS* America.'

'Oh for fucks' sake.' The three of them said at once, 'Shut up, Thomas.' He smiled at them in turn. They took everything off of him and tossed most of it back in the room. Paul hung on to the box.

'Alright, we just need to go up those stairs, down one hallway.' Chelsea closed her eyes, 'And there's a door right behind where the front table is. This is perfect. We have a reason to be walking him there. Right?'

'I don't want to be seen or connected to this.' Paul said.

'That's a good point. Still operating on shove him in and run.'

'Let's go!' Lily led the way, getting in front of a caterer at the top of the steps and distracting him with a confusing thirty step dance on which way they would pass one another. Paul and Chelsea/Tom walked around them, the poor caterer so discombobulated by Lily he didn't see them. They were there, the door ahead, in the stretch. The three of them were carried along in the moment. They stood at the door, hallway clear in both directions.

'Chelsea,' Paul asked as they were walking, 'am I the only person on staff that didn't know Lily before this evening?'

'I mean, her face is on pretty much every piece of lit.' They stood at the door, hallway clear in both directions.

'We can't just *shove* him in.' Chelsea said, slowing as she spoke, considering how effectively she wanted to protest the idea, 'What if he falls down?'

'We are committed to this course of action, Le. It is time to move, Lily can only keep people distracted for,' Paul looked back, where he saw the caterer still twisting and turning, 'probably a really long time. But come on.'

'*America. When we commit to action, we follow through. A reliable friend and a worrisome enemy.*'

'What he said.' Paul hitched a thumb at Sexton.

'I'm riding this until the vine lets out. I'm ready.'

Max opened the door in front of them. 'Oh fuck you, you found him. You're the best Le. I owe you.' Max took Sexton firmly by the elbow and walked him into the room to applause. He beamed at the crowd.

Hurt

→2 ↓1

October 21

A cold drizzle dripped from the nicotine stained concrete sky. Sarah watched the Crew dress, pulling the inexpensive sweatshirts over their heads. She helped tape down the foam rubber that Carrie had wrapped around herself so she could be Rush Limbaugh and smoked a 'slave rolled' cigarette that one of the Billionaires for Bush had given Her. Carrie looked absurd and waddled in circles, trying to pick up the pom poms that were part of her costume. Her thighs were bound together by the foam. As the prisoner in the skit Sarah felt uneasy, nagging at her was the thought that she was parodying the man and his suffering, referencing it but standing separate. She wore the black poncho and hood of the Abu Ghraib prisoner over flesh toned tights, necessary in the unseasonably chill air. Albert held her hand as she stepped atop the crate, blind to all and alone within the crowd. The dance music sounded around her and she heard people cheering her and her friends on as Republicans turned into the parking lot. She shivered and whispered apologies to the man she was portraying. She raised her arms away from her body as the Beach Boys sang.

'Fuck this,' She dropped to the ground and stripped off the bodysuit, just her bralette and underwear under the poncho and hood, all black. Her tattoos flashed, uncovered. The wind bit into her skin and she redonned the poncho and hood. She quickly mounted the crate; hoping this would horrify those supporters driving in, that her pain would affect them deeper than any of the protest signs and chants. That something would reach them. As the SUVs and luxury cars slowed to turn into the parking lot they would have enough time to examine the person on the crate, and she hoped to be their nightmare. Her friends danced on with their backs to her, oblivious. Albert watched from where he stood by the boombox but did not interfere. The cheering from other protesters diminished. She had turned the goofy spectacle to a grotesquery worthy of Poe. She added the element that it needed. Inside now in the cold dark her iliocostalis muscle spasmed, jerking her right foot off the crate. The protesters began chanting 'Bush is a Joke! He did too much Coke!' A cutting edge came out in the new round of chants around her. Her shoulders inadvertently pulled towards one another. The cut ends of the wires Sarah held out at arms length dug into Her fingertips as her hands reflexively tightened. Tears hung on her face in the darkness, she shivered and her limbs convulsed by inches. She felt the Danse Macabre.

Hands pulled at her, the singing had ended and voices had replaced it. She heard Albert's voice, he was denying to someone that he'd put her up to it. Carrie had taken off her oversized mask and with one hand removed the hood She wore. She squinted against the sunlight.

'Are you okay? Sarah?' Carrie held her arms, concern on her face. Carrie was rubbing her biceps. 'Get some clothes on.' The police officer standing next to Carrie watched her quizzically, saying nothing. He pressed unopened heat packs into her hands.

'Thank you.' She whispered.

The first officer said to Albert, 'You can be out here, do whatever you gotta do. But that can't go on, do you understand?'

A murmur went through the crowd. Cheney's motorcade was nearing. The police moved away, the Crew stood in groups of two and three discussing the next go with the skit. She sat up and looked in the direction that people were focusing on. He'd come right by them, turn just ahead. She eyed distances. She saw Stephen, he hadn't put back on the Alberto Gonzalez mask. They made eye contact, a knowing smile grew on Stephen's face. 'What do you think Carrie, steal their seconds, right?' Timing, seeing the roofs of the lead SUVs now. 'Steal enough of their seconds from enough of them and they can't meet, can't make decisions that don't include us but affect us.' Carrie watched as she stood up, holding the black hood in her hands. She ran towards the road.

12:53 p.m. Carrie Catherine
  <She ran in front of the Motorcade. She's hurt, and arrested. I'm trying to find wehre they've taken Her.>

12:54 p.m. Carrie Catherine
  <The event was canceled. Cheney got banged up when the limo swerved.>

12:54 p.m. Carrie Catherine
  <Bravest fucking thing I've ever seen.>

Dozens of volunteers, from all parties and for nearly all of the races on the ballot, crowded the entrance ramp leaving downtown. They began arriving at three to human billboard, by four thirty they'd halved, halved, and halved again, crowding together, so the back of their hands were scratched by the signs their neighbors held. They thought they were doing some of the most important work of the campaign. Sharp elbows meant preferred sightlines were taken by tougher volunteers. Sexton volunteers that wouldn't do any direct voter contact were sent to the line to hold three foot by five foot supersigns and wave at cars. Today, an old green hardtop Jeep came to a halt in the parking lot across from the crowd. Three men got out and pulled worn Democratic candidate supersigns from the back, one for a candidate who wasn't on the ballot. They scanned the crowd and saw the Sexton volunteers. They walked diagonally across the street, dragging the signs behind them. Cars slammed on their brakes and honked. They posted up in front of the Sexton volunteers, blocking them. The Sexton volunteers moved, the second crew shifted to block them. One Sexton volunteer asked for some space, thinking it was unintentional. The heavy turned and told him to fuck off. The volunteer walked backwards and went to the end of the crowd, still thinking it was an escalation of the normal fight for space. The heavy followed him. The volunteer, frightened now, held up one hand, palm out, holding the sign with his other hand. It see-sawed in the wind. The crowd of volunteers were watching now. The heavy stood in front of the volunteer, facing him, holding the sign to block his face. 'Alright man, whatever your fucking problem is I'm out of here.' The heavy shoved him with both hands, he stumbled and caught his balance, the signs they were holding lost and sliding into traffic. Volunteers ran over and pulled them apart. The Sexton volunteers, scared, took off for their office.

'No. No one got a plate number. They didn't have one on their truck.' Paul said into his cell. 'He's going to be fine, rattled.. He's pretty bruised. When the pushing started the others came in. The other two vols are here and they're scared. I closed the phonebank and sent everyone home.' he listened, 'No, yeah. The police did come, but our people were on their way back here. I got a call from someone I know down there. I don't know if they're coming here, it was forty five minutes ago now so I don't think so.' 'Yeah, they walked, our office is right down the street from where it happened.' he listened, 'I asked them to write down statements' Paul paused, 'Just something I learned a long time ago, to write down what you remember right away.' pause, 'Thank you I was going to try to get Corey,' pause, 'Yeah he's the vol that got jumped. I want to ask him to write down a statement too. Okay, I'll stay here until you arrive. Thank you Steve. Sir. Mr. Foliot. Sorry.' Paul hung up.

Entered Data

↓3 ↑2

Paul checked the address posted in wrought iron over the door, this had to be her apartment. The building was built in the late 1800s as a luxury hotel. It never opened, sat vacant and was converted, and converted again. Finally to small apartments. It was nearing ten, Steve had driven straight from his house in Delaware, north of Columbus. Still nearly eight when he got to the office. He'd thanked and relieved Paul, indicating he should go. Paul didn't get it but left him with an extra key and drove towards Michigan. He rung up and waited at the bottom of the steps for her to come down. He walked back down to the sidewalk and sniffed his armpits and debated whether he should have a cigarette. He'd been at work since six that morning. All that time, he marveled, Chloe was an hour away. He sighed, knowing that tomorrow he would have to chase wherever HQ told him to go in their attempt to settle the matter. He felt ill. He looked sallow and peaked from the stress he was under. At Carrie's prompting he'd texted Her and She had agreed to meet up, seemed excited but Paul wasn't sure if he was reading into a few lines. Regardless, not until the weekend, and it'd been weeks since she dropped by unannounced.

The fox was staring at the hound before he knew she was there. He looked up and Chloe was standing next to the mailboxes for the building, watching him. The local college sweatshirt was many sizes too large, coming down nearly to her knees and her legs were bare under it. She walked noiselessly down the steps, but said nothing. From her neighbor's open window Paul could hear *One Love* by Bob Marley playing. Chloe stopped in front of Paul and waited for him to speak, nerves shimmering the air around her. To Paul she was absolutely magnetic, everything that genes and instinct scream at a man to attempt to impregnate at the earliest possible moment. He felt like his body was made of iron filings and he was being pulled to shape around her. 'I'm Paul.' Paul whispered, afraid that she would shoo him away if he spoke too loud.

'You really drove all this way.' She didn't seem to believe it. She hadn't taken her eyes off him at all, she was trying to decide if he was crazy or not. Who knows which one she hoped for? Paul stared.

'It's just an hour. I'm glad I did. I wish I had sooner.'

'Now was the right time to. Earlier wouldn't have been.' They had never exchanged any photos, indeed Chloe would have stopped conversing with Paul if he had asked, and everything she had put online was heavily Photoshopped with lenses and distortions added. Some of Paul's friends do that, the same reason they fill their profiles with quotes from other people – to hide their mediocrity. She was beautiful though. And seemed to have nothing to say but her own thoughts.

'Well, I wanted to meet you. I had the night off.' The boy said lamely.

'Have you eaten?' She walked back up the stairs, holding the door open for him to follow. Chloe led Paul to her apartment, 4C. The stairway was a mix of work and modifications from over a hundred and twenty years, all done cheaply. Her apartment – just one room – was small. Originally the main sitting room for a suite, now half of the original space because the landlord wanted to squeeze as much money off of the college in town as possible and put a stud wall across it to make two. It was just one room with a kitchen boxed in the front door and a bathroom accessed through a closet. They sat down on the loveseat at the foot of Chloe's bed and after a few false starts their conversation really got underway, when they both realized that the person they'd been talking to nearly anonymously online was sitting in front of them. We'll pick up at a moment where Chloe is speaking.

'Well, before I decide to date anyone I make them read *The Crying of Lot 49.* Whether or not they think Trystero is real determines how much time I'll spend with them. I see it as my *Pass this get access* test.'

'That's a pretty slim book, not something like *House of Leaves*, though I think just handing that to somebody would present a clear insight on how determined they are to spend time with you.' Paul opines.

'Ah, true, I would never get in anybody's pants. Would you like to watch a movie? Go pick one out.'

Paul crouches in front of her movie collection. "Have you seen *Adaptation* recently?' He

mispronounces the title as *Adaption*. Normally Chloe would have tallied a strike against him, but smiles instead.

Paul glanced back at Chloe. She was sitting cross-legged on her couch with the hood of the oversized sweatshirt she was wearing pulled up and her hands tucked into the pocket. So

353

still, symmetrical, patient. She looked steadily back at him.

'No I haven't.' She answered.

He puts in the movie and sits down on the couch. Chloe moves to lean against him, putting her arm through his. 'Televisions are transitory, early attempts to make them look like furniture were ill-conceived because they're meant to be swapped out when they become outdated and replaced. So we live with plastic. But here we are, staring at this television, but it's not aesthetically pleasing. Just designed to disappear until I buy another which will be designed to disappear. But there's always a place set aside for them.'

'What's that cloth?' Paul pointed at a large patchwork blue and brown cloth Chloe had hanging. It was nearly as tall as the wall and three or four feet wide. It hung on a frame of canvas just larger than it was.

'Boro. It's rare. It's indigo cloth from Japan. Seventy, eighty years old, I think. Before the war things were repaired, mended over generations, so they ended up looking like that. It's a futon cover, I think. It's so beautiful. How the mendings create something so sublime. They're art. Art made by generations of people. It's not utilitarian, it's more. After the war new things were so easily accessible from the West this practice ended. I stretched the canvas and sewed it on myself.' Paul looked impressed. 'Not that big a deal. Painters build our canvasses. Though I'm thinking of getting into panels. Lot cheaper. Can get plywood cut down at the hardware store.' Before even the point in the movie where Chris Cooper explains to an actor portraying a Park Ranger the intricacies of the law in relation to Seminole Indians, Paul is simply watching Chloe watch the movie. Paul wanted to kiss Chloe, but didn't know if that would be reciprocated or if

354

he was reading too much into friendly intimacy. Impulsively he turned towards her and blew on her hair - making a soft *puh* sound. Chloe turned to him. 'That was totally glaucoma test.' Paul kisses her. She puts her hand on the back of his head and kisses him back.

After a few moments, Paul slid his arm out from hers and wraps it around behind her, pulling her closer. A few moments more and he slides his hand from where it was on her waist up the side of her body. Realizing then that she wasn't wearing anything under the hooded sweatshirt.

'I just got off work when you called, I didn't have time to really change.' Chloe said, embarrassed.

'I think the Trystero organization is a fiction, in the universe of the book. Do I pass?'

'Not under normal circumstances. Perhaps you have thought of constructing an elaborate maze of riddles to torment an ex-lover after your death? Perhaps?'

Though both soon took part in an act that would have, under alternate circumstances, caused a zygote to form within a few hours from the combination of an egg cell from Chloe and a spermatozoon from Paul. This was avoided and they were not stricken with a **Big Decision** in a few months because Chloe was on the pill and hadn't missed her dose earlier that afternoon, while Paul was sending cheerful volunteers who wouldn't do anything else out to human billboard next to an expressway on-ramp in northern Ohio. While Paul was unbuttoning his pants Chloe pushed Paul's face away gently and said 'I don't normally do this.' Paul smiled, not sure if she was serious or protecting herself. Both of the Republicans who were vying for their party's nomination in the Senate race would have rolled their eyes and condemned the acts that were occurring for numerous reasons. That it happened outside of Ohio would probably not be one of them. And their condemnation would probably have gained them some votes in important areas of the state.

As they lay on the bed, she answers his silent question as he traced the faint lines on her body. 'I've always had them. There's not really any name for them unless it's tied to worse outcomes. Chimerism, Mosaicism.'

The Republican platform has no mention of dermatological rarities like this. there are no votes to be won amongst important conservative demographics.

'What do they mean?' Paul asked quietly.

'Nothing really, just a quirk of my skin. An ex called them my *tiger stripes*. My pediatrician told my parents that I might have had a twin, one that fused with me.'

'You're more than one person?'

'In a way.'

'You're so beautiful.'

Chloe just looked at him. She said nothing but kissed him on the mouth. She cried a little, though Paul wanted to have sex again she softly rebuffed him.

Paul saw the time on her phone, laying flat beside the bed. 'I think we're getting to the main part of the eclipse, do you want to go watch it?" Paul asked her.

'When does it peak?'

'Not for another half hour I think.'

'Well, lay here, are you hungry? I'll make you something.'

'Don't cook on my account. I'll eat if you're hungry.'

Naked, she left the bed and walked across the room to the kitchen. 'I don't have much, some carrots.'

He leaned over the counter and watched the muscles in her

back move as she prepared baby carrots and chopped green onions in honey, reaching up to put the bowl in her microwave.

'This is my favorite dish.' Chloe said, 'I only make it for myself.'

'You don't have any of your prog rock paintings here? I kind of expected to see them.'

'All locked up at my studio. Have to do it, keep it compart-mentalized or it'll overwhelm me.' On her refrigerator Chloe had a picture of a man doing a cartwheel on a snow covered street. His smile was the kind that stretched out without going up, so even upside-down it was wide and happy. Paul was staring at it. 'That doesn't reflect anything. That's Jack. He isn't as sweet or spontaneous as you might believe from looking at that.' She tipped her head towards the photo to indicate it. 'It's a lie. Photos are not to be trusted. They don't record anything but a fraction of the light in a tiny window. What he's thinking, the events that led us there, where we would go. None of that is captured.' She looked at Paul. 'What's She like? Your girlfriend?'

'You watch the news?'

'Some.'

'You may have seen Her then. The protester that interrupted the Vice President's motorcade.'

'Her? Wow. She's tough. And really pretty.'

'I don't want to talk about either of these two with you. Not now.' Paul chewed the soft carrots slowly. 'This is really, really good. I think it's my new favorite dish. Thank you for making it.' Chloe walked out of the kitchen. He handed her the bowl. Steam passed backwards out of the bowl cupped in her hands, up over her faintly striped breasts as she walked to the loveseat. Paul walked to the french doors and drew the curtain aside a small amount. Looking up he said to her, 'The moon is a tiny sliver, kind of reddish on one side. Kind of interesting.'

'Oh, then the best part is close.' She responded. 'Let's put the loveseat on my balcony.' Naked, Chloe opens the french doors, as wide as the balcony was, and quickly brings her sole deck chair inside and drags the lemon tree she had in a five gallon plant pot there, rolling it instead of picking it up. Paul picks up the loveseat and walks it over, it barely fit in the opening. 'Searched all over town for one that would fit.' She walked to the bed and pulled the comforter off. Paul climbed over the back of the loveseat, Chloe after and over him, pulling the down comforter and arranging it so they were covered. 'This is all I want, my little pod here. I'd have groceries delivered if someone would do it.' she cuddled into Paul, 'I love the internet. It's so much better online with all of human knowledge available to me. Finding people all over the world, even as far as an hour away.' she smiled at the night. They spooned and watched the sky over the bright sodium lamps below. The neighbor downstairs was still playing Bob Marley, other songs and conversations could be heard, quieter, from other apartments. Overhead the moon went dark for a moment, then glowed a dull copper.

They have sex again during totality. Barely moving. They lay for a long time afterwards.

They dress. As they are walking out *Redemption Song* comes through the tightly closed door in the first floor hallway. 'It doesn't ever stop.' Chloe shrugged. They walk to a boat dock at the end of the street. In the pond a family of ducks paddles aimlessly near shore, ignoring the two invaders.

'I only smoke Parliaments. And then, only rarely.' She put two in her mouth and lit them

together, handing one to Paul.

'Thank you.'

'I learned that from Jerry Durrance.' Chloe quipped.

'Who's that?' Paul looked down from the moon.

Holding her cigarette delicately Chloe kissed Paul on the mouth, 'Sweetheart, if you weren't so very adorable.'

The night was chilly, the boy and girl pulled one another close as they sat on the worn wooden dock. *hm hm hm* Chloe mewed melodically as she nestled into Paul's arm. 'So what does your tattoo mean?'

'It's the cover of a book by Hemmingway. The bull almost always dies. But that is due to

the system. The bull learns quickly and given a few minutes would certainly kill the matador. I got that a couple years ago when I really felt strongly about people power. That if we are united we are stronger than those who control our society.'

'The strength of a united rabble?'

'Yeah I guess. I have a hard time feeling that anymore. That anything is strong enough.'

'Well, without tattoos how will we know we're getting older? Everyone gets wrinkles and

loses their hair. But tattoos can tell you that you are no longer the person you were when you

were young.'

'You know you're old when you regret what you've done to yourself?'

'Yeah. Light flashes on your palm and you're off to the surface.'

'Well. That's why I smoke! We get more conservative as we

get older and I want to kill

at least one Republican.'

'You are a dark person.' She tapped Paul's forearm. 'Who wrote that? *Text me when you get home.*'

'A friend wrote it. It's what we always say when we are going home. Has just become shorthand between us. You just got the one tattoo?'

'I will go back for the other two, but I couldn't take the pain. Made them finish the one and stop. So until then I just have the first law, the description of an orbit with the main body at one focus of an ellipse. The other focus can be, and usually is, empty.'

'That's the smaller open circle?'

'Yes.'

They sat silently as the stars processioned overhead. A car turned the corner behind them and for a moment, they cast shadows onto trees hundreds of meters across the lake. Paul whispered, 'I have to remind myself often that the moon is an orb. That it isn't a painting

affixed in the sky for us to admire.' Chloe smiled at this.

'Do you realize, that we're floating in space? The sun doesn't go down, it's just an illusion caused by the world spinning 'round?' She sang quietly, so only they could hear.

'Do you realize, that you have, the most, beautiful face?' Paul didn't sing, but enunciated it to the rhythm.

'I'm cold. I want to wear you like a scarf. Or eat you. Can I chew on you a little bit?' Chloe nipped Paul's shoulder. 'What is your secret, Paul? Everyone has one that they won't ever share with anyone, not even the love of their life.'

'I don't know if I have one.'

'Everyone has one.'

He told her his.

They sat quietly, for minutes that were hours.

'What's the worst event to happen to you in this past year?' Chloe asked later.

Paul took a long time to answer, 'I think it just happened recently. I crashed my car. I was driving home from the bar and hit a curb.' he took a drag on his cigarette. 'I got out of a DUI because the police didn't have me in the car. I came out of my apartment when they were there. They were furious. But it scared me. And my car's totaled and I feel out of control more and more often. Drinking was fun but there are more bad nights, more,' he paused, 'just solemn nights. More nights by myself.' He looked out at the water, 'Two years ago I nearly died. Halloween. I got blackout drunk and went behind the bar and passed out. I wasn't really wearing anything and would have frozen overnight. My best friend came looking for me, the one who wrote *Text Me When You Get Home*? We never leave one another when we're out. I don't like to think what the other outcome would have been. Got better for a long time but I feel like I'm slipping.'

'He's a good friend. You're not going to get another like that.'

'She. Her name's Carrie.'

Chloe smiled. 'Lady best friends are a green flag. If it's stable.'

'I don't know if it is. I'm the unstable element.'

'How long have you had feelings for her?'

Paul was surprised and answered without thinking, 'Since the beginning,' he caught himself, 'I guess. But it's not reciprocated.'

'Just because she doesn't love you like that doesn't mean she doesn't love you in a way that's important.'

'I don't like this line we're on. Since you asked, what about you? What's the worst thing to happen to you in two thousand and four? So far, I guess. Two months to go.'

Chloe leaned into Paul's chest, still watching the moon. 'I didn't think of you as an SUV type.' Paul looked at her, a half smile forming. 'I was watching the parking lot ever since you messaged me. The worst thing though? An ex boyfriend posted some photos that we took together to an amateur sex site. That's not the right description for what they do, but it's all I have. That guy who called my skin condition *tiger stripes*? I don't know what motivated him. His dick was in some of the photos and he was always self-involved so it could be narcissism, or revenge against me, or maybe he saw an opportunity to get paid. But I got a call from a cousin I haven't seen in years and he told me that he recognized me and sent me the link. It has been humiliating and I haven't been able to get them to take the pictures down, they're still up there. I've got a lawyer but they are lost with this. They're spreading too, other sites are copying them. I've traced them around and they've been posted to three different sites now. I've become obsessed with their travels. A different ex called a few weeks ago letting me know, thinking I haven't seen them. I think he wanted to hook up. I feel so disgusting. I'm just waiting for a call from my dad or brother asking me about this.'

It seems like everyone who ends up on amateur porn passes through the same set of rooms, Paul thought, the boring suburban painted drywall with white carpet and doors, lacking anything interesting from a design standpoint. You never see photos from people living in a refurbished Victorian. He wondered if he had scraped any of her photos in his compulsive behavior. He didn't think so.

'What are you thinking? You're distant.'

'I'm here with you.' He said, hugging her close.

Paul woke up to the sounds of the morning in an apartment. Waterworks, radios, reggae from downstairs, car doors. He saw the balcony doors were still open, the thick comforter kept him warm away from the cold air. Blinking, he rolls over. His arm, prickly and needling him from the way he was sleeping, flops across his body and he accidentally backhands Chloe full on the face. She gasps and sits up.

'Oh, shit. Are you okay? Did I hurt you?'

'What was that?' Chloe rubs and wiggles her nose.

'I rolled over, I'm sorry. I was asleep.'

Chloe laughs and kisses Paul. He liked her morning breath. He pulls her over on top of him. She follows his direction and to Paul it felt like fingertip pressure was all it took for her to move. That is, until she hits her head on the wall while they were having sex.

'Oh God. I'm sorry. I'm sorry.' Paul closes his hands into fists and puts them against his mouth. Chloe laughs again, 'It's okay sweetheart. It was an accident.' Another kiss. She puts her hands on his shoulders and presses him into the mattress, holding her body still. 'I'm honestly glad you woke up, Jack is coming by at ten and I forgot to set my alarm last night.'

'Jack, I thought you two had broken up?'

'We did, sort of. We're not moving in together. We're not letting it get more serious. Going back a step, maybe all of them.' She looked down at Paul, starting to gently move again. 'I should have told you last night.'

'I should get going then, shouldn't I?'

'Soon. For now.' Half an hour later Paul admitted to himself he had to go. Chloe had tucked her head under Paul's chin and they pressed tightly together. They were laying very still, memorizing the moment.

'I've got to go to work. I'll be online as much as I can.' Chloe felt his body separate from hers. Chloe watched Paul dress from under the comforter. He crossed and recrossed the room.

Chloe got up when he was done, wrapping the comforter around herself and walked him to the door. 'Goodbye,' the girl says, and they kiss once more as the boy stands in the hall.

Paul drove to his apartment. He knew he had to shower but dreaded it. She was still covering him and when he washed she'd be gone. He did, slowly under hot water, going over the time with Chloe. He masturbated in the shower to her. Brushing his teeth last, the last part of her with him, he asked himself what the day would hold. What he should do.

Paul saw Steve's light blue Lincoln Town Car parked outside the office. He realized he should have warned him about leaving it here. And a brand new car too. He didn't understand why it wasn't at his hotel. He angled in to park next to it and walked to the door.

Steve was asleep on the ragged couch, still dressed in the clothes he had on the night before. A tea towel wrapped around the blocky ice pack that someone had left in the freezer from a previous tenant lay on the floor next to him. Paul's office whiskey bottle was empty on the floor with cigarette butts in it. He stirred and sat up as Paul opened the door.

'Morning. Paul, can you put on some coffee?' He had a black eye. Paul looked closer, no two black eyes from a broken nose.

'Are you okay, sir? You slept here?'

'Fine. Just fine. Yeah, I miss crashing in offices. Coffee and breakfast and I'll head back south. You've got a big day working for me though. We're in this position because of things I've missed, so I'm playing catch up.' Steve stood and stretched. Knuckles on his left hand were abraded and there was blood splattered on his white dress shirt. He carefully touched his face, 'They say that reflexes and reaction times get slower when people get older, but you'd be surprised.'

Paul brought him coffee, intimidated, he had a cup too. He sipped at it. He realized the few times he'd seen Mr. Foliot that the big cone-shaped man was always smiling, joking with people. But that was camouflage. He was a violent man acting professional.

'First, shred those statements you had the volunteers write. Good initiative. Honestly, that's a good best practice, but I need you to shred them now before I leave. I tried to find them last night but didn't. I did find all the data entry that hasn't been put in. If you would, please get to that soon.' Paul looked to the chair next to his desk. There sat a pile of unsorted walk lists two feet tall. Underneath, the continuation of the pile brushed the support for the foam pad. Paul had camouflaged this scene from investigation by an empty manila folder labeled *Entered Data* set on top. Paul had begun to fall behind weeks ago and had never, ever been able to catch up. 'Hey Paul, listen.' Steve was smiling, his bruised and swollen face distorting it, 'Everything's fine! You're not in trouble. Just

365

put a pin in that, okay?' He turned and pulled couch cushions out until he found the pack of cigarettes he was looking for. Paul recognized it as his brand, and expected they'd come from his stash in his desk. 'What else? A runner is coming up from Columbus with a letter in a sealed envelope. Tommy's finishing it up now. They're going to park here and hand that to you. You're going to take that letter to Lou Martel as soon as you get it. Text me when you have it in your hands and when you deliver it. Don't lose sight of it, don't blink if you can avoid it. That letter is more important than anything you've touched this year.' Steve paused, 'You know Lou right?' Paul nodded, 'Good, he seemed to recognize your name. You're going to bring that in to him, don't leave it with a secretary or anything. Text me when you leave his office. I want you to make sure he sees the envelope. Understood?' Paul nodded, 'Last thing, the runner is going to have a manila envelope – doing this so you don't mix them up – with two checks in it. The Sexton Campaign has decided it is important to bring Lou on as a consultant and donate to the local Party to give Field a boost. So go to their Treasurer after Lou sees it. We talked things over last night and that's important to him.' Paul had no idea what he was into. 'Simple: Letter, don't blink, See Lou see it, Lou gets consultant fee, deliver other to local Dem treasurer. Text me each step. Take my cell number down.'

Steve walked to the bathroom. On the way he said, 'You tell the vols that what's been happening is over. Everybody's safe now. Hey, you hear the Red Sox won? Maybe it's a sign!'

He came out of the bathroom. Paul showed him the statements and shredded them as Steve watched. Steve gave Paul three hundred dollars from his wallet in twenties, and fifties, saying to give it to the vols, as cash or gift cards, whatever he decided. It was a gift for what they went through.

The runner handed the two envelopes over to Paul an hour after Steve left, they must have passed one another on the highway. Paul wondered if the runner felt Steve's smiling, deceptive, bruised face staring at him and drove faster because of it. Paul had no doubt Steve felt the runner close on him.

10:43 a.m. Isaac Scheer
  <Martel's office? What do you
  need to know where that's at for?
  It's painless to use a booth.>

10:44 a.m. Isaac Scheer
  <outro: Theme from MASH w/lyrics>

The runner was gone. The office smelled like cigarettes and whiskey. He didn't know what to do about that, but walked outside to his Mom's SUV, locking the office behind him. He laid both envelopes on the passenger seat, and set a book on top of them to make sure they didn't blow away. He was afraid his phone would buzz with a friendly and threatening text from Foliot if he broke eye contact.

Isaac told him Martel was mainly working from the Port Authority, he'd been appointed and held regular office hours there. Official work only. But he split his time, he did consulting work from a century old arcade that was mostly filled with aging lawyers closing on the end of solo careers. Paul expected this was the right office to start at. He parked, free lunchtime parking and carefully, theatrically, picked up both envelopes and went inside, gripping them tightly enough to wrinkle the paper. The revolving doors spun over chipped linoleum, he walked into the nearly empty first floor. A middle-aged guard slash custodian slash maintenance tech in a light blue short sleeve workshirt leaned over the original help desk, reading. Paul looked down the arcade, most of the storefronts were empty. The few that remained were a hard wearing motley of services. A convenience store, a clock and watch repair shop with the sole proprietor there running a lathe turning pen blanks in hopes of selling gifts. Tiny, shiny, low-value items in glass cases. A storefront that sold domestic and foreign magazines and newspapers, a travel agent. The overhead lights were off, the light in the arcade came from the shops. Paul stopped looking at the space and turned to the board, it listed *Martel LTD* upstairs, fifth floor. Jesus Saves was written in neat typewriter script on the frame of the board. He ascended the cupped white marble stairs.

'Come in!' Paul's knock on the solid core door got an immediate response. He opened it. The reception desk was empty, large blinds sent stripes of sunlight onto the old green carpet. To his left was another empty space with a conference table. 'Back here!' From an open door at the back of the conference room. He walked through. Lou Martel was sat behind his desk, with a black eye. His right hand was bandaged. A great oak thing, the desk, with a maroon leather pad taking up the center. Lou was old, weathered, wearing a mustard cardigan over a blue dress shirt. A gold chain lay in gray chest hairs that crawled up his neck. The room smelled like what it was, one where an old man spent days alone. Martel's I Love Me wall had some people Paul recognized, but most he didn't. It was a mixture of black and white photos, sepia, grainy midcentury color, and modern prints. Metal filing cabinets took up one wall in the office. A table had property surveys, building blueprints, and other materials open and piled on it. 'You're from Foliot?'

'I'm Paul, sir.'

'Yeah, I remember you. You're keeping out of trouble nowadays?'

'Yes, sir.'

'We got off on the wrong foot. Never got a chance to clear the air with you after that campaign.'

'No worries, sir. I understand. It's a long time ago.'

'You got something for me?'

Paul handed over the sealed envelope. Martel took a gold letter-opener-scale sword from a stand on his desk - Paul realized they were souvenirs from Toledo Spain - and slit the letter open. He read it through. He sat it aside. 'Apologies for insults are important. Even if they are a decade after. That's why I wanted to apologize.' He looked at the letter.

'I've got this envelope for you too?' Paul said.

'Indeed you do. Let me see it.'

Paul handed over the manila envelope. Martel opened the clasp and shook out the checks. They floated and skirted over the desk onto the floor. Martel grunted and picked them up off the floor beside his desk. He looked at them, putting one back in the envelope.

'Thank you sir.'

'Yeah. Take my card. Give me a call after this campaign wraps up before the Muni fields comes out next year. If you're working in this town I want to know what you're looking

369

at.' Martel paused, 'Tell Steve that I'll call the chairman today and Exec will reconsider the endorsement. Expect that we'll put your signs up on Dawn Patrol alongside McAllen's. Check in with the Party after tomorrow evening. They'll need two hundred twenty signs.' Paul was surprised Martel knew something so granular off the top of his head. He looked through the dirty window at Executive Plaza a block away, the offices for every government bureaucracy that touched the county from School Board to Congress. 'Actually, since I'm consulting on this campaign now. I've got a project for you Monday night. Call me that afternoon.'

Paul drove. He'd seen the number on the check when Martel was putting it back in the envelope. Two thirds of what he was looking to make this year. He'd never had that much money, and here it was on his passenger seat. He arrived at the lawyer who was the Party's treasurer. Wondered what he was supposed to do. Just walk in and hand it over?

Booth

←2 →2

Paul stepped out the front of the bar. He liked smoking outside. He liked smoking inside too, but he was in a mood to wander. It was midnight, early. He pulled his pack of cigarettes and a lighter from his rust-colored jacket. Paul looked to the sky and the moon was there, nearly full. Waning Gibbous. His bladder pressed on him. He walked across the street. Gold and orange leaves piled along the curbs, strewn over the sidewalk, the Reagan Booth was there, door still broken. It smelled like rotted piss and sun-baked garbage, and worse. He looked up and down the street. Other bars had customers in and out off the sidewalk. He could hear the quiet murmur of their conversations, with rising elements of jokes and laughter. He held the cigarette in his mouth and unzipped his pants, squinting at the smoke rising into his eyes, making them water. In the sky the moon was clear and not hazy, for the first time since the wildfire had been extinguished. Paul put an arm up on the doorframe for support and urinated into the booth. He shivered and hung his head in relief. He opened his eyes, saw that someone had filled the intake of the breathalyzer with cigarette stubs.

371

Halloween

↓1 →2

Saturday, October 30

grammateia: I've been really wobbly since you left. Jack and I broke up for good.

g: Well, I broke up with Jack. To be clear. I chose it.

g: It was wonderful with you Paul.

g: I want you to know I have feelings for you. Important feelings that are not just a hook up or friends that came together one night and are friends after. It's hard to describe.

g: We don't even have a word for it. I'm trying to describe Pink in the Fifteenth Century. I feel 'wine‑dark sea' for you Paul. It's not love, but it's real and it's a precursor.

g: Please say something.

'I appreciate everyone coming in today to make calls!' Paul shouted to reach the room, 'Like we discussed when we were signing up shifts! Because it's a holiday we're going to wrap up now before dusk so no one gets annoyed with calls during Trick or Treating! I appreciate all of you and what you're doing for the Sexton campaign! This is how we win!'

The volunteers filtered out. The sun hung low, crosshatched with branches. A chill underlined the breeze. The afternoon lacked the tales songbirds tell all summer. Most had left, and those that remained had no time for gossip. The sun tired itself and only could mount a low pass. Cicadas buzzed the rat-a-tat of approaching shadow. Fall felt the world wearing out.

Paul, alone, wrote his weekly report. He looked at the messages from Chloe. The office was quiet, Paul could hear wind whistling through the gaps in the plywood covering the front window.

bkp971: I had a wonderful time with you.

b: I'm having a hard time with things right now and we live far apart.

On a bed in Michigan, a girl pulled a comforter closer around herself with both her hands.

g: An hour isn't as far as what a lot of people make work.

b: I know. I'm afraid. I told you I'm struggling right now. This could be too much. We're both immature.

g: We could be more than ourselves together. We could be more than we could be with anyone else.

He heard a knock on the door.

b: I have to go. I am going out with friends and they're here. I want to talk to you about this.

'Trick or Treat.' Carrie said, beaming at him when he opened it. 'Am I the first you've gotten tonight? Give me weed, candy, and cheap beer or I'll TP this place.' She wore a black nylon baseball jacket over an A-shirt and faded jeans. Her French bob was somehow pulled into a semblance of a mullet and she'd drawn a five o'clock shadow on. She wore aviator sunglasses and Converse to complete the look.

'Come on in. I'm finishing up.'

'I think the best remedy is to get drunk and party and work

on what I have left in the morning. Thoughts?' Paul went on, 'There is beer in the back of the back fridge, I have some whiskey in my desk if you want some before we head out.'

'No, not till I get to the bar.' Carrie said. She walked the perimeter of the office. Trying side doors and finding them locked.

'Space is way larger than we needed. Most of it is locked up.' Paul said when he noticed her investigation.

'Spooky though, all this space. Isn't a locked door scarier somehow?' She said from the far part of the room.

'Yeah, well I'll think about that when I'm here alone at night thanks!'

'How was the parade?'

'It was not good. Two hours out, two hours back, and the locals said I didn't bring enough candy. All of which I've got to be reimbursed for. I just gritted my teeth and smiled. Came back to the phone bank. What's the Crew doing now?'

'Lot of interviews since the Cheney visit. National press. We're basically Her media team now. Paul, you should have seen it. I thought the lead SUV was going to roll swerving around Her.'

'I saw the footage.'

'Cheney still hasn't appeared in public. Got banged up pretty bad.'

'Yeah, I've been following it.'

'You okay? Is this a nerve? I'm sorry.'

'Is She going to be out tonight?'

'I expect Her to be. But you know how She is. Let's go. We're leaving cars at your place and walking down right? I want to drink tonight and you're a terrible DD.'

'Excuse me a moment Carrie. I have to go flirt with that flower.' Paul walked across the bar. She stood talking to someone, finally turning when She saw Paul. The petals of Her costume were thin cardboard, stapled together.

'It's been a while stranger. How have you been? Want to sign my cast?' Her arm was encased in a plaster cast up to Her shoulder.

'I'm good. Running in to the end of this election. Sorry I haven't been around much.'

'All good.' She said.

'I want to hear about it from you. It's all been secondhand and the video the local stations keep running.'

'Just had the opportunity. I just saw it there.' She laughed, 'The cops were so pissed off. A bunch of local ACLU lawyers were at County before I was even out of booking. I spent the night there but the next day they got the judge to release me on OR bond.' She kicked Her leg out and pulled up the loose jeans She wore. 'Well, not totally on my own. I had to go buy jeans that'd go over this fucking thing. And they're making me rent it. Still better than the alternative.'

'So the ACLU is covering you?'

'Oh my god, yes. I don't think they'd stop crying if I didn't. We're working on a media strategy and legal strategy together with the foundation that Albert and Stephen are here with. I'm fucking stoked that it's spreading. I think the media hits are making people think deeper about protesting. I've heard there have been three similar actions since I did that. Tuesday, couple people camped out at Rumsfeld's house and forced his official car to turn around. The DoD didn't have a press conference that day.'

'So you're going to be okay then? I feel like I let you down.

Like, as your boyfriend.'

The shock on Her face was palpable, 'Shit what? I don't think that's a good word to use anymore Paul. A lot has happened since you split. I don't know what you think is here, but that's a...wow. Yeah, no boyfriend girlfriend, man. It's good seeing you. Don't get me wrong. I just have a whole thing going on and you're not part of it.'

'Oh. I guess. I just thought.' He trailed off, 'Sorry. I'm just surprised. I thought we'd drifted as all this was going on and.' He stammered, 'You haven't said anything to me. Carrie hasn't said anything about it.'

'Paul, seriously. I forgot, man. I'm sorry. Other things happened! I broke my arm getting hit by the Vice President's car! I've been fucking busy! I didn't reach out or cry on Carrie's shoulder cause I just thought it was over. Not everything needs a big closing speech. I figured you saw it that way too and had just moved on. Sorry.'

'No. It's cool. Just miscommunication.' He looked around for an exit, 'I'll see you later.'

'Yeah, Paul. Later.' She hugged him and walked out to the patio.

'Who was that dopey dude with the caution tape wrapped around His head that you were talking to? Sarah's sister asked.

'He's a guy I used to hang out with. Nice dude but a lot different than I thought He was when we first met.'

'Oh. Yeah that makes sense now.' Carrie said. 'I thought She wasn't talking about you because you all are pretty private. I'm sorry. You're going to be okay.'

'Yeah. Just shocked.' They leaned against the upstairs bar

as the room filled further and further with people out to enjoy the night.

'Don't drink to forget. Okay? I want to have a good night tonight. My costume isn't *The Unequal Emotional Labor I Carry In Our Friendship.*'

'Yeah.' he sipped his tequila and Sprite.

'What are the next couple days for you?'

'Run the plan. Reconnect with IDs we've made. Chase voters out. What about you?'

'We're rolling in under ACT. All the Crew will be field captains. We got trained up last weekend. Running vans of paid canvassers to knock doors through the day. Coordinating with the local lead. Trying to reach new registrants and those unlikely to vote. We've each got two dozen vans, five canvassers each. I'm pretty excited.'

'Do you think I'm selfish Carrie?'

'Questions like that lead to nights where I'm pouring you through the door of your apartment and I don't want to deal with that tonight.'

'Seriously.'

'No. I don't think you're any more selfish than most people are. I don't think you are that, sorry to say, coherent. You're directionless though. You just grab and you tease people and you crash around but none of it benefits anyone. Not even yourself.' She sipped her drink. 'That was harsher than I meant it to sound.'

'I'm really down.'

'Goddamnit Paul. I'm sorry She told you it was over. But I want to enjoy tonight. Please?' Carrie hugged him, at best a yearly occurrence between them. 'Please, just be my buddy and we'll pick up this depressive spiral tomorrow when liquor sales aren't allowed.'

He smiled at her. 'I'm sorry Carrie. I will.'

'I like seeing your smile.' She pointed at his cocktail. 'Just tequila and Sprite's tonight. Singles. And pace them out. No shots and nothing stiffer.'

Under Pressure

←4 ↑1

Max toyed with his weighty panniculus as he looked through the venetian blinds towards the asphalt lot, where a bitter wind whipped the light sleety rain across the ground. The mass across his stomach was made up of the following: a notepad, four pens and one pencil, two packs of filter cigarettes with nine remaining in the opened box, a scarf, woolen gloves, a blue and yellow striped cardboard box labeled as originally containing fifteen hundred toothpicks, napkins from a fast food restaurant that he was using as tissues, two cell phones - one for campaign work and one for government business - and a hand-assembled, precision-made, forty three piece striker operated cigarette lighter that he bought for a dollar and thirty nine cents. It was too cold for any more snow to be created. 'I like living in areas that have seasons, but winter kills people.'

Chelsea, reading a spreadsheet and not catching his tone, grunted. 'People die in the summer. Summer kills old people.'

'Let me be wrong before you correct me. Anyway, a lot of things kill old people, sometimes I consider doing it myself with how they vote.'

'And kids.' Chelsea decided to antagonize Max. 'There have

been deaths from heat stroke when kids are out training for sports, and in the spring there is flooding. People die then.'

'Well, I survived childhood. If others can't figure out how to, that is their fault. Let people know that the Sun will just kill you if you stand in it too long most anywhere in the world. Okay, winter could kill me. I guess that is the point I am trying to make.'

Chelsea reviewed the Tick-Tock she'd created for the close of the campaign. It was running. Just over fifty-six hours until polls closed.

'Whatever Steve did up north worked. Chairman from Toledo Pareto up there called Jamie today to say they'd rescinded the endorsement of McAllen.' Max said, 'Treating them as equals. Two others called from Northwest Ohio. Same thing. Another county flipped their endorsement. Fuck all good it'll do here Sunday before the election. Have you seen Steve?'

'No. What's up?'

'Face is all busted up. I was here working when he came in. Clearly was trying to get some things from the office when people wouldn't be here. He's working from home for the duration.'

Joshua sat on the blue all weather carpet sucking on his fingers where he had touched the live wire. 'Fucking hot wire J.' He chastised himself, reaching for his beer. The Chris Craft Catalina he'd decided on made him giddy. Twin three-fifties in the back. Loads of electronics - some of which he'd just gotten sideways with - but a nice radar and other goodies he needed to poke at. And room enough for a dozen people. A couch! Television! Head! Galley! And it looked like a thousand other boats on the lake, he reminded himself. It's anonymous. And he had a lead on a good exhaust for quiet nights. He still needed an inflatable tender for options, he thought. He stood and looked down as his Islander, still smiling. 'This is it.' He needed to call Robert to show him the new Q Ship.

'Headquarters staff!' Max boomed. 'Relevant campaign update here Monday Election Eve! Our tracker that is not employed by the campaign to follow a fellow Democratic candidate just called me from our Democratic opponent's press conference that I have paid them to attend in order to get footage. McAllen called a press conference at an abandoned factory to talk about the plight of the working man! Incidentally I think he had his acoustic guitar with him. He and his crew set up and he's halfway through his speech to the cameras when a semi turns in and nearly runs him and the media over.' Max paused, 'The place wasn't as vacant as the advance team thought it was, two companies still operate out of there.'

'There is a trick to making sure that doesn't happen.' Chelsea said from her desk.

'Oh yeah?'

'Yeah, the trick is called being good at your job.'

'I didn't fucking do it!'

'Yeah but tomorrow is Election Day, I thought of that a while ago and have been saving it and at this point don't think I'll have a chance to hit you with it this cycle.'

'Mr. Martel,' Paul said into his phone, he stood in front of the office, smoking. 'You told me to call you this afternoon.' He listened,' Tonight?' pause, 'No. Yes, sir.' Martel gave him an address. 'Thank you again, sir.'

Paul parked the small SUV at the location he'd been directed to. It was a space in a strip mall anchored by a convenience store. Most of the storefronts were empty and dark. He walked to the one on the end opposite the convenience store. The front windows were papered over with newspaper and lit from inside. He heard people talking and laughing inside. The door was locked. After some time standing he heard someone yell through the glass to park in the back. He parked next to an old hardtop Jeep, green but difficult to discern in the dark. He walked through the steel security door into the bright light of the store, in reverse of a customer. All through the space men milled around laughing and drinking beer. All wearing a mix of Carhartt jackets, knit skullcaps, lined hooded sweatshirts, and denim. The abandoned painter's equipment was pushed up along the walls. Incomplete roller marks on the walls made it look like the job was called as work was going on. A burly young man offered Paul a beer from a bucket filled with ice. He recognized Martel, laughing with a cluster of tough looking older men. Paul was unsettled that his one point of contact in this scene was Lou. No one else knew he belonged. One of the men Martel was talking to looked at his watch and shouted at the room. 'Alright boys! We're here to make sure everyone that requested a yard sign gets one!' Laughter, 'Now we're not looking for Sexton anymore.' Boos. Paul saw Martel scanning the room, his eyes landed on Paul and he nudged the speaker and pointed. 'Ah, we got the Sexton campaign here tonight with us! Welcome to the Midnight Canvass!' Paul flinched. 'No writing down the names we're looking for, alright? Everybody grab a razor if you don't have one and if you need a partner raise your hand! Grab a road beer if you want one and get to it!'

Paul was assigned with Jimmy. He said he was an apprentice but neither he nor Paul wanted to go into detail introducing themselves. Their triangular region was bounded by the Turnpike, the County Line to the West, and the road to the airport. Jimmy drove his new GMC pickup, Paul looked for signs. At the first cluster of signs they found Jimmy parked to block them from passing cars and hopped out, extending the blade of his razor as he walked over. Paul followed him, uneasy. Jimmy sliced the first supersign in half down the center then bent the U-channels over with his foot. 'Fifty bucks gone.' He scanned for more targets, pulling up small signs and frisbeeing them into the weeds. 'You getting in on this or are you a narc?' Jimmy asked Paul, who still stood uneasily. Paul extended his razorknife and walked towards a Maxie sign.

Rain set in as they made their way around the region. A semi truck's blurred red taillights in the night rain ahead of them. They stopped at a golf course, sprinklers running in the night rain. The work was done quickly and they moved on. Paul was chilled and welcomed the hot cab, Jimmy blasted the heater and nu metal. Paul watched the road, pointing at target signs. A neon pink cross lit the road juncture in front of a modified gas station now church in an unincorporated cluster of houses. Jimmy looked both ways, the few houses here each had Maxie and Maguire supersigns. Jimmy was thinking. Rain tapped on the truck.

'We're going to fucking get shot if we go after those.' Paul said.

'Yeah, that's what I was thinking. There's an old boy with a rifle waiting for this.'

'Let's call it. We did our part.'

They drove, Jimmy's nu metal overwhelming any opportunity for complex conversation.

'You doing dawn patrol?'

'Yeah, three thirty right?' Paul saw it was already two.

'Guys are headed straight there. I'll drop you off at your truck.'

3:17 a.m. Carrie Catherine
  <Election Day Paul! Paul It's Election Day! It's Election Day Paul!>

3:17 a.m. Carrie Catherine
  <Paul, Election Day!>

3:18 a.m. SENT Carrie Catherine
  <Hey carrie, I hear it's election day>

3:19 a.m. Carrie Catherine
  <IT'S ELECTION DAY!!!>

He read Carrie's text standing outside the union hall under an awning out of the rain. He finished his cigarette and walked inside the western wing of the building. This was the hall proper, this entire extension was one large room, the other through the short corridor was offices. The windows were black and reflected the activity inside. Hundreds of bundles of small yard signs, thousands total, were lined up. Volunteers and volun-tolds were carrying them to trucks outside along with route maps. Polling locations in two counties would be covered from this one site. Polls were set to open in three hours, ten minutes. He yawned and found the cooler with sodas.

Paul opened the office at six, half an hour ahead of polls opening. Paid canvassers would be in at eight, that had blown up. Expanding to a division of thirty out of this office, hundreds around the state. They'd be out by nine, all day on the doors. Volunteer phonebank starts at eleven. Volunteer canvass would be in at noon. Reconnecting and confirming today. No new IDs. GOTV, get out the vote. Paul felt strung out already, cold and damp from the rain, wearing the clothes he was working in the day before. He giggled, delirious.

His phone vibrated, Le was sending texts to all the regional staff.

6:13 a.m. Le Boss
<Topline reminders: One set of callsheets today. First pass red ink, second pass blue, last pass black.>

6:15 a.m. Le Boss
<If locals are distroing street money then you need to track it so we can report it correctly.>

Paul remembered getting chewed out cycles before when he refused to give cash to a local for vague promises. Isaac had fixed it. 'You're against street money? You don't like winning elections do you?' he'd said at the time, incredulously. 'How do you think we take care of the people that get our candidates elected? We give them gas cards, we give the tickets to games, we send meals home. People need shit like that. Really fucking bougie to think people don't need something for their time.'

6:17 a.m. Le Boss
<I'm in the boiler room all day. Call if there are any voting issues in your region.

6:18 a.m. Isaac Scheer
<Slaughter. It's going to be Rough today. Good luck.>

6:19 a.m. Le Boss
<Send contact reports at 11, 2, and 5. Include the BOE posts when those go up.>

Le's workstation in the Columbus boiler room - a union hall - was in the center of the stage. She'd taken silvery pulldown projection screens and angled them behind her so no one could approach her. Her cell and laptop were plugged into an extension cord that snaked in from behind her. She faced out at the hall. On the floor below tables were arranged for Media (Max alone with a semi-circle of laptops), Data and Targeting, Finance doubled up with Paid Media (low-level, the top consultants were upstairs with Sexton fundraising for the final leg that would start tomorrow.) Fred Ryan and Steve Foliot were in, their table was unused aside from their coffees. They were standing with Jamie, who was centered in the hall opposite Le. Max was right about Steve's face, Le thought to herself. Six televisions on carts were lined up on the wall to Le's left, all muted but tuned to different stations that would have news today. The largest set of tables was for Legal, lawyers who were watching the news and ready to field calls from anywhere in the state. They had contacts and friends who were no more than a half hour away from any polling location. She closed her eyes, stretching her senses through her staff across the state.

Her alarm went off, it was six thirty and polls were open. She sent one more text.

UNDER PRESSURE

Final Act

Scene 1

Sexton Campaign Boiler Room, Columbus Ohio, Day

LE is center stage rear at desk on elevated platform. Laptop should be clear plexi or open frame so audience can see actor. LE cycles through holding head in hands/reading or sending texts/typing/reading computer screen in this scene when not speaking.

Text Messages are shown on projection screen at back of stage, spotlight character sending/reading text. On main stage visibly-worn folding tables with folding chairs flank her. Stairs rise outwards from base of platform with wooden doors visible.

6:30 a.m. SENT DFDs RFDs
<Polls open. Tell your door teams
if they see suppression lit, call it in.
We'll fight for them if they take it down.>

LE

That last sentence was probably unwise.

ACT Canvass Launch, Toledo Ohio, Outside, Day

Spotlight CARRIE standing stage right front. She wears a black hiking vest. Play recording of static to simulate rain in outdoor segments.

6:48 a.m. JimJam the Man
<I'm here at Glenwood and
no one is able to vote. Couple
dozen people around. You know
about this?>

Typing on phone.

6:51 a.m. SENT PaulPants 6:51 a.m. Carrie Catherine
<FYI.Voters can't get in <FYI.Voters can't get in
at Glenwood. I'm sending at Glenwood. I'm sending
it up with ACT, just it up with ACT, just
thought you should know.> thought you should know.>

Sexton Regional Office, Toledo Ohio, Inside, Day
Second spotlight on PAUL sitting at folding table stage left rear. He scowls reading text from CARRIE.

PAUL

Thank you Carrie but you're the third person to tell me and the first that's illegal to talk to right now.

Spotlight LE. Canvassers walk up to PAUL as she picks up phone.
6:55 a.m. SENT Le Boss 6:55 a.m. Paul Toledo Pareto
<Legal Issue. Keep hearing <Legal Issue. Keep hearing
about Glenwood in Toledo. about Glenwood in Toledo.
Still closed.> Still closed.>

Spotlight CARRIE

> **7:16 a.m. Sarah CREWfriend**
> **<Dude, half the canvassers**
> **I've got are Republicans. You**
> **seeing this?>**
> **7:18 a.m. SENT Sarah CREWfriend**
> **<Watch them. Walk with them**
> **if you can. I don't like it but it's**
> **what we've got.>**
> **7:20 a.m. Sarah CREWfriend**
> **<Fuckers don't give a shit about**
> **us until we've got a job for them.>**

CANVASSERS go up and down stairs repeatedly. Cycle cardigans, vests, coats, hoodies, etc in order to look like a large group. Leave flyers on each door going up. Infrequently, others mime conversation with them at doorways. Mix of visibly positive and negative interactions. This continues through scene unless stairs are needed for a specific action. Speed up action through scene.

Spotlight on interaction on stairs. Static rain.

ANGRY MALE VOTER

Get the fuck off my property and don't fucking come back here! I see you or anyone else I'm going to kick your ass! I don't need to be harassed to vote!

Crumple up and throw flyer as canvasser retreats.

CANVASSER

I'm just. Sorry! Sorry! Sorry!

Spotlight LE.

LE

Legal! I just got a report from East Cleveland. A polling location is out of pencils for their Scantrons and no one from the BOE is working to fix it. You got anyone near Fairfax?

Spotlight stage right front. Voters walking past conservatively but well-dressed ELECTION PROTECTION and VOLUNTEER wearing campaign shirt. Static rain.

ELECTION PROTECTION

Just, here take this. It's all the cash I have. Go buy as many pencils as you can and bring them back here.

LE

Glenwood in Toledo is open! Machines were locked in Principal's office. Keyholder arrived. Eight Fifteen. One Fifty voters estimated walked.

MAX stage left front covers scratches in a black-metal podium with a permanent marker. He is dressed in a worn suit. A blue light is on beside him over a door. The light goes off and he opens the door.

MAX

Congressman, you're leaving to vote in fifteen minutes. Your wife is here. I'll follow in my car.

LOW LEVEL HQ STAFF approaches LE from stage floor.

HQ STAFFER

Le, the copier isn't working again.

LE

I can't fix it. I'm busy.

HQ STAFFER

When can you?

LE

I'll have a break at...

LE looks at her phone indicating she is checking the time.
tomorrow.

HQ STAFFER

Can you please help? Finance needs to print call sheets for when Sexton comes back. It's saying there's a paper jam, but there's no paper jam.

LE is visibly agitated. Lowers laptop screen.

LE

Is the paper feeding from the letter tray correctly?

HQ STAFFER exits stage and returns.

HQ STAFFER

There are actually two reasons why the printer is broken!

10:11 a.m. SENT DFDs RFDs
<Check EVERYWHERE in your offices
AND cars in case someone left an
Absentee ballot with you on accident.
Get those in!>

PAUL sat at folding table stage left rear. VOLUNTEERS murmur quietly making calls at both sets of tables. Picking up and setting down phones rhythmically. He stretches.

PAUL

Everything is stable here. I just got an urgent text to get some materials out to canvassers. The phonebank captain is in charge. Call if you need me. I'll be about two hours.

PAUL stands and walks offstage. He ascends stairs stage right behind LE and into apartment door. He reappears on stage floor carrying pillow and blanket and walks to center stage and lies down.

Phonebank VOLUNTEERS continue calling, CANVASSERS resume on stairs. LE picks up pace of calls/texts/computer/head in hands. CARRIE stage right front mimes instructions to CANVASSER.

MAX and SEXTON appear stage left front. Spotlight on them. SEXTON at podium. SEXTON in suit with American Flag on lapel.

SEXTON

I cast my ballot just now for a better future for America. We have to change direction and set a new course. A new and better course that takes us in a new direction. Not this course that is taking us the wrong direction. So we need a new direction, on a new course. Thank you.

Spotlight PAUL

11:49 a.m. Le BOSS
<This is GOTV. Tell your
people to knock until
someone answers, dial
until someone picks up.>

CARRIE enters stage right with SARAH. Stop center stage front. Both wear black hiking vests. SARAH has an ankle monitor and her left arm is in a cast to the shoulder. Static rain.

CARRIE

I've got a bad feeling. The news is reporting issues all over the state. Lines are already forming in college towns where they've pulled machines.

SARAH

Election Protection nearly had to physically separate a Republican goon from voters. I watched it. He was blocking the entrance screaming at people. Black people. As they were walking in.

CARRIE

They're going to do it. This is what it looks like.

DELIVERY DRIVER approaches LE. They hand up a white styro-foam food container.

LE

What's this?

DELIVERY DRIVER

It's an order from Max? That's who paid for it. There's a message with it. It says Because you're going to forget to eat.

PAUL stands up and retraces route, returning to phonebank. A phone is ringing. He picks it up.

PAUL

Ma'am I assure you Congressman Sexton is on the ballot.
Pause.

PAUL

It's a special primary. You had to request the ballot, the BOE should have asked you if you wanted to vote and which...
He pauses, cut off.

PAUL

Okay, I understand. If you saw Maguire and Maxie then that means you received the Republican ballot.
Pause.

PAUL

Okay, so you requested that one. No, Congressman Sexton

is a Democrat. He...
 Pause.

PAUL

Hello? Hello?

SEBASTIAN, downcast, sits wearing an orange jumpsuit at the table stage right rear. Across from him is a person in a rumpled suit. They may be a LAWYER, they may be a DETECTIVE. They mime conversation. Visibly tense.

LE appears frustrated. She sends a text.

2:18 p.m. SENT DFDs RFDs
<People! Are you even looking
at the TickTock? Where are
my midday turnout reports?
How is it possible you're all
late?>

LE

Legal! CM! Blackwell sent a directive late morning telling the County BOEs not to post any more turnout reports! We're flying blind!

Tables stage left front, two people are standing talking. One has a clipboard.

LEGAL

Those Return Service Requested letters we caught? The other shoe dropped. Republicans have challengers all over the state with lists of names that came back to them. They're at AfAm and Dem polling locations.

JAMIE

Interference? Can we challenge their right to be there? Are they harassing anyone?

LEGAL

Challenge the challengers? I like it. They are overstepping, but we can only tackle it one by one. We can't get an injunction. Election Protection is doing their work as a neutral party but they're outmanned.

LE

Yo! Legal! CM! BOEs are sending all our people to vote provisional! This is growing! I'm hearing it from multiple cities!

CANVASSERS continue cycling up and down stairs. Moving fast.
Stage right front CARRIE and SARAH.
Stage right rear SEBASTIAN and LAWYER/DETECTIVE.
Stage left front LEGAL MAX SEXTON JAMIE.
Stage left rear PAUL and VOLUNTEERS. Calls being made.
All mime silently work and conversations.

LE

This is it people!

All but CANVASSERS, SEBASTIAN, and LAWYER/DETECTIVE look to LE. CANVASSERS continue cycling up and down stairs.

CANVASSERS freeze midstride. Descend stairs and go to center stage rear. Softly.

Polls are closed.

'Fuck. Did your ears pop?' Max asked Le. He was rolling his jaw and sucking in breaths.

'Pressure drop.' Le answered. The world felt like it had been let out by millimeters. She was closing her tragus over her ear canal and shaking her head. 'I forgot to chew gum.'

'We have a month to go to the General. Fuck, Le we shouldn't feel the pressure drop! Fuck!' Around the room people were shaking their heads and sucking in air to fight the decompression. They were all coming to the realization that Max and Le had. *Fuck. No.* could be heard from everyone. Jamie took off running towards the offices where Sexton was barricaded with Finance.

Steve was on the phone. Ken started packing up. Others closed laptops and pulled boxes out and began filling them.

'We have hours before results are in.' Le said, desperately.

'It's over. McAllen is moving forward. Get your people. Some of them may have just lost for the first time.'

'You the only one here?' Max walked into the campaign office at noon to Le sitting at her desk. The lights were off for the first time since they rented it. She was scrolling through a spreadsheet, now dead. Her Hangover was steering clear of her and Max saw it in the next room twisting the blinds closed and open.

'Got to be here for my people to drop off their materials and equipment. I'll be here through the weekend at least.'

'Anyone else in?'

'Ken came through for his computers and was gone by ten. Finance disappeared in the night, their offices are empty and smell like whatever it is a vampire leaves behind. Good perfume over brimstone.'

Max lit a cigarette. Le flicked a look of disapproval and he shrugged and offered her one. She took it. He pulled over a chair and put his feet up on her desk. She leaned back and did as well. They ashed onto the cheap carpet.

'It's a lonely spot to be, losing after all the support you could have asked for was given to you.' Max said.

'Our Field plan was a work of fiction. We always underper-formed because the goals weren't based in reality.'

'Sure yeah. I don't know what that means but I feel for you. Carry lessons forward to the next one.'

'What's that for you?'

'Back to the Hill. Fuck this shit.'

'Until you get called out again.'

'I'll have at least a year until the Oh-Six Senate races. No more Specials.'

'Fuck Specials.'

'Fuck Sexton.' Max shrugged at the glance from Le.

'We need that vote in the Senate.'

'Going to have to find it somewhere else.'

Jamie walked into the main office, blinking at the dim light. Her Hangover was wearing a Sexton for Ohio t-shirt. Max and Le threw anything that came to hand at it until it retreated to a corner to sulk.

'Steve took me out to get shitfaced last night. Guy kept up with me and I couldn't even tell he was drinking.'

'What are you doing here?'

'Walked from my hotel. Wanted to see it again. Tell your people they can work for McAllen. Welcomed with open arms. One level down from what they had here though. And Steve says everyone who doesn't have a clause already in their contract is going to be paid through the end of the month. We got more money than we can spend.' She coughed. 'I'm going to go vomit.'

Carrie, Sarah, and the rest of the local Crew hugged Stephen and Albert goodbye outside the house they'd been working from. Tearfully promising to stay connected, even as interviews for Sarah were becoming scarce, and collaborate and support. 'Think globally, act locally. Love you all.' Albert said, turning to walk to the truck.

Paul was alone in the regional office. All afternoon he had been carrying load after load of boxes of lit, call sheets, signs, all the detritus of the campaign to the dumpster. He'd found half a dozen absentee ballots in their envelopes in a desk drawer some volunteer had collected. After staring at them for a long time he took them to the dumpster as well. Unions came by for their tables and chairs. Joshua came by to be morose, leaving after a few hours. Some things he saved for his own use or reference. Not much though. The boarded up window rattled in the wind. His computer was open and he saw that Chloe had responded to him.

bkp971: hey
  grammateia: Hi
  b: how are you?
  g: I'm fine, thanks. How are you?
  b: i'm well.
  g: That's good.
  b: i'm sorry i upset you. it all came out wrong and i want to try this.
  b: i'm really just a bunch of fireworks
  b: with unreliable fuses
  b: set off by some kid
  g: It's late, Paul. I try not to let anything upset me too much anymore. Don't worry about it.

g: Goodnight, Paul.

b: goodnight chloe

grammateia has gone offline

###